AN0MAL0US

THE END OF RA
BOOK 1

WILLIAM BELTRE

CONTENTS

PART I
Bonds

Ends and Beginnings	3
Karal	5
Clara	10
Visitors	13
Village of Gallow (image)	19
Confessions	20
Ives	25
Lies	29
Hate	34
Lost	38
Mercy	41
Threshold	49
Escape from Gallow (image)	53
Flight	54
Fento	61
Flee the Klenzeer (image)	69
Escapism	70
Into the Fire	78
Paldor	92
Thievery	99
Pursuit	107
Bolt from Paldor (image)	115
Challenges	116
Near Death	123
Capture	132
Triad	136
Forward	145
Destination: Ormant (image)	155
Midnight	156
Extraction	164
Centerfugue	173
Fragility	182

Scatter   193

Choices   200

Junction   206

PART II
Snares

Portent   217

Solemnity   222

Sentence   224

Desperation   229

Town of Ormant (image)   237

Beo   238

Recon   246

Cycle 240   256

Damned   263

Invitation   270

Unusual Encounters   275

Decisions   280

Knock, knock   283

According to Plan   290

Absolution   296

Expectation   302

Justice   306

About the Author   311

ANoMALoUS

This is a work of fiction. Names, characters, places, and incidents are either the product of the author's imagination or are used fictitiously. Any resemblance to actual persons, living or dead, events, or locales is entirely coincidental.

ISBN 979-8-9952955-0-1 (eBook)

ISBN 979-8-9952955-1-8 (Paperback)

ISBN 979-8-9952955-2-5 (Hardcover)

Cover design 2026 by William Beltre

Edited by: Sarah Chorn

https://sarahchornedits.com/

First edition: 2026

Published by Rho Alpha Press, Brentwood, NH

❀ Formatted with Vellum

Dedicated to the dreamers captivated by a single spark, who possess the resolve to follow its light into the unknown.

And to my family and friends who allowed me to pursue this crazy venture with the love and support needed to see it through.

"He who is brave is free." — Seneca

PART I

BONDS

ENDS AND BEGINNINGS

Ragged gasps escape. His lungs burn.

The dirt path cuts into his pads. Rocks and roots jar his trembling legs with every strike. He shoves through the agony.

Sweat and saliva slick his chin as he pants into the night. His shoulders scream under the weight of the pack, but he pushes—he has to reach—

The memory wavers.

Think, Fento, remember!

He growls through clenched teeth.

A silhouette flickers in his mind—a broad-shouldered figure standing beside him. A friend. A hand reaching out, offering something vital—

The image dissolves.

Focus!

A warning echoes in his skull.

Your memories of the mission will vanish if you sleep.

Now, exhaustion makes them slip through his mind like dreams dissolving at dawn.

An ancient log blocks the path. He leaps. His landing is clumsy, bone-rattling. Woods thick with decay stretch endlessly around him, downed trunks crumbling into the muck. Rot saturates the air. Only the crunch of dead leaves under his paws breaks the silence.

Ahead, the canopy thins. Moonlight slices through the branches in cold, sharp slivers.

He tilts his head back. The moon hangs full and heavy, glowing deep yellow. The Cycle ends when it reaches its zenith. Always at the zenith. When the light hits the peak, the world falls still.

No, please—I'm so close.

Days of running blur together. He's nearing one of them. He has to be. One of them is going to kill the world. Everyone dies unless he—

A low branch whips out of the dark. Quick reflexes save him, but the sudden, violent pivot is too much. The pack's weight yanks him sideways.

Down he goes, rolling into the dirt. He catches himself on clawed paws—black nails gouging the earth, his momentum never quite breaking.

Moonlight thickens to a deep red, bathing the world in crimson.

It's happening!

The Cycle's end always comes this way—the moon shifts color, then comes the sound. His focus fractures. Blood fills his mouth as teeth bite tongue.

Stay awake—just until I reach—

A low, booming gong shudders through the forest. It vibrates through him to the marrow.

His vision blurs.

The forest tilts.

His knees strike the earth.

The world goes black.

KARAL

Pounding fills Karal's skull like a smith's hammer on an anvil. He burrows deeper beneath the covers, trying to smother the sensation.

Oh feng, what did I do?

The tavern had seemed like a good idea—just a meal and a fizzle. Then Ives and Soma showed up, talking him into several more. *Stick to water, they say. Don't end the Cycle drunk, they say.*

"This is horrible," he moans to no one in particular.

Memories from the tavern door to his bed are adrift. Work clothes still cover him head to toe, boots mercifully off. Reaching from under the nest of blankets, his fingers grope for the ceramic pitcher near the bed. It slides away. He lunges—his hand catches only the handle.

Crash!

"FENG!" He winces, the sound of his own voice splintering his brain.

Groaning, he smothers his head with a pillow, bracing against the inevitable. Clara is coming today. She can't see him like this. There's so much to prepare.

His eyes burn as he peels back the covers. Daylight floods the room.

Late. So late!

Squinting, shuffling toward the window, bare feet crunch something underfoot. His jaw clenches, holding back a list of curses. No blood—just shards of the pitcher scattered across the floor. A small blessing.

With the shades jerked shut, the dimness offers a grim inventory: overturned chairs, a sprawl of laundry, and a puddle of vomit souring the floor near the hearth.

"Heck of a grown-up you've turned into, Karal," he mutters, rubbing sleep from his eyes.

A memory surfaces: Ives, steady and sober, removing his boots by the door, stacking them with care, helping him into bed. Then, nothing.

Last time I drink, I swear. A vow he's broken countless times.

He's appreciative of Ives and his family. When Karal's mother died during childbirth, the Law of Balance would have required him to be removed from his dad's care—one parent can't work their trade and provide adequate care for a child. That's when Ives' family stepped in. They tended to him while his dad worked. Dad still raised him, but Ives' parents made it possible. The village Headman, Lindor, falsified the records so it looked proper. Gladys Stillburn remained alive on paper with a child lost at birth. Karal was never registered. They were never caught.

He forces his feet into his boots, the leather stiff and unforgiving; water won't fetch itself.

Bucket in hand, the cool doorknob feels solid under his palm. Light stabs through the gap as he cracks it open. He squints against it, hazel eyes watering, then pulls the door wide.

The hammer and anvil in his head ring louder.

The worn dirt path to the well stretches like an eternity, each step sending fresh spikes to his temples. The bucket drops two floors down—a long hollow rattle into the dark, but better than walking to the river. His house sits on Gallow's far east edge for good reason. Smithing means flames and sparks. Out here, backed by the southern forest and sparse neighbors, a stray ember won't burn down half the village.

Back inside, he sets water to boil and stares at the bed. Fragments drift back from the night before: Soma swigging fizzles and telling tales from their youth. Somehow, the tunku chase story came up. Everyone laughed at its ridiculousness.

When they were seven, an older boy told them about a rite of passage to prove their manhood: tip over a tunka. Seemed simple enough. So late one night the three of them snuck out, heading to the Magnus farm. Several of those large, feathery beasts stood out there in the dark—broad as all three boys combined, plump and unmoving, asleep on short legs. Under the new moon's darkness, they targeted a smaller isolated tunka and ran at it, ramming the dark shape with all their might.

The wall of muscle didn't budge.

The creature let out an annoyed, piercing bellow and turned toward them. In the near dark, the silhouetted spiral horns of a young male looked menacing.

Realization hit: they'd just tried to tip a tunku, known for their irritable tempers. They ran.

The beast chased them through the darkness until they found a tree to climb. Ives swore it chased them two miles. Soma vouched for four. The distances grew with each retelling.

A warm grin spreads across Karal's face.

Boiling water snaps him back to the moment. Fumbling with dried yubu leaves, several flecks miss the filter and spill into the mug. He pours the water anyway. It turns deep orange, foaming as the leaves wrinkle into hard little balls. A bitter aroma fills the room. Karal swallows the warm liquid, jolted by its intense flavor and caffeinated qualities. The yubu helps the worst of the headache retreat.

He manages runny eggs, burnt fatty jambo, and decent toast despite his poor cooking skills. Eating stirs more memories— including Soma vomiting on his floor.

"That stinking truga!"

Fortified, he tackles the mess: straightens furniture, gathers clothes, sweeps up ceramic shards, and scrubs away Soma's foul contribution last.

His final chore is tidying himself. By the light, maybe an hour remains before Clara arrives. With warm, soapy water in the basin, he runs his razor along the sides of his head in quick passes. Scissors tame the long brown hair on top—no precision, just short, modest curls.

Rubbing the crusts from his eyes with soapy fingers stings them shut. A litany of curses escapes as he splashes and wipes clean.

He dunks his head in the remaining water from the bucket, scrubbing away the soot and the lingering scent of the tavern. His skin emerges honey-colored and freckled, but a dull pain flares near his cheekbone. He traces a rising knot with a cautious fingertip.

"Did Ives and I fight again?"

He moves to the mirror and examines the lump, shaking his head —no memory of how he earned it. Thank goodness for the Cycle's end—accelerated healing is an unexpected benefit amid its otherwise jarring effects. The last thing he needs on top of the hangover is Clara arriving with a million questions.

Sniffing through a pile of clothes, he finds some that don't make him turn green. When there's a chance, they'll get soaked and restored to a semi-stained but functional state.

He pauses at the mirror—a rare moment of vanity. He doesn't look bad, though his face is too round, his lips too soft. Still can't grow even a light mustache. At least he's rugged and built. He flexes. The muscles grow taut beneath his shirt as the mirror fogs.

When he wipes it clean, he catches sight of the untouched bed next to his.

He pauses.

He fills his lungs and lets out a long, profound sigh.

In that bed, a fever dragged on, taking his father's life. Months later, the pain still lingers. So many days were spent in agony, watching Dad waste away, until a Cycle's end did him in.

Sweating and moaning, sometimes delirious, Dad spoke about

the shop—maintaining it, running it properly, like he knew what was coming. Pragmatic as ever. It drove Karal crazy, though watching him fade gave his words weight.

Dad was his sole blood relative in the village. Lessons about being strong, both inside and out, came from him, but his most valuable teaching was smithing. From a young age, Karal knew he wanted to become a blacksmith, just like his father. The scent of iron, the warmth of the forge, shaping metal into whatever form he chose—it was love at first sight.

At seventeen, he's likely the youngest blacksmith in Ra, running his own shop. Most begin apprenticing around twelve. Karal was forging his own hammer by that age.

Dad's words return when doubt grows. *You're good at this. Let your skills speak for themselves. Don't let anyone tell you different. Don't let them take your identity.*

He'd give anything to hear that voice one more time.

Wiping away a stray tear, Karal straightens. Mourning does his dad a disservice. Honoring him means being the finest smith possible.

The walk to the shop's door is cathartic. He presses his palm against the worn wood, summoning a shared ritual.

"This is more than my home," Karal whispers. "This is my heritage. My lifeblood. My joy. I will honor it by crafting the finest wares with my hands and heart."

The headache doesn't vanish, but it retreats as he crosses the threshold. Everything feels right. Every tool sits where it should. The job list holds tight in his mind. Every ounce of ore accounted for. When he was younger, dreams of exploring the island of Ra were a daily occurrence. Seeing the world beyond the village was a goal.

That doesn't matter anymore. He belongs here.

There are no regrets.

A knock on the outside door breaks the silence.

Unbidden, a smile rises. Clara.

CLARA

Clara bursts through the door, her grin fading. Her eyes widen as they sweep over him.

"Karal, you look terrible! Did you cut your own hair again? I told you I'd do it. How are you feeling? What did you do to yourself? Can I get you some water?"

"A little quieter, please, Clara. It's been a slow morning."

"Oh, had some fun last night, did you?" A mischievous smirk crosses her face. "You know you're not supposed to drink fizzle at the end of a Cycle. You could die! What if you didn't eat enough or dried out, or fell at the wrong moment? Look at what happened to Charlee Rosson."

Karal sighs, rolling his eyes. "Charlee had a problem with his heart. You remember—he used to get winded easily. It wasn't the Cycle that did him in; it was his poor health."

Silence drops between them. The ghost of Charlee lingers for a heartbeat—he'd been a good kid.

Clara shakes it off and flits about the shop, red braid bouncing as she snags safety gear—gloves, heavy apron, boots, thick shirt. She's seen Karal's scars. She knows better. Her green eyes—bright jade, almost luminous in the morning light—shift between the workbench and Karal as she preps.

"So, who did you meet up with? Anyone new?" Being just twelve and the eldest of five, she's held to the highest standards by her parents. Fun is a rare currency for her.

"Just me and Soma. Oh, and Ives, I guess. We were celebrating with old Ruffalo and his boys. They got a good trade for their pumatee in village Pastoral, so they bought us some drinks." Smiling, he winks and preps the forge.

Clara can't wait to be old enough to join Karal at the inn. At least he doesn't talk about girls all the time. "Are you and Ives talking again? I can't believe you didn't talk for months." She pauses, hoping to hear the story. "Why won't you tell me what happened? You know I'm good with secrets."

Karal ignores the probing and focuses on the forge.

"Come on, he's your best friend. What happened? You can trust me. Was it over a girl?"

A chuckle escapes as he shakes his head. "Water under the bridge, Clara. Took a few drinks to loosen us up, but we fell back into old habits soon enough." Rubbing his cheek, he spreads soot across the bump. "We were singing *Ye Old Bunghee* before long."

Frustration flickers as Clara rolls her eyes. Ignoring the slight, she shifts gears. "Guess what?!" She drops the apron she's holding. "There's a stranger in town."

Karal raises an eyebrow.

"He was with old Augustine, riding a giant cambra, and he had a Sinna with him. I got a look as they walked by the farm. When I came here, I saw their cambras at Headman Lindor's house. That thing was massive—all scales and fins. I've never seen anything like it."

Karal pauses, curious. "No one comes to Gallow. We're the dead end of the south." He shrugs. "Maybe they're from the Census."

"Yeah, but they had a Sinna with them. They mostly work the fields for farmers." Freckled cheeks flush with excitement. "Augustine comes around every month for trades, but why did he bring some-one?" She gasps, her eyes lighting up. "Maybe they're starting a new settlement! There could be a lottery for who gets to go. I'd volunteer —you'd have to come, Karal!"

Karal smirks, sarcasm rising. "So you and I go to some new place and build a village? Now you're just being silly." He shakes his head.

Clara wrinkles her nose. "Oh, come on, Karal. I come twice a week to help you organize, set up orders, and be there when you need an extra hand. We're a great team." Pleading lines into her voice. "We always talk about exploring Ra and leaving the village. This could be a terrific adventure—and you know I'm good at cooking!" She sticks her tongue out.

He hesitates before he responds. "I wanted to explore Ra and still do sometimes. But this shop, Clara—it's all I've got left of my dad." Staring at the anvil, his voice softens. "Leaving would mean abandoning his legacy, and—"

Three steady knocks thud against the outside door.

Karal and Clara exchange glances.

"Master Karal, are you there? May I come in? It's Augustine from Pastoral." The voice is stripped of its usual warmth.

"Come in—we haven't started work yet. We're full of chatter today." Calling back, Karal sticks his tongue out at Clara, returning her earlier gesture.

Old Augustine enters with a dour expression etched on his weathered face.

Behind him, a shadow falls over the floor. An enormous man stoops to clear the doorway.

VISITORS

Karal's breath hitches as the massive figure fills the entryway, blocking the light. Darkness swallows the shop. Though Karal is solidly built from years at the forge, this man dwarfs him.

He stands six and a half feet tall, towering over any villager in Gallow. Midnight robes with gold lattice stretch across broad shoulders. A thin black shirt with matching filigree clings to his chest. Black riding pants bear the same intricate pattern.

Despite arriving by cambra, his uniform remains pristine—no dust, no wrinkles.

In his right hand, an ebony staff topped with a polished sphere gleams like a black mirror.

But it's his face that holds Karal frozen. Slicked-back hair frames a pale, sharp visage. His eyes are flat, dark voids—lacking the jewel-tones common to Ones. They look less like eyes and more like holes in a mask.

Augustine clears his throat, his expression muted. "Good Morning, Karal. I'm pleased to see you. We are fortunate you smith wares with as much quality as your father did before you." A tepid smile rises on his face.

Karal shifts his eyes to Augustine, but the older man won't meet his gaze.

"Well, it's my pleasure to help the villages. Gallow benefits from trade with your village." Karal turns back to the dark man, who roams the shop, inspecting tools and unfinished orders. "What can I help you with? Have you brought a new customer in need of something?"

"I am not a customer." A harsh, baritone voice escapes the man in black. His eyes reflect little light—small white dots from deep within their sockets.

Augustine pales. Fear flickers across his face. "I'm here in a formal capacity. I've been tasked with bringing an official to this shop based on a complaint received from a villager."

Karal frowns and crosses his arms. "If this is about Swazey's axe, I told him that if he left it out in the rain, it would eventually rust. He's been complaining ever since. Left it out in the dead of winter and 'forgot about it'. What am I—"

"It's not that!"

Augustine's desperate interruption stops him. Heavy boots creak against the floorboards. The stranger stops directly behind Augustine, a shadow looming over them both.

"This is about a violation of the Laws," Augustine whispers.

Clara's breath catches. She stumbles back as the stranger looks their way. Karal edges toward her, blocking her from his view.

"We haven't done nothing wrong. This shop operates according to the Laws. Why isn't Lindor here? He's the Headman in Gallow. Who made this complaint?"

"Lindor wouldn't follow up on the complaint, so they went around him to me," Augustine says, his voice cracking. "I had no choice but to report it."

Karal opens his mouth, then hesitates. An uneasy feeling rises in his gut. "And who are you? A constable?"

A mocking smile crosses the stranger's face, exposing dull, yellow teeth and black gums. He lopes toward Karal, each step pounding like a hammer on the creaky floor.

"I am a Klenzeer, the hands of the Overseers." Pride drips from his voice.

Karal's heart skips. His father's warnings flash through his mind. *Scourge* and other colorful words were used to describe these despicable tools of the Overseers.

"And what Law is being broken?" Karal's confidence slips.

Silence stretches as the Klenzeer glares. Narrowing his eyes, his lips curl into a faint grin. "The Law of Duty."

"No!" Clara whimpers. "It can't be! I help out here in exchange for the services Karal provides my pa. We can't be violating the Law." Her voice cracks, lacking its usual charm.

Dark eyes fix on Clara. A sneer grows. "And who are you?"

She swallows hard. "Clara Braeger, sir."

The Klenzeer approaches with slow steps. Clara seems to shrink into herself. "And what are you doing in this shop, Clara Braeger? Are you training to become a smith?"

Her eyes go wide. "No, no, no, sir. I know the Laws. I'm here to help. That's all."

"Recite the Law, child. We shall see if your Headman has instilled the proper lessons in his village."

Clara glances at Karal, then at Augustine, who nods. She straightens her back, her voice trembling.

"The Law states that all Ones shall perform their trades and attend to their duties as designated by their genders and roles. None shall deviate to ensure the strengthening of our bloodlines in the generations to come."

Silence falls, heavy and suffocating. The Klenzeer stands unmoving, eyes set on Clara.

"Leave."

The command is firm.

She stumbles into Karal. Fear fills her eyes as they lock with his. Grabbing her belongings, she nods at Augustine, tearful, as she rushes out of the shop.

Augustine tries to speak.

"Leave us, Augustine. You have done your part."

Worry crosses his face. He nods toward Karal and backs through the door, defeated.

Alone with the Klenzeer, Karal's heart thunders. He crosses his arms and hardens his expression. The Klenzeer begins prowling the shop, touching tools and wares as he circles, eyes never leaving the blacksmith of Gallow.

Karal waits, growing impatient. "What can I do for yo—"

"What is your name?" A pause. "Boy."

"Karal Stillburn," he snaps.

"And how long have you been smithing in this village?"

"I started learning the trade around the time I was five. But what does that hav—"

"Where is your mother?"

The question cuts through his rising confidence. He recites a practiced lie. "She left when Dad died. She and I didn't get along much."

The Klenzeer's face shows nothing.

"Where did she leave to, smith?"

"I don't know. Family, I guess. She had some relatives in—"

"Pastoral, Raymens, and Bentwood."

Karal's jaw tightens. He shifts his feet.

"Gladys Young has an interesting lineage that can be traced back generations. I checked every village she had family in." A pause. "Gallow's records were incomplete concerning your mother. Other villages were not."

A stifled inhale is all Karal manages before the Klenzeer continues.

"Do you know what I found when I questioned her relatives, boy?"

Karal gulps, shaking his head, staying quiet.

"Nothing."

His voice drops in pitch. "She hasn't been heard from in over seventeen years. Isn't that curious?" The grim smile returns.

Karal lowers his eyes and reaches for another lie. "She must not have gotten along with many people. Family can be a fickle thing."

Laughter erupts—a hollow grating sound.

Karal wants to cover his ears but won't. "What does all this have to do with me?! I haven't broken any La—"

"Seventeen is young to run a shop. How proud you must be to operate this shanty on your own."

Karal stifles a growl. "I do alright in this shanty."

"You must be proud to inherit it from your father. A tradition passed on from father to—"

"Get to the point!"

The Klenzeer returns his glare—a hollow smile rising. Turning away, he retreats into the shadows of the forge, eyes catching the dim light like two white sparks.

"Of all the Laws, Duty is the easiest to follow. You are given a choice of trades and execute them as per the roles designated by our Overseers. Farmers, Carpenters, Blacksmiths—"

"I know all of this! What does it have to do with me?!"

"EVERYTHING!"

A flash of light erupts from the staff, blinding and violent. Karal stumbles, blinking away the white spots. The Klenzeer's voice comes from somewhere close.

"Lindor's records might not have been valuable regarding your mother, but the undertaker's records were much more telling. Gladys Stillburn died during childbirth. No child was recorded as being born. Yet somehow, Leone Stillburn raised a son!"

A shuffle of steps, then an iron grip seizes Karal's throat. He's slammed into the wall with bone-cracking force, feet lifting off the floor. Choking. Gasping. Tools crash to the ground as dust showers them.

"WHO ARE YOU?!" the Klenzeer growls.

Karal struggles for breath.

"You might think yourself strong, but the Will of the Overseers is stronger! Do you believe what you do here goes unnoticed? We hear everything, see everything. No one remains hidden for long." The Klenzeer leans in, breath reeking, somehow both acrid and sweet, like rotting fruit.

"Where did you come from?"

Karal fights the iron grip. Spots crowd his vision.

Ther Klenzeer presses close, lips slick. "I will expose your secrets!"

He releases him. Karal crashes to the floor in a heap, lungs screaming for air. Desperation and fear burn away into rage.

A fallen cross-peen hammer lies within reach. Trembling, he looks up at the brute. Lightning quick, he grabs it, turns the pointed end toward the Klenzeer, and roars as he swings with everything he has.

The Klenzeer catches him mid-swing, lazily blocking with his staff. He drives Karal to the ground with such force that his head cracks against the wood. Light explodes across his vision. Air leaves his lungs.

A knee drops onto his throat. The Klenzeer's massive weight crushes the life out of him.

The door bursts open.

The Klenzeer yells at the Sinna, ignoring Karal. As consciousness fades, his final words echo.

"Prepare him for judgment!"

Gallow

CONFESSIONS

A bell rings.

Karal jolts awake. Blinding sunlight forces his eyes shut. The familiar scent of iron is gone—he's not in the shop. His head throbs. All he craves is darkness. Buzzing resonates in the background somewhere behind him. Panic rises as he struggles to piece thoughts together.

Deep breath. Calm down.

He quells the fear somehow, heart still pounding. It settles in a cold knot in his stomach as he finds his center. The bell continues tolling.

He tries to shift, but his arms won't move. Iron chains rattle. His wrists are bound. As he adjusts to the light, he recognizes the buzzing as the Raymonde River rushing behind him. A few yards away, old Augustine pulls the rope of the meeting bell, his eyes fixed firmly on the dirt. Villagers gather in a semicircle around them, staring at Karal.

Clarity hits. He's on the Posts.

They're required in every settlement by Law: two sturdy wooden posts buried deep, eight feet tall, iron chains ending in manacles.

Gallow hasn't seen a Judgment in over twenty Cycles. A dispute over land led to an argument over livestock: one farmer slaughtered a young tunku he claimed as his own before a decision was rendered. Headman Lindor was forced to whip the man ten times on these same posts.

Chained between them, Karal's arms are held high while his body slumps below. The manacles bite into his wrists, forming dark bruises. Peering through narrowed eyes, villagers stare back. Their gazes pierce through him, exposing the vulnerability beneath his tough exterior. The bell stops tolling as Gallow finishes assembling.

He scans the crowd searching for a sympathetic face. Amber eyes, violet eyes, storm-grey—the varied hues of Gallow bloodlines. Solid folk weathered by labor. Over a hundred Ones gathered in judgment, and not a soul will meet his gaze.

From Headman Lindor's home near the village center, the Klenzeer emerges, followed by Lindor on his heels, wearing a troubled expression. Dressed in black, the Klenzeer resembles a living shadow in the daylight as he marches out, stopping a few feet from the Posts. The ebony staff in his left hand seems to swallow the sunlight. Villagers watch him with curiosity. Many avert their eyes, while others gawk. Gallow has never hosted a representative of the mysterious Overseers.

Striding toward Karal, he towers imposingly. A deep-set frown etches his face, and his eyes have a sharp glint. He leans in, his voice a private, venomous murmur.

"You have an audience. Is this what you wanted when you attacked me?" He lowers until they are face-to-face. "My masters want examples, not corpses. They want to grow the population, not shrink it." Closer still. "Stop this charade. Whoever you are, admit to this farce and make it clear that this violation should never happen here or anywhere else. I will ensure your reassignment is smooth and peaceful. All you need to do is confess to your origin and whatever deception is occurring in this village."

Karal's head clears as his predicament crystallizes. He has nothing. No power. No leverage. Everything he is—everything his father was—is back in that shop. A single tear tracks through the soot on his cheek—a moment of weakness he regrets instantly.

"Go ahead and cry." The Klenzeer's voice drips with satisfaction. "The village will learn your secrets soon enough, and they will understand." He wipes the tear with his gloved hand, wearing a vile smirk.

Karal winces from his touch. Silence stretches between them. They lock eyes until Karal looks away. "I'll confess," he whispers. The words taste like ash.

"Good. Be loud and quick. I tire of this simple village. I'll take you to a town where you'll enjoy your reassignment." He turns to address Gallow, voice booming over the crowd.

"People of Gallow, I am a Klenzeer, a representative of your benevolent Overseers who give much and ask for little in return. They have created Laws to guide you into prosperity and ascension. I am here to enforce those Laws when they are broken." He gestures toward Karal. "Beside me is Karal Stillburn—a neighbor, a villager, and a liar." He spits the last word. "He has been caught breaking an essential Law and is here to confess his wrongdoings. Listen well, so you do not follow him into ruin." He turns to Karal, lips curling.

Karal scans the crowd. Familiar faces appear stricken and confused. Soma. Clara. Ives. Mind wavering between haze and clarity, he closes his eyes, inhaling a deep breath, the Raymonde roaring behind him.

Bracing himself, preparing to yell, he shuts his eyes. "Gallow Village! My name is Karal Stillburn, and I—" He pauses, opening his eyes to glare at the Klenzeer. "I am the rightful blacksmith of Gallow! I am Leone Stillburn's heir and have lived my life to serve Gallow with my forge. I will always—"

Thud!

A fist slams into his cheek. Blood sprays from his mouth along with a pair of broken teeth. He clings to consciousness. Cheek and lip swell. The assembly cries out in shock.

The Klenzeer comes within inches of his face, enraged. Blood drips from Kara's split lips, breath labored. Acid fills the Klenzeer's voice. "You are prideful, and that will be your end. I will be there when the Council of Wisdom eviscerates your mind. I will be the last thing you see when you disappear from this world. And when you are a blank slate, I will make you suffer any way that I choose."

Turning to the village, a twisted smile grows. "It appears we will have a judgment today, and punishment will be served. Who has accused Karal Stillburn of breaking our Laws?"

A dirty hand shoots up from the crowd. Villagers part to reveal Laramy Uphill—chubby-faced, scraggly-bearded, belly pushing out ahead of thin arms and legs. A boy pretending to be a man. Behind him, his father Amarus beams with pride. Karal recognizes Laramy and shoots daggers at him. The lazy apprentice his father had fired. The boy whom Clara replaced.

Laramy stops several paces from the Klenzeer, trembling but triumphant. The Klenzeer clears his throat. "State your name for your fellow villagers and tell us your accusation."

"I am Laramy Uphill of Gallow." His voice shakes. "My pa is Amarus Uphill, and we live up the hill there." Pointing west, he continues. "I accuse Karal Stillburn of lying to steal the position of village blacksmith."

Murmurs ripple through the crowd. People turn to each other, pointing, rumors spreading. A stiff pounding of the Klenzeer's rod settles the chatter. Silence returns.

"The Law of Duty requires that each of you execute your trade as designated by your roles. Yet, some form of deception lies here. Karal Stillburn shouldn't exist, yet here he is. Records have been falsified!" The Klenzeer's eyes dart to Headman Lindor. "His existence denies villagers the right to become the proper blacksmith of Gallow."

Faces watch with rapt attention. His command over Gallow is absolute.

"And why do you suspect Karal is hiding something, young Laramy?"

"I heard it at the inn from that one." Laramy points a finger.

The villagers scramble back as if the boy's finger were a brand. Left standing alone in the center of the clearing is Ives.

Karal's best friend.

IVES

Karal stares at Ives, searching for a trace of guilt. Ives stands still, unblinking.

All Karal feels is the crushing weight of regret. This is all his fault. If he hadn't—

The memory hits him, unbidden and sharp.

MONTHS AGO, Karal surprised Ives with a party at the inn. All their friends gathered to celebrate his seventeenth birthday. Soma kept their mugs full of fizzle all night. Not surprisingly, they both got drunk. When the innkeeper kicked them out towards midnight, Karal and Ives stumbled through the cool, crisp air to his place. Singing and laughing at the top of their lungs, they managed to make it over the threshold before collapsing onto his bed.

The room spun, the ceiling seeming to drift sideways. Just as Ives was settling into sleep, Karal burst into song.

"—they ended up with itchy mouths and ugly red hives and blamed it all on the nasty man they called Ives!"

Ives laughed so hard he almost fell off the bed. Karal saved him, extending his hand to keep him from the edge.

Laughter ebbed to a comfortable silence. Ives turned and found Karal gazing at him, looking pensive. They stalled on releasing each other's hands. Ives lay on his side. Karal mirrored him, never breaking eye contact.

Growing up as friends—siblings, really—they'd known each other since they could crawl. Karal was rough-and-tumble like all the other boys, yet more impulsive and prone to getting into trouble. It made their friendship fun and sometimes dangerous. Wounds, bruises, and near-drownings were a weekly occurrence.

As teenagers, things changed. Their friendship became strained. Karal grew secretive and distant, yet Ives never stopped reaching for him.

Now, as older teens, not much had changed. Karal was still impulsive and reckless, but he cared for Ives like a brother, which made it confusing when Ives lunged to kiss him, and Karal didn't pull back.

Their tongues met and danced clumsily. Shifting on top of him, Ives caressed Karal's face and neck. Warmth flooded Karal's skin under his touch. His neck burned. He rubbed Ives' arms, feeling his strength as Ives held himself above him.

They kissed with more urgency, passion intensifying, barely holding back. Ives pulled away, then bit Karal's lips with a light pull. Karal gasped. The moment felt perfect—but then Karal snapped, pushing Ives away.

"Stop! We have to stop! I'm sorry." Karal spoke the words, exasperated.

"What's wrong? What did I do?" Ives' voice was full of concern.

"No—we can't. This is a mistake."

"I don't understand, Karal. Don't you want this?" The heat between them cooled.

"I do, Ives, but not like this. You don't understand what I've gone through—"

"No, I don't understand, Karal!" Ives stumbled up from the bed. "You've grown so distant for years now. Since we were ten. Not only did you shut out all our friends, but you've shut me out, too. We were best friends!"

"We still are! You're my closest friend, Ives. I've been going through—" Karal got up, reaching for Ives' hand, drawing him close, their eyes meeting. "I love you, Ives. I have to tell yo—"

Ives lunged to kiss Karal. Alcohol, emotion, passion—whatever the reason, it was out of character but god's damned enthralling. Karal kissed back, rubbing Ives' back and hair with his calloused hands.

The kissing escalated.

Karal abruptly stopped it, pushing Ives away again.

"What is wrong, Karal?!" Ives shouted, anger pulsing in his gaze. "Why are you doing this? We love each other, Karal. This is what happens next. I don't care if the Laws forbid males to love each other. I still love you." Desperation grew on his face. "What is—what is wrong with you?"

The words hit like a slap. Karal withdrew into himself, turning away. "You don't understand, Ives. You'll never understand."

Ives moved closer. "How am I supposed to understand if you keep shutting me out! We're friends, but it doesn't work if we can't trust each other."

Silence.

"Don't you trust me, Karal?"

Karal's eyes moved to the floor. A long exhale escaped him.

"Ives, of course I trus—"

"You don't—you don't trust me?" Ives' voice cracked. "All this time together, and you can't look me in the eyes and tell me that you do? We've been sticking up for each other for years! Through mischief, fights, stolen treats, teasing girls—all of it. All of it means nothing if we can't trust each other."

The hurt in his eyes was heartbreaking, but he didn't stop there.

"You and your dad—"

"Leave him out of this. He had nothing to do with us."

"No, he had everything to do with us." Ives' face twisted with anger as he let go of all that built-up resentment. "Your dad controlled you. Once you got older, he kept you away from your friends and from me. Bolted you inside so you could be a smith, just like him."

Shaking, Ives continued. "Do you know how many times I knocked on your door just to see you, and he denied me?" Ives mimicked Leone's voice: "'Karal's busy learning his trade, Ives.' 'Sorry son, a tricky pour today.' 'Karal's busy hammering, Ives. Go play with the other boys.' He denied you, and he denied me. Your dad—"

"Enough! He did what he had to do. He helped me be the best version of myself."

"Karal, he was a truga, and he's no longer here!"

"That's enough, Ives. Leave!"

Ives stood his ground, crossing his arms—a stubborn look planted on his face. "No."

"GET OUT!" Karal screamed, done with the moment, done with the emotions, done with all of it.

"No! Not until you tell me what is wrong with yo—"

Karal's fist flew out before he could stop himself. Ives took it square on the cheek and fell against the dining room table, smacking his head on the way down.

"Nothing is wrong with me! Not a god's—damned—thing!"

Face beet red, fists clenched, tears streamed down Karal's cheeks.

Ives got up. The damage wasn't just physical. Fresh tears spilled from his eyes. In all the years they had known each other, Karal had never seen Ives cry. Not once.

"Ives, I—I'm sorr—"

"Don't bother. I wouldn't trust your apology anyway."

Ives turned and left.

Now, staring at Karal chained between the Posts, Ives blinks—the first sign of life—but his face reveals nothing.

"Come forth, villager." The Klenzeer's voice is condescending and loud.

LIES

Karal watches Ives stride toward the Klenzeer, toolbelt clanking at his waist. Villagers whisper as he passes. Ives doesn't flinch. Only the slight tremor in his left hand betrays him.

"Turn." The Klenzeer's voice carries across the crowd. "State your name for all to hear."

"I'm Ivan Scolas, Jr. I'm a junior carpenter here in Gallow. I have lived here all my life."

"And what did you tell Mr. Uphill that caused this accusation to be brought before me?"

Ives pauses. His eyes find Karal, who holds on to consciousness by will alone. Then he looks back at the Klenzeer, and a familiar, disarming smile rises on his face.

Karal has seen this expression dozens of times. Whenever they fleeced a baker or farmer after stealing treats, Ives had always been the one to calm their ire. "I don't remember much of that night. I was pretty drunk." He relaxes. "I was probably going on about Karal holding back secrets about smithing. If I remember correctly, it was about something Karal was forging. Not to spoil a surprise or anything, but he was making a jewelry box for Clara. Being all quiet about it and wouldn't tell his best friend." He huffs. "We got into a fight, and there may have been fizzle involved." He shifts his gaze to Karal. "Trust is hard to come by. Maybe he lost trust in me, but you know, it happens." Returning his gaze to the Klenzeer, a solemn expression grows. "I've known Karal all my life, and if there's anything he's hiding, I think I'd know about it."

A ripple of hope stirs in Karal's chest. The villagers nod. Ives stands clean-shaven, speaking with ease. Laramy appears disheveled and shifty-eyed.

Pacing before the two men, the Klenzeer scrutinizes them. Laramy lowers his eyes while Ives meets his gaze. Moving on, he studies Karal. The blood dripping from his lip and mouth has stopped. Drenched in sweat, he's still clothed in his smithing gear—a leather apron, heavy hemp shirt, wool breeches, and boots. The sun bakes him on the Posts.

The Klenzeer is about to turn back to the crowd when he stops. He approaches Karal with a look of doubt, angling for a better view, and catches sight of something beneath the shirt. A cruel smile crosses his face. Realizing something is wrong, Karal tries to shift position, but it's too late.

The Klenzeer dismisses Ives and Laramy with a brusque wave, then pivots to address the villagers, his voice tinged with snark. "Who am I to believe? There are two stories here. What decision must I make to ensure that justice is upheld?" He paces. "Perhaps there is deception here, but by which party? Who gains the most by lying to me?"

Without warning, he slams his staff on the ground and grips the dark orb at its peak. It begins glowing a deep plum. A quarter twist unscrews it to reveal a wicked dagger attached to it—a serpentine blade curving to a fine point, the metal drinking daylight and gleaming purple. It vibrates in his hand, blurring the metal, making a disturbing sound like a swarm of angry buzzles. The crowd gasps at its sudden appearance. Turning to Karal, he lowers the weapon and closes the gap between them, lips pursed in a grim smile. "We will now expose you for the liar that you are."

Karal's eyes widen. His heart races as the blade rises. Scanning the crowd, he recognizes several friends he grew up with. Their fear mirrors his own. His hands clench into fists. Tears form.

With a deft swipe, the ties binding Karal's leather apron are cut. It drops silently to the ground. Next is the heavy shirt. The loose drawstrings that close the top are severed one by one as the Klenzeer savors each cut. When no more strings remain, he slices the shirt with little effort to its hem. Opening up the frayed halves exposes flesh and a wooden binder held together by string.

He laughs at the contraption and cuts the strings. It falls to the ground, revealing Karal's breasts.

Silence blankets the square. Some gape; others look away. Ives stares at the ground, his face twisted in a shame that looks like death. Karal stares at the dirt and gives them nothing.

Not satisfied, the Klenzeer works on the drawstring of her breeches, cutting it with precise, clean snaps of his wrist. The wool is sliced from hip to toe down each leg, dropping them to the ground. He kicks away the unlaced boots. With a metallic click, he sheaths his weapon in the staff and faces the crowd, Karal's body on display behind him.

"It would seem I have exposed the truth, does it not? A woman serving in a man's role, denying others this right. A birth hidden and manipulated, from the Census to perpetuate a lie!" He surveys the crowd with satisfaction, then yells, almost foaming at the mouth. "Know this, Gallow! You are not above the Law! We do not forget you here at the ends of Ra! You are charged with telling the truth at all times and exposing lies!" His voice builds. "Our Laws are written to create a greater population. You will obey, or you will suffer the same fate as this!" The last word hisses as he points to Karal.

"Headman Lindor, come!" The command rings out from the Klenzeer, spitting.

From the crowd shuffles the aging headman. Tidy, braided white hair frames a weathered face. Lindor stands a few inches shorter than the Klenzeer and walks with the proud gait of a man who has worked hard all his life. A farmer, father of four—generations of his family, founded Gallow. His face is defiant. He opens his mouth to speak, but the Klenzeer silences him with a finger to his lips.

"Lindor Raymonde, you have been charged with lying to our Overseers, allowing this deception to continue under your watch, and therefore defying the very Laws that you and your family have sworn to uphold. You have been found guilty and will serve your punishment."

The move is lightning fast. The Klenzeer draws the dagger and tears it across Lindor's throat. The blade thrums once. In one fluid motion, the dagger slides back into the staff. Blood hits the ground.

"NO!" The sound tears from Karal's lungs.

Panic erupts. Blood flows from Lindor's neck—a single spurt, then a stream down his tunic. He drops to his knees, hands clutching his throat, convulsing, trying to speak. He falls forward into the pooling blood, wheezes, and goes still.

The crowd breaks into vulgar shouts. The Klenzeer studies the commotion, then slams the dull end of his staff on the ground.

"SILENCE!"

The orb burns a brief, dull red. Every villager, save Karal, winces in agony as if struck. The silence is profound. The Klenzeer speaks, his voice dark, surveying his flock. "Gallow, you have fallen low in the eyes of the Overseers. Forty-two days from now, when the current Cycle completes, your taxes will rise. This will continue for the next twenty Cycles." He gestures toward the crowd. "Amarus Uphill, you will collect this levy as the new Village Headman. Your family will inherit the lands of family Raymonde, and they shall toil under your boot for twenty Cycles hence. The price of truth is leadership and gifts from the Overseers. The price for deceit and lies is death and forfeiture of rights."

He pauses, looking at Karal. "However, in your case, girl, you shall have your mind cleansed, and you will bear fruit for the greater good."

He surveys the cowering crowd with satisfaction. A wicked smile crosses his face when he turns back to Karal.

CRACK!

A rock strikes him on the temple. He staggers, dropping to a knee.

HATE

The rock strikes true.

The Klenzeer staggers, stunned, dropping his staff and relinquishing the hold on Gallow.

Guilt crystallizes into action. Ives sprints to Karal, his hand diving for the hammer at his belt. He pounds the right manacle. *Ping.* Metal shrieks against metal with each swing. Villagers find their voices, their cheers rising in a ragged wave.

A grunt. The Klenzeer's Sinna lumbers toward them, aggression in its black, recessed eyes. The creature is massive—gray-skinned, arms thick with muscle. Its awkward gait leaves divots in the ground with each step. It growls from its toothless maw, hunched forward.

Ives's hands shake. He looks at the beast, then back at the manacle.

A hail of stones pelts the Sinna. Soma and Clara lead the charge, screaming curses as they drive the creature back. The barrage buys Ives the seconds he needs.

He swings again. The right manacle shatters. Karal collapses towards the dirt, held up only by her left arm. Ives catches her, concern etched on his face. "I'm sorry," he stammers, voice breaking. "I'm so sorry, Karal. This is all my fault."

Behind them, the Klenzeer rises on slow legs. Ives's jaw sets as he attacks the remaining manacle.

Rocks continue pelting the Sinna, driving it to a halt with roars of frustration. Ives works, frantic. Karal mutters in a haze, her words slurring together—Lindor... the blood...

The clang of the left manacle breaking echoes. Karal falls into Ives' arms. He pulls her close, his lips brushing her forehead in a desperate, silent apology.

Villagers charge the square, swinging tools and fists at the Klenzeer and his beast. Ives hauls Karal toward the bridge, her steps hobbling and uncertain.

"ENOUGH!"

The Klenzeer's voice thunders through the turmoil. The orb pulses a violent red. All of Gallow staggers—except Karal. Villagers clutch their heads in pain. Some cry out. Ives collapses, writhing on the wooden planks of the bridge.

The Klenzeer stands, staff in hand, blood dripping from the welt on his temple. Murder shines in his eyes. He glares at the writhing villagers. Wobbling as he stands to his full height, he turns, searching for Karal. A guttural snarl escapes as he spots her and stalks toward the bridge.

Ives forces himself up. His head throbs with a sickening pulse, but he reaches for Karal, pulling her onto the bridge. She shuffles, bewildered, recognizing the approaching danger. Their footsteps echo—hollow, frantic thuds against the wood. The Klenzeer's longer stride cuts the distance in an instant. They make it halfway across before he reaches for Karal.

Ives releases her and swings his hammer in a protective arc. The Klenzeer flinches back. Ives swings again, but the Klenzeer is faster. He blocks the hammer with his rod and seizes Ives by the throat.

He lifts Ives off the ground as if he weighs nothing. Ives kicks, fingers clawing at the iron grip, the hammer clattering away. Karal screams his name.

Looking down at her, no mercy lives in the Klenzeer's gaze.

"This is the price of your lies."

He unhooks the orb-handled knife from his rod with one deft turn of his right hand. A hum sounds as it flares to life. The rod clatters to the ground, and the spell over Gallow lifts. Grinning with sinister joy, he plunges the dagger into Ives's chest, the blade piercing through his back. Ives's body jerks. Blood floods his lungs, spewing from his mouth in a hot spray. He spasms, then looks at Karal one last time, the light in his eyes dimming into a dull, gray stare.

The Klenzeer drops him.

KARAL SCREAMS. She snatches up the hammer, plants, and swings. The heavy head connects with the Klenzeer's cheek, raking his nose and shattering bone. She swings again, but he catches her wrist and backhands her. The force sends her spinning, her face hitting the bridge with a sickening crack.

The Klenzeer takes his time assessing his wounds. The Sinna has pinned several villagers to the ground, holding them captive—awaiting its master's orders. The Klenzeer grips the dagger, its vibrations steady and menacing. Karal backs away, rising to her feet with the hammer in hand, using the bridge's railing for leverage. Her mouth is a mess of copper-tasting blood.

"This is your fault, Karal Stillburn." The Klenzeer gestures around at the chaos. "You could have prevented it all but for your pride. When we take your name and memories, know that I will be there. They will brand my face in your dreams." His voice drops to a hiss. "You will remember me."

Karal spits a glob of blood at his face. He takes his time wiping the spittle away. Her hazel eyes burn every detail into memory—every scar, every crease on his face. She snarls with determination.

"I will kill you!"

She hurls the hammer.

The Klenzeer dodges, the heavy iron whistling past his ear. Karal turns and runs.

Rage contorts the Klenzeer's face as he swings the blade wide, missing her by inches.

Karal vaults over the railing of the bridge. Behind her, the Klenzeer crashes into the railing, fingers grazing the hairs on her neck.

She curls into a ball, taking one last, searing breath.

Splash!

Cold, dark water swallows her. The current pulls her under.

LOST

When Karal surfaces, the bridge is already distant. The Klenzeer watches, unmoving, his features twisted with rancor. Frigid water shocks her dulled mind awake. Gallow recedes in seconds, the village swallowed by the treeline as the river sweeps her downstream.

The Raymonde is relentless and swift. The current spins her as she fights to regain her bearings. One breath, then under again, struggling to stay afloat. Naked, the cold water stiffens her muscles and slows her movement. She shoves her heartache deep into her gut and strokes hard, breaking the surface with a jagged gasp.

Ahead, the old southern forest looms. Ancient trees overhang the river like a gaping mouth. Rapids churn where submerged boulders break the surface. Karal strains to swim clear, but her limbs feel sluggish, disconnected.

The current quickens. She slams into a boulder. Air bursts from her lungs as the stone strikes her right arm. She stays afloat, stroking hard, her resolve fading. Reaching the bank is no longer a choice; it's a necessity. She spots a gap in the white water on the left. Her lungs burn, the air feeling thin and useless.

Partway to the far bank, her leg strikes a low rock. Pain lances through her limb, spinning her counterclockwise. Another rock slams into her shoulder—numbness floods the joint.

Tree branches flash past overhead, blurring into a ceiling of green. The shade provides a brief respite. Bushes line the riverbank, branches dipping into the water.

She lunges for a low-lying branch of an ironweed bush and latches on. The current whips her. Sharp thorns pierce her palm as the water pulls at her. Blood swirls in the dark current.

Bruised and battered, she fights as the river drags with sweeping strength. Tensing her injured shoulder to keep from being swept away, she lifts her other arm out of the water and onto the bush. *So close.* Fingertips brush against an upper branch. She pulls. Thorns tear at her fingertips and embed deep—Karal grunts from the effort. Sharp points burrow deeper into the meat of her hand.

She lunges and grabs with her left hand. The branch holds, and she grips for dear life. Water pulls her downstream. Back muscles scream as she hauls herself up. The water threatens to drag her away, eroding her.

Crack!

The lower branch rips away. The sudden loss of tension sends her splashing back into the depths.

Racing away at dangerous speeds, she crashes into a large, flat-faced rock. Her face strikes stone. Vision dims. Pain engulfs her. Her mind flickers in and out of awareness. She thrashes as control slips away. Water floods her mouth, choking her. She's drowning.

A trill sounds overhead—a flitter darts through the canopy. She opens her eyes. Branches rush past impossibly fast. Then nothing. Weightless, she tumbles through the air, spinning as the cascading torrent fills her vision. She snatches one last breath before splashing into a deep, churning pool.

Fresh pain assaults her, but she fights on. Reaching bottom, she pushes upward, lungs screaming as she reemerges.

She keeps swimming, but freezing numbness overwhelms her. Limbs shake. Floating down the Raymonde, exhaustion wins. She is a passenger now.

As consciousness begins slipping away, her thoughts drift to Ives —his final moments, blood spreading across his chest, the light dying in his eyes.

His sacrifice was for nothing.

Her head goes under. Arms flail as consciousness begins to fade. Her hand strikes something solid—rough wood, debris. She squeezes. Pure instinct. Survival reflex. Whatever it is pulls her through the water, but the world is already fading to black.

A final breath slips away. Her grip fails. The river takes the rest.

MERCY

Karal awakens with a slow, heavy blink. Darkness surrounds her, broken by the glorious night sky above. It shimmers with countless stars.

Floating on her back, warm water undulates beneath her, waves buoying her. Her arms and legs are weightless, free of pain—she feels whole. Nothing hurts. Lucid in mind and body, an unexpected calm settles over her.

She turns her head. More sky in every direction. Water stretches from horizon to horizon, a mirror for the heavens.

Is this death?

A sound captures her attention. Lights on a wave disturb the calm. She stops floating and treads water. An image of her dad from childhood crashes into her—detailed and surreal, like a living memory, backlit by soft lights that shift with the ripples. She feels the stubble on his face. A sweet taste reaches her lips before it dissipates.

Behind her, another familiar sound signals a different memory. This wave carries her forging her first hammer, Dad guiding her through every step. Tears fall as she watches. Dad has that loving look of pride shining in his eyes.

Crashing from behind, a swell carries Ives's profile within it. A memory of her and Ives stealing treats cooling on a sill, repeating over and over. They giggle as they run away to eat their spoils. Sweetness fills her mouth.

Light bursts from the water's edge, illuminating the horizon. The sun highlights pastel hues that fill the sky—purples and blues blending with orange and yellow in a fusion of soft tones. Karal watches, captivated.

More memories flow past—climbing trees with Ives and Soma in the dead of night, her father's face when she told him about punching a boy, moments of joy from her life in Gallow. Each wave brings sweetness and longing.

Then a loud boom disrupts the harmony. Lightning threatens as waves begin to roil. Dark clouds roll in, and the temperature drops. Swells toss her about. The emotions of her fight with Ives crash into her, harsh words filtering through. Another wave blindsides her. Her dad, dying in his bed, delirium and sickness robbing him of his senses. The water tastes like smoke.

Her lips tremble. Ice crystals form on her lashes. Dark clouds obscure the sun while turbulent water threatens to drown her. Towering waves rise behind her. She can't swim away—the current pulls her back. A tidal wave forms, the world darkening unnaturally. The faded image of the Klenzeer appears within the wave. It looms over her, threatening to crush her. She clenches her jaw as it breaks. The impact feels like boulders as the surge tosses her around in flips and tumbles. Her lungs scream as cold water floods in.

She's dying.

The icy water drags her down until even the nightmare visions fade to black silence.

～

HER EYES FLUTTER OPEN. It's night. A canopy of trees fills her vision, illuminated by dull firelight and distant starlight. Everything feels muted and numb. Sleep threatens to pull her back. Moving her head triggers a spasm. Pain floods her body, overwhelming every sense. She wants to cry out, but has no strength.

She raises her hands to her face. Crude bandages wrap around them, covered in a foul-smelling substance.

"The salve will dull the pain. It should help you sleep," a voice says from behind her. She tries to move, but her body won't respond. Everything is delayed.

"I rubbed some crushed navid on your wounds. It has medicinal qualities, but it also dulls the mind. You were in rough shape."

"Did you pull me out?" Hearing her own voice, Karal notices how dry and raspy it sounds.

"I happened to be casting when you came into view. You're the oddest finny I've ever caught." A light chuckle accompanies the comment.

She is alive, somehow. Everything she's feeling is real. Her memories of the day's events threaten to drown her happiness, but she pushes them away. "Thank you. You saved my life." Each word hurts. Tears threaten to fall. "Can I have some water? My mouth is so dry."

"Ah, yes, the navid will do that. Give me a second." Sounds of movement mixed with the swish of water come from behind. A pale hand brings a canteen into view. Another hand supports her head as she drinks. She tries to see her rescuer, but pain forces her eyes shut. Cold water flows down her throat, flooding her with relief. The hand eases her head back to the ground. Her eyelids lift, revealing a blurry figure. She whispers, "Thank you," and falls asleep.

IN THE EARLY MORNING, sunlight filters through the canopy in narrow rays. One streak lands on Karal's face as she wakes. Shifting away from the light, pain stabs near her neck, waning in small steps. A weak grunt escapes as she adjusts further. She blinks away drowsiness and stifles a yawn. Shivers run down to her feet as the morning air chills her. A rough, worn blanket itches her skin, yet doesn't keep the cold fully at bay. Thankfully, a presence behind her provides welcome warmth.

Sounds of nature fill her senses. Flitters sing their melodic songs from nearby branches while the occasional critter leaps between overhead limbs. Trees, both old and young, encircle her in a tight ring. The scent of an extinguished campfire drifts on a gentle breeze. She finds herself in a small clearing set up as a camp. A large pack rests nearby. Firewood is stacked in a neat pile. A weathered casting pole leans against a tree. The peaceful setting brings a faint grin.

Flexing her right hand, she realizes that it aches, though the cuts have healed somewhat, and her fingers wiggle without issue. Moving her arm triggers shooting sensations from the shoulder joint. The pain subsides, though it now creaks with movement.

She raises her torso while twisting, placing a hand on the earth. The blanket slips down partway, exposing ugly bruises on her midsection. Deep purple and yellow marks highlight the area where she struck the rocks. A noise behind her makes her turn too quickly. Pain explodes behind her eyes. She takes slow, deep breaths to ward it off.

When the sensations calm, she gradually turns, seeking the source of the sound. A figure draped in a rough, woven tunic whispers in their sleep. The garb is comically large on them, meant for a bigger frame. She spots a pale white hand extending from a long sleeve. A closer inspection makes her gasp.

Resembling a paw, the hand features five long, thin fingers covered in white fur, ending in short, sharp-looking black claws. Calluses and scars mark the inner pad. From the bottom of the tunic, lengthy, flat feet protrude—a mix of paw and foot with curved black claws. A fluffy tail is tucked between the feet.

Curiosity overtakes her. She leans forward, seeking a better view, but her back muscles spasm, forcing her to ease into a sitting position. Releasing a soft exhale, she backs up, wincing and rising on shaky legs, head protesting, sending waves of nausea to her stomach. Rasping for air and exhausted by the effort, she closes her eyes until the sensations ebb.

"You can open your eyes now." A light, friendly voice sounds from nearby.

She raises her lids, startles, and almost falls over. If not for the stranger's quick actions, she would be sprawled on the ground. They have one paw on her mid-back to stabilize her, and the other grips her wrist.

Awe shapes her wide eyes and open mouth. Before her stands a beast somehow merged with a One. Tall ears twitch atop their head. Rather than a typical nose, theirs ends in a black button snout, but maintains a jawline and lips like hers. Fur covers the cheeks and forehead, and whiskers frame the short, wet nose. Their teeth are jagged and sharp, yet they smile as she does. Stunning blue eyes gaze back at her—large and shining like diamonds.

Karal whispers, "You're so beautiful."

The stranger smiles. "You and my mother share the same opinion."

They pull her forward with gentleness until her balance returns. "You are a rather strange One, young lady." Their smile deepens. "And you seem to have misplaced your clothes."

Suddenly aware of her nudity, Karal reaches for the fallen blanket. The stranger beats her to it, saving her the trouble of falling over. They hand it to her and turn around.

"I'm so embarrassed!"

"I haven't seen many naked Ones, but you have nothing to be embarrassed about."

"You're going to think I'm a joot fruit, I'm so red." There's the first hint of a smile on her lips. "You can turn around now, Mr. or Mrs.—I don't know what you are."

"The last I checked, I was most definitely male, and have you never seen a Fen before?"

"A Fen? Is that what you are? The only other non-One I've ever seen is a Sinna."

"Oh, those dull things. Walk with their hands, eat ironweed all day, barely talk? They're the least intelligent non-Ones. I can't believe you've never seen a Fen. Do you live in a cave?"

She hesitates. Her mouth opens, but no words spill out.

The Fen responds, saving her from the awkwardness. "You don't have to tell me. I know I'm a stranger to you. I understand." The Fen raises his hands and steps back. "I'm not insulted, but at least tell me your name. 'Nude girl' doesn't suit you. I'm Fento." He bows.

A wide smile grows. "I'm Karal."

His smirk slips. "That's an unusual name. I've heard it before. 'Kuh' and 'ral', right?" He tilts his head, scratching his chin. "What's its origin?"

She shakes her head, embarrassed. "It's dumb, but my dad hated the Laws. He said they smothered happiness, so he took the word 'lark,' reversed it, and added the 'a.' He figured I would be the joy he could cause mischief with." She shrugs. "Adding insult to it all, 'Ra' is in the name as a snub to the island." A gentle, forced smile grows on her lips, though it quickly vanishes. "I am forever thankful to have met you." She offers him her hand, which he takes but doesn't shake. Instead, he inspects the wrappings and sniffs.

"Something about you, Karal. I'll figure it out. My memory's all jumbled, but you remind me of someone." He looks at her hands. "You heal quickly. You version threes are quite the marvel."

"Version threes? What does that mean?" She wobbles, still weak from her injuries. Throbbing sensations return, breaking her delicate balance.

Concern grows on Fento's face. "Shh, you've gone through a lot. It takes time to recover. Even Ones aren't unbreakable. Sit, let's have some breakfast."

She obeys, easing to the ground, panting from the effort. Fento moves to and fro in her wonder. Shorter than her by a few inches and thin, he moves on fleet paws. Pulling back his long sleeves reveals arms as white as the rest of him. He walks to the large pack and retrieves cooking tools and cured meat, then restokes the fire with a few well-placed puffs and some kindling. His eyes dart upwards, and she follows his gaze, becoming dizzy. Grinning, he scampers up a tree, black claws digging into bark, finding purchase with little effort.

Paws work in concert, propelling him ever upward at an impressive rate—his tail swings to balance his momentum. Halfway up in seconds, he disappears behind stout limbs and reddish-brown leaves, then reemerges seconds later, bounding down with a flitter trailing him, trilling with an agitated voice.

"I think mama flitter is cursing me." He reveals three small spotted green eggs in his paws. Karal laughs, wincing when the ache sets in.

The flitter chases him comically as he dodges her tiny teeth and barbed tail, eventually returning to the nest to protect her remaining clutch, complaining with loud chirps.

Several minutes later, they begin eating a breakfast of eggs, meat, and fresh-picked fruit.

Karal moans at the taste of the eggs. "I've never had a flitter egg before. It's so full of flavor. Where I come from, we only have ground flapper eggs."

Fento smiles. "Well, when you're raised from the land, you get exposed to many different things. Have you never heard the rhyme about the different fliers?"

Karal responds with a shrug and a shake of her head, mouth crammed with egg.

Clearing his throat, Fento nods, recalling the words. When his eyes light up with recognition, he begins to sing, his voice cracking:

> *Flitters are small, they bite the hardest,*
> *Their eggs are tiny, but their taste the largest,*
> *Flutters are bigger, everywhere in forests,*
> *Yummy are their eggs, though their vision is poorest,*
> *Flappers are next, so docile and boring,*
> *Their eggs are quite bland, they'll leave you snoring,*
> *Gliders are largest, floating in the skies,*
> *If you snag their eggs, now that is a prize.*

Karal claps and laughs at the ridiculous rhymes. Fento bows modestly from the praise, stuffing himself with more fruit.

Midway through their meal, Fento stops, his blue eyes searching her face.

"What? Is there something wrong?" Karal looks around, expecting to see something.

He shakes his head. "No—I—you seemed really familiar for a second. I had this feeling of déjà vu. Like we had met before."

"Well, I would definitely remember someone as unique as you." She looks away, red-faced.

He pops a berry in his mouth. "Never mind, it's early. Haven't had any yubu yet."

They fall into a comfortable silence, the breeze filtering through the trees, the morning chill held at bay by the warmth of the fire.

THRESHOLD

"So, Karal, were you swimming for fun? Left your clothes on another bank?" Fento licks his fingers, inspecting them with a playful tilt of his head.

Her face falls as she swallows, staring at the ground. "I—it's hard to—I don't want to lie to you. Everything happened so fast. I didn't know it would come to something like this. I should be dead." Her eyes fill. "I'm running away. I was caught breaking a Law, and they came for me. He came for me. I jumped in the river to escape."

Fento stops mid-bite, eyes and mouth widening as his ears perk up. A tremble courses through him. "Who is this 'he', Karal? Does he wear all black? A One with strength beyond reason?"

Karal offers a slight, jagged nod.

Fento's demeanor cracks—the friendly, playful Fen becomes distraught. He stands up in a rush, backing away. "Where did you last see him? Was it where you came from? Was he on a cambra? How long ago was this?"

She speaks, words thick, confused. "It was yesterday, I think? Did you rescue me yesterday? I think he had a cambra. Yes, he rode in on one. I'm from Gallow. I think it's upriver if this is the southern forest."

Fento begins packing, his movements brisk and desperate. Panic pulses in Karal's voice. "Are you leaving me?" Fear rises. She has nothing. Is nothing. As far as she knows, she has ceased to exist.

"You have a Klenzeer after you?! They are beyond reason. They hunt and hunt until they find or kill their prey. He will come after you until he finds your body. And he will find you! I cannot—" He stops, his voice breaking. "It would have been better to let you drown."

His words stab her gut, collapsing the last of her hope. Everything is gone, and she's being abandoned. "Please, Fento! I have no one left." Tears flow in rivulets. "He's killed people I loved. I don't want to put you in harm's way, but I'm alone." Strength ebbing, she swoons, begging.

Fento changes his clothes, rushing, dropping the tunic for her at his feet. Pity slips through the fear on his face. His anguished look grows, his snout twitching as his expression shifts through several emotions.

Then he goes rigid.

A blank stare overtakes him. He stands unmoving. No breath escapes. Drool slips from a corner of his mouth. Unblinking, whispered words spill out. "Fento, remember Amity."

Karal strains to hear him, her sobs drowning out his voice. Trembling, she calls his name. "Fento?"

He snaps out of his stupor, aware and awake again. Panic returns, wild and unfettered. He grabs the pack and runs.

Karal collapses in a heap, crying.

Despair drains her. She can't fathom continuing alone. The ghost of her dad yells, *Get up! Keep fighting,* but this final abandonment saps her resolve. She curls into herself. Consciousness slips away, and she passes out.

"KARAL, Karal, wake up! We have to go!" Fento shakes her back and forth.

She blinks her eyes open, bewildered. She doesn't know if it's been seconds or hours. Fento's face hovers over hers, full of fear, breath raspy, eyes darting left and right.

"I saw him by the riverbank. He's on the opposite side with his Sinna. He'll have to double back to get to this side. You have a chance." Violent tremors shake him. "We have to run. Now."

Tears blur her vision as he offers his paw. Hopelessness turns into gratitude. The offered succor reignites her will to persevere.

Taking his paw in her hand, its warmth confirms that this is real, not a dream, that she has a chance. Now she must fight to survive.

Fento tugs her up onto unsteady legs. She pulls on the tunic he left—it clings tight to her frame, but it's clothing. Protection. Her first steps toward freedom are reaffirming.

Together, they turn from the light and delve deep into the suffocating green of the woods.

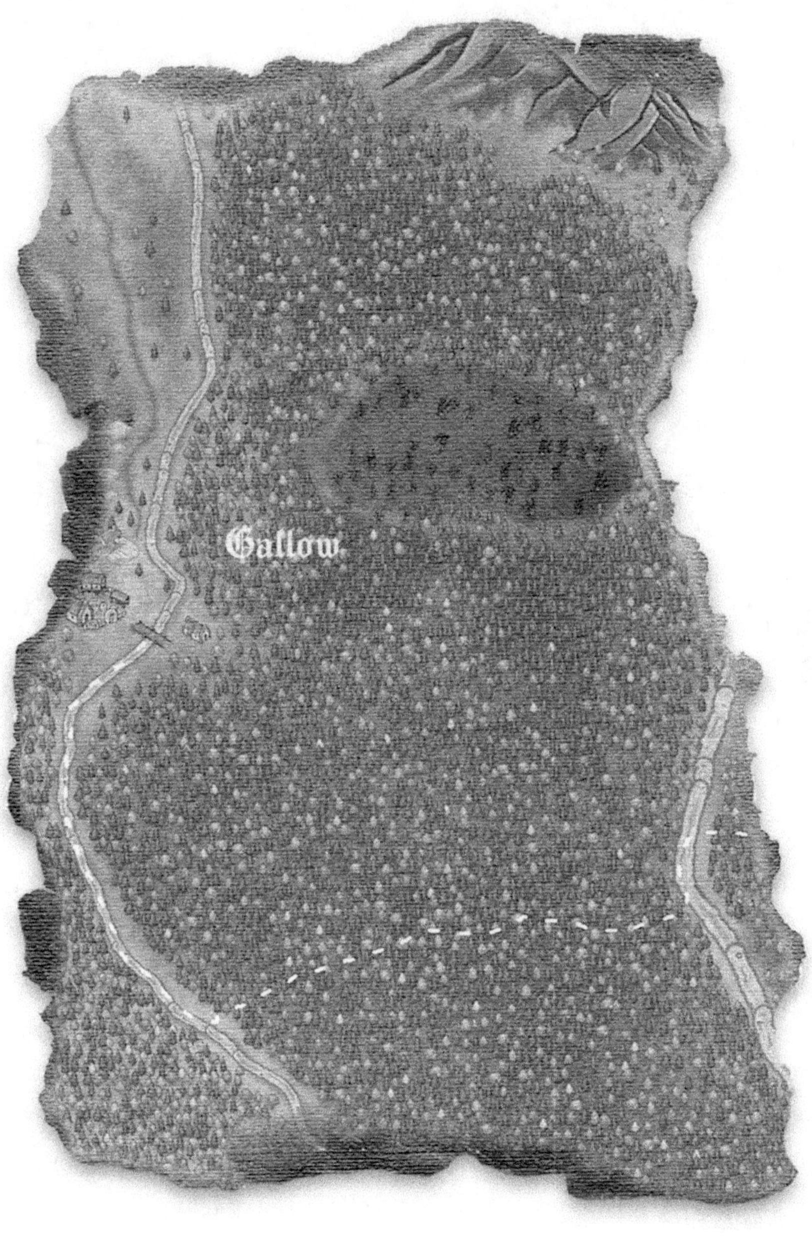

Gallow

FLIGHT

Every step sends fresh agony through Karal's frame. Her head, back, and shoulder radiate pain. She steels herself as they half-run, half-walk through the forest. An hour in, the stabbing sensations win, and she has to beg Fento to stop. Breakfast comes up, warm and curdled. Fento watches with concern, his cheerful demeanor forgotten. His ears flick left and right, scanning for pursuit.

She wipes her mouth, still bent over.

"How did you come across the Klenzeer? What did you do?" Fento demands.

Karal avoids his eyes, staring at the dirt. "I can't talk about it. I don't want to—" She retches again. "It hurts so much. I'm sorry." Her eyes water.

He huffs. "I am risking everything for you! I need to know why."

"I swear I'll tell you once we're safe. Not now. This headache—" She cradles her head in her hands, on the verge of tears.

He turns away, digging at a small bush with red flowers and blue spots. Pulling a knife from his bag, he hacks at it. In a few minutes, he produces a blackened, white-spotted tuber, which he rinses with his canteen. "Suck on this. It's called Ovega. It will help with the nausea, not that you have anything left to vomit. It should also help your head. We have to go. He will have to backtrack to the other side of the river, but you haven't been careful with your steps. He'll pick up your tracks. The farther away we can get, the better." He holds out his paw, and she takes it.

The next few hours are a blur of brisk walks interspersed with short breaks. Tall leafy trees give way to thinner ones with dense foliage. The forest transitions—a mix of leaves and needles, lighter-colored trunks, deepening shade. The darkness alleviates her headache. Nausea dissipates with the root wedged between her teeth, though her hunger and thirst surge.

Timidity creeps into her voice. "Is there anything to eat or drink? I'm sorry."

Fento shares his canteen without comment. She drinks, savoring the water as it soothes her parched throat. Digging into his pack, he produces a larger knife and approaches a thick tree, leaning near collapse. He shaves off a few layers of bark from the trunk, uncovering a nest of goop. Several sticky, large white grubs with luminous sap surrounding them nestle within the inner rot.

"These are coojak larvae. The adults eat into the trees, then lay their eggs. These probably hatched a few weeks ago, but you can eat them." He moves away, peering into the forest. "We should make it to the Loren before nightfall. It's another river, but shallow and passable if we're careful. I'm going to scout ahead while you eat." He nods. "They're tastier than they look—almost sweet. I'll return shortly." He disappears into the forest, leaving Karal by the tree.

Hunger pangs flare as she stares at the gooey meal. She's starving but has never encountered anything less appetizing. Pressing her finger against the sap, she pulls away, and a sticky residue stretches from it. The smell is disgusting—like old earth mixed with spoiled vegetables. Eyes shut, she scrapes several larvae away with her hands and stuffs them into her mouth. The urge to vomit returns as they burst against her tongue—a sickening, fatty explosion. By the time Fento returns, the tree is stripped clean. Karal squats near the ground, forcing her mouth closed, looking green.

"Your definition of sweet is vastly different than mine," she chokes out.

"Would you have eaten them if I said they were disgusting?" He looks at her with reproach. "You needed to eat, and I stretched the truth. In my experience, Ones can be difficult."

She licks her fingers, grimacing. "I am far from the typical One."

He rolls his eyes, bordering on a smile, then extends his paw, which she takes.

The afternoon wanes, but becomes more manageable. With sustenance, Karal's head clears, and breaks come with less frequency. Bushes of tangleberries along the way help alleviate further hunger; their juice sweet this time of year. At dusk, they arrive at the Loren. Its width is impressive, though it flows slower and gentler than the Raymonde. When they step into it, Karal gasps. "This is even colder than the Raymonde. How is that possible?"

"It's mountain-fed and runs underground for a portion of its path. The sun doesn't warm it much. We have to follow it north." He squeezes her hand, and she nods.

"Why north?"

Fento's whiskers twitch as he walks against the flow. "South will take us toward the ocean. There's less places to hide and the forest thins. This will be safer."

"I've never seen the ocean."

"And you shouldn't. There's nothing there. Waves and water bash the shore all day." His tone is ominous.

Trudging up the river, they stay close to the western bank in the shallows. Once Fento feels satisfied with their track, he finds a shallow section, and they ford it. By the time they exit the waters, Karal trembles, freezing, her feet numb. A couple of steps in, she stumbles to the ground.

Fento lowers himself to her level, meeting her eyes, his voice softer. "Thank you for fighting through your pain. I know it wasn't easy." He looks away, guilt growing on his face. "I'm sorry I abandoned you. I'm a coward. My past—we'll talk later." He takes the blanket from his pack and wraps it around her.

Fento prepares the camp with practiced skill. Karal offers to look for wood, but he insists she warm up instead. In short order, he collects wood, lights a fire, catches some finnies from the river, and erects a campfire tripod. From his pack, he produces a chain and a small metal pot, hanging them over the fire. Water, a selection of herbs, and dried root vegetables are thrown in to stew. Before long, he sits beside her.

"You're amazing! I wish I could create a camp as easily." Karal sits by the fire, sensation returning to her toes. "I need to learn new skills —" Her voice trails off, and her face falls. She will never be a black-smith again.

"Very few tricks here. Just lots of time alone wandering the woods." Fento's grin fades. He salts the finny tentacles and adds some to the stew. The two stare at the fire in silence. He turns to her, sighing. "So, what brought you to my casting line?"

Karal hesitates, finding it difficult to raise her eyes. "I don't know that I'm ready yet, Fento. After dinner? Please."

"I understand this is all still raw to you, plus you mentioned losing people. I won't push just yet, but I need to know what you are up against. You don't look like a murderer, but context matters." Rummaging through his pack, he digs out a small bottle and two thumb-sized cups. "Do you drink fizzle? This is much worse! It's fermented joot juice." He chuckles. "This isn't meant for you. It's for me. I haven't had a reason to drink in a long time." He fills a cup for Karal, who downs it in one gulp. Eyes wide, he does the same and refills their cups. "A toast to memories we'd sooner forget but keep close to our hearts." The beverage burns warmer than the fire down their throats with the second draught.

Karal studies Fento as the world mellows and slows. His fur reflects yellow-orange in the firelight. Thin and wiry, he wears worn shorts and a stained shirt. His tail arcs behind him in a graceful curve. Staring at the fire, his eyes blaze gold with hints of blue. He cuts a handsome profile.

Warmth settles inside her, coupled with unexpected contentment. When she realizes Fento is offering her a cooked finny and a bowl of stew, she accepts them, grateful. They eat in silence for several minutes. The warm meal tastes incredible after their harried flight and the coojak larvae. Events of the previous day replay in her mind as she stares at the fire.

"I was a blacksmith—a good one, too. My dad taught me. He died a while ago." Her words are slurred but intelligible. "Only four people knew I was a woman. Maybe some suspected, but I never hinted at it. I held that secret tight." She sips more of the drink, continuing. "That was until Ives—Ives—" Tears slip as her composure breaks. "It's my fault."

"Who is this Ives fellow? What did he do?"

Karal swallows, streams flowing from her eyes. "He was my best friend."

"Not much of a friend, if he summoned a Klenzeer." Fento watches Karal.

The comment hits hard—her face crumples. Mouth trembling, she struggles to form words. They slip out as a whisper, "He—he didn't do it, but he must have blurted something to the wrong person when he was drunk." More tears fall, which she wipes away with a rough swipe. She starts again, with control in her voice, though it wavers, "We argued. He wanted something I could never give him, and we both struggled with how to move forward. I—I handled it wrong. I shut him out, and we should have talked. It's my fault."

"Hey, no. He was your friend. He betrayed you."

"He died trying to save me!" she shouts. Her hand shakes, face damp with sweat and tears. "If I had told him that I trusted him, none of this would have happened."

"Did you trust him?"

She doesn't answer, wiping her eyes with a sleeve. "It doesn't matter anymore." Fresh waves of emotion hit. "The Klenzeer killed him." She looks away, feeling the weight of her guilt.

Fento approaches, offering a warm paw on her back, his voice is apologetic. "I'm sorry for your loss, Karal. I've never had a friend that I could—well, actually, I don't know that I've ever had a friend. Isn't that curious? Look at the company you fell into." He gives a wide smile and lies on the ground next to her.

Despite the tears, she sighs, continuing her story. "That monster took him from me, and I never got a chance to say goodbye." She wipes her eyes, her expression hardening. "I told him I'd kill him, and I'll find a way. I wounded him. He can bleed."

Fento gasps. "I saw him. His nose was broken, and he had fresh wounds on his face. Was that you?"

She smirks and nods. Slurring, she sits up. "You and your drink. The next thing I know, you'll try to seduce me." She raises her brows, giving him a crooked look, and they both erupt in laughter.

"Any more of this stuff, and you'll wish you had your headache back." Fento's words come in slow steps, yet remarkably clear. He lies on the ground, near Karal, both of them looking up at the sky. It's a dry cloud cover, with no sign of rain. "Can you pass some water? I need to clear my head a bit."

She crawls over to his pack and retrieves the canteen. Dragging it behind her, she collapses next to him and snuggles his tail.

"Hey, that's private property! I'm sure this is a violation of some Law." She laughs and squeezes. Fento pretends to pull back but relents. "You have a lovely laugh for a One. It reminds me of someone."

She returns the compliment. "You have a lovely tail for a Fen. It reminds me of a soft blanket." She giggles, and she never giggles. "Don't think I'm being romantic."

Fento retorts, "I've already seen you naked." The comment earns him a flick on the ear and prompts more giggles from Karal. He takes a swig of water and offers her his shoulder. She obliges by leaning her head on it. His fur, warmed by the fire, feels nice against her cheek.

Their laughter ebbs. Ashes from the fire dance up in the air on warm currents, drifting into the dark. Karal turns to Fento, her eyes losing focus, blinking slowly. Her mouth opens, a question forming.

"Why are you so afraid of Klenzeer? What did they do to you?" Her tone is innocent, though the words are heavy.

For a moment, he doesn't respond. The crackle of the campfire fills the silence. She's about to apologize for asking when Fento replies. "I've never told the story. There's no one to tell when you're alone." He takes a swig of water, missing most of his mouth. Another moment of silence passes as he scans the dark sky, lost in thought. When he speaks again, his voice carries a somber weight. "Don't fall asleep. I'll only share because you asked. Consider yourself special or just very unlucky."

"I am special, Fento. We both are."

Inhaling deeply, he holds his breath. His body trembles as he exhales. "My history started at least seventy Cycles ago. And before you comment, I know I'm old. There's gray mixed in with the white." A half smile crosses his lips before his face turns serious, his voice dropping to a notch above a whisper. "I lived in the Central Gardens among them, Karal. I was their pet. I belonged to the cruelest of all the Klenzeer. Her title was D874651. I had been captured after my skulk abandoned me. I had done a terrible thing that no Fen should ever do." He looks at her, his eyes hollow. "I killed Ones."

FENTO

Fento gazes at Karal, his body taut with the expectation of judgment. Her eyes reflect the firelight, mouth parted to a line. He is about to abandon his story when she responds.

"I'm listening. I'll try not to judge. We all have reasons for our actions. I want to hear yours." Her voice is gentle.

He takes a long swig of water and settles into the dirt.

"We Fen were a peaceful nomadic people, but we didn't contribute. We took. We consumed from an area and moved on. My skulk—my family—contained around thirty members. We would raid farms at night when we came across villages. My mother, Loana, and my siblings were responsible for the ground flappers and eggs. In the dark, we would sneak in and take what was necessary without overstepping our needs. The rest of my skulk stole vegetables, fruits, and the occasional livestock for slaughter."

He pauses to drink water. "I'm sure some skulks ranged far south in those days, though you'd have heard nothing of raids in Gallow—Fen are careful."

Karal shakes her head. "I have never heard of anything like this in Gallow. News traveled fast in my village."

Fento arches an eyebrow. "Does a farmer notice when a ground flapper lays fewer eggs in a day or when a wooly goes missing? The larger the farm, the less is noticed."

He shrugs, reflecting on the next part of his story.

"It was a moonlit night when my mother died. We were raiding a large farm that reeked of manure. It should have been a warning, but our elder insisted it was a sign of a productive farm. We assumed our roles and snuck on quiet paws. My mother entered the enclosure while my oldest brother acted as lookout. Time was always against us, and my brother investigated when my mother delayed. His screams alerted us to danger. Arrows rained down around us, piercing my fleeing skulk members. It was an ambush. The Ones were lying in wait. Several Fen fell that night beyond my mother and brother. My next eldest sibling, Bondoo, died running away—an arrow through her chest. From thirty, only ten of us survived. My immediate family went from five to two." His voice cracks.

Sympathy crosses Karal's face. She reaches out to offer comfort, but Fento flinches. He goes rigid, his fur bristling. Recognizing her intent, he calms. "I'm sorry. You've done nothing wrong. I was—abused."

Distress grows on her face. "You don't have to continue. Whatever happened, you don't need to relive it for my sake."

"No, I must confront this. Your touch is welcome. Necessary, really. Understanding will come." When he pauses, Karal places her hand on his arm and strokes with a soft touch. Nodding, Fento wipes his eyes and looks up at the canopy. "The elder was blamed for his shortsightedness. Anger filled the survivors. He, in turn, deflected those accusations to me. He accused my white fur of reflecting the moonlight and giving away our intent. It was a weak argument, but his words held weight for my superstitious kin. I am not colored right."

"What does that mean?"

"No Fen are white, Karal. I am an anomaly. We are typically red, gray, brown, or a mix of these colors with some white. Pure white is a curse. You are more visible and give away your skulk. My mother named me Fendan. Dan is the word for blessing, for I was her child.

That night, I was renamed Fento—the cursed Fen." Anger bubbles up in his voice. "My skulk turned their backs on me; even my only remaining sister, Reyna, would not approach me. I slept alone for the first time in my life." He swallows hard. "This is not normal, Karal. Fen need physical touch. From a young age, we sleep in a heap with our families. We hold hands when we walk. It is a requirement—a weakness, really. We're not meant to be alone."

Karal hesitates. Her hand hovers in the air between them. The pause is noticeable. Fento is about to abandon his tale when she shifts her body unexpectedly, hugging him with gentle strength. "You're not a curse. You're a blessing. You held my fate in your hands, and not only did you save me, but you risked your safety for me. I can only repay your kindness with my own."

Warmth spreads through him in relaxing waves as he melts into her. Her warmth overwhelms him. He thought he had let go of the need to be touched long ago. "Thank you" is all he can manage for several minutes. He smiles. Tears disappear into his fur.

After a moment, he clears his throat, breaking the embrace, pushing forward. "I was not right the following morning. I was young, naive, and newly abandoned. My skulk left without me. I sat in the last place I saw my mother before the raid, unable to reconcile my situation. When I smelled smoke on the breeze, I followed it to its source. Near that same horrid farm, bodies were burned in a pile while several Ones watched, mocking my people. My kin's tails hung like trophies from the side of a barn. It was a warning to most, but a provocation to me. I fumed." His voice rises, quickening with anger. "Fen are not like this, Karal. We are docile and submissive. I would rather run than confront something I fear or hate, but that day, I was possessed.

"I caked myself in mud throughout the day and hatched a plan to be welcomed back to my skulk. When night arrived, I assaulted the farm like a shadow. I placed piles of hay around the home and its surrounding structures, barring doors where possible. I then took an ember from the burnt pile of bodies and lit everything. I ran away with a dead ground flapper in my hands, turning once to revel in my revenge. The flames were so bright. Screams could be heard as windows were smashed and fire raged around the home. A horrid smile crossed my lips as I followed the path my skulk had taken earlier that day."

Karal remains silent, not shifting or moving away. Fento glances up, hoping she has fallen asleep, but her gaze meets his unblinking. He can feel her judging him, ready to abandon him for this act. Worry lingers in his eyes. This shame has festered in him for so long. When her mouth opens, her voice is low and calm; a weighted whisper. "They earned it."

"Why are you not angry? I murdered your kind. I felt no regret."

Dark emotion colors Karal's voice. "We are not all family, Fento. I have met loathsome people, even in my small village. You avenged a wrong. I can see myself doing the same for my father or friends, so I won't judge you."

Silence follows. Zizzers chirr, and twinklebugs sparkle near the waning flames. A gentle breeze rustles leaves. There is an unexpected peace at their campsite.

Karal breaks it. "What happened next?"

Continuing, he swallows, knowing where the story leads. "I found my skulk the next day. I walked straight to the elder and dropped the dead flapper at his feet, declaring my actions to them all, expecting praise. Instead, shock crossed the elder's face. He started crying. I was beside myself. This was far from the reaction I expected. The elder spoke between sobs. 'Fool, you have doomed us! You have killed the Overseer's precious Ones. They will send their Klenzeer and kill us! You are a curse, Fento!' He picked up a rock and threw it at me. Several others followed suit, even Reyna. They screamed my name with such hatred. I ran away more alone and desperate than ever before. I wandered for days, lost in nature. I shook from the lack of touch, almost withdrawn from reality. It wasn't a surprise when a rider on a cambra ran me down. A Klenzeer had found me."

Tremors wrack Fento. Karal reaches for him, and he doesn't resist submitting to her embrace. He stammers, "I—I—"

"You don't have to, Fento. I've heard enough. You don't need to relive this."

"NO!" His shout stills the night. "You have to understand what they are, Karal. Your vengeance is not worth this! They are not people. They are monsters!" He grits his teeth as he utters the last word. Grabbing more drink, he pours another glass for himself and Karal, then downs it, letting it settle in his stomach. He exhales a slow breath.

Restoring control of himself, he continues. "The one who found me was named D874651. They are all named like this. They are tools for the Overseers and are titled as such. Their rankings are found on their collars. You may not have noticed a small insignia on your Klenzeer, but they are designated F through B, then ascend to the Alpha level. They always start as an F and work their way up. The Alphas wear all white and comprise the Council of Wisdom. They are the elite. They are the vilest of them all."

He swallows, regaining his composure.

"D874651 dragged me to the Central Gardens, bound by rope to her cambra. I ran behind it until my feet bled, and when I could not go on, I continued to be dragged. I was clinging to life when she shoved me into a cell scarcely large enough to hold me. There, I shook in the dark for three days, dying. When she remembered me, she beat me, yelling curses the whole time. I became immune to suffering faster than I expected. She wanted to know how I had done it. How I had killed without reserve—no Fen had ever hurt so much as a fly. How did I break my nature?

"When no answer came, she threatened me with more violence. When none of these tactics were effective, she changed her approach. She stroked me like you would a pet. For all her cruelty, I somehow responded to this the most. She traded her fists for pats." He stops his storytelling, sitting up and breaking the embrace. All signs of anger lost, he whimpers, "I'm so weak, Karal. Your savior is a coward who was so easily cowed. It took an ounce of kindness to break me. At first, I was given small tasks, and she traded them for scratches. When I failed, she would beat me within an inch of my life.

"Her enslavement of me continued for countless Cycles. One day, a kindness; another, a throttling. Day in and day out, I didn't know what to expect. Nine times out of ten, I would be injured in some capacity. It wasn't long before I forgot who I was and just became a tool. When they experimented on me, I became utterly lost." His words fragment as his lower lip trembles. "They figured out that Fen are susceptible to suggestion. We are highly impressionable. One day, I awoke with blood on my hands and feet, not knowing where it came from. Another day, I had somehow lost a toe and already been healed. I had no memory of this. Nothing. Sometimes, ghostly images flit through my dreams. Karal, I live a nightmare."

She doesn't respond, her eyes fixed on him. When she speaks, her words are weak and small. "I'm so sorry, Fento. You suffered so much, yet you came back and took pity on me." Her eyes fill with tears. "I brought you back into this hell, but I won't let him hurt you."

This time, he hugs her, grateful for her presence and acceptance of his past. No one has treated him like a friend before. He whispers in her ear. "I was abandoned once, and it led to my suffering. When you told me what happened to you, I ran away in fear. It was my first instinct, and I'm so sorry for that. I ran to the river, bent on heading north or south, but then I spotted the Klenzeer looking for you across the way. He never saw me, though I recognized him. I hid. But while I cowered in that bush, waiting for a chance to slink away, I realized that the same pattern was repeating. I couldn't let their cruelty break you like it did me, and I ran back."

The warmth of their embrace is cleansing. Fento feels calm with her arms wrapped around him. Her scent is pleasant and somehow familiar, reminding him of—something shifts in his mind. The campfire dims, and for a moment, he's somewhere else. A being swathed in shadows watches him from a wooden chair, dressed in tattered robes —a dim ethereal light illuminates parts of their frame. They shout: "REMEMBER, FENTO!" It echoes through him as the vision flickers. He blinks, finding himself back by the dying fire with Karal still in his arms. The strange memory slips away like smoke, leaving only a faint unease he can't quite place.

When they break the embrace, the fire is low. Quiet follows. Karal preps for bed while Fento cleans their camp. They don't speak. Everything necessary has already been said. Karal eases to the earth, with a padded blanket beneath her, adjusting to its thin comfort. She breaks the silent spell when Fento begins lying down opposite her by the fire. "Don't sleep on the ground by yourself. We can sleep beside each other and share the blanket. It'll be warmer." She pats the ground near her, smiling.

Fento considers her invitation. He can't summon any reason to reject her, but is apprehensive. As he approaches her, her smile eases his worries. Something about her familiarity warms his heart. He lies down near her, back to back; the warmth of her presence fills him with such peace. Sleep overtakes him faster than expected, and for once, his dreams are pleasant.

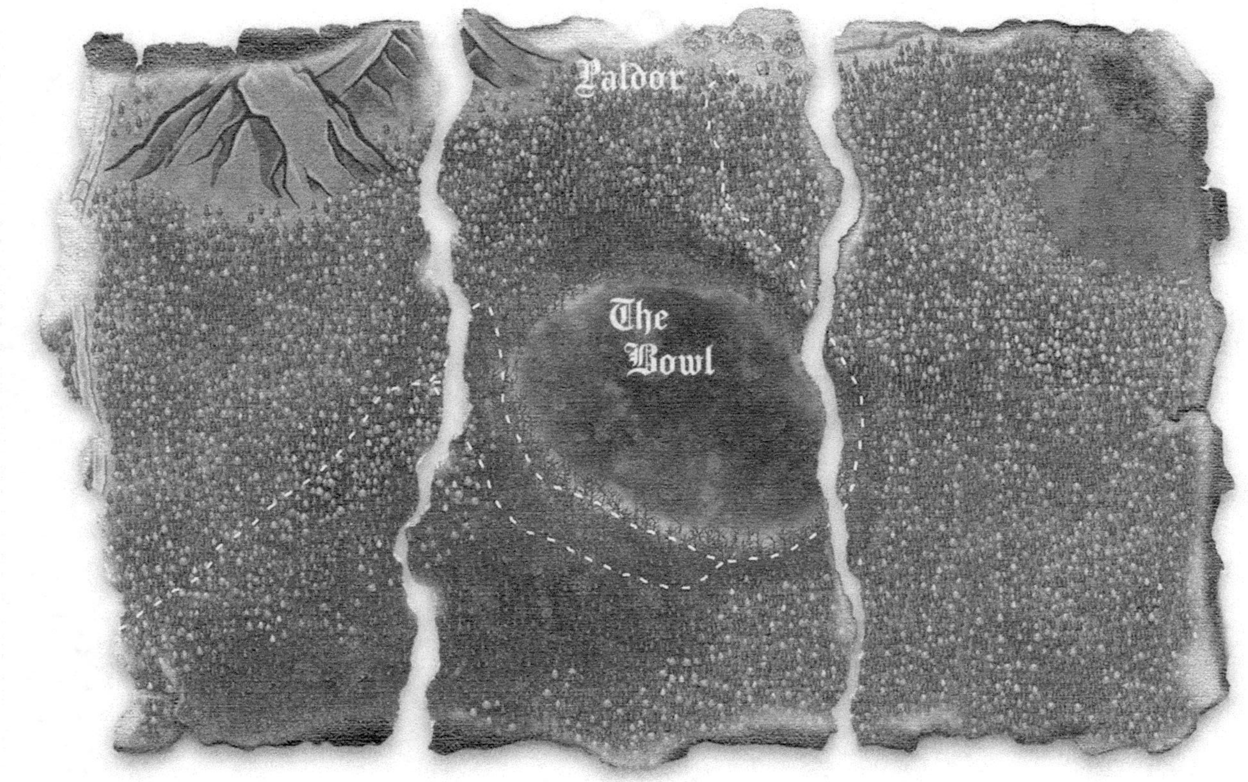

Paldor
The
Bowl

ESCAPISM

Karal blinks awake as dawn breaks. A mild hangover pulses behind her eyes. She finds herself snuggling Fento, his back pressed against her chest. Somehow, during the night, they found each other. It should feel strange, but instead it's comforting. Steady breathing indicates he is still sleeping.

Yesterday, she didn't know Fens existed. Up close, he gives off a pleasant, earthy scent. His fur is soft to the touch. Looking closer, she notices a map of unsettling scars on the skin beneath his coat. There are hundreds of them, varying in size and shape, covering his entire body. They healed a bit off-white, blending beneath his fur. The fact that he has survived for this long is admirable.

Reflecting on the previous evening, his story mirrors her own trauma at the hands of the Klenzeer. Her heart aches for him. He has suffered a lifetime under their cruelty, while she has endured a handful of moments. He carries so much grief, yet he endures.

She slips away, uncurling from their embrace. When she stands and stretches, aches resonate from her slumber. The ground is unforgiving. Her back and shoulders protest—years of smithing and falling from trees have also left their mark. Her joints crack and pop as she moves. She smirks at feeling old at such a young age.

Yawning, she walks toward the river to wash up. The morning sky is a calming blue with a slight haze. Dark clouds drift southward, disrupting the serenity. The air is crisp, but scents of ash and smoke fill the breeze.

Something is wrong.

"Fento! Wake up! I smell smoke."

He snaps awake, nostrils flaring. Panic widens his eyes. "Where do you smell it the most?"

Together, they rush to the river. The scent is more potent to the south, drifting on errant breezes. Fento nods and scales the nearest tree, digging his claws into the thick bark with precision.

Karal follows his movements as he disappears among the boughs, circling the tree, trying to catch a glimpse of him. All she smells now is the overwhelming scent of burning wood.

Fento descends rapidly, almost colliding with her. He's panting, unnerved. "We need to pack and head north. He's set the forest on fire!"

They gather loose items, frantically stuffing them into Fento's pack. Breakfast is an afterthought as they dash north.

Karal trails Fento as he leads them north, then turns east. The unfamiliar woods scatter her sense of direction when the canopy grows thick, obscuring the sun. Their zigzag trek continues for over an hour. Her bare feet throb, her soles unaccustomed to the raw bite of roots and jagged stone. Having worn boots for most of her life, the stumbles and collisions are excruciating. She grits her teeth, holding back moans, focusing on escape rather than complaint.

By mid-morning, she is exhausted, collapsing to her knees, gasping for breath. She sputters, "I have to stop. I need rest."

Fento nods, sniffing and scouting ahead while Karal sips from the canteen. He returns with handfuls of wild tangleberries and some firm white fruit she's never seen before.

"I'm sorry I didn't stop sooner. Here, eat. I'm going to climb and check the fire. Hopefully, we've gotten ahead of it." He disappears with little effort up a tree just as before.

Karal devours the berries, still weak and recovering. If she pushes too hard, she'll become a hindrance. When Fento clambers down, he looks focused, calculating.

"What did you see? Is it bad? I'm sorry I'm so useless to you." Her hands flex open and shut. "I have no idea where we are, how far I can go, or how to help you. Please, tell me something!"

Fento's face softens. "I'm sorry, Karal. My first instinct has always been to run. I haven't had anyone accompany me before." His breath slows as he controls his fear. "We've been heading northeast. We're ahead of the fire, though it's spreading into a massive blaze. I'm aiming for Paldor, a village similar to yours. We can resupply there and maybe lose our enemy. If we're lucky, he hasn't realized you're not alone." Fento stops, taking bites of berries, though more of the white fruit. With a mouthful of food, he continues, "I haven't taken your state into account, and I'm sorry for that. You're struggling and unwell. I'm pushing so hard." He grabs her hands in his paws. "I appreciate your fight. I'll slow down to spare you the strain, okay?"

Karal smiles, grateful. "Thank you." She focuses on the ground, feeling guilty. "I'm sorry for being a burden."

"Nonsense!" He lowers his face to meet her gaze. "We are on the same side of this. Survival." He continues eating, giving her a quizzical look as he points at the white fruit. "Don't like moonies?"

Karal looks away, embarrassed. "I've never seen one before. I didn't know how to eat it."

A grin rises on Fento's face. "You are sheltered. Moonies are delicious. They grow on the ground, usually near damp areas. Though they have a tart outer flesh, which most animals ignore, the pit is edible and incredibly sweet. Try it."

She takes a bite of the flesh and grimaces, prepared to spit it out, but holds judgment until the sweet pit crunches in her mouth. She devours the rest with haste. Fento arches an eyebrow. "Well?"

She grabs another moonie and bows her head.

"That reminds me of the first time—" He pauses, lost in thought. A confused look crosses his face as he tilts his head at Karal. "Odd. I was going to say my sister, but it didn't sound right. Someone else was with me when they tasted it for the first time. A cousin, maybe." He hums to himself, shrugging. "Tells you how old I am."

Between bites, Karal asks, "Where do we go from here?"

Fento shakes his head, refocusing. "We'll head to the Bowl. It's a depression with a lake at its center. I casted out of there once. It's pleasant with tons of wildlife. We might be able to hide somewhere in it. It's wild country, so no easy trails to follow and animals like rackers and growlers aplenty. If we're lucky, it'll throw them off."

"But what about the fire? Won't it burn everything down?"

Fento shakes his head, confident, though worry weighs in his eyes. "I saw dark clouds on the horizon, so I'm praying for rain later on. If it doesn't, then we'll change course."

Rising, Fento looks forward, drawing a deep breath. He urges Karal to stand. "Are you ready?" As she nods, he directs her to follow, lowering his voice as she matches his stride. "We'll continue northeast to throw them off. I'll be focused ahead while you watch our tail. We'll slow down to leave fewer tracks. The more difficult we make this for them, the better our odds. Sound good?"

Extending his paw, she grabs it, and they venture farther into the woods.

Their journey continues for several hours, alternating between north and then east. Soft terrain is avoided, with purposeful steps near tree roots and rocks. At times, Fento uses his tail to sweep away areas disturbed by their feet. Breaks are taken at least once an hour, or when Fento spots bushes that can be picked. Karal collects berries and edible leaves that Fento points out along the way. Several creeks along their path provide water to refill the canteen and quench parched throats.

Dark gray clouds drift above as the day slips into the early evening. Fento climbs the tallest tree they find to get their bearings. Karal waits at the bottom, nerves heightened, breath held. The forest is dense and too quiet. Darkness grows by the minute. Finding a safe refuge for the night will be difficult with the Klenzeer searching for them.

While hunting for moonies, a disturbing screech shatters the silence, startling Karal. It's a mix of a shrill, tortured scream mixed with a loud caw. She looks up at the canopy and watches Fento race down the tree. Terror fills his face.

"What was that sound?!"

Fento crouches beside her, urging her to stoop low. He speaks above a whisper as if the forest is listening. "A Silva is flying above. They have sharp vision, though I'm unsure about their hearing."

"What's a Silva?" she murmurs, peering through the breaks in the trees, attempting to spot the creature.

"A winged One—one of the Overseers' worst creations. It is a blend of a One and a large, black glider. They're abominations with an appetite for raw meat." His eyes search above. The Silva's cry echoes again, this time farther away. Fento stands, and Karal follows suit. He continues in a whisper, "When I was up top, I spotted the fire south of us. It was closer than I anticipated, but rain is coming. We're close to the Bowl now, but we have to be more careful. Now we have three pursuers. The Silva covers a wide area from the sky."

Anxiety creeps onto Karal's face, fear growing. "It's going to be night soon. How are we going to stay safe? What should we do?"

Fento's voice remains calm. "I have an idea to hide us, but it will take some work. We need to venture deeper into the forest, where there are more trees and a thicker canopy. This will take us closer to the Bowl and hopefully keep us safe tonight. Come on, we must be quiet." Leading them northeast, they take careful steps, slower and more purposeful.

When darkness nearly overtakes them, Fento finds a dense cluster of trees and empties his bag. Halfway down, he pulls out a sizable green blanket made from a stretchy thread and black rope. "Can you climb, Karal?"

"Not as well as you, but I can manage."

"Good. Repack my pack, strap it on, and start climbing that tree." He points to a medium-sized tree with thick limbs that start low. "I'll be up there already. Come find me. If you struggle, yell for me." He bites on some rope and straps the blanket onto his back, ascending the thickest of the trees with ease.

A raindrop hits Karal's arm, bringing relief from her worry about the fire. A steady patter wets the canopy, though only a rare drop penetrates. Karal gathers the items from the ground and straps the pack on. Fatigue drains her as she leans against a tree. The morning's headache persisted all day, and her limbs quake. Nervous about the climb, she bites her lip. Memories of childhood falls come back as she reaches for a low branch and pulls herself up. Hand over hand, she scales, groping for handholds in the near dark. Her bruised feet help her balance better than any boots could. Moving like a ground crawler, she inches upward toward Fento.

High in the tree, he's securing the blanket to the branches with black cord. The sound of Karal's panting startles him. "You're a natural! I am impressed!" A weak grimace crosses her lips, modest pride warming her from his praise.

"What are you making? Is this a shelter?" She studies Fento, tying a loose corner, breath escaping in spurts.

Finishing off his final knot, he looks up, pushing down on the fabric. "This is the safest way to avoid detection. Hopefully, our pursuers aren't looking up. The color should help us at night. I call it my aerie. I've used it in many dangerous forests where ground sleeping isn't safe. It should be sturdy enough even for someone of your size." He winks at her.

Karal eyes it with unease. "My size? I'd be insulted if I weren't so impressed. Will it hold both of us?"

Fento nods. "I am sure of it. Give it a try."

Cautiously, she places a foot on the fabric and grips a branch above her, feeling the material flex as she tiptoes toward the center. Fingers release inch by inch as she relaxes her hold, feeling the fabric sink beneath her feet until it stabilizes, supporting her weight. Nothing creaks, and the cords tighten at the corners. A few branches sway, but nothing shifts. Her held breath releases as she lowers herself into a seated position. A relaxed expression emerges as the tension leaves her face. It grows into a smile as she bounces with tepid movement, appreciating the stability of it all. She unstraps the pack, sighing with relief, and lies back against the surface, spent.

She declares with a wink, "You are part bushtail and flutter."

"I prefer part growler, part glider, but I'll take it." He grins.

Crawling to the center, he speaks just above a whisper. "We should be quiet and not move much to avoid shaking the top branches." He offers some edible leaves and moonies for dinner, coupled with some jerky.

In the darkness, they lie side by side, eating. A steady rain drips through in certain spots that are easy to avoid, allowing them both a chance to lie back and unwind. Looking up at the canopy, they discuss Karal's childhood and upbringing, omitting Fento's past.

"I can't believe you wound up sleeping in a tree because of a tunku. The horns didn't give it away?"

She groans. "It was dark, and we were seven. I never said we were smart back then. If you gave me a dare, I didn't hesitate."

"You're lucky they have short legs, or it would've rammed you all the way home." He laughs. Steady drips lull them into stillness, the rain's sounds mesmerizing. Fento turns to his side, a faint smirk on his lips. "We Fen are good at climbing, hiding, and stealth, though all of us are cowards. We were created weak, as the Overseers planned."

Karal retorts, "Weakness in body, maybe, but Fento, you're resilient! You survived abuse from the Klenzeer. That takes grit and courage. You have strengths you aren't acknowledging." Pride fills her voice. Fento looks away, embarrassed.

"What do you mean by 'as the Overseers planned'?"

"It's something I overheard once when I was first captured. I only know small parts of it. It goes 'Sinna are the helpers, Fen the disruptors, and Lopers the mistake.'" He speaks into the darkness, his voice quiet. "We were meant to make the lives of you Ones difficult. You all had it too easy and became lazy. We were created to be weak but inconvenient, forcing your kind to work harder."

Reflecting on his statement, Karal hums to herself. "They must hate anything that isn't according to their plans. Look at how you were treated. You are different from what they intended. Your Klenzeer must have been angry at you for it."

Fento shakes his head. "No, Karal. My treatment was the result of a horrible, twisted person. I should have been killed or experimented on. I was the only pet at the Central Gardens. I gave my Klenzeer a strange sense of satisfaction. I represented something to her. She is morally corrupt and unstable. I was fortunate to survive as long as I did." He sighs before continuing. "The Klenzeer who pursues you is intense. He is known for his cunning and anger. Be wary of him."

"Why would anyone pursue me with such determination? He set a forest on fire. He's insane!"

Fento sits up, his expression serious. "He can't return empty-handed, and with a wounded face, Karal. You hurt him, and you're a female. You can't imagine how arrogant these fiends are. The Overseers grant them all this power, yet you somehow got away. I am sure his fury is boundless."

She beams despite Fento's caution. "Then I'll enjoy every second I infuriate him with my freedom." Fento rolls his eyes, chuckling under his breath.

Stifling a yawn, Karal stretches, feeling exhaustion drawing her to sleep. "What are Lope—"

Fento paw slips over her mouth, his expression harried. Above them, the sudden shrill cry of the Silva pierces the night. Flapping wings can be distinctly heard, continuing for several seconds. The sound intensifies while the flapping slows. Something heavy lands to their left, shaking branches and dropping loose leaves. Karal's eyes widen, muscles tensing. Fento releases his grip on her mouth, thrusting his paw into the pack, retrieving his larger knife, and placing it in her hand. He grabs his shorter knife from the pack, trembling. Together, they lie in wait, listening. Seconds turn to minutes.

Then, a low, rhythmic snore echoes from the darkness.

Eyes wide, Fento dares to whisper in Karal's ear. "I'll take the first watch. You need rest. I won't sleep until it's gone." The Silva's snores rumble uninterrupted.

Karal shakes her head no, but Fento insists, body tense, crawling to a post near a stout tree.

Exhaustion finally wins. As the Silva rumbles in its sleep, Karal's eyes close, and she slips into a deep slumber.

INTO THE FIRE

Thunder startles Karal awake. Remnants of a nightmare fade as she sits up, shaking the feeling. The handle of Fento's knife is a cold, wooden weight in her hand. White-hot lightning flashes, highlighting Fento sitting at the edge of the aerie, staring outward. Rumbles of thunder vibrate in her chest. Another arc of light sparks nearby, and she notices the terror on Fento's face. Less than ten feet away, dirty yellow-black talons grip a wide branch, moving closer with each flare in the sky.

She crawls to him achingly slow, praying she doesn't shift any branches with her movement. Fento's eyes flick toward her, acknowledging her approach. His paw clutches his small knife. When she reaches his position, she crouches low, their bodies touching. Ragged breath escapes from Fento, his body trembling.

Low, guttural sounds—resembling the common language—come from the Silva as it talks to itself. Lightning sizzles overhead, driving the beast closer to within a handful of feet. Rain begins falling in large, fat drops, occasionally piercing the canopy, dampening the aerie. Wind drives leaves and rain horizontally at them, the sounds masking the pounding of Karal's heart. She swallows, her throat dry from the tension. The knife in her hand weighs heavily in this moment. She tests its sharpness against a branch, slicing a thin layer of wood with forced effort.

Movement catches her eyes as a talon moves down from the canopy, seeking shelter from the deluge. The lower half of the dark body presents itself, mere feet away. A stray lightning bolt illuminates a scarred torso with wet, black, leathery feathers. Her grip tightens on her weapon.

Unnoticed, Fento's paw feels for her hand and directs her attention to him. Using hand signals, he gestures a slow slashing sign across his throat just as the sky lights up. Thunder rolls overhead.

Breath elevated, heart racing, she readies herself. Fento's free paw lifts, displaying five fingers. Then four. Three. Her hand lifts, preparing to stab. Two. Fento's knife raises high, bent on stabbing down into the torso. One. Breaths are held as the decisive moment arrives.

Static electricity raises the hairs on their bodies. Pressure and heat blast through the air. A mere fifteen feet away, a jagged streak of white tears through leaf and limb, burning and splitting wood. Bark scatters like white-hot coals, striking their bodies. Gritting her teeth, Karal rolls onto the aerie, extinguishing flames, muffling her reactions to the sparks of pain. The Silva emits a surprised, high-pitched caw, flapping backward across the canopy. A wave of sound reverberates through them, forcing trees to shift and splinter—a deafening roar. The aerie bounds up as its edges tighten from the shifting trunks. Karal rolls to the center, breathing rapidly. In a corner sits Fento, his paw pressed against his chest, the other clutching the small knife. No one speaks as the cacophony fades. In the distance, the distinct, chilling cry of the Silva can be heard growing softer.

Fento is near collapse as the tension eases. He slides down to her. Karal breaks the silence in disbelief. "I can't believe we survived that. I've never been that close to killing anything."

"It's been a long time since I took a life." Fento swallows, rolling onto his back, staring into the dark canopy. Gradual raindrops filter through. "If the Silva had fallen by our hands, the Klenzeer might have become aware of us. This is the best-case scenario."

Karal pats him gently. "I know I only saw the lower half of its body, but that Silva was frightening. It had so many scars, and it smelled foul."

"It likely ate not long ago. They are supposed to be scavengers, but several rebelled and devoured Ones. Most were destroyed." He shakes his head. "The scars are from the abuse they receive. Few creatures survive unscathed from the Gardens." He yawns.

"You need sleep, and I'm too awake to rest right now. I can watch out for our visitor if he decides to return."

Nodding, eyes half-mast, Fento moves an inch or two before curling up in the center of the aerie. Exhaustion weighs on his face. Within seconds, he's snoring.

Wiggling her way to the edge, Karal leans against a gnarled tree in a semi-comfortable position. Refreshing rain cools her. Pitter-patter splashes form a soothing chorus. The occasional stray bolt lights up the sky, though no thunder follows.

Rainy days in Gallow come to mind as she sits in quiet repose. Splashing in puddles and chasing wooden boats down channels was always fun. Ives often baited her outside in the rain with promises of adventures, though they almost always ended up flinging mud at each other.

Ives.

Fento's question comes to mind. *Did I trust him?*

There's so much to consider. Closer than anyone beside her dad, he knew almost everything about her. Even Soma didn't know half the things Ives knew. Kissing him that night felt so good. There was passion and excitement, but none of it was real. Ives didn't know her secret. Only her dad, Ives' parents, and Lindor knew. The midwife was already old when Karal was born and died not long thereafter.

Her dad cut her hair short before she could walk and dressed her in boys' clothes. He decided her future without her input. Once her mom died, she was the only heir her father would ever have. To his benefit, she was willing to make the sacrifices to become that person for him.

It's hard to know if she did it for him or for herself. It didn't matter. She grew up as wild and carefree as any boy. Being a girl, chained to expected behaviors, would have been troublesome. She would have rebelled. The thought brings a light smile to her lips.

Returning to Ives, she realizes she trusted him. What she didn't trust was how he would react to her being a woman. Would he have felt betrayed? Disappointed? Disgusted? It was a mistake to kiss him back—a mistake to give him hope for something more. He deserved to know who she truly was, not the way he did. Raindrops mix with salty tears as her emotions float on the lip of a bursting dam.

Crack!

She stiffens, both alert and frightened. The sound of splintering wood rings out from below. Fento's snores are low, motionless, unaware. Everything is dark beneath them. Was it an animal? A falling limb, perhaps?

Braced against a tree, she peers down, seeking the source, and then she spots it—a blue orb floating above the ground in the distance. She gasps to herself as the faint silhouette of the Klenzeer comes into focus, visible in the eerie glow, with the Sinna trailing behind. He lifts and lowers his black rod, with the lit sphere perched atop. It illuminates the ground and trees in a dull, eerie blue shade. His face is haggard and worn. She remains still as she watches him walk hunched forward. Every few seconds, he refocuses on the orb, reading something from it.

She shifts from her perch for a better view, and the light intensifies. An alarmed look grows on the Klenzeer's face as he looks about excited, his expression turning fierce. Karal turns to stone, unmoving. His head turns left, then right, then angles upward toward the trees, the orb's glow chasing shadows away.

A sudden sound to his left diverts his attention, and he directs the Sinna in a flanking move. The orb brightens again, and he bends low, ready to pounce. The Sinna dives into a bush, and a loud squeal rings out. A small rodent-like creature squirms in their hands, which they crush without mercy. The Klenzeer growls, cursing the Sinna for their uselessness. They continue skulking north, their steps cautious and hushed. Minutes pass, but the glow fades. Karal lets out a long-held breath.

Morning finds Karal snoring, slumped against a tree. Movement on the aerie's fabric jolts her awake, her knife hand coming up swinging as the veil of sleep lifts. Fento abruptly halts his approach.

"That is quite the greeting. I'd hate to wake up near you on a bad day." He sits several feet away with an impish smile.

Karal shakes off the cobwebs, squinting away the daylight. A look of shock rises when she turns her knife hand over. Strapped tight with a cord, the knife handle is cinched to her palm. "How I avoided stabbing myself in my sleep is a miracle." She unravels the binding layer by layer. "I was worried either the knife or I was going to fall to our death last night. I might have been overly cautious when I wrapped myself up." She smiles at the indent left by the cord on her skin. When she looks down, she unties the cord wrapped around her chest and the tree that kept her from moving or falling.

She yawns. "Did you sleep well? You almost shook all the leaves out of the tree last night."

"Ha! You should talk. I felt the aerie vibrating with your heavy breathing this morning." Fento chuckles. "I am better now. Last night, I was paralyzed with fear. I'm sorry I didn't wake you."

"Don't feel sorry for anything. You hardly give yourself enough credit. It takes courage to face your enemies without running away. You inspire me."

Flustered, Fento looks away. "I am lucky to have a partner who tolerates my fearfulness."

A hush takes over as they both pause, unable to meet each other's gaze. Karal winds the cord while Fento fidgets with the small knife in his hand. Clearing his throat, he changes the subject. "We need to discuss our next steps. We don't know where our enemies are or what they have planned and—"

"I saw them last night. The Klenzeer and his Sinna." Karal's interrupts. Fento sits straighter, eager to hear. "He was using his rod, and the orb on top glowed blue. He was waving it around like a light. I stayed still as I watched him sneak around below us. When I moved to track him, the orb lit up. I stopped moving after that. He found a critter that bounded from the bush, and the orb glowed bright again. I think it's tracking movement."

Fento's mouth opens, ready to comment, but pauses. When he speaks, there's doubt in his voice. "Where was he heading? Did he go north?"

"I think so. Is that north?" She points in the direction she tracked last night. "If it is, he didn't stray much. I watched him and his light follow a straight path. Just a few twists for going around trees."

"That puts us in a bind, Karal. We were heading in that direction, and now we can't. He could be hiding or waiting for us at an intersection. Plus, that Silva is going to be difficult to avoid. I wish the lightning had fried them last night." He digs into the pack, scrounging up some breakfast.

"Then let's head back south or go west? I know you mentioned a village in this direction, but wouldn't it be safest to avoid it?"

Fento quiets as he contemplates her words, rummaging through the pack for something they can eat. He looks up, voice strained. "We could consider those options, but the Silva makes it difficult. To the northwest lies a decent-sized mountain, which is an option, but there would be no cover, and the Silva would spot us instantly. Plus, you're in no condition to go mountaineering. Your feet look rough, and that's a lot of tough terrain."

Karal looks down at her dirty, bruised feet, sighing with defeat.

"Heading back south isn't ideal either," he continues, his face worried. Retrieving some bread, he shares half. "There's nothing but burnt forest now and hardly any ground cover. Plus, the Silva could spot us and raise the alarm. If we head east, we'll hit the woods and the lake, but we'd go hungry if we had to hide for too long. We have to find a way around the Klenzeer somehow."

Hunger keeps Karal silent. She devours the stale bread. Her face scrunches up when thoughts of her simple, well-fed life in Gallow intrude. She'd give anything to eat more of her own crummy cooking right now.

Shaking the thought away, she focuses on the charred remains of the lightning strike to avoid dwelling on her growling belly. She had never been so close to lightning before. Its raw power was terrifying. If not for the rain, flames might have consumed—

An idea forms. She turns to Fento, opening her mouth as if to say something, and stops. Her brow furrows.

"What?" he studies her expression, puzzled. "Do you have an idea? You look mischievous."

Her lips close, eyes widening with childlike wonder. She hums before speaking. "What if we found a way to focus them on the wrong thing. Maybe create a diversion."

"How? They'll be watching from the air and ground. There are very few avenues of escape."

"It was just a joke when I called you a bushtail, but can you jump from tree to tree?" She raises a brow.

"I've done it many times before. It's called tree striding."

"And can you be stealthy when you do it?"

He contemplates, hedging on his response. "If I try, I suppose. I haven't really needed to before."

She hums again.

"Just tell me already! You're making me anxious." He smiles.

"Well, what if we split up to confuse them. I'm leaning on the idea that they don't know about you, and if they don't, it will make our plan easier." Karal pauses as Fento passes a moonie, which she devours, tart flesh and all. He watches her, his patience waning. Between bites, she continues. "You mentioned that the Bowl has lots of wildlife. You called it wild country."

"Yes, it's a thick forest with lots of life, so there's a good mix of both."

She hums a third time. "Well, what if we set a tree on fire. Maybe a dead one. It could distract them enough to investigate the source. It would definitely get the Silva's attention. When it goes to investigate, someone makes a counter-distraction in the opposite direction, stirring up the wildlife. That way, the Silva is flying back and forth, focused on two different things. That's when we can try to escape or hide somewhere. We'll have to meet up somehow."

Fento's eyes light up. "I have something that makes lovely fires. I've been meaning to use it. An apothecary sold it to me. She said I could light a river with it if I had enough. Plus, look at us, we're not soaked. I'm guessing other trees survived in a similar shape."

"That could work. But you'd have to know where the Klenzeer and his Sinna are, so you know which way to escape. It's the reason I mentioned the tree jumping."

"I can do it as long as I am focused. But what about you? How are you going to make a counter-distraction?"

She quiets, thinking, before Fento jerks, excited. "My pots! They're old and clatter when I don't pack them right. You can take them. If you bang them hard enough, you could stir half the forest to run from you."

Fento teems with excitement now. "Head south until you hit the edge of whatever got burnt yesterday, then turn inwards and head toward the water. When you see the lake, look for a marshy section with tall grasses, float pads, and such. I am sure there are tons of flutters near there. In fact, we can meet up there. It would make a great spot to hide. You can't miss it."

"Do you think this will work?"

He nods. "If they're distracted, it'll be difficult for them to find us. From our hiding spot, we can wait them out. They're bound to think we got away somehow and chase in a different direction." His face lights up, showing all teeth. "You're brilliant!"

Karal beams with pride. "Ives and I perfected our craft when stealing freshly baked treats. A distraction and a theft were our favorite tricks."

"You live up to your name, Karal." He stands. "Help me loosen these ties and pack up. The sun is still climbing. We have an advantage while it's not quite above us."

Together, they break apart the aerie and descend to the ground. Fento removes his flint and steel, along with the vial of thick fluid.

It smells foul as he opens and presents it. "This should do the trick."

Karal cinches the pack and puts it on, inhaling a deep breath as she steadies her nerves. Fento smiles at her before unexpectedly hugging her. They take several moments before breaking the comfort of their embrace. "Good luck and be careful. We have many roads ahead of us still." He winks.

"Give me some time to head south and prepare. I'll go slow on the off chance they doubled back." She parts ways with Fento, crouching low and heading south. Fento climbs up a nearby tree and leaps from its branches to another, heading north with as much stealth as he can muster.

Karal hikes south, looking skyward for the Silva through the breaks in the trees. She is slow as she heads toward the southern part of the Bowl. Before long, she encounters the edge of the burnt forest. She pauses to cover herself in ash and soot. Crouching low, she makes her way into denser woods. Her movements slow to a crawl as she listens and watches. Nothing stirs. She inches forward as the center of the Bowl comes into view, encountering piles of scat and bushes stripped bare of leaves—a promising sign of the dense wildlife Fento mentioned. The marshy area Fento mentioned comes into view not far from her position.

Movement catches her eye: the Silva flying above the water, searching for them.

She waits.

Twenty minutes, thirty. *Where are you, Fento?* Then she sees it. A column of dark smoke rises above the canopy. A tree is on fire on the northern side of the bowl. There's a flurry of movement across the water with flutters shooting out from their perches. But then a tree suddenly erupts in a ball of flames, followed by another. She shudders, her heart stuck in her throat. The Silva flies in the direction of the commotion, leaving her free.

She waits several seconds before she bangs the pots with as much ferocity as she can muster, running around creating a ruckus, stirring animals into movement. A family of wild ground flappers darts to the skies, honking. Flutters, with their short wings, flap away as they take off. Even a racker jumps out, its horns marking its path as it leaps away. She runs toward the water while various animals scamper.

The Silva's caw echoes like an agonized scream. They glide in the sky and adjust their heading with a wide turn. Karal drops the pots just as they reach the halfway point of their turn and then runs in the opposite direction. The disturbed animals flee east.

Taking the bait, the Silva follows the animals' movements. With their attention diverted, Karal dashes toward the marsh, stepping with care to avoid disturbing the otherwise calm lake. The reeds and tall grass shift as she quiets, settling in. Feeling the muddy bottom, she grabs handfuls and spreads a generous amount on her head and face for camouflage.

A stream of black smoke continues rising from the north. She turns within her shelter, seeking signs of Fento, when he emerges in a sprint from a thicket with a panicked expression on his face. He hurriedly enters the water, causing splashes and ripples to expand from the shore.

She approaches him on silent movement, whispering his name. "Fento. I'm here."

He yelps in shock, but calms when he recognizes her voice. "You scared me!"

"Calm yourself, don't move so much. That Silva won't be distracted for long."

Fento's breath slows as he settles in. He swallows and closes his mouth, breathing through his snout. A light tremor courses through him every few seconds. When he finally releases a long exhale, his face reflects greater calm. "Sorry."

He settles next to her and accepts the mud she covers him with. They both hover in the water, with just their heads sticking out. She submerges the pack, hoping it won't ruin anything of value.

"Did you get hurt? What was that explosion? I saw two trees go up in flames!" she whispers as they venture deeper into the reeds and tall grass. White and pink flowers bloom around them. A haze of green pollen and brown debris floats on the surface.

Fento surveys the area before speaking in a low whisper. "As we planned, I followed north, then turned east. That's when I found the Sinna acting as a sentry along a worn trail toward Paldor. He stood out easily enough. Not far from him was the Klenzeer. He was waving his rod around, and the orb glowed as you mentioned. I watched him point it southward, as if he didn't notice me sitting in the tree. Bush-tails were about, so he must have ignored me as one of them."

The unsettling cry of the Silva echoes, interrupting their conversation. Karal and Fento monitor the Silva's flight as their path narrows to circling overhead. The Silva's cries intensify as they drift lower.

A swoop from above freezes them. The screeches become loud, almost ear-piercing. The Silva turns abruptly, altering their path, floating on short bursts of their arms. Their wails slow to a guttural scream, eyes staring down. "HERE! They're here! I have found—"

BOOM!

An ear-splitting sound from the north ripples the water. A black orb rockets into the sky above the Bowl, trailing a ribbon of dark smoke. The Silva face stretches with fear. They gasp, "No!" and flap away in a hurry.

Shadows lengthen as the orb expands, gaining height, eclipsing the sun's rays. When it reaches the peak of its arc, it explodes like a starburst.

CRACK-THOOM!

A wave of force hits, causing the lake to undulate. Karal and Fento jolt as they're pushed back. Dark fingers of vapor spread blinking sparks in a circular pattern above the Bowl. They float down to the earth buoyed by the air, streaming like fireworks.

The display is breathtaking. Beautiful.

Just as the wisps touch the tallest trees—

WHOOSH!

Brilliant golden flames erupt from every branch. Trees are

engulfed in an instant. Black sparks shoot out, igniting neighboring trees. Animals panic, fleeing. Anything touched by a spark flares, producing more sparks. Tiny embers fall into the water, hissing and sizzling as they produce steam. Karal and Fento huddle, horrified. They take a deep breath and submerge for as long as they can. When they surface, the remaining falling embers wither and die. The Bowl transforms into an inferno, smoke blackening the sky. Charred animals rush to the water, dying inches from the edge. Black silhouettes line the shore. Trees billow thick ash into the sky. Even the marsh suffers modest burning, though not enough to be engulfed, given its proximity to the water. Smoke swirls up, lacking any wind.

The sounds of wings flapping overhead force Karal and Fento low into the water. The Silva crashes onto the nearby shore with a heavy splash, trailing ash and flames.

Karal freezes, eyes wide, as she watches the Silva struggle to breathe. Their body smolders, and they cough violently.

A shadow approaches along the water's edge, followed by another figure. The Klenzeer marches along the shore, unfazed by the firestorm around him. His rod is sooty—the orb atop gone. Ash darkens his face.

When he speaks, his voice is heavy with fury. "Get up! Search the sky. I must know that they did not escape." He kicks the Silva in the ribs.

The Silva moans and stirs. Achingly, they sit on their knees, gasping for air. Blood and wet soot seep from their beaked mouth, lined with teeth, as they glare at the Klenzeer. When they speak, an intelligible, husky voice emerges. "I am hurt." They cough, with ash dribbling from their chin. "I must recover. You shot your flame without warning me. Why? We help the Klenzeer."

"Time was pressing, and I did not want them to escape. You should have avoided the Ashthrok. It is limited in scope but effective in killing. Confirm their deaths." Another kick from the Klenzeer crunches bones, collapsing the Silva.

Coughing black ichor, they gradually stoop to their knees on shaky, leathery arms lined with black feathers. They turn their beaked face toward Karal's hiding spot, inky black eyes boring into her.

Fento shakes his head next to Karal, recognition and surprise on his face. He balls a fist, biting it with his mouth, trembling, hyperventilating.

"I will find them." The rough words escape the Silva as they flap their smoking wings.

In the firelight, Karal watches their beaked mouth open and shut, expelling more spit. Their bald pate drips sweaty soot. Dark eyes flare with an orange glow reflecting the flames. They're thin in body, but long in length, with a scaled, slithery tail. A lone, pale white stripe along their left wing, the only color on their dark body.

Several limping steps are taken toward Karal and Fento's hiding spot before they pause and look back at the Klenzeer. The Silva flexes their bloodied, dark yellow, taloned feet.

Screeching, they run straight for them.

Karal steels herself, ready to fight. Fento sinks lower into the water, frozen with fear.

The Silva hops, face wild with anger, and takes off into the sky just before reaching them.

As they gain altitude, they circle ominously for several rotations, lowering with each turn and gaining speed.

Fento and Karal watch as they accelerate, talons shifting forward to attack. With one final turn, they dive.

The Klenzeer is unprepared for an attack as the Silva shrieks with vitriol, talons scraping and piercing his shoulders, lifting him off the ground, before throwing him onto the dirt. He gets up lightning quick, reaching for the Silva's tail, snatching at the scaly extension, but missing.

Flying upward, the Silva banks north before disappearing from sight, a final caw piercing the sounds of burning.

The Klenzeer roars, incensed, ignoring his wounds. "Damn these worthless tools! Come, Sinna, you are still useful. We head to Paldor. If there is no sign of them on the road, we'll retrieve the cambra and return to the Gardens to await the Sorumjah. It will find them." The Klenzeer wastes no time admiring the destruction, walking inches from the marsh, the Sinna trudging dutifully behind him.

Fento and Karal watch him melt into the distance. They do not move. Neither does anything else. They are ghosts in a garden of ash.

PALDOR

Ash falls for hours, like winter flurries. Karal and Fento linger in the lake watching the Bowl turn gray until late afternoon. Dead finnies float on the now cloudy surface, intolerant of the warmed waters.

Black stains mar the lakefront. Carcasses of burnt animals litter what was once a beach, their outlines vague in the soot. Skeletal trees stand black against a cloudless, blue sky. A haze of gray dims the sunlight.

When they feel brave enough to leave the safety of their refuge, they wade to the shore, making it a few feet before the ground becomes too hot to traverse. Fento's tough paw pads offer some resistance, but Karal, barefoot, comes close to burning her soles and retreats to the water's edge.

She stares in shock at the surrounding devastation. Her mouth hangs open. She approaches slowly, close enough to make out the vague outlines scorched into the shore.

"How could he do this, Fento?" Her voice cracks. A tear slips down her cheek. "This was a living, breathing forest." She shudders. "He destroyed it all looking for me. I'm just one person."

Fento places his paw on her shoulder. "They are extremists,

Karal." He swallows. "The Overseers encourage them to be nothing less. If they kill anything other than a One, they are justified."

"Is he going to keep destroying forests and lives to get to me? There's no logic to any of this." She drops to the ground. "I don't want to cause any more harm or destruction."

"Don't give up." Fento shakes his head. "No one stands up to them or their laws. You staying alive means something, even if it's just defiance." He walks to the bloodied indentation where the Silva landed on the beach. "We were so close to losing everything. And I froze."

"Don't do that to yourself, Fento. My heart was beating just as fast as yours. I was ready to run away."

He snickers. "You don't have to lie for me. I know I lack the mettle. You looked ready to fight. I was ready to run."

"We got lucky. That Silva spared us because of the Klenzeer."

"Maybe." He twitches his snout. "I recognized him, the Silva. His striped wing is unique."

Karal turns, tilting her head. "You met him before? At the Gardens?" She stares at the impression on the beach. "Do you think he saw you?"

Fento shrugs. "He found us because I was careless. Scared. The ripples." He huffs. "Luck or not, that was a close call." He sheds the thought. "We should eat. Find whatever sticks you can. We'll make a fire and cook these finnies."

A few floating branches are all they manage to find, but it's enough. They eat their fill that night, as the fear of the Klenzeer returning fades with time. An unnatural quiet settles over everything —no bugs, no sounds from the lake, no rustling in the underbrush. The silence stretches between them until Karal can't stand it.

"What was that fire, Fento? It consumed anything it touched." She gapes at the burnt horizon. Few trees remain standing for a considerable ring around them. She shivers despite the radiating warmth around them. Her tunic dries by their campfire along with the strewn contents of the pack. A semi-damp blanket drapes over her shoulders.

Fento cups his chin. "I've never seen anything like it. He shot at me twice. Trees exploded behind me. I felt the heat so close to me, like it was propelled." He shivers. "They have many tools at their disposal. My Klenzeer's weapons were throwing knives—deadly accurate, precise and clean. She would never use anything like this. Each of them specializes in a specific type of weapon. It's what makes them unique. They can all hurt you in a brutally different way." He spits out black phlegm. "The Overseers built Ra. Did you know that? It's a place they maintain for a purpose. You Ones are the reason they built all this. This destruction is nothing. They can rebuild it, I suppose."

The revelation lands like a blow. "Everything was so simple before," Karal says, her voice unsteady. "You're saying, Gallow, my shop, and my friends could easily be wiped away and rebuilt at a whim? How is that possible?

"Karal, they can replace the land, but not the people." Fento's voice is resolute.

"But what are the Overseers? I don't even understand who they are. No one I know has ever seen them. Dad hated their Laws, but he never saw them or knew much about them. What do you know?"

Fento shakes his head. "I'm afraid as much as you do. In all my time at the Gardens, I may have heard of the Overseers making an appearance once or twice, but I was never allowed anywhere near them. I was a pet. An experiment. Unimportant and disposable in all their eyes." His gaze drops to the ground.

Karal exhales slowly. She shakes her head, trying to clear the dark thoughts forming. "So, where do we go from here? Paldor? Do you think it'll be safe? Is there anywhere else that would be safer?"

"I don't know that we have a choice. It has to be Paldor. Our supplies are low, and we'll need to replace a few things. For instance, you owe me some pots." He grimaces. "Paldor is our best chance. If what the Klenzeer said is true, he will be gone long before we arrive. From there, I think we find a town. It'll be easier to lose the Klenzeer in a populated area if we're careful. We have the advantage. He doesn't know if we're alive. We stand a better chance if we can avoid whatever the Sorumjah is."

"Yes! What is a So—rum—jah?" Karal stumbles over the syllables between bites of charred finny.

Fento shrugs. "I've never heard of it. It certainly doesn't sound familiar from my time at the Gardens. The Klenzeer used me for various tasks, but none involved anything that sounded remotely like this. I don't know how this relates to finding us."

"Maybe it's an animal or something that hunts us. We should increase our watches. It might be seeking us from anywhere." She looks out at the dark. "It doesn't sound natural, whatever it is."

Fento nods. "Yes. Whatever it is, I have no desire to encounter it. If we're lucky, we'll avoid the Klenzeer and his destructive staff. Once in a lifetime is enough for me."

For the rest of the evening, they chat, with Fento describing the Central Gardens. Nothing moves in the devastated landscape. Occasional movement sounds from the waters, but not much else. Few creatures survived.

That night, sleep comes in fits on the soot-covered ground, broken by hacking coughs and the struggle to breathe. When it eventually comes, it is brief and restless.

MORNING BRINGS a hazy sun over the Bowl, as particles of ash continue blotting the sky. Fento and Karal leave at daybreak. Between their labored breathing and coughing, their slumber did little to aid their recovery. On their way out, they scan for the discarded pots and find only their melted remains.

Thankfully, the swath of destruction is limited to the inner Bowl. As soon as they leave the charred ring, nature returns. The sight of living things loosens something in both of them. When they find a bush of ripe berries, they strip it clean, relishing the flavors. Along the way, small trickles of cold, clean water soothe their parched throats. By the time they reach the Bowl's edge, they move with lighter feet.

With the Klenzeer no longer looming, their tensions ease—

though every precaution is still taken on their journey to Paldor. Roads are avoided in favor of trekking through the woods on a parallel path. Fento scouts ahead, watching for whatever the Sorumjah might be, but finds nothing out of the ordinary.

Sometime before noon, signs of a village begin to appear. Woolies graze on a hill herded by waggers. An orchard and rows of plants and bushes come into view. Buildings rise on the horizon with each step. The signs of civilization make Fento grin.

Having never seen another village, Karal's face lights up with excitement, but it's short-lived. Paldor resembles Gallow in almost every way.

From their outskirts, she watches villagers move about, either working or chatting. Children run to and fro, playing with sticks and wooden toys. Mothers lead young families around trade houses constructed in familiar styles. Karal spots a bakery, a tavern, and—her breath catches—a smithy. Wooden signs hang outside shops and homes. The layout resembles Gallow. Farms are located on the outskirts, while commerce thrives toward the center, and the village square, with the despised Posts, lies in the middle. Even the people wear similar clothing, just in different colors.

"I've never seen another village, but it's all the same." Disappointment colors her voice. "If they didn't look different, I'd expect the same people as in Gallow. Are they all like this?" She regards it, expecting to find a twin of herself walking along the main road.

"Yes." There's sorrow in Fento's voice. "They all resemble each other. Little room for uniqueness in Ra. There is only the approved template of life. I'm sorry, Karal." He grimaces. "You may even notice patterns in the personalities and actions of the Ones here. Consider yourself informed of Ra's ways. You exist in it, yet you truly never live." He lowers himself to the ground, searching for fuzzfruit. Finding a ripe one, he begins to chew and speak. "Not all hope is lost, though. You are unique, and that is valuable. I was born different because of my coloring. You were born different because of your heart and mind. Treasure those."

She looks away, heat rising in her cheeks. Pride fills her as she asks, "What should we do?" She grabs a fuzzfruit and sidles next to him. "I imagine that either you or I walking in might cause a bit of a stir. Villagers love to gossip. At least we did in Gallow. The Klenzeer might even have laid a trap or informed the villagers to look out for us."

A smug grin rises on his face. "We're going to walk in there, get what we need, and get out."

She cocks an eyebrow. "And how do you propose we do that?"

"We're going to do some late-night shopping." Fento discards the pit and stands. "Time to make our shopping list. Come with me." He leads her to a higher vantage point. From there, they observe the villagers' routines as they go about their day. Fento takes mental notes, while Karal identifies tradesmen and their destinations. As night approaches, they dine on wild berries and leftover cold finny.

With a mouthful of berries, Karal asks, "Aren't you worried about getting caught? What if there's a guard or someone roaming around?"

Fento shakes his head. "Villages like these tend to be quiet late at night. They hardly lock their doors, much less have guards roaming about. Was Gallow any different?"

She considers this. Safety was never a concern, even after dark. "Ok. You have a point. But should we have a signal if we're separated or if there's danger? You know, while we're being quiet and sneaking around."

He smiles. "If it makes you feel better, we can—" He shuts his eyes as he taps his finger against his temple. "Can you whistle?" She nods. "Ok, then, using your best whistle, imitate a wibbler."

"A wibbler? Hmm." She blows out a low, sorrowful note, followed by two quick, high-pitched blows. She smirks, embarrassed.

Fento's shoulders drop, while he arches a brow.

"I never said I was good at whistling." She crosses her arms. "Can you do any better?"

Flawlessly, he imitates the melodic low, then double high whistle of a wibbler. He manages this three times, then nods at Karal, with a snarky smile rising.

She tries again, somehow sounding worse.

"Tell you what, Karal. I can make the whistle if there's trouble, or if I'm trying to grab your attention. You get into trouble, just shout my name out. I'll come running."

Nodding, she turns away from him and starts whistling to herself to pass the time.

Darkness settles as the daylight wanes. Karal dozes. Fento rouses her with a gentle shake. He looks into the sky and nods when he sees clouds forming overhead. "Good, patchy moonlight tonight. This will make things easier. Are you ready?" He extends his paw, which she takes. He leads them into the heart of Paldor.

THIEVERY

Paldor could be Gallow's twin. The village center sprawls before them—single-story buildings of wood and stone, a handful rising to two stories with more robust construction. Karal's stomach tightens at the uncanny familiarity. Ahead, Fento slinks from shadow to shadow on silent paws. She follows.

They start at one of the carpenter's homes. According to the Laws, signs outside must indicate both trade and family name for the census. Fento approaches what he assumes is the younger carpenter's home—the sign less weathered, the joinery novice. "Karal, you are the lookout. If you see any movement, whisper my name. I'll hear it if you're loud enough."

She nods. Her pulse drums in her ears.

He tests the main door. It opens with little effort.

In her youth, she stole small things—treats, fruit from orchards. Tonight, she and Fento raid a village for supplies. Guilt and excitement twist in her gut. When Fento emerges with only a handheld oilcan, she relaxes, raising an eyebrow. They'd discussed their route and practiced her stealth, but the order and specific items remained vague. She whispers, "Is that it?"

He nods.

Their quiet steps lead them to the butchery for cured meats and discarded fats, then to the bakery for day-old bread and mouthwatering tarts. Fento oils rusted hinges and locks as they navigate the various buildings, slipping through shops and homes as if he'd known them all his life. Watching him work, she marvels at how simple he makes it seem.

As they make their way to the nearest farm, she falls in beside him. "Have you ever been to Paldor before? How are you so familiar with everything?"

A smug grin. "I have lived in Ra for a long time. There is little I haven't seen recurring in these villages. I am certain Gallow is no more unique than Paldor." His pale face catches moonlight. "When I enter a village, I see the patterns repeated. The buildings' layouts are similar because that is how they've done it for countless Cycles. Butchers, bakers, homemakers. All of them follow the same pattern. It's what's expected. They inherit this from their parents and their parents before that. You've witnessed this, haven't you?"

His face recedes into shadow. She turns away, heaviness settling in her chest. "I have, but it saddens me. I thought there might be more to see outside Gallow. All I see is my old life."

Fento brightens. "Many aspects of Ra are repetitious, but there is more than just villages and people. There are beautiful landscapes and fascinating species. The cities are spectacles and house many interesting things. You will see."

"I hope so," she murmurs.

At the farm's edge, Fento slows to a crawl and signals her to follow. They stay low, sneaking onto the property. He has her stop several feet from the two-story barn while he advances around a corner with fatty meat in hand.

She surveys the barn. Zizzers chirr in steady choruses while night flutters flap overhead, catching pests in the dark. Small scurriers skitter through the grass. The familiar sounds ease some of her tension.

Fento's soft whistle signals it's safe.

When she rounds the corner, she freezes.

A massive black and brown wagger sprawls on its side, enjoying Fento's belly scratches. Its forked tongue lolls. All muscle and scales, it rolls on its back playfully, bony tail wagging. An undercoat of short fur contrasts with leathery skin, which radiates warmth. It stares at the meat Fento dangles, transfixed. The beast must weigh a hundred pounds or more, but it cannot resist the affections and tempting treat.

Fento nods toward the barn.

She gathers eggs, tunka nectar, fresh fruit, unripe popnuts, root vegetables, and grains, placing them in containers within the pack. When she returns, Fento tosses the remaining meat into the distance, and they scurry away from the distracted wagger.

Walking back to the village center, Fento inspects her work and nods. "We will make you a proper thief yet." He cinches the backpack and passes it to her.

Her face falls. "Is this how you survive? Stealing to keep from starving? Moving from location to location?" Her throat tightens. "How do you do it? Don't you need the comfort of a home? Somewhere to settle? I'm trying to find my place in all this, but I worry more with each moment."

Fento stops. He studies her face as the sky begins clearing and reaches out to wipe a tear inching down her cheek. "You've been off tonight. What's troubling you?"

The words stick, but she forces them out. "I'm—I'm lost, Fento. I had everything ahead of me, and now I have nothing. I don't know where I'm going or what I am doing." She sniffles. "If not for your kindness, I'd be dead or erased."

Fento pats her back as she leans against his shoulder, weeping quiet tears. "I sympathize with you, Karal. It's hard to trade all your experiences and comforts for this uncertainty. This path you are on is lonely. I understand your sadness. I faced it once."

A lengthy pause. He drifts somewhere distant. "When I was discarded from the Central Gardens, I had nothing. I was nothing. There was a hollow in me because I had no purpose." He looks to the moon. "I almost ran back to it."

She looks up, wiping tears away. "Back to her? To all that hardship?"

"Yes! I didn't know who I was without that misery. It wasn't longing but rather an absence of purpose." He meets her gaze as the moon escapes between clouds, bathing them in cool light. "You have to learn to redefine yourself, Karal. Smithing is in your blood, and you will work iron someday. I am sure of it. But who are you without it? That is what's scariest—not knowing yourself, losing your identity. You need to experience yourself again."

She wipes away the last of her tears. "Will you help me?"

"Gladly." His expression softens. "I will happily be your companion and guide if you allow it. You give me friendship—it's more than I could hope for." He reaches out his paw.

She takes it, and he gently guides them forward. With each step, the ache lifts. "I'm not usually like this. You must think I'm a mess all the time."

"Change is hard," Fento says. "And always worse at the start."

Their footsteps grow quiet as they walk back into Paldor's heart.

THE MOON HANGS LOWER NOW. Shadows loom darker on the quiet main road. Everything is tranquil. They stroll with ease, approaching the seamstresses' home when a dull clack sounds behind them.

They duck behind a corner, pressed against the wall. Karal steals a glance—nothing. All is quiet. They wait. One minute. Two. Silence presses in.

"What was that?" Karal whispers. "It sounded like a rock got kicked, didn't it?"

Fento stays low beside her, watching. The night remains hushed.

"I thought I heard it, too." He backs away from their hiding spot. "We need to finish. I'm ready to leave."

She follows as they slink around the next home.

The structure is small. Multiple snores rumble through the walls.

Fento studies their surroundings as he oils the door's joints and locks, slipping in without a sound. Karal watches.

He returns holding a needle and thread. "Anything?"

"I only hear my own heart at this point." Her hands won't stop trembling. "Let's hurry. I'm spooked."

They slink forward, quiet as scurriers, but no unexpected sounds come. Walking down the main road, Karal suddenly stops. A sign draws her in.

Set back from the road, a smaller, dark house blends stone and wood, a large stone chimney rising from one end. She softens as they approach. Her fingers trace the curves of the symbols—a hammer and anvil displayed prominently.

Fento checks their surroundings. Paldor is serene. A chilly wind picks up. He oils the hinges, picks the lock, then cracks open the door, listening. Nodding to Karal, he enters. She follows.

A single lantern burns low on a shelf, casting a warm glow. Dying red embers illuminate the forge. When she steps inside, her chest constricts.

Several pieces of iron rest on tables, in various stages of completion. Tools are strewn about with no regard for order, making her frown. She fights the urge to tidy the shop, then strokes every tool within reach. She rests her head on the cold anvil and breathes in the familiar scent.

The weight of the tools, the scent of iron and coal, the warmth from the dying forge—all of it calls to something in her that she can never answer. She could easily live in Paldor and resume her life, but it's just a cruel dream. She was born a woman, not a man. This will never be for her.

Fento startles her with a touch. His face is kind. "I'm sorry, but we have to go. The night will end before long."

She nods, and they turn toward the exit. On the way out, she spots something in a dusty corner—a cross-peen hammer with a split handle, gathering rust. She picks it up. It warms her hand. Well-balanced and worn. It won't be missed.

She places it carefully in the pack and heads out, resisting the urge to look back. Fento closes the door behind them.

"Thank you for letting me do that. It means a lot. I'm ready to leave Paldor. There's one more house, right? Let's finish up."

"Agreed, let's go."

He takes her hand and leads her to the last house—a large two-story home. The sign on the post is unfamiliar: a cambra-drawn cart with squares in the back.

"Local trader," Fento says. "Bigger villages need supplies, so this villager travels to other villages and towns to obtain them. Generally, it's a profitable business, but it carries risks from thieves and the like."

"People steal on the road?"

Fento pats her head. "Oh, you naïve Gallowers. Ones are far from perfect. Even the Klenzeer can't catch every immoral act." He inspects the main door, testing his weight on it. "This one feels bolted. Follow me."

Rifling through his bag, he retrieves his small knife and unlatches a kitchen window. He slips through as quietly as possible, then closes and relatches it behind him.

Outside, Karal observes her surroundings. The night air has cooled. The moon sits clear of the clouds now. Shadows press against doorways and alleys.

The window above opens and she startles. Fento hands down two worn pots to replace the ones that melted. "I'm going to look for more," he murmurs, ducking back in.

She stores the pots carefully to avoid clanging and waits as Fento resumes his search. She yawns. The nighttime raid has been less exciting than expected. Nothing moves. Everything is still. A howler screeches in the distance, echoing eerily.

Then she spots a mewler crossing the main road. She watches idly. It's pretty, with its long, soft black undercoat trailing a sleek, athletic body. If not for their horns and spiky skin, they would be perfect to cuddle. At least they keep the scurriers in check.

Just as she is about to look away, it stops and growls.

She stiffens.

It spits a low warning, tail erect and vibrating, backing away from a dark alley where shadows pool thickest. Whatever spooked it stays hidden. The mewler doesn't wait—it scampers away without looking back.

Karal fixes on the alley. Clouds filter overhead, dulling the light. The breeze picks up. Nothing else stirs.

She sidesteps with the building pressed against her back, caution guiding every move. Her eyes remain trained on the alley as she rounds a corner, hiding herself at an angle.

The sound of a wibbler makes her jump.

Seconds pass.

The wibbler whistles again, this time louder. It takes a second to register that it's Fento whistling. He hangs from the window, face tight with worry. She approaches and presses a finger to her lips, then points to the darkened alley. He narrows his eyes and stares for several seconds before shrugging. She waves him on, her nerves spent.

He hands her worn boots and winks, beaming, ducking back inside. She's about to try them on when she hears the window stick—

It slams shut.

Glass rattles in the frame. Through the panes, Fento's startled face disappears into the house. *Feng!*

She retreats to her hidden corner, breath quick, eyes moving between the alley and the shuttered window. Minutes pass before a bright light flares behind the glass. She swallows and holds her breath. The frame rattles. The lock is applied. The light fades.

She exhales.

She angles away from the home and looks up at the second story. Dark windows return pale reflections from the hazy moon. She turns a corner, searching. *Where are you, Fento?*

Every few seconds, her eyes go back to the alley. She dons the boots and nearly swoons, though they're cavernous for her feet. She looks up. Nothing moves. A howler screeches nearby. She startles.

A grating sound from above shifts her focus. A window opens. Fento dangles a pair of trousers and a heavy shirt. When she catches them, his alarm is plain. He scurries out onto the roof and uses a foot to shut the window behind him. She presses herself against the side of the house and edges around the corner, breath shallow and fast. The upstairs window rattles.

When she dares to peek, the room is dark. She releases the breath trapped in her lungs.

Stepping away from the house, she searches the roofline. When she finds Fento, he's whistling, arms outstretched, pointing toward the alley she'd been watching.

A shape emerges, bulky and imposing. Sunken eyes catch the moonlight like dead coals.

A Sinna.

It makes a loud, throaty sound and turns toward Karal.

Her legs move before her mind catches up.

She runs.

PURSUIT

Sharp clacks echo behind Karal—needle-tipped legs striking stone. The Sinna's heavy fists pound the earth. She drives her legs hard, arms pumping. The new boots grip each stride, while the backpack jostles on her back. Pots clang, rousing villagers from their deepest dreams.

To her right, paws thud across rooftops. A glance reveals Fento sprinting down a roof slope. An acrobatic leap sends him rolling onto the ground, sprinting just behind her. His labored breathing cuts through the night air.

She doesn't break stride.

When the village fades from sight, she risks a glance back. Fento runs beside her, breathless in the moonlight. The clatter from the pack startles sleeping animals in the tall grasses surrounding them. Flutters fly away. Rackers leap as though pursued. Turning her head further, Karal finds only darkness.

She slows. Fento passes her, glancing back at the same emptiness. Several flitters take flight as Karal stops. The clatter ceases.

"Quick, to the grasses." Fento guides her into high growth, breaths heaving. They crouch low and watch the road from a few feet into the dense stalks. Between sips of air, he manages, "Where did it go?" His eyes dart in several directions. The moon sits low, casting deep shadows. Wisps of clouds pass before it, dimming the pale light.

"I don't know." Karal pants, skull throbbing. "I heard it coming toward me, but then the pots took over. I should have tucked them in better. Half of Paldor heard us." She stares up the road. Nothing approaches.

Fento stays alert. "Are you sure you didn't see anything else? Not the Klenzeer or any other sign of attack?" He keeps watching, muscles tense.

"I don't think it was his Sinna. It was different, and it looked smaller." She holds her watch, not daring to look away.

"Are you sure?"

"It was a quick glance, but I would know his Sinna in a heartbeat. This one wasn't as stocky and wore clothing. I'm mostly sure." Her breathing evens out, but her pulse still hammers. "Why would a Sinna watch us from the shadows?"

Fento's ears relax. "Perhaps it was curious? We made an odd pair in the middle of the night, and we were stealing. I would watch us too, if I were unsure."

"I considered that. It could be a misunderstanding. It made a funny noise before it came toward me. Maybe it was trying to say something?"

He gasps. "What if it was the Sorumjah? We have no idea what it might be. Could it be a Sinna?"

"Then why not attack us? Wouldn't that make more sense? It feels like the Sorumjah would be something threatening." Karal readjusts the pack for a quieter walk.

"Hmm, that's a valid point. Maybe it's a system for watching. It might use different creatures to find what it's looking for."

Karal quiets, considering the Klenzeer's overwhelming weaponry. A network of observers isn't too far-fetched. "Let's head back to the nest. We can plan for it, or at least we can hide for the remainder of the night. I'm exhausted."

"It's called the aerie." Fento stifles a yawn as he steers them toward camp. "And I agree. I can barely keep my eyes open."

They walk through the grass to the edge of the surrounding forest and disappear into the darkness. Paldor looms behind them, quiet and dark. The forest is undisturbed—chirrs and squeaks filling the background, masking their passing. When they reach the cluster of trees that anchor their temporary home, Fento stays on the ground while Karal climbs up. When she looks, his eyes are closed, face intent, listening for any disturbances.

She whispers down. "Fento, come up. I think we lost them."

He opens his eyes but doesn't move.

"Fento!" she whispers louder.

He jolts, then turns to climb. "Sorry, I was lost in my mind for a second. I felt like I had been here before."

"You mean Paldor?"

He shakes his head. "This spot. This moment. It all felt so familiar." A sigh. "It's nothing. Aftereffects from everything they did to my mind." He shifts back to an earlier thread. "So are you sure the Sinna was different? My eyesight isn't as sharp in moonlight. You likely saw it clearer than I did."

"I'm mostly sure. The moonlight was patchy." She turns the Sinna over in her mind. Arching her back, she sinks into the aerie's fabric and lets out a terrific exhale. Her eyelids grow heavy. She pats a spot beside her. "Come on."

Fento releases a quiet yawn as he crawls toward her, rubbing his face as he lies down.

"Thank you for finding clothes for me. Did you almost get caught?" She hugs him and kisses the back of his head. "The welts on my feet thank you the most."

He warms from the affection. "Almost, but it was worth it. I couldn't let you keep stretching out my oversized tunic. I had plans of growing into it someday." He chortles.

He peers into the dark forest, watching for any sign of the Sinna. When nothing stirs, his eyes close and his breathing slows. "Goodnight, Karal."

She responds with soft snores.

He falls asleep moments later.

〜

LATE MORNING FINDS them piled together in an embrace. Karal wakes first, her chin resting on the back of Fento's head. She slips out carefully while he shifts in his sleep and rummages through the pack to examine the haul from the previous night.

The hammer rests on her lap. She palms it. Heavier than her old ones, a little unbalanced. Rust can be cleaned off. The handle will take some work to repair. Practicing a few swings, she imagines the Klenzeer standing before her.

"He won't know what hit him." Fento watches with one eye open.

Heat rushes to her cheeks. "I can't believe you saw that. I'm like a child receiving a toy. You would think I was fighting a growler." She laughs. "This gives me a chance to fight back if we get backed into a corner."

"I do not doubt that the growler would go running." Fento sits up. "But if we ever run into a Klenzeer, we should run in the opposite direction. There is no beating a Klenzeer, Karal. I've only seen a dead one up close, once."

A pause.

"There was a Class D once. He tried to take on a Loper in heat. It was right before the end of a Cycle. The Loper was mating with a One. Against the Laws, of course, so this Klenzeer tried to stop him. Do you know the Laws, Karal?"

"Of course. We are forced to memorize them. The Headman expects it, so no one can break a Law and claim ignorance. This would be the Law of Purity." Her voice shifts into recitation: "No species will mate with a species not of their own. The traits of all Ones and lesser beings will stay pure to ensure the proper behaviors and traits of that species. Any species not found to be pure will be destroyed."

Back to her normal cadence, she adds, "I always thought they were talking about Sinna, but who would mate with a Sinna?" She shudders. "You've mentioned Lopers before but never explained what they are. You said they were a mistake."

"They have an interesting history. The short version is that Lopers are larger versions of slopebacks, but they can shift their bodies into Ones. It's painful for them, so they do so reluctantly. However, at the end of each Cycle they must do this to mate. They go into heat near the full moon. Afterwards, they revert to their slopeback form. Have you never heard the rhyme?"

She shakes her head. "I can hardly believe something can transform from a slopeback into a One, much less hearing a rhyme about it."

"You're very sheltered." He sticks out his tongue. "It goes like this." He clears his throat:

> *"Hide yourself when the moon is full,*
> *Or you will feel the touch of lust.*
> *A Loper is lurking, and you they'll fool,*
> *When they charge you with their tusts."*

She blinks. "Tusts?"

Fento blushes. "Have you never heard that word? Tusts are your— you know, things that you have sex with. Common slang at the brothels."

"Brothel? What's that?" Innocence radiates from her expression.

He looks away. "Never mind that. Lopers are dangerous. When in heat, they get aggressive. This Klenzeer thought he could stop this Loper from mating with a One, and they tussled. He managed to wound it before the Loper disemboweled him. I caught sight of the Klenzeer's wounds. They were a mix of bones and flesh, but also metal fused to the exposed bone. He died not long after. They didn't even bother pursuing the Loper."

He meets her eyes. "My point is, Klenzeer are not like us. Don't fight. Run."

Silence follows the story. Karal's expression turns stony. She refuses to look up.

Fento abruptly changes the subject. "So where do we go from here?"

She stirs. "I was going to ask you the same thing. I don't know much beyond Gallow. Where will we be safe? How do we avoid getting caught?"

"Well, we did talk about heading to a populated place, like a town. Or maybe we can aim for a city." Karal moves to interject, but Fento stops her. "We have been running in forests for days and are both starving and dirty. What if we change our appearance and disappear among the Ones and other Fen? A town or a city will hide us better than a forest or the mountains. There will be supplies and food, and we can find a place to stay." He catches her gaze. "We are surviving on berries and stolen food. We will have more options."

She looks down at herself and sees how filthy she's become. They've been running since she left Gallow—only days, not weeks. What would weeks on the run look like? She nods. "Ok. Is it common practice for people to go to these centers? Will I fit in?"

Fento smiles. "You'll fit in just fine. Do you think you're the only villager to leave home? There's constantly an influx of people in towns. It's the reason the census was created. They initially wanted to track every individual but opted to evaluate the changes in population size. As long as Ones are having babies, that's all they truly care about. There are places in towns where Ones get together for that purpose."

"Oh, you mean brothels? Yeah, my dad told me about them. He said I'd end up at one if I were discovered being a blacksmith." She giggles and winks at Fento.

"You little scamp! Not as innocent as you pretend to be. You knew all along, didn't you? And tusts too?"

Karal nods, grinning.

Fento chuckles with delight. "You're full of mischief."

After a few moments, he redirects their conversation. "What about last night? Did you think about the Sinna?"

She nods. "I was wondering if maybe it lived in that village. We occasionally had some pass through Gallow and work plowing fields or moving stones. We were sneaking around in the middle of the night. It might have seen us at the farm and become curious."

"Maybe." Fento's whiskers twitch. "It makes sense from that perspective. They speak the common tongue in bits and are fairly docile. I was running so fast that I didn't even notice if it gave chase. Oh, that reminds me." He looks at his foot pad. A bloody slice runs from his heel to midfoot. Not deep, but annoying enough to be inconvenient.

"Ooh, how did you do that? That looks painful." Karal examines it, poking it with a finger.

"Careful there. I might bleed out if you keep doing that." He snorts. "I was so focused on running away, I didn't notice when I cut it on a roof somewhere. It'll heal in a few days. I've faced worse."

He refocuses. "Are we agreed? Shall we go to a town? Villages are too small, and we would stand out. Plus, I don't imagine you want to become the permanent resident thief of Paldor. I'm sure the villagers will gossip about last night's escape for months to come."

"Yes. A town. I want to start small. A city sounds overwhelming. They are three times the size of a town, right?" Karal starts retrieving food for breakfast.

"Wait! I want eggs. They're best fresh. Let's pack up the aerie and cook a hot meal first." Fento licks his lips. "A town is about three times the size of a village. A city is about ten times the size of a town. They're impressive."

Karal's jaw drops. "That's too big. A town. Let's go to a town and see how it goes."

Together, they pack up the aerie and climb down. Karal digs a small fire pit and collects wood while Fento begins preparing breakfast. When she returns to camp, she finds him staring at the base of the trees.

"What did you find? Anything interesting?"

He inspects the tough bark, touching fresh gouges where sap weeps. Deep impressions mark the trunk, resembling a large hand and thick fingers. Small round holes dot the ground in deep indentations. Similar depressions spiral midway up the tree.

He turns to Karal. All color drains from his face.

"We have to go. Now!"

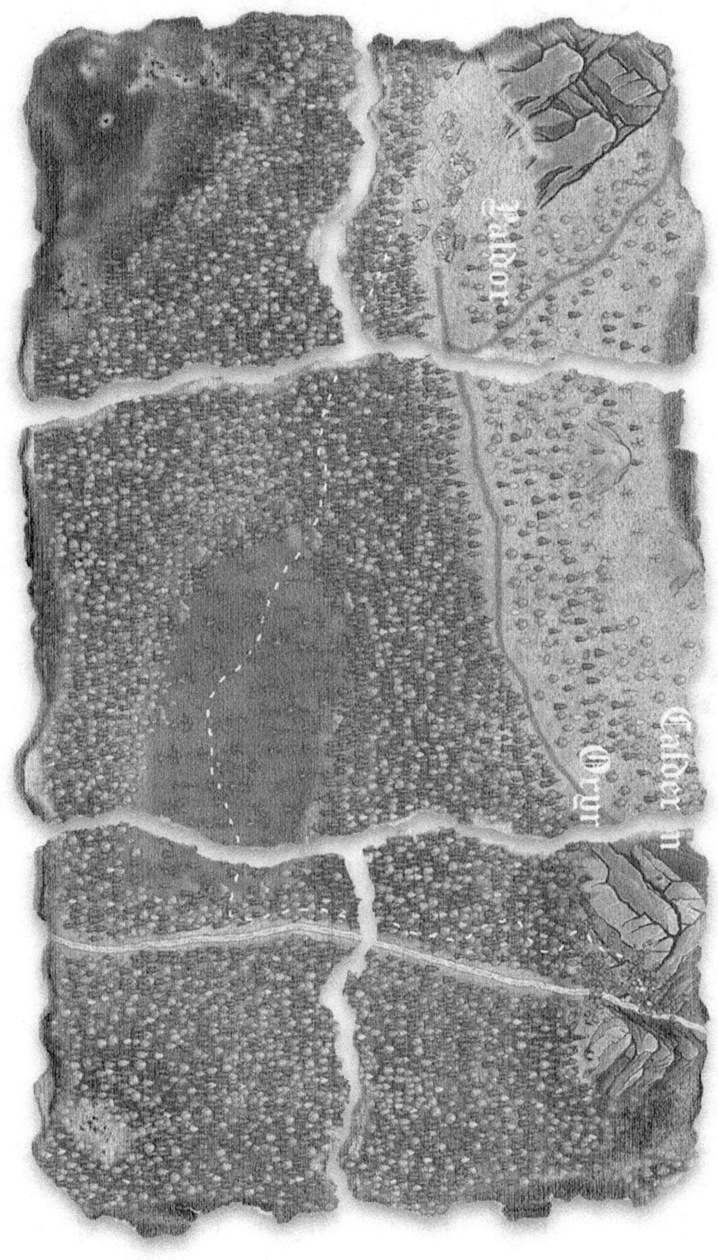
Pathor
Oryr
Cader in

CHALLENGES

Karal crashes through the woods, branches whipping at her face, Fento close behind. They've been half-running, half-walking for hours. Her face is flushed, lungs burning. Mercifully, the injuries from her escape from Gallow have faded to yellow bruises and distant memory. A glance behind reveals no pursuing figure—no trace of anyone.

"Fento, stop! I'm spooked like you are, but we need to rest. There's no one behind us." She slows to a walk.

He matches her pace, huffing. The words tumble out. "Karal, Sinna don't climb trees! But this thing—whatever it was—almost made it halfway up!"

"How do you know it happened last night? What if it was a coincidence? What if the tree trunk was always like this?"

Fento paces, paws pumping. "Sinna have large, thick hands, and their legs end in fine points. You saw the tree. The bark was crushed around the edges with the imprint of fingers. The holes climbing up the bark were its legs digging in. It had to be recent; sap leaked from the holes. This Sinna, or whatever it was, made an impressive attempt at climbing, and it was stealthy enough to do it while we slept. It made it halfway up!"

Karal's mouth tightens. "We were exhausted. Our journey to Paldor had been torturous. Of course, we didn't stir."

"Contrary to what we believed, we're being chased by that Sinna. It's likely the Sorumjah. This thing is clever and almost got to us while we slept. I don't understand how it found us."

"Maybe it followed us last night. We made too much noise. Either way, there are two of us. We can face it together. I have my hammer. You have your knives. We can take on a Sinna."

"No, no, no! Sinna are no pushovers. They are hardy, strong, and tough-skinned. Whatever you think we can do together, forget it." His voice drops. "I've seen one injure five armed Ones and walk away with a few scratches. It's better to avoid this and find a way to Ormant."

Karal kicks a tree. "Where have we been running to? You haven't told me anything besides we're heading to Ormant. Where are we right now?"

Fento turns in a circle, taking a few whiffs. When he catches a strong scent, he winces. "We're near a swamp. I'm afraid we'll be sleeping in there tonight. It'll be our safest route." He sighs. "Sinna aren't elegant or limber. They are about brute strength and toughness. They won't enter a swamp. Their dense bodies will get stuck or sink. The more we throw this thing off, the better our odds."

"Can't we go another way? Maybe a less active road?"

Fento shakes his head. "I'm sorry."

She kicks the tree again and curses. "Let's go."

THEY CONTINUE EAST until they near the edge of a swamp. The stench is overwhelming. Rot and stagnant water assault Karal's senses. Downed trees and a wet landscape enclose the bug-infested area. She wrinkles her nose. "Are you sure about this? We can go around and save ourselves the headache."

"Karal, I want us to be safe. Trust me, I don't want to do this either, but no other route makes sense."

"Fine!" She takes the first step into the muck. Her new boot fills with mud and water. She cries out in disgust and takes a second step. Fento follows, stepping into her bootprints to avoid leaving more tracks.

Nitnits swarm them, biting viciously. They swat at their faces and exposed necks. Karal still wears the tunic Fento gave her at the beginning of their journey. The bugs bite through the fabric, leaving large welts.

Swinging his tail, Fento tries to ward off the pests. "Karal, get some mud and put it on your skin. It will act as a repellent." He pauses, lathering mud on his fur, then gags as the odor intensifies. Bugs continue to harass him. "Never mind." He retches. "It's not worth it."

They trudge on for hours. Deeper in, the mire swallows their existence. Dead trees, half-broken and cracked, surround them like a wooden graveyard. Thick mud threatens to cement them in place. Without warning, a deluge of rain falls. Cold, heavy drops make the journey more miserable but alleviate the bug problem.

Minutes feel like hours. Before long, the sun sinks toward the horizon. Their progress slows to a crawl.

Karal shivers. Cold, wet, and hungry, she scans the waterlogged landscape. There's almost no dry ground and hardly a tree sturdy enough to shelter under. "Can we at least make a fire? Something to warm us up. Maybe make dinner?" Her words tremble with her body.

Fento shakes his head. "There's no dry wood. I'm not even sure if this soaked wood would burn. We'll have to suffer tonight. It's just one night." His belly rumbles.

"But we have your fire-starting liquid. I bet you can make anything burn with it." She scratches at the welts on her arm. "I'm on this dumb detour. You can at least indulge me."

"It's not dumb. We're trying to be safe. Look, I don't want to be here either, but we're here, so let's make the best of it."

Karal drops onto a stump, glowering at the ground. "Can we at least eat something?" A beat of silence, then a quiet, "Sorry."

Fento grabs his bag and searches for the hard bread. "Feng!" His hands come out covered in wet egg yolk. "Why are these packed so high? I thought you moved them?"

"I thought you moved them! You packed up the aerie, so you should have moved them."

"No, I asked you to—never mind." He rubs his hands on his pants. Insects swarm immediately, drawn by the yolk. He growls and swats them. "Go away, you nasty things."

Walking toward Karal with the bread, he slips and loses his footing. Half his body splashes into the mud. He curses.

Karal chuckles, then laughs, loud and hearty. She's about to reply when mud splatters across her leg and back. Her laughter dies. "What the—why would you—"

More mud hits her back.

She scoops handfuls of sludge and flings them at Fento. He dodges the first volley but takes the second on the tail.

He retaliates.

She ducks behind a tree.

Mud flies. It cakes the trees around them. It spatters across limbs, chests, and hair. Both of them reek from head to toes.

Karal stomps to the opposite side of a tree, refusing to speak. Her hair and hands smell like dirt and decay—a combination that steals her appetite. She punches the tree solidly, grunting. The pain in her knuckles does nothing to ease the frustration coiled in her chest.

Her mouth twitches as rage turns into anguish.

A gentle touch surprises her. Fento stands there offering a blanket, his ears drooping. "I'm sorry," he whispers.

The firm line of her mouth relaxes over quiet seconds. When she lifts her face to his, she mutters, "Truga." But there's no venom in it.

Fento nods and says nothing. Karal extends her hand, palm up. He places his paw in hers. She guides him beside her and wraps the blanket around them both.

A long sigh escapes her. A yawn follows. Fento echoes with one of his own. They lean their heads together and welcome the night.

Miserable, but together.

~

Morning brings a frigid fog. Karal wakes chilled beside Fento, who snores deeply. The back half of an animal hangs from the pack across the way. She gets up and frightens it off, yelling. Her voice snaps Fento awake. As she inspects the damage, he rubs his eyes, yawning. "Did it eat all our food?"

"It nibbled on the popnuts and some of our tangleberries. Looks like I caught it early enough. We should have hung the pack or kept it closer. This place is full of nasty surprises." She cracks her neck. "Do you think we'll get out of here today?"

"If we can power through, yes. It's not as large as most forests. It gets fed by the Ormanti river, so it will lead us there, assuming we don't get lost. All this fog isn't going to help." He steps forward with a slight limp.

"Is there a problem with your foot? Got a splinter?" She teases while shouldering the pack.

Fento smirks. "My injury might be infected. I must have reopened the wound yesterday, and this foul mud has done a number on it. I can feel the warmth spreading up my leg. I have a salve I can apply, but not if we're knee-deep in this muck."

Karal loosens the pack's straps and tightens them again, ready to go. "Which direction? I'm so tired of this place. The stink is in my blood."

Fento studies the fog and points. "There? I have no clue without the sun."

Karal shrugs and heads that way. They probe ahead with sticks, testing what lies ahead. The fog sits thick and impenetrable. Fento grimaces with every step. After an hour, the landscape shifts. The water reaches their knees, then climbs higher. Float pads and murky water surround them. Bugs dive-bomb exposed skin. Karal groans with each new bite.

When a sliver of sun pokes through, Fento adjusts their course without a word. Karal watches him. He's too quiet.

Midway through the morning, the fog lightens over an area of fallen logs and tall grasses. The water is chest-deep now. They slow to a crawl, unsure whether the next step will submerge them. Karal balances the pack on her head with one hand while probing ahead with a stick.

Fento drags behind.

A splash to the left spreads ripples that fade. *Croak.* Karal's eyes shift right, chasing the sound. Something bumps her leg, and she goes rigid, stabbing at the water with her stick. Finding nothing, she relaxes and moves on. When she turns to check, Fento is catching up, his movements labored.

"Are you alright?"

He shakes his head. "No." His face is slack. The brightness in his eyes has dimmed. Dark circles shadow beneath them. His white fur looks almost ghostly.

"Get on my back." She hands him the pack to strap on and crouches. He wraps his arms weakly around her neck.

She moves forward, probing ahead with her stick. His warmth against her back worries her—he's too hot. His head bobs with each step. They continue past midday until the ground begins to firm, water receding with each step. The mud fights every stride. She grunts against it, energy dwindling. Fento's grip loosens. The pack slips sideways on his back.

Late afternoon, the sun breaks cover. Keeping it at her back, Karal marches east across ground that has grown rockier and firmer.

Fento is silent. His arms are barely holding on.

"Fento?"

A low hum. She leans forward to ease his balance and pushes harder.

As the sky darkens, the sound of running water fills her ears. Everything else had fallen away hours ago—only Fento, only forward. The Ormanti flows ahead, hidden behind overgrown bushes. Her steps quicken. The burdens of the last few days lift with each stride.

So close now.

Without warning, Fento's arms drop from her neck. She starts to turn—too slow. He falls backward and hits the ground with a heavy thump.

His eyes roll back. He doesn't move.

"Fento?"

Nothing.

"FENTO!"

He doesn't move.

NEAR DEATH

"DO NOT FORGET!"

The haunting voice jolts Fento's eyes open. Semi-darkness surrounds him. Above, a domed ceiling curves into shadow. Light begins to glow around him, illuminating the walls in a deep, dark red.

He's in the middle of a circular room. Near one wall, an unidentifiable being sits in a large wooden chair, leaning forward as if struggling to stay upright. Several layers of cloth—blankets or robes—drape over them. Long white hair cascades to the stone floor, hiding their face.

A sudden boom echoes to his left. A thick metal door several feet from the chair vibrates on its hinges. Large dents bow out from its center. Another boom follows, like a hammer striking metal.

The figure speaks in a clear voice with an unexpectedly young tone. "Are you ready, Fento?"

"Ready for what?" His words come fast, unsteady. "I don't understand. Where am I? What is this about?"

The voice sharpens. "You must save us, Fento! Do not waste time. Four tasks shall come naturally, but the last will prove most difficult. That one—you cannot fail."

"What is difficult? What am I to—"

The room quakes as if rocked by an explosion. Hairline cracks race along the walls to the domed top. In a curved section of the ceiling, bright white light streams through a hole the size of a fist. Angry cries issue from the gap like animals braying.

"You must do what is necessary when the time comes." The voice lowers, tenderness entering it. "It will be difficult, but you must not let—"

Another blast. The door buckles, held by threads. Hands burst through gaps—twisted and bloody. Dirty, chipped nails grasp at the air.

"What am I to do? I don't understand!" Fento approaches the chair, each step careful.

Ancient arms lift from the robed figure, revealing gnarled fingers tipped with black talons. The dry, cracking hands come together and rub vigorously like sandpaper on wood. When they part, five lights bloom at the chamber's center—disc-shaped, hovering at ground level in a perfect circle. Each oval expands to Fento's height, radiating an eerie yellow-white glow.

"Stand in the center of the chamber."

Fento hesitates but complies, uncertain what else to do. Another explosion echoes from above. The ceiling shows signs of collapse. Dust falls from new cracks.

The twisted hands come together again, rubbing with that same gritty sound. Fire courses through Fento's veins. He screams as every cell in his body stretches and pulls apart, as if being torn in half. Heat spreads through his limbs and head, threatening to melt him from within.

The door shakes and nearly flies open. Bloody limbs pry at the gap.

The ancient figure spreads their arms, and Fento feels himself pulled apart. Five identical copies of him collapse to the ground, each staring at the others in surprise.

"GO!" The figure screams as the door finally fractures and falls. Dark-robed beings flood the chamber, streaming toward the chair, ignoring the Fentos. Tall, dark, nondescript—growling and tearing at their own flesh. There is but one thing that will satisfy them.

"GO!"

The robed beings reach the chair. The Fentos watch as the ancient figure disappears under a wave of bodies. The light dulls from the glowing discs. He and his doppelgangers turn toward them. Unsure what else to do, they leap.

FENTO'S chest constricts as he jolts awake. Quick, shallow breaths fill his lungs. "What was that?" he whispers, grasping for memories that are already fading like morning fog.

Five lights—red room—something about saving—

The details slip through his mind like water through cupped hands. By his second blink, only the lingering sense of urgency remains.

A nearby fire pulls his attention; the crackle of wood and a familiar scent invade his senses. He lies face-up on a thin blanket, staring at a canopy of leaves. Beyond them, a field of stars twinkles. The warmth of a figure beside him offers comfort. Fento recognizes her scent and calms.

As his mind clears, he surveys his surroundings. Weak-limbed trees encircle them, short and reedy. The ground is covered with dry needles and dead leaves. He suspects they are at the swamp's edge, near the Ormanti. The rushing waters enhance the night's ambiance.

Sitting up, a headache assaults him, forcing his eyes shut. He reaches for his head and feels a sizable bump at the back. The sensation of falling comes to mind, but nothing more. He'll need the details from Karal.

Wiggling his toes, he feels a slight sting in his injured foot. Angling it into view, he finds neat stitches held together with thread. He looks at Karal's sleeping form and smiles. She is full of surprises.

His belly rumbles. Within reach, a bowl and a pot filled with liquid sit near the fire, steaming—kept warm but not cooking. He pours a generous helping, salivating. The first swallow makes him gag. There's hardly any spice. Something that might be finnies mingles with what resembles stones or burnt vegetables. Hedging, he drains the bowl and pours another. He drains that one without tasting it, but denies himself a third.

Mental note: deny Karal cooking privileges going forward.

Glancing around, he notices Karal's done an admirable job setting up camp. The casting gear rests in a neat pile, while logs and cooking tools are stacked near the fire. A blanket spreads over them in a snug arrangement. Chuckling quietly, he marvels at the reversal—he'd always assumed he would be the one protecting her.

A yawn escapes, sleep still pulling at him. Stretching, he looks around for the canteen and spots it sitting between him and Karal. As he takes a swig, his gaze drifts across the river.

Two glowing eyes stare back.

He chokes, coughing. Karal wakes with the long knife already in hand, swinging—Fento ducks just in time.

Recognition floods her face. She drops the knife and crushes him in an embrace.

"Fento! You're alive! I thought I was going to lose you." She holds him tight, their warmth mingling.

He hesitates to let go. Peering behind her across the water—nothing. The space is dark and empty.

"You saved me this time. I suppose the swamp seems like a bad decision in hindsight." He feels a flick on his ear and takes it willingly. "I didn't mean to wake you. I was drinking water and thought I saw something watching us across the river. I must have imagined it."

Karal breaks the embrace and meets his gaze. "It has been watching us for two days." No panic in her voice. No fear. "I have only seen it at night, always from the same spot. It's been hiding in bushes across the way. I've yelled at it several times, and it disappears for a while, but always comes back. I've thrown rocks, invited it to speak, and even left food out, but it just watches."

Fento's fur bristles. "We need to move. There is no time to waste. I'm awake." He assesses what needs packing, but she holds him firm.

"There is no need to overreact. Whatever this is, be it Sinna or something else, it just watches. No aggression. No assaults. It has had two whole days while you recovered to attack me." She holds his gaze. "Nothing has happened."

Her hazel eyes lock on him, reflecting the vibrant dance of the flames. His anxiousness ebbs.

"I've taken precautions. This knife is strapped to me, and my hammer is on my side. Whatever happens, I'm ready."

Something catches in Fento's throat. "I am—thank you. You are a good friend." He looks away.

Karal smiles. "We can talk more in the morning." She turns and pauses. "Oh, you drank the soup! How was it?"

"Oh, yes, it was wonderful! You seem to have a—gift. I'm ashamed to have put you out like this. I'll cook for several nights to make up for your kindness." Fento's smile is all teeth.

She beams. "Don't sleep with one eye open. I am here and ready to do what is necessary. Relax. We can chat in the morning." She lies down and pats the ground beside her.

He settles next to her warmth. "Thank you," he whispers.

Karal kisses his forehead, then rubs his ears, as is her habit, and closes her eyes.

A grin spreads across his face—childlike and touching. He tries to compose himself, huffing quietly. It stays anyway. He whispers, "Good night, Karal."

Her soft snores already blend with the night sounds.

Old fool. Be her friend and nothing else. The Laws.

But as sleep takes him, the mirth never fades.

THE FIRE BURNS down to glowing coals, generating waning light and heat. Across the river, nothing stirs. The sounds of the Ormanti mask the chirr of nighttime creatures.

Deep within the cooling coals, something stirs. A dark, amorphous shape rises like a shadow given form, imperceptible except for two perfect orbs of red light that gleam like tiny stars.

For a heartbeat, it watches Karal and Fento, then sinks back into ash.

The crimson lights fade to nothing.

PALE SUNSHINE BRIGHTENS the morning as Fento rises, feeling rested. He surprises himself by waking before Karal. His first instinct is to check that she didn't gut herself on accident overnight. His second is to look across the Ormanti. The expected scenery remains undisturbed, just as Karal assured him. He grunts softly and stands. To his surprise, his head doesn't protest. The lump remains, but the worst has passed. He checks their supplies. If he can help it, Karal won't cook again anytime soon.

What luck! A single egg survived their trek across the swamp. He poaches it for her benefit, rebuilding the fire with kindling and careful breaths. Next, he retrieves water from the Ormanti, scrutinizing every surface on the opposite shore, examining every crevice. Nothing. He turns away reluctantly.

He prepares a decent breakfast: poached egg, berries, and dried meat. The scent stirs Karal from her slumber, and she rubs her hands in anticipation. He can tell her breakfasts have been subpar for the past few days. She practically drools when he presents it.

With a mouth full of egg, she asks, "How far do you think we are from Ormant? Oh, and you have to tell me all about towns. I don't want to sound too dumb when we get there."

He laughs. "Don't worry, you're going to fit in just fine." He gives her a wink that makes her roll her eyes. "The size can be daunting to anyone used to small, comfortable spaces. Also, the variety of townsfolk is overwhelming. There are more shades of skin, accented speech, and non-Ones. You'll be surprised when you see it." A pleasant smile grows. "Nothing truly prepares you for a new place.

You have to experience it. Plenty of folks like you leave their villages to seek their futures in a town. Don't worry."

She smirks. "You just want a good laugh watching me react to things." She sticks out her tongue. "I'm not as naïve as you think."

"It will be a joy to watch you explore somewhere new. Especially after being in the woods with me this long." He snickers.

They finish breakfast in comfortable silence. Fento appreciates the unexpected calm after so many harrowing days. Occasionally, he glances across the river, but spots nothing alarming. When his eyes drift to the casting pole, curiosity stirs. "How did casting go?"

She lowers her voice. "I don't know what's wrong, but I think the finnies in the Ormanti might be sick." She looks to the river and back. "After I got you comfortable, I decided to try casting. Mind you, I don't know much about the Ormanti, but it seems like a decent river. When I got the bramble bait in the water, it wasn't long before I got a finny on the line. I gave it a few tugs, but then the fight just disappeared. I reeled it in, and it was a decent size, but it didn't fight or flop about, though it still breathed. I tried again with fresh bait. It wasn't long before I saw a finny float up with the bramble attached to its tentacles. I was scratching my head at that point. So, I decided to try a third time, and this time, I saw a lively finny struggling with its tentacles tied up in the bramble and some of the bait in its mouth. I was excited because it was a good size. So I grabbed the pole, and the line went dead. I thought I had lost the finny, but when I reeled it in, it was unmoving, like dead, but still breathing." Her voice drops. "What in the world is wrong with this river?"

Fento studies her with a queer look, leaning back. Then an idea strikes. "Show me the casting gear."

He sniffs the rod and brambles and smiles, then rushes to the pack and rummages until he finds a cracked bottle filled with a viscous liquid.

He cackles.

"What? Did I do something wrong?" She stands with her hands on her hips. "Fento, tell me! Now you're just laughing at something I did." Growing annoyed, she tackles him and pins him with her weight.

Fento grins up at her. "You have become the greatest caster in Ra. I will forever call you Castburn."

She tickles him until he relents.

Between chuckles, he explains the trick. "I was once sold the contents of that little bottle. An apothecary said I could use this oil to capture animals. It smells harmless to us and has little effect unless ingested in the saliva, but it's sweet to animals. It has a few useful properties, but its key ingredient is a natural paralytic. You can douse some on a berry or other treat for a hopper or bushtail, and within minutes, they'd be unresponsive. I don't use it because when the animals are affected, they've gone to ground before I can retrieve them. It so happens that the bottle cracked, and some must have dribbled onto the brambles and bait." He returns to cackling.

Karal rolls her eyes and gets off him.

"Castburn? I'm never going to live that down." She grins despite herself.

They take their time breaking camp. Karal observes him as he moves about.

"I'm fine," Fento says. "You don't have to mother me. I'm mostly healed." He pokes out his foot. "You should consider becoming a healer. Your stitching is top-notch."

She examines her handiwork. "I had enough injuries as a child that it was cheaper to just patch myself. Before long, I was sewing up my friends. We were accident-prone. You could almost call it a hobby."

When they're packed, Fento scans around for anything left behind. The fire has been extinguished, and the campsite is cleared of any traces of their passing. Karal looks at him expectantly.

"So, how far are we?" She bounces on her feet, ready to leave. "I don't want to be stuck in the woods when a Cycle's end occurs."

"Right, you asked that earlier. Sorry, I forgot." He draws a crude map with a rock on the ground. "If we're lucky, we should reach Ormant in a few days. Four, maybe five. Well below the forty-two days between Cycles. As we follow the river, we will eventually reach the twin mountains, Oryn and Calderan. The river runs by them in a narrow pass. There are manageable sections. It should—"

Karal places a hand over his mouth and tilts her head toward the river.

At the edge of a distant tree, hidden against the ashen bark, stands a gray figure. The Sinna's mottled skin blends with stone and wood.

Dark, unblinking eyes fix on them.

Karal reaches for his paw as she turns back to him. "What do we do, Fento?" Calm. Fearless.

He gulps.

He looks into her eyes and recognizes the determination there, then steals a glance toward the Sinna. He steadies his breath. When their eyes meet again, he squeezes her hand and utters one word.

"Run!"

CAPTURE

Turning northward, Karal sprints along the river with Fento close behind. They stop when breath runs short. She looks back across the water and sees nothing.

"I don't see any sign of it." The words come between breaths. "How does it keep finding us?"

"I don't know, and I'm not going to ask. If they're on that side of the river, let's keep them there. Who knows what would happen if they crossed?" Fento drinks from his canteen, chest heaving. "I'm hoping we can lose them in the mountains or, if we have to, in Ormant."

Karal watches his labored breathing. "Are you going to be able to hold up? You're not fully healed."

"That's unimportant right now. We need to outpace this thing." His jaw tightens.

"Okay, let's go." She extends her hand to him. He takes it, and they start anew.

The day continues in bursts—running, resting, walking, then running again. By evening, they're spent. Fento moves them inland, searching for trees to rebuild the aerie. They climb high into the branches—no fires, no laughter, just silence. They bed down early, intent on leaving with the sunrise.

Morning breaks in violent gray.

A distant thunderclap rouses them. Karal stirs from slumber, still foggy. As they pack, the wind picks up, forcing them out of the aerie for fear of their safety. Rain falls in sheets. By the time their gear is secured, they're drenched. Against the wind, they walk to the Ormanti, which is swollen and breaking past its banks.

"We have to pull back from the river!" Fento yells over the heavy wind. "A nasty swell could pull us in!"

Walking north several paces from the swollen river, they watch trees bow alarmingly. Creaking trunks groan, threatening to uproot or crack. As the ground elevates, trees thin until they reach the base of the mountains, where the Ormanti flows alongside the peaks. Mountainous torrents swell the river as it rushes south. Raindrops pelt them like tiny stones.

Karal looks back at the forest. The trees sway near splitting. "What do we do?" She has to yell to be heard.

"We need to find a cave or an outcropping. The forest is too dangerous. We have to go up." Fento points to a clear trail following the slope upward. Thunder echoes overhead. "We have to hurry before the storm overtakes us."

Oryn and Calderan loom above them. The Ormanti runs wildly past the mountains, bashing against their sides. Fallen trees bridge the gap between shores while more sway dangerously in the wind. Both mountains bear dark stone with scattered trees climbing their lower levels. Bare peaks tower against the landscape.

Fento leads them up Oryn. The terrain shifts from gentle rises and thickets to barren fields of large rocks and hard ground. The slope steepens, and they slip on slick stone. Rain pounds down, driving them back when they try to shelter under a rocky outcrop.

"Where do we go from here?!" Karal yells through gusts.

"Higher might be better!" Fento shouts, fur whipping in all directions. "These mountains were mined—there could be caves!"

They struggle uphill against violent blasts. Trees become shorter and sparser. The wind howls the higher they climb. Rivulets flow down the mountain, swelling as they ascend. Their pace slows to a crawl. Karal bends forward, hands on the ground for stability.

Frustrated, she veers off the trail to circumnavigate Oryn. The dense rocks thin, but now they face long grass and mud.

"Karal, you have to stay on trail. This will—"

She missteps.

The soft ground slides beneath her feet. Fento reaches out but misses her hand as she tumbles sideways down Oryn's slope. Clawing for a handhold, she tears off a nail while rocks and mud cascade around her. She slides down the mountain with Fento chasing from above. Gritting her teeth, she digs her heels in, managing to find enough purchase to slow to a stop. The debris flows past her, crashing at the bottom. Her legs bleed from the rocks. Her breath sounds loud in her ears.

"Feng!" she yells.

"Are you alright, Karal?!" Fento reaches her side.

"I'm fine! Nothing's broken, at least not yet." She picks tiny rocks from her scraped legs. "We need to get out of this mess."

"Let's keep moving and—"

A streak of brilliant white lights up the sky, followed by rolling thunder.

"We've got to go! We're too exposed. I don't want to be on this mountain in a thunderstorm. Let's head down."

The way down is treacherous. Feet slip. Loose rocks roll with each footfall. Another crack of lightning lights up the sky, followed by thunder that reverberates in their chests.

Karal speeds up, risking her footing, leaping over rocks, stumbling. Vegetation turns mossy beneath their feet, hiding the rocks beneath. She trips as a strike sparks and hums overhead.

Fento scans the area, desperate. His ears perk up when he spots something. "There!" He points at a dark gap near the bottom of a scree field. The opening contrasts sharply with the green-gray land-scape—potentially a cave, not just shadow.

They navigate down the loose rocks. Each footfall shifts the rubble, threatening larger slides. The daunting slope angles down like a half-bowl, every step precarious. Rain pounds again, joined by hail bouncing off them. They zigzag down the slick surface, slipping often.

Suddenly, Fento's fur bristles.

"Run!"

He pushes Karal away from him. Both tumble down the stones as electricity crackles behind them, illuminating their desperate flight, before a thunderous bellow shatters the air. The sound resonates in their chests. Rocks vibrate all around.

They leap from stone to stone, trusting their footing to chance.

A dark cave opening greets them at the bottom.

They rush inside and tumble to the floor in a heap, gasping. Thunder rumbles like a beast while lightning flares at the entrance. As their breathing slows, Karal bursts into wild laughter.

"That was amazing!" She grins at Fento in the darkness. "What a rush!"

Fento tilts his head. "Amazing?! We were almost turned into twin-klebugs! That was terrifying! My tail might be singed."

She keeps giggling and grabs his tail. He wrests it from her grasp and scrutinizes it. Unable to help herself, she tackles him. They roll across the cave floor, her strength against his slick, wriggling body.

Their laughter echoes off the stone walls.

Then a low voice cuts through.

"You two are curious."

TRIAD

Karal bounds to one side of the cave opening while Fento mirrors her on the opposite side, each hugging a wall. Two eyes gleam from the darkness. Lightning illuminates grayish skin and the faint silhouette of a Sinna.

No one moves.

"Hello, One and Fen. We meet at last." The Sinna's voice is calm, deep, and clear. "We are together here in this cave by luck. Do you not think so?"

Fento edges toward the pack. "Why have you been chasing us? It was you, wasn't it? In Paldor that night? And you tried to climb the trees?"

"Yes. I tried to climb up to meet you. I was curious. I have never climbed a tree before. It is hard to do." Their tongue comes out and licks their face. "You do not have to be afraid. I do not want to harm you."

"Who said we're scared?" Fento retorts.

Karal notices Fento edging toward the pack. Their weapons are tucked in the outside pockets. She moves in his direction, her steps careful. "Why have you been following us?"

"You are scared. I can taste your fear. I only want to talk."

"Well, you have us cornered." Fento's words come out rough.

"I am a Sinna. I am stronger than you both, and I have not touched you. I was in this cave first. I cannot corner you. You came here." They offer their hand and point toward the opening. "You may leave if you'd like."

"Who are you?" Karal asks. "Why didn't you come when I called for you? I tried to meet you before."

The Sinna casts their eyes to the ground. "I can be scary. Your friend was hurt. I did not wish to make you afraid. It was not the right time. But now, in this cave, we are together. We were meant to meet." Their tone remains even, nonthreatening.

The storm rages on outside. Wind and hail drive pellets into the cave opening.

"Come, I have fire in this cave. It goes deeper." The Sinna stands and walks into the darkness. Faint firelight glows ahead.

"What should we do?" Karal whispers.

Fento hesitates. "I'm at a loss. Sinnas don't talk like that." He raises his hands. "I don't know."

Karal reaches for the pack but straps it on rather than pulling out her hammer. She looks at Fento. "They don't seem threatening. I'm willing to hear what they have to say."

H peers into the dark—faint traces of fire illuminate walls in the distance. "We can hear them out, but be prepared to fight." He glances back at the cave exit. "I've never met a Sinna like this one."

Together, they walk toward the light. Smooth cavern walls with small dimples meet their hands. Broken rocks make walking difficult.

As they round a corner, a vast cavern emerges. Stalagmites and stalactites divide the room. A fire burns, illuminating the rocks. A natural chimney in the western corner draws rainwater down while allowing smoke to escape.

The Sinna stands near the fire, beckoning them closer. In the flickering light, Karal studies them. This Sinna resembles the Klenzeer's, though not as stocky. Their gray skin looks rough and thick in the firelight. About Fento's height, they are twice as broad, with a dense look suggesting exceptional strength. They stand on long, thin, bent legs that end in fine points. Their angled thighs and shins taper to hardened bones resembling rods.

A sizable upper torso forces them to bend at the waist, supported by large, calloused hands and muscled arms. Their face is elongated, with deep-set black eyes and a broad brow. A flat, broad nose with two large nostrils sits above their wide, toothless mouth. Their dirty pink tongue slips in and out repeatedly.

As they approach the fire, their ovoid head bobs up and down. They wear a stained, soft white shirt, torn past the shoulders, but hanging to their lower torso. Wiry black hair spots their head and arms.

Fento and Karal sit opposite the Sinna. Silence stretches between them while rain echoes in the chamber and pooling water drains through rocky fissures.

Karal breaks the quiet first. "Who are you? Is this your home?"

The Sinna watches her, tongue hanging as they take long breaths. When they retract it, their words are measured. "You are a One who looks male, but you are female. Is this correct?"

Karal opens her mouth, but Fento cuts in. "You've been watching us. Why?"

The tongue comes out again and retracts. "You do not need to be afraid. As I said, I do not wish to harm you. I am curious. I follow you because you are like me. Different."

"Different, how?" Karal asks.

"We are not like the rest of our kind. We act different and live different." The Sinna puts their hand to their chest and points to Fento and Karal. "The black ones do not understand us. They wish to harm us."

Karal stiffens. "You mean the Klenzeer? Have you dealt with them?"

"I was taken by one and chased by another. They want to use my kind." The Sinna drops their gaze to the fire. A low, mournful sound escapes somewhere between a wail and a sigh. "I do not wish to be used."

Fento's rigid posture softens. "We have a common enemy, then." He studies the Sinna. "Why are you so different, Sinna?"

They point to themselves. "I have learned to be knowing. My father taught me."

"What is knowing? How did you become it?" Karal tilts her head. "What is your name?"

The Sinna opens their mouth, emitting a guttural sound full of chuffs and yowls. Fento and Karal exchange perplexed looks. When the sound ends, the Sinna speaks. "That is my name. It is hard for your tongue. Father gave me my name as he heard it. You may call me Xytel."

Winds whistle outside. Thunder rumbles. Flashes of light reflect in the chimney. Drips resonate in the cavern's silence.

Fento stares at Xytel. "Have we met before, Xytel? Is there a chance we crossed paths? Something about your name is familiar."

Xytel shakes their head. "You do not look familiar. I would remember."

"How are you knowing? Your speech is unlike any Sinna's I have ever encountered. What did your father do? Who is your father?"

Xytel stares at the flames when he mentions their father. "Father is no more. A man in black killed him for teaching me."

Karal's expression shifts. "I'm sorry for your loss. The Klenzeer are cruel." Her hands tighten and loosen. "How did your father learn common so well? I haven't met any Sinna who can speak like you."

"My father was a One, like you." Xytel's mouth opens in the shape of an attempted smile.

"Oh?" Karal straightens.

Fento leans forward. "Did your father take you in? It is a rare thing."

Xytel shakes their head. "No, no. Father did not take. He saved." Their voice drops. "I was dying. He rescued me from—" The words catch.

"From what? You can tell us." Karal smiles to ease the tension.

"The big death."

Xytel shrinks back after saying the words.

"What is the big death? I have never heard of such a thing." Karal scoots closer. Fento goes still, his face grave.

Xytel makes a wheezing sound, then a grunt, and stands, moving away from the fire, sniffling. "Bodies of many things. Death and more death floating together down the river." A tear rolls down their tough gray skin. They wipe it away with trembling hands.

Fento's hands rise slowly to his mouth. His eyes fix on Xytel and don't let go. Tremors run through him. Karal watches him. "What's wrong? Fento, what am I missing?"

"You know of this, Fen? Have you floated, too?" Xytel asks.

Fento nods. He begins to speak, but a sudden boom jolts them to their feet. It sounds like boulders crashing in a thunderous blast. Walls vibrate. Rocks rattle on the ground. The torrent of sound lasts several seconds, then stops.

They hold still as the rumble subsides, then halts altogether. They ease back into their seats, watching the walls and ceiling. When nothing further occurs, their tension eases.

The fire crackles in the quiet.

Fento speaks, his voice registering above a whisper. "You were at the Gardens, weren't you, Xytel?"

They nod.

"When I was let go from my service to my Klenzeer, I was unceremoniously dumped down a hole with all the refuse." He pauses. "It is where Klenzeer discard the waste from their experiments." Another nod from Xytel. "It is an island of corpses floating on rank waters. A floating grave." He swallows. "I was there countless days, surviving on trash and other things."

He looks away, breath elevated.

"I almost gave up—many times—but I was afraid to die." He squeezes Karal's hand and forces himself on. "When they finally flushed the housing clean, I hung onto the dead flesh of unrecognizable things." He looks up and finds understanding in Xytel's eyes, a mirror of his own sadness. Tears track down his cheeks. "As we left the vicinity of the Gardens, I swam away with whatever strength I had left and made it to shore." He shudders and goes quiet.

Karal bites her lip and squeezes his hand.

"Sinna cannot swim." Xytel's voice pierces the stillness. "I was alone on the island, dying and hungry. When we floated to a dam of a village, that is when Father rescued me."

"Why were you in the Gardens? What brought you there?" Karal keeps her voice gentle.

Xytel exhales—a vague noise escapes their mouth. "I was taken with many other child Sinna. The young are left to grow alone. We are not a community like Ones. A black one took many."

Karal's jaw tightens. "Was he tall and strong with dark hair?" Xytel nods hesitantly. "Did he carry a large staff topped with a shiny orb?" This time, they nod with confidence.

"That monster!" The words grind between Karal's teeth.

Fento's voice is steady. "Sinna are not Ones, Karal. It does not matter to Klenzeer." He looks at Xytel and softens. "Do you know why you were discarded?"

"Yes." They gulp. "I am female."

Karal opens her mouth and stops. Xytel turns to her. "You may ask. Do not be afraid."

"Why does being female matter?"

"Males are stronger and fiercer when they rut. He wanted males for tests and fighting." Xytel's dark eyes moisten. "Young Sinna are difficult to judge the sex of, so our blood was tested. Females were thrown away." A mournful sound. "Many were thrown away. One survived." She points to herself.

Karal's brows furrow. Fento puts a hand on her shoulder and changes the subject. "How did you learn so much from your father? He saved you, and he taught you. He must have been special."

Xytel's tips forward and back. "Yes, yes. He was a good teacher. He helped me learn why I was wrong."

Fento tilts his head. "What do you mean by wrong?"

"Sinna eat wrong. We dull our heads. We eat only ironweed." She stands and walks to a dirty sack on the ground and retrieves various vegetables. "If we eat good food, we make our heads good." She points to her belly. "Come eat."

"Oh, are you sharing your food with us?" Karal perks up. "Can we make a soup or a stew? Do you drink these things? Can you?"

Xytel nods. "Yes, father did this. He cooked good. No meat. It is not good for bellies."

Fento smiles. "We can certainly share in a meal if you desire. May I cook it?" He catches Karal's eye. "No offense, but I'd like to keep Xytel on friendly terms." His comment earns him a flick on his ear.

With some effort, the fire is stoked higher with dry logs Xytel brought in before the storm. Karal fills a pot with water from the chimney, while Fento cuts and peels vegetables. Before long, a savory aroma drifts through the chamber. Mouths water as the flavors meld.

"So your dad fed you fruits and vegetables to make you smarter?" Karal asks.

Xytel nods. "Sinna only eat ironweed. Day and night. Father had none when he took me to his home. He tried meat, but it is bad for us. I would not eat it. He then gave leaves, and I ate it quick. He gave me more, and I ate more. I came to see things like new. My head cleared."

"Soup is ready," Fento pulls a pair of bowls from his bag while Xytel digs from her sack and extracts a dented metal bowl.

"Your hands will get hot." Karal offers her bowl in exchange.

"No, no. Hands are strong. No hurt. No burn. I will eat from bowl." Xytel doesn't flinch as the warm meal fills her bowl. "Sinna are strong and thick. We do not hurt easy."

"I am starting to pick up on that." Karal returns a warm smile.

A satisfied sound escapes Xytel's mouth as she eats. The contentment in her voice warms them both. "Good food, friend Fen. You cook like Father."

"I picked it up from my many years on the road. It was a forced education." Fento chuckles, then glances at the scars covering his arms and hands.

"You have pain. I taste it from you." Xytel's tongue hangs as she studies him.

"Hmm, yes. Old pain." He looks up. "What are you tasting?"

"You. I taste you where you go. I taste air and trees and river. It guides me. The tastes tell me many things. It tells me you are not bad. I can taste badness. I avoid it."

Karal slaps her forehead. "That's how you found us! No wonder we couldn't lose you. Your tongue is so sensitive, like tasting scents." Her expression shifts. "Wait, can all Sinna do this?"

"Only females," Xytel answers. "Males are strong but follow females for food. Females find the ironweed and danger."

Karal stands, bouncing on her heels. "Fento, he doesn't know! That stupid Klenzeer has ignored females in favor of strength. Xytel can help us avoid him. If she is as sensitive as she says, she can taste for him before he gets near us."

Fento regards Xytel with new interest. "Are you sure you can tell? It could benefit us. We are heading to a town. You can help us get there." He tilts his head. "But what about you? Where are you heading?"

"I am alone. I have nowhere to go. Sinna will not gather with me. They say I smell like Ones. I am ignored. They will not rut with me." She slumps.

"Is this because you are educated now? Because of your time with your father?"

"No, I do not taste of ironweed. I taste of good food. Smart food. They dislike this taste." She pounds her chest. "I will not be dumb again. I will be smart."

Karal shakes her head. "So that's the penalty of your diet. You're different from them now, and they abandon you." She looks to Fento. "We can relate to that. We are both unique in some way."

Fento goes quiet, looking from Karal to Xytel. His mouth opens, then closes. He shakes his head.

"What do you wish to say, friend Fen?"

Karal turns to him. "What is it? Are you thinking of something?"

He clears his throat as if unsure what to say, wavering for several seconds.

"Spit it out already. You're making me nervous." She flicks his ear. "I won't stop until you do." She raises her finger in warning.

Fento lifts his hands. "Okay, okay. I hesitate because it's unusual."

He looks at them both. "We are what the Overseers consider anomalous. Different from what was intended. To them we are fractured. Broken." A pause. "No, forget it. It's stupid."

"Just say it, Fento. Please."

He sighs. "It's probably a bad idea, but with Xytel's abilities—we might actually have a chance." Karal and Xytel stare. He gathers himself.

Fento stands and begins pacing. "Ages ago, I accompanied a group of Klenzeer on searches that lasted several Cycles. We scoured the northern edge of Ra for something that remained hidden." He sits, dropping his voice to a whisper. "Someone created a refuge long ago—a place so well concealed that even the Klenzeer couldn't find it. Somewhere in the northern snow lies the Village of Any, where all anomalous are welcome."

Karal's jaw drops.

"What?!"

FORWARD

Xytel leans back while Karal stands and begins pacing. "There's a place that would accept us?" She points to her chest. "A place where we could be ourselves? Be accepted?" Her voice rises with each question. "But how? How does it exist? What do you know about it? Why haven't you told me about it before?"

"Calm down, Karal. This is just me thinking out loud." Fento raises his hands. "I can't say for sure how or where to find it. It is hidden. We searched for many Cycles and found no traces. Klenzeer are thorough and have tools provided by the Overseers, and they couldn't find a hint of it." He stands. "I think Xytel holds promise. If she is as unique as we believe, she could potentially find something hidden." When he looks at Xytel, she nods eagerly.

"What do you know about this Village?" Karal sits, enraptured.

Fento squats down, leaning forward. Outside, the wind howls while distant thunder peals and fades. Occasional streaks of lightning reflect down the chimney. The firelight casts dancing shadows across the gray walls.

"When I became more trusted by my Klenzeer, she would use me on missions. Sometimes with other Klenzeer, sometimes alone with her. Before long, it became common.

"One time, she kicked my cage and told me to prepare to head north. She said they had found a promising lead to something important. We were to assemble immediately to search for the hidden village of the anomalous. The Overseers knew it existed then, but didn't know where.

"Sometimes, they would pursue fugitives labeled as anomalous, but these people would simply vanish. However, this time, there was a clue. An anomalous carrying a note was captured. They were tortured for days." Fento stops. His eyes drift somewhere distant. His ears droop.

"You have much sadness, friend Fen. I am sorry for you," Xytel says.

"Thank you. I have moments where I cannot help but relive the pain." He swallows before continuing. "This anomalous was a Twun. I saw her but once. She begged for mercy, insisting she knew nothing more about the village." He clears his throat. "I'm sorry—the note. I was given it to read, and the words stayed with me. I memorized every line:

"Welcome all who seek freedom from the oppression of Laws and Overseers. We gather in the north in the place that Cycles forgot. Be you a Fen, a One, or a Fantil, we do not place titles on our brethren, for we are all members of this land and share it equally. Find your place with those who have no place in the Village of Any. We accept those who come with open hearts and minds. Meet us at journey's end, where there is nothing and everything in front of you.

"It was vague, but it pointed us north. So, we bundled up and headed that direction. We spent hundreds of hours freezing and searching. Nothing was found. Not a trace."

"Then we need to go north. We can start tomorrow." Karal's jaw sets.

"We can't just go!" Fento's voice rises. "What if this is a misdirection? We can't just run toward something. We have to plan this, get supplies, prepare."

"Why didn't you mention this place before?" The question comes out quiet.

Fento rubs his face. "We've been trying to outrun a Klenzeer for days now. This is the closest we have been to safety since this began. What would we be able to find on our own? I'm just worried about making it to tomorrow, Karal, much less finding a hidden village."

She moves next to him and wraps an arm around his thin frame. "I'm sorry. You're right. I'm just excited." She catches his gaze. "Fento, this is hope. I haven't had much since this began. The moment that Klenzeer walked into my life, everything became darker. You just offered me a light." She kisses his forehead. "You are the best thing that's happened to me since this nightmare began. And now you're offering us a chance to be free of everything horrible this world has thrown at us. I can't help but want to run toward that hope." She smiles. "Don't you want to go too?"

He stares at the ground. "I do, Karal. It has stayed in the back of my mind, like a wish, but I've never been brave enough to act on it." He looks up. "You're a fighter. I'm a coward. I never knew how to start looking. But now, with you and Xytel, a part of me thinks there's a small chance."

"Friend Fen, friend One. I wish to go. This would be good for us. I want to see this village and find more Sinna like me. I wish to not be alone." Xytel's rigid face mimics a smile as best she can.

"Karal, call me Karal. If we are to be friends, call me that." She extends her hand to shake. Xytel shakes it. Her large, rough hand dwarfs Karal's calloused, dirty one.

"Fento." He extends his paw, which she palms.

Karal rubs her hands. "Well, now that we have the formalities out of the way, we can start planning. We should go to Ormant and get supplies. We can even ask around—"

"No!" Fento shoots to his feet. "We can't talk to people about this. Towns have spies everywhere." His voice drops to just above a whisper. "Towns are centers of commerce and information, but also dangerous. Something like this needs to be handled with care. We can't trust people in towns. They're a backstabbing lot. It would be wise to stay in Ormant for some time, keep our heads down, earn what we need."

"But we can just go north—" Karal starts.

"Karal, we can't just steal from a town. A village is a simple thing. Towns have more people who work at all hours. There are constables and more suspicion. Dangers are everywhere, and the Klenzeer frequent them. I was used as a spy. Many times, I was forced to expose people who skirted the Laws. Do not trust anyone."

"Then what do we do?" Her shoulders sag.

"We should find jobs and raise money. We can know each other, but not keep the same company. It would be unusual to see us together. We are conspicuous." He sighs. "Hope is a strong emotion. It can guide us through these difficult moments. We will need enough money to buy supplies to reach another town further north. A Cycle, maybe two." He turns to Xytel. "Can you blend in at a town? Are you known to the Klenzeer? Are they hunting you? You mentioned more than one."

Xytel shakes her head. "When my father was killed, I fought a Klenzeer. I wounded him so he could not walk, and then I ran. No one follows me. The Klenzeer do not care for Sinna."

Karal whispers, "Good for you. I hope you maimed that monster permanently."

"I can be a dumb Sinna. I was once. I will work and earn credits. Then we will leave when we are ready. I will not talk to many." Xytel nods, accepting her role.

Fento smiles. "Then we are agreed. This is the start of our journey north. Let's rest—tomorrow will be a new day."

They bed down with excitement that evening, warmth and light waning with time. The wind howls throughout the night. They talk about their past until sleep overtakes them.

WHEN ONLY DIM COALS REMAIN, an unusual ashy shape emerges in the dying embers. Short and squat, with two pinpricks of glowing crimson, it watches their sleeping forms.

It stays unmoving, a grin slowly forming on a barely perceptible mouth, until the embers finally die.

The presence dissolves back into ash, leaving no trace.

MORNING DAWNS MUGGY, the air damp with a slight chill. Fento and Karal lie huddled under a blanket while Xytel sleeps curled nearby. A dull yellow glow of sunshine brightens the chimney and the cave.

The trio rises and shares a light breakfast over resurrected coals. Water boils for hearty oats, while Fento steers the conversation on their route forward. "So from here, we should be able to climb the trail up Oryn and come down the backside of Calderan. I expect the Ormanti to be swollen from the rain, so the safest route should be up and over the mountains. If we're lucky, we will be about a day or so away from Ormant."

The walk out to the sun is filled with enthusiasm. The cave opening reveals bright sunlight.

Disaster greets them outside.

Massive boulders are wedged beneath the cave's edge. A large rockslide covers parts of their exit—bushes, rocks, and mud mar the landscape. Vast swaths of debris hang precariously above.

"We need to hurry." Fento rushes his companions forward. "The storm we escaped battered Oryn. Everything is unstable."

Walking parallel to the debris field, they carefully navigate loose rocks and deep, muddy soil. Several missteps make the descent challenging and slow. Yesterday's landmarks have vanished—Oryn has been reshaped. As they descend, flooding appears in the lower vale. The Ormanti breached its banks. Disaster afflicts the surrounding area. They escaped it all by sheer luck.

The sound of debris shifting behind them triggers panic. Violent crashes boom above and below, and the ground trembles. Large rock fields slide down in whole chunks.

None of them looks back.

They run. Legs pump through mud and chaos, feet slipping and sliding. They don't stop until they reach Oryn's calmer backside, where the ground levels and the mountain quiets.

Karal collapses, red-faced and drenched. "How did we survive that?"

Fento bends over, eyes shut. "I can't believe we weren't buried."

"For once, we were lucky." Karal's smile comes easily.

"It is a good sign. Good friends. Good results." Xytel rests with her fists on the ground. "Which direction is the town from here?"

Fento examines the region's layout and gestures north. The land is wet, with water pooling all around. Xytel points out a road in the distance. Karal squints and finds the unnatural scar winding near the mountain's edge. The road continues north in and out of the forest and foothills past the far edge of Calderan.

Fento turns back. "This is where we must be careful. The road offers an accessible route, but we will be exposed. Or, we can follow Oryn's edge to Calderan, but it will be messy and slow. All this debris and mud will be difficult to traverse. We will have to trudge through downed trees and loose stone. What do you think? We are a trio now. We should make decisions together."

"It is harder, but mountainside is best." Xytel observes the treacherous route, tongue waggling out. "It is safe from others."

Karal grimaces. "I was going to say road, but I already know what you're going to vote." She points to Fento, who grins unapologetically. "Don't blame me if you trip on a log and break your bushy tail. Cautious Fen." She mumbles the last two words. "Can we at least stop to pick fruit? I'm hungry, and this path looks grueling."

Fento nods, and they break to eat. Karal searches for food with

Xytel while the sun approaches its zenith. The light illuminates the western side of Calderan, its dull gray sheen glowing bright. While admiring the landscape, Karal spots a dark smudge that mars the rock face. She squints. The detail eludes her, so she pulls Fento in to look. Xytel joins them.

"That shadow in the rock face. It looks like an opening. Do you think it might be a doorway or a cave?"

Fento perks his ears. He hums. "Well, many Cycles ago, Calderan used to be mined for iron ore. It is part of the reason that Ormant became a town. Workers would take boats down the Ormanti and work the mines. They would enter from the Ormanti side and exit onto the road. Wagons full of ore came back to Ormant on this road. The mine was a boon for many Cycles until the ore ran out. It has been abandoned ever since. That might be the exit that leads to the road."

"If it were functional, we would cut through and regain the river and follow it north. That way, we could avoid the road to Ormant. It would save us some time, but we can't use it. We could get lost for days or encounter some hazard. Who knows what state it's in?"

"I can guide us," Xytel stares at the shadow.

Fento cocks his head. "How?"

"I can taste for the exit. There is air in entrance and air out exit."

Silence. Fento looks toward the entrance, then back to Xytel. Karal speaks first. "I trust her." She straightens. "This can be a test before our journey north."

Fento's mouth opens several times. Nothing comes.

"What's wrong? What are you worried about?"

"That mine could be our end. We might get lost. Loose rocks could cause a cave-in. Dangerous creatures might be living in it. The list goes on. This test could prove fatal." His ears droop as he looks at Xytel. "Are you certain you can do this? Our lives hang on your answer. Any doubt whatsoever, and we should reconsider."

She places her large hand on his shoulder and squeezes. "I will find the exit." Her dark eyes shine dully at his and don't let go.

"I will listen to our group." He swallows. "And I will follow you, Xytel."

~

SCOUTING AHEAD, Fento takes the lead. Oryn's edges are wet and muddy, layered with debris. There is little evidence of pursuit or life around them—a disturbing quiet manifests. Several uprooted bushes provide berries. Drowned animals along the way provide meat for future meals. Karal collects three wet hoppers, a considerable boon given their dwindling supplies.

The road shows no recent traffic. The storm likely kept travelers away, to their benefit. When the mine entrance comes into focus, it resembles a dark mouth carved into Calderan's face. Cover is abundant along Oryn's edge, but the ascent to the mine is exposed with no protection from watchful eyes. Several switchbacks make the climb long but manageable.

Fento watches the sky and waits. "When cloud cover comes again, we will run up this path. Be sure to stay low to avoid exposure." He looks at the sun as clouds threaten to block it. The cry of gliders drifting overhead can be heard. When the sun fades, Fento grunts, "Go!"

They make a mad dash up the trail, dust swirling behind them as they charge up the incline and turn at each switchback. Karal leads while Xytel follows. Fento huffs from the rear, glancing back every few seconds. It takes nearly ten minutes, but they reach the entrance just as the sun re-emerges.

Inside, the air smells stale. The walls loom pitch black. A subtle breeze blows from within, emerging as a mournful howl.

"It is dark in here." Karal's voice drops low. She pushes forward in tiny steps, hands out, fingers trembling.

"Are you okay?" Fento reaches for her arm. She jumps at his touch.

She looks back at him, framed by dull sunlight. The bare silhouette of his face is visible. "This is not what I expected." The words waver.

"Karal, be still. The cave is good, not bad. I can taste it—I taste the other side. We can use this safely." Xytel's voice is steady. Her large hand settles on Karal's shoulder.

Fento removes his pack and rummages through it. "I have a torch we can use. It should have some life left." Several seconds pass. He finds a wooden handle wrapped in cloth. When he pulls it out, a heavy oil scent fills their noses. He takes flint and steel and strikes.

The seconds stretch.

When it flares to life, Karal's shoulders drop.

"I'm sorry," she gulps. "This is more unnerving than I expected. I'm not afraid of the dark, but this is beyond that. I've never seen such darkness." She winces. "Are there scramblers here?" Her eyes turn to Xytel.

Xytel nods. "We will avoid if we can. They do not bother most." She starts walking forward. "There are many things here, but not big dangers. You will see. I will guide us to the exit. I trust. You trust." She opens her large hand and invites Karal to take it.

Karal does.

"Lead the way, friend." Fento breathes out, steadying his nerves. He bows toward the darkness ahead. The tunnel stretches wide enough for two to stand side by side, almost eight feet high, with rotting wooden beams framing the walls and ceiling every twenty feet.

Karal squeezes Xytel's hand as they take their first steps into the unknown.

Behind them, the light grows distant.

Ormant
Sendowa

MIDNIGHT

Karal's hand slides across hewn rock as she walks forward in short steps. Her other hand grips Xytel's. She searches the darkness, breath sharp and quick. Fento's torch casts dancing shadows before them as they venture deeper into the mountain. Silky webs drift on a steady draft. Each step takes them farther from daylight. Powdered stone beneath their feet makes almost no sound.

A chittering noise causes Karal to pause. The sound is high-pitched and quick, echoing from ahead. Another answers it. "What's that?" Her muscles tense.

"Scramblers," Fento whispers. "I expect there to be many here. They like to gather in dark spaces. In my experience, if you leave them alone, they will leave you alone. Just don't make much noise."

Karal drops to the ground, palms touching fine rock dust. "I'm terrified of them." The words shake. "I got locked in a room with one once on a dare. I never screamed so loud in my life. Are they nearby?"

"No, they are far." Xytel helps her up and dusts her off. "We will go around."

"What about them scares you so much?" Fento asks, curious.

"Everything." A high-pitched whisper. "Their hairless tails. Long, swooping ears. Short, black hair. The slimy exterior. The way they walk on ceilings and walls—those jagged little teeth. And the mouth is the worst."

"But they only eat bugs and small creatures."

"I don't care. They're gross. I saw one eat a scurrier once. It opened its mouth, sucked it in, and collapsed its mouth like two slabs of stone shut together. Smash! Blood spilled out from the impact before it started crunching bones. It was disgusting and left an impression."

"But they're no bigger than a mewler, and—"

"Don't care. Let's stop talking about them."

Xytel guides them forward. The tunnel remains straight with a pair of bends. An unexpected hush takes hold. Occasional broken tools or debris from fallen rocks obstruct their path. After a sharp curve, the passage descends to an intersection. There are two options: one to the left with a draft, or to the right, ascending and sharply veering farther ahead. Xytel extends her tongue and points right, heading in that direction.

"Wait! Let's mark the paths we choose. If we end up stuck, we can always find our way back." Fento scrapes a rough arrow against the rock face with a piece of stone.

Karal brightens at this. Having a way back settles her nerves.

Their slow march continues in dead calm, each turn revealing passages identical to the last. Several mirror-image intersections follow Xytel's guidance as the maze stretches on.

As they walk, Xytel speaks to distract Karal. "I hear and taste many things. Scramblers and air. I take way with no ywaaywaatwee." A low whistle follows her words.

Karal whispers, "What's that? Sinna for scrambler?" Xytel nods. "Why do you make the sounds if you have words?"

"We use sounds for heart. Words come before or after."

"Heart? Do you mean emotion? Like you give the feeling of the words before or after you say them?"

Xytel nods again. "Yes. Different but good."

"What is friend? You are my friend." Karal's face relaxes.

Xytel considers it. "Cheen cheen yaun." She pounds her chest twice and lets out a low yowl.

Karal repeats the words and motions, with measured practice. Fento mimics them in hushed tones and raises the torch to provide more light. Aging wooden beams brace the walls and ceilings. A thick layer of dust covers the floors.

As they round a corner, Karal lets out a surprised gasp. A lump of cloth and bones lies ahead. As they draw close, Fento notes that it has been there for many Cycles. The torchlight reveals the body of what appears to be a Fen in a red and white robe eaten away by time. A bony face lies forward on the ground. One hand holds a lantern with a small well of oil at the bottom. The other clutches a small wooden box, ornately painted with unrecognizable symbols in repeating patterns. Its construction is curious—multiple wood types fitted together in angled pieces that form intricate geometric designs. A prominent keyhole marks one face, though no hinges are visible anywhere.

Karal grabs the lantern and moves it toward the torch, attempting to light the wick. It flickers to life—a welcome second source of light.

Xytel picks up the box and hands it to Fento. When their hands meet, he goes rigid.

"Are you okay, friend Fento?" Xytel watches him with concern.

He whispers as if to himself. "I have been here before. This moment is oddly familiar." His voice sounds distant. "A broad-shouldered figure standing beside me. A friend. A hand reaching out, offering something vital—they are giving you something important, Fento." He looks down at the curious box. He sniffs at it and shakes it —a small, dull sound returns from within. He turns it over several times, bewildered.

Karal touches his arm. "Are you okay? You seem out of it."

He shakes away the haze. "I'm fine. Just trapped in an odd memory." He lets out a frustrated huff. "Well, there's something in this thing. Does this fellow have a key on them? If not, I'll work on it some other time."

Xytel searches through the pockets and finds a few weathered matches, nothing else. A closer inspection reveals a circular pattern of red near the chest, blooming from a hole. "This Fen was killed. They did not die happy." Her examination reveals nothing else.

"That's unusual." Fento scratches his head.

"What?" Karal asks.

"This Fen is missing a toe, just like me. On the same foot."

She snickers.

"What?" he asks.

"If your Fen feet weren't so big, you'd keep all your toes." It's her first smile since they entered the tunnels.

Without warning, Xytel makes a strange sound they've never heard. It is low-pitched with gurgles and pops. It is so unexpected that Fento bursts into laughter. Karal joins in despite everything.

Their laughter echoes through the tunnel.

A clamor of movement answers it.

Fento quiets first. "Scramblers!"

Hundreds of the small creatures run toward them like a wave, clinging to the walls and ceiling. Xytel pulls Karal close as she hyper-ventilates. Fento swings the torch, driving them back around Karal. Several hiss at the light, pale white eyes blinded. Their sleek black bodies undulate overhead. Karal bats at them with the lantern, hand trembling, as high-pitched screeches fill the tunnel.

A groan from a support beam. The scramblers' combined weight shifts the precarious balance above.

Stone grinds against stone.

Dust drops.

Fento yells, "Run!"

Karal takes off, stepping over scramblers on the ground, Xytel just behind. The grinding grows. Dust falls around them. Scramblers hiss as they swerve clear of the moving figures. Rocks begin tumbling.

A thunderous boom drives them to sprint. Karal leads with the lantern, Fento's torch falling behind. Scramblers scatter in all directions. Fine dust chokes the trio as they barrel forward.

Xytel coughs something like 'left,' and Karal takes the turn. She runs hard as a mountain of stone drops behind her.

The rumble fades. Calderan settles.

Karal crashes to her knees. She coughs as dust clouds bloom around her. Blindly, she reaches for her friends and stops.

Where are Fento and Xytel?

She backtracks as her eyes adjust. A wall of stone blocks her way back.

"FENTO! XYTEL!" Her voice rebounds back to her. Dust makes her cough. *They have to be alive.* Yelling until her voice grows raw, tears form. She can't lose them.

Her hands shake as she reaches for the wall, shoving rocks aside. Blood drips as her nails chip and break. She digs mindlessly, tossing debris behind her. One of the thrown rocks catches the lantern. Glass shatters. Oil seeps out, flaring bright, and dies in a wisp of smoke.

Everything goes black.

She screams.

~

FENTO FEELS the ground with his hands. Sharp stones greet his palms. A steady drip of blood pools from a gash near his eye. He hears Karal's voice, distant, muffled, directionless. He fumbles in the dark until his hand encounters something stiff. "Xytel, is that you?" He keeps his voice low, afraid of triggering another fall.

An unintelligible sound responds. He paws at the body, feeling the head and torso, then a rock wall. "Be still. Get your bearings, and then we'll try to move you."

"What happened? Where is Karal?" Xytel's voice sounds thick.

"She's on the other side of this wall. We can't get to her." His words come fast. "I don't know if she's alive!"

"We will find our friend. She is not lost." Xytel speaks calmly, pulling her legs free of the rubble without disturbing it. She stands.

Fento coughs, spitting out dust. "How do we find her? We can't even see!"

"You cannot, Fento." A brief, sharp inhale, then a long exhale. "But I can." She finds his paw. "Let us find our friend."

SHAKING, Karal struggles to breathe. Bright spots dance before her. She fights to keep it together. Several minutes feel like hours.

"Breathe!" She forces the words out. Her pulse slows. The tension eases. "Have faith, Karal. Your friends are alive." She makes herself believe it. "You have to keep going."

Eyes open or closed make no difference. She crawls forward on her hands and knees, using the wall as her guide. Moving settles her. She inches along, listening for any signs of life. She talks to herself against the silence.

"Why do you do this to yourself, Karal? Always looking for trouble." She forces herself back to happier times. "Remember that buckleberry pie you and Ives stole? The baker chased you both all over the village while you ate it. When she caught you, the pie was gone, and your stomachs ached. Dad made you work in her kitchen for a week." A shaky smile. "I could use some pie right now."

Her eyes fill. Thinking of happier times was a mistake. Her focus shifts to Ives. So much has happened since she escaped Gallow, and there hasn't been time to mourn him properly. She sheds tears in the dark, holding herself. Her mind returns to the despair on his face when the Klenzeer killed him. The brutal dumping of his body.

It's all her fault. All the death and pain. Ives didn't deserve that.

And then a stray memory surfaces, hazy at the edges.

SHE'S DRUNK. Ives is helping her home, guiding her through the door, removing her boots with gentle hands. He helps her with her tunic so she doesn't sleep in her work clothes, but he stops when he encounters the binder.

He backs away. Surprise fills his face. His eyes dart from Karal's face to her chest and back. She tumbles into him, unbalanced. Tears fall. She panics, apologizing, begging. Ives says nothing. He pushes her away. There is so much hurt on his face. She tries to hug him. He pushes her away again. A third time, and frustration overtakes him. He punches her.

She falls onto her bed.

The memory goes white at the edges and dissolves.

SHE TOUCHES HER CHEEK, remembering the bruise she woke with the day the Cycle ended. The morning the Klenzeer came.

Her sobs echo back in the silence. Minutes pass. She grows quiet. Why didn't she tell him? Why did she deny him her truth? All those lost moments.

Then, in the quiet:

"Yes."

The word surprises her as it leaves her mouth. It's what her heart has always known—her decisions were the right ones. She loved everything about Ives but could never face losing him. Their bond was brotherly, yet she never wanted him to carry the burden of her secret. She wants to feel guilty about this, but no anger rises.

Her dad had cried at her feet before the onset of puberty, begging forgiveness. He told her she could quit the lie before it was too late. Selfishly, he wanted an heir, but the gravity of that decision weighed on him. The awkwardness of blossoming into a woman brought about more secrecy and challenges, but she was prepared to endure it because she loved who she was—a blacksmith of Gallow. She thanked him for letting her smith with him.

Fento's words strike her. *You will smith again.* The confidence behind them pulled her back from the darkness threatening to swallow her. Without him, she would be a poor, broken shell.

A smile grows in the dark. Feelings for Fento are developing that she's not ready to name. The comfort of his presence has let her sorrow for Ives fade in slow drips. He has known who she was from the beginning. There are no secrets with him.

She swallows and pushes on.

THE WALL ENDS AT AN INTERSECTION. She sits for a moment, deciding. She closes her eyes, sticks out her tongue, and pretends she is Xytel. It doesn't help. A slight breeze blows from her right. She goes right.

The journey stretches on. Intersections force her to guess. Crawling through the dark, she begins to fracture. She can't see anything, has no supplies, no water, just endless darkness.

Anger rises. She wants to live. To seek vengeance. To see the Klenzeer suffer for what he did. She punches the air. "Why was I so stubborn?" Another punch. "I had to be proud and defy that monster. And now I'm going to die in this pit!" She bangs her hands against the ground until the frustration drains out. Then she sits, breathing hard.

When she flexes her hand, she winces. The ground is harder than before. The powdery dust has changed—it feels different. Sifting through it, she finds a rougher texture, something coarse mixed with the fine rock dust. Pawing at the ground, she feels the grittiness between her fingers. *Could it be iron flecks from the old mining operations?*

Little by little, she follows the grit. When she reaches an intersection, she sifts a handful of dust in her palm. Whatever path has the roughest texture, she follows. Nothing sways her. Each new intersection follows the same pattern.

The sound of trickling water stops her. She stands. Arms extended, she walks forward, tracing the wall. When she rounds a corner, a soft glow blinds her.

She squints as her eyes adjust. A tall, cavernous room opens before her. Pale sunlight reflects off a mirrored device mounted to the ceiling. Water streams through a basin carved into the wall, entering through a hole on her left and exiting through one on her right.

She rushes to it, stumbles, catches herself, then plunges her head under. When she comes up gasping, the world feels vivid.

An unexpected voice speaks behind her.

"Are you going to share that?"

EXTRACTION

Karal gasps as Fento and Xytel rush to her, arms wide open as they embrace in a three-way hug. *They're alive. They're here.* A scrambler's screech brings tension back to the group as hundreds of them crawl above them on the ceiling.

Whispering, Fento asks, "How did you get here?! We just found this place."

"You're hurt!" Karal touches Fento's wound. Dried blood mars his white fur and face.

"I've been hurt worse. This is just another scar to add to the collection. Never mind me. Tell us how you found this place!"

A warm smile spreads on Karal's face. "I used my tongue. I licked the ground and followed the trail here."

Fento nearly belly laughs before catching himself. His eyes light with mirth, matching Karal's.

"It was by accident, really. I was angry and lost and in the dark." Her face scrunches. "I thought I lost you both." She takes a moment to collect herself, then continues. "I followed the walls for a while and tried following what felt like a breeze. But then I got frustrated after I turned left for what felt like the hundredth time. I felt no closer to anything, and I stopped, got angry, and pounded the dirt.

"That's when I noticed the difference in texture. The ground was rougher. It was a mixture of that soft, powdery rock, but now it had grit. I followed this to an intersection and chose the path with the most grit. I latched onto the idea that it might lead me somewhere. It makes more sense now. Anything carted from here might be flecking off pieces of iron ore. There would be more in this direction than toward the cave exit. I didn't expect to find this place. It just appeared in front of me." She looks around at the breadth of it all. "It's amazing."

The cavern suddenly darkens as the sunlight fades. Fento pipes up. "We need a fire or a light source before the sun sets!" He points to the contraption above. "I've seen something similar before. It reflects sunlight from a distance. If it's setting, we need to supplement the light. Karal, Xytel, spread out and look for torches or combustible wood. I'll dig a pit and prep a fire."

As the light fades, Xytel returns with several lanterns while Karal brings a container reeking of oil. Working quickly, Fento lights a lantern with a nearly empty well, while Karal fills the spares. Within minutes, they have three lanterns lit and more filled with oil; the warm, yellow glow provides enough visibility for Fento to start a proper fire with a few discarded wooden logs strewn about. Once lit, the group relaxes around the bright flames, worn out from the day's events.

Fento exhales a long breath. "Let's get some food cooking and explore this place. It might have some hidden treasures." He retrieves his cooking gear as Xytel and Karal gather water. He then begins gutting the dead hoppers they collected earlier in the day, while Xytel and Karal cut vegetables left over from Xytel's stash. While the stew cooks, Karal wanders off to explore the expansive cavern.

Ladders leading to upper and lower adjacent tunnels are bolted to the walls. Large, rusted metal carts sit empty on rails leading in various directions. Pickaxes layered with dust lie in a neat pile stacked against the smooth rock walls. Having time to look, Karal stares at the large contraption on the ceiling. It resembles mirrors but appears to be glass. She recalls her dad telling her about objects that can bend light. Whoever built this was clever. They figured out a way to bring sunlight from outside down to the center of this chamber. The craftsmanship must be exceptional to have lasted this long.

Puddles of feces litter the ground. She looks up, spying hundreds of scramblers hanging from the top of the cavern. They occasionally hiss at each other as they readjust their positions or clamber over one another. They vary in length and girth, being black or dark grey, and are the largest community she has ever witnessed. She watches with interest as they slip noiselessly into burrowed holes or escape through an opening near the chamber's top. Their nighttime hunting ritual will soon draw many out.

As fascinating as the vermin are, the day's events have left her feeling jittery. Preferring to pretend they don't exist, she continues her exploration. She spots a map of the mine hanging askew on a wall. It shows a network of tunnels that intersect with this main chamber. The entire layout resembles a buzzle hive. Miles of tunnels cross paths in concentric circles. Several outlets lead to dead ends. She tries to trace back the route they took from the opening, but gives up after backtracking a few steps. Shaking her head, she laughs at the possibilities. Without Xytel, they could have been wandering in here for days.

Next to the basin, she finds garments left behind by the miners. They're made from a tough weave, though most have large holes and pull apart at the seams with little effort. Still, she salvages some trousers that a thread and needle might be able to mend. The best find, however, is a pair of boots. Although worn, they are more comfortable than her current ones. She tries on several pairs until she finds ones that fit. Adding to her haul, she also finds gloves and suspenders to hold up the trousers.

When she returns to the fire, Fento and Xytel work on more Sinna words. "Yeench, yuhan, yak—yak." Fento coughs, attempting to make a sound that emulates choking. Karal chuckles at his attempt, though Xytel praises him for the effort and promises to teach him more soon.

There is light banter as dinner is served. The hopper meat is cooked on skewers, while a stew is made from leftover vegetables from Xytel's cache. Karal shows off her findings from the mine and shares details about the map she discovered. Fento lines up parts of the mine's history with Karal's description.

Dinner is cozy and filling, easy around the fire. Exhausted, they lie on their blankets. The air is warm and stagnant, keeping any chill at bay.

Karal yawns first, triggering a wave of yawns from her friends. Xytel falls asleep in seconds, snoring loudly, her mouth wide. Karal tries to lie on her side, heavy with sleep. She uses leftover shirts and trousers as a pillow. Just as her eyes are starting to fall, a dull light shines on a wall, followed by another and another.

The fog of sleep lifts as her eyes shoot open.

The cavern sparkles with pinpricks of light all over the walls. Tiny dots twinkle like stars. She gets up, amazed, sleep temporarily forgotten. Touching a nearby wall, the glittering rock dims. When she inspects the stone, Fento speaks with a soft voice behind her.

"You are touching moonstone. It's often found near iron deposits and is likely the reason that this mine was found." He pauses as he approaches Karal. "Certain acids in the stone are released when sufficient pressure is applied. It creates a chemical reaction when it touches iron, which melts away some of its density. This creates a new material, moonstone. It's not useful for anything beyond providing light. It only reacts to moonlight, not sunlight. Something about the intensity of the moon's rays versus the sun: we use them to mark graves. It's a beacon for the mother Fen to find her fallen children and bring them to her skulk."

Karal looks up at the ceiling. The contraption reflects moonlight into the cavern. Fento watches her. Wonder fills her expression—eyes wide, lips parted.

"You've seen so much, Fento." Her tone is gentle. Smiling, she reaches for his paw, which he gives willingly.

She turns and looks into his soulful blue eyes. They reflect the cavern's beauty, while his pale fur glows in the moonlight. Drawing closer to him, she moves beyond a friendly hug, yet he doesn't pull away. Warmth radiates from their joined hands. Her free hand slides to his chest. His lips part a thread's width, but no words escape.

They remain locked in each other's gaze.

The moonlight fades, and the bewitching glow subsides, yet they are rooted to the spot. Only the flickering embers of the waning fire provide any light.

Karal squeezes Fento's paw.

Fento closes the gap between their faces, drawing near, and then stops moving. His eyes fix on something beyond her.

"Fento." A pause. "Fento?" She speaks to him, but there's no reaction. His eyes stare at a wall, unseeing, and then his body goes slack.

"Fento!" She catches him as he collapses, guiding him to the ground.

His eyes never close. He starts speaking under his breath. "Tree, fire, bridge, Klenzeer, tree, fire, bridge, Klenzeer, tree, fire—"

She calls his name, sharper, "Fento!"

Scramblers squeal, forcing her to look up.

He breaks from the trance, body shuddering, blinking rapidly. "What, what happened? Why are we on the ground? Is everything okay?"

Tears threaten, but Karal blinks them back. "You stopped. Everything about you stopped, and you were unresponsive, repeating words. Are you okay? Has this happened before?"

Fento is slow to speak. "I—I don't know. It's all so confusing, Karal. All my memories are scrambled. I've seen things, but don't know if they're real. Moments are missing. Sometimes it feels like there's a hole in my past." He stares at her hazel eyes by the waning firelight. "It's hard to believe, but I know you, Karal. Or someone just like you. You were the trigger." He closes his eyes and shakes his head. "They damaged me in the Gardens. I pray these are just aftereffects and nothing more. I'm sorry. I didn't mean to frighten you."

"No, don't be sorry. I was worried." A weak smile.

He sighs. "I'm okay, but I don't want to hurt you. I don't know what these memories could trigger."

He gets up, moving away toward camp. Karal reaches out to him, but he slips out of reach, continuing toward the waning fire without looking back.

She exhales. Her usual friendly tone takes effort to maintain. "I understand." She makes her way back to camp.

～

As LIGHT SNORES sound around the flickering fire, something stirs in the dimming flames. A dark shape rises from the ashes—more cohesive this time, resembling a small, leafless black tree, no taller than a foot or two. Glowing red eyes emerge from the bark along with a twisted, toothy mouth.

Two branches move like arms and extend outward and upward, fingers shaped from twigs. It remains motionless as it closes its eyes, focusing.

A faint tremor shakes the cavern. Scramblers squeal from above. Loose pebbles drop. Karal shifts in her sleep but never awakens. The quaking subsides after a minute. The red eyes reopen. The mouth curls into a smile as the tree-like shape begins to lose its form.

Ash drops as the figure crumbles, extinguishing embers and leaving no trace of its presence.

～

MORNING ARRIVES WITH FITFUL LIGHT. As Karal walks back to camp with a filled canteen, Fento studies the old map, identifying the exit. "It looks like we need to follow that tunnel over there, and we will finally be out of this darkness. I've had my fill of tunnels and scramblers."

Xytel points to a separate path labeled *outlet*. "This goes out too. To a new place." She follows the line with her eyes as it winds south before heading northeast.

"I think it's an emergency exit. Like an alternate if the main way in is blocked. It certainly goes out a ways." Karal winds her finger along the path. It leads them away from the Ormanti.

The three finish a light breakfast and gather their belongings. Karal leaves her old boots for the next weary traveler and puts on the more comfortable ones. She glances one last time at the scramblers above and makes a rude gesture to them as they depart. They walk into the exit tunnel when Xytel stops. Her tongue hangs out. She shakes her head. "No air there. It is not open. We must go a different way."

Fento slumps at the news. "Are you sure? This will be so much closer than the other way. I'll scout ahead to check." He disappears down the tunnel with a lantern. There's a noticeable dip before it turns right. He returns moments later, his feet sloshing with each step. "The tunnel is flooded, likely from the storm and the swelling river. We can't pass this way. You are right as always, Xytel. Lead the way."

Xytel returns to the main cavern and veers right. Karal looks up at the scramblers, which squeak back. She imagines them mocking her. They follow Xytel down a narrow tunnel, each carrying a lantern. A faint breeze blows from afar, carrying a musty, stale scent with a strong undertone of bitterness.

"Do you recognize that smell?" Karal inhales deeply.

Fento shakes his head. "No, should I?"

"It's familiar." She takes another deep breath. "It reminds me of something the herbalist gave my dad towards the end, when he was suffering the most. It gave him vivid dreams."

"Like a sedative to help him sleep?" Fento asks.

She shakes her head, her voice solemn. "No, much stronger."

Xytel shrugs. "There are many things I have not tried. I do not know this one."

They move forward with renewed determination. Karal's desire to escape the darkness grows with each step. After an hour, doubt starts to creep in. The tunnel narrows considerably, and they march in single file. Xytel leads, with Karal behind and Fento bringing up the rear. Another hour passes as they continue in quiet desperation, the weight of the mountain pressing down with each step.

The ceiling lowers. The walls close in. Karal's breathing quickens as rough stone walls rub against her clothes. Her lantern light dims in the confined space. Thoughts of being trapped flood her mind. The hand gripping the lantern begins to tremble. She closes her eyes—it only makes it worse.

Whispers invade her mind.

She gasps. "Do you hear that?!"

"Hear what?" Fento's voice vibrates unnaturally.

She whispers, "The voices."

"I do not hear anything, Karal." Xytel sounds distant.

Karal draws a slow breath, settling herself. "Keep going." She trembles. "I want to get out of here."

They continue, but the whispers intensify, coming from all around her, faint and overlapping:

> *Come to us.*
> *We'll show you the way.*
> *Lost forever.*
> *Do not stray.*
> *Mind your steps.*
> *Straight on the path.*

The litany repeat endlessly, voices talking over each other, sometimes faster, other times slower.

Exhausted, she narrows her eyes and tries to speak, but the whispers drown her out. Her lantern dims further. The world feels like it's collapsing inward. Each step becomes muffled and slow as the rocks grip tighter. She can't turn her head to see Fento; only Xytel ahead.

She drops her lantern. Her hands fly up to plug her ears. Pressure builds. Fear builds. She has to scream. Her mouth opens—

"Karal?"

Fento's voice cuts through. Light appears just ahead. The cave opens to a clearing of soft grass along a babbling brook. Her hands drop. The lantern lies discarded on the ground.

"Are you okay?" Fento guides her forward out of the darkness, his voice careful.

Karal breathes her first lungful of fresh air. When she looks back at the dark opening, it appears wide and inviting, with no trace of that unexpected darkness or tightness.

She looks away.

Fento lightens the mood by sharing leftover fruit. Xytel fills a canteen and takes in the surroundings. A wide path lies before them, well-worn and slightly overgrown—thick bushes filled with fruit line the trail on either side. Ripe berries swell with juice.

To the left, Calderan's walls are unclimbable. They rise thirty feet vertically before the slope begins to level off. On the opposite side, strongly scented, thorny bushes form an impenetrable barrier. The bitter smell that Karal noticed in the tunnel is overwhelming out here.

Ahead, tall trees blot out the sun. Wide at the base, they rise like columns into the sky, casting shifting shadows below. Light filters through the canopy. No moss or lichen mars their dark bark, and tall overgrown grasses spread in all directions across the spongy ground.

Fento looks about. "I've never seen or heard of a forest like this." He touches the sturdy bark of one of the tall trees. "I don't think we have many options for our route. Looks like we can only follow the path. What do you detect, Xytel?"

She walks about, touching trunks and tasting the air. Her expression is uneasy. "I feel the trees, but they are strange. They have no old scent. They are fresh, like saplings. It does not feel real." She looks at her friends. "I do not like them."

Karal looks ahead. The forest seems to dare them to enter, and she wouldn't dare go back the way they came. Part of her wants to panic, but the rational part reminds her that a forest is just trees. They don't move. As long as they stay together, they'll be fine.

Steeling her resolve, she extends her hands. "We'll be careful. We have no choice. Take my hands."

Xytel and Fento comply.

Putting on a brave face, she leads them forward into the woods.

CENTERFUGUE

Karal feels Xytel's grip on her hand tighten as they step farther into the forest. "That hurts, Xytel." The hand loosens. "Is something wrong?" She stops.

Xytel pushes ahead, head bowed down, tongue out a sliver. She looks back, a frown growing. "This forest is wrong. Feels wrong."

"I don't understand." Fento sounds apprehensive. "What kind of feeling is it?

Xytel turns in a circle, eyes darting to several features of the woods around them. "It is green. Healthy. But no animals. No songs. It is empty. Unnatural."

Karal's lips part, but she stays silent. She lifts her eyes to the trees. "No nests." Xytel nods.

Fento approaches the bushes, which are producing ripe, delicious-looking fruit. Moonies line the path in exotic colors and sizes. "Nothing is picked over. Everything is untouched. There is no rotten fruit anywhere in these bushes."

"This is not a good place," Xytel whispers.

No wind penetrates. Everything is very still.

"What do we do?" Fento asks.

"We can't go back!" Karal is quick to reply, her eyes wide.

Xytel nods. "We follow the path."

Karal swallows, then extends her hand. Xytel takes it. Fento falls in line on her other side. She studies the dense canopy above as they move forward. Large leaves and thick branches block most of the sunlight. Various leaf shapes and sizes sit on stiff, almost-black branches. When her gaze drops, she notices something unusual. "There are no dead leaves on the ground—no dead brush. Nothing."

Xytel remains silent, tongue out, eyes fixed ahead.

"What do you taste, Xytel?" Fento asks, hushed.

"It is strange. The tree tastes do not change. They are the same here."

"Do all trees taste differently?" Karal asks, looking at the upper branches.

"Yes. Each tree is different. Unique. These all taste exactly the same." She gazes up at several trunks to their treetops. "Old trees have old smells. These look old, but are like new."

They walk a straight path for what feels like ages. The forest remains unnaturally quiet, their footfalls making the sole sounds. The immaculate woods are unnerving.

An hour passes before the trail curves left and leads to an intersection with eight distinct directions. Xytel stops in the middle, turning about.

"Where to?" Fento asks.

She draws her tongue in, gulping. "I cannot taste anything. The air is quiet." She moves forward, turning in a circle. "The tastes have never—YAGHHH!"

Xytel drops to the ground. A guttural scream escapes. Grunts and chuffs follow. Her hands cover her ears. Fento and Karal run to her.

"Shouting!" Xytel squints, voice darkened with pain. When she opens her mouth, all that comes is a choking sound. Between sputters, she gasps, "Voices sh—shout!" She rolls on the ground and starts yelling, "Go to tree! Go to tree! Go to tree!"

Fento yells, "Where? Where do we go?!"

Xytel shakily points to one of the paths.

"Quick, grab her!" They each take an arm and drag. She slackens as they reach the designated path, releasing an exhausted breath, then goes still, breath shallow.

"XYTEL! XYTEL!" Karal looms over her, tapping her cheek, trying to rouse her.

Several moments pass before Xytel stirs, eyelids creeping open.

Fento holds her hand, stroking her arm. "What happened? Are you okay?"

She blinks, disoriented. When she blinks again, a red tear drips from her left eye. Her voice is weak. "You could not hear them?"

Fento and Karal shake their heads.

Xytel's twitches. Her eyes lose focus. "Who's there?" she says to no one. Fear is in her voice.

Karal looks at Fento, then back. "It's just us. Fento and I."

"Who are you? Get out of my mind!" Xytel snaps, eyes distant.

"I don't understand, Xytel." Karal turns to Fento. "What do we do?"

His ears flatten. Hesitant, he says, "Cheen cheen yaun," then pounds his chest twice and lets out a low yowl. Xytel looks at him, recognition returning. She blinks several times.

"Fento?" The word slurs.

"We're here. Karal and I." He squeezes her hand. She returns it.

Slowly, Xytel rises to a sitting position. Her eyes blink faster. She looks about. Her tongue creeps out and quickly retracts.

"You had us worried." Karal caresses Xytel's brow, ending on her cheek. "What happened to you? One moment you were talking, the next you fell."

"Wh—when I reached the middle of the path, all the tastes went away. It has never happened before." She looks at each in turn, regaining her voice. "A loud sound started. A buzz. It hurt so much." She swallows. "With it came voices. Many voices. Screaming. They all yelled the same thing." Her voice cracks. "Go to tree." She lifts her hand and points ahead of them. "And they came from there."

Fento's breath quickens. He looks ahead, his face tight.

"What about the last part? You looked lost. Confused." Karal watches her carefully.

Xytel flinches. Fento and Karal's eyes dart to each other. "There was someone there. A voice. A—" She hesitates. "A presence." She points to her head. "A different voice. A mean voice."

Fento trembles, fear and anger warring. "Someone? Something?"

Xytel nods.

"So now they want us to go where they say?" He stands, eyes flicking left, then right. "We should take a different path. Somewhere far from here." He looks around. "I'll climb to the top and figure out where we are. Then we can reassess."

He runs to the nearest tree and attempts to climb it. Digging in, he gets about five feet off the ground before falling flat on his back. He dusts himself off, looking at his claws. Growling, he says, "I'll have to dig deeper." He tries again, making it about seven feet up before stumbling to the ground. He stares at the spot where he tried to find purchase.

Nothing marks the tree. He cannot penetrate the bark. It's unclimbable.

He looks from tree to tree. None of them has low-hanging branches; all seem to have the same bark. He shakes his head. "I've never met a tree I couldn't climb. Maybe we should turn back."

Xytel shakes her head vigorously. "We cannot! They yell when I look at different paths now. Even now I hear them."

Fento looks at Karal. She shakes her head. He acquiesces. "Let's see where this forest wants us to go."

They prepare before moving on. Karal palms her hammer, Fento his knives, and Xytel clenches her fists.

With trepidation, they walk the prescribed path. It winds and curves across the flat landscape, lined with trees of similar bark. The trail narrows to no wider than two abreast, and the ground grows rockier—pockets of grass sprout in smaller increments. Browning shrubbery dots the landscape. Long after the first intersection, another appears. Xytel points in the direction the voices guide, and they follow.

"The voices have changed."

"What do they say?" Karal asks.

"Now they hum low. A quiet song. A dark song." She walks on.

The flora darkens as they go. Trees are sparser, twisted into unnatural shapes. Dead leaves litter the ground, yet still no animals. Rocks now jut from the trail beside tree roots. Another intersection leads them onto a murkier path. The sun hides behind clouds. The day grows gloomier and cooler. Sparse trees occupy less space on the forest floor. Some are dead, while others bear dark green leaves. Shrubs are nonexistent.

Xytel huffs as the trail begins to climb. Her breath grows heavy with each step as rocks protrude precariously. All the trees here are dead, appearing as short, sickly husks with dark bark. They resemble Ones frozen in agonized poses.

Karal whispers, "I don't understand this place." Fento says nothing.

Xytel reaches the top and stops. She makes an unusual sound, like a breath catching.

Karal summits breathless. "What's the matt—" The word hangs as her eyes fixate on the vista.

Before her spreads a plateau, dark brown grasses swaying with the wind. Further ahead, a ring of blackened grass encircles a shape resembling a tree. Its enormity is hard to take in. One hundred feet tall, no, two hundred, it's hard to determine from this distance.

A bulbous, striated trunk, impossibly wide, grows from the ground, surrounded by meaty roots that coil and stab into the dark soil. Hundreds arch in and out of the earth. Midway up, the trunk splits into two enormous halves. Countless, thick boughs twist outward like tentacles in insanely curved shapes. Leafless branches and twigs scatter, forming a lattice of interwoven tendrils—hundreds stabbing at the gray sky. Its color is as dark as night, save for light-colored tendrils that trace the silhouette of a face on the trunk.

The tree looms statuesque as the wind picks up. Grass billows.

Karal stays rooted. She turns to Fento, who is stiff and unmoving, eyes fixed, fur rippling in the breeze. Xytel releases a held breath, her tongue dangling along the left side of her mouth.

"What do you taste?" Karal's voice falters.

Xytel remains quiet before a single word escapes. "Poison."

The wind blows harder. Gray clouds drift towards them. Thunder rumbles in the distance.

Karal shakes her head. "Let's turn around. I don't like it here."

"I agree. This place reeks of evil. We should leave." Fento's eyes stay fixed on the tree.

Xytel stares at the misshapen aberration in silence. She opens her mouth to speak, closes it, and exhales. Her fingers flex, knuckles cracking before clenching into fists. "I hear it. I feel it." A pause. "HIM."

"Who? Karal whispers.

"The presence. The tree."

Eyes shut, shaking, Xytel takes a step back.

"YAAAAAAGHHG!"

She falls to the ground, hands clamped over her ears, convulsing as if shockwaves are battering her. Blood drips from her eyes, ears, and nose.

Fento springs into action. "Grab her legs! Quick, drag her to the tree!"

Karal takes hold of Xytel's thin legs as they kick, dragging her heavy body across the ground, leaving a bloody trail. As they cross the boundary of the dark ring, Xytel goes still. A low sigh escapes her mouth. Fento and Karal lower themselves beside her.

"Xytel?!" Karal whispers, tapping her cheek, but she doesn't respond.

Fento produces a rag from his pack. He dabs at Xytel's face, cleaning off the blood, whispering her name. Her rhythmic, shallow breath is the only sign that she's still alive. Karal hovers nearby, looking about, frenzied. Fento strokes Xytel's hand. Their vigil lasts several minutes before Xytel suddenly spasms and draws a deep breath. She coughs as she exhales. A tremor ripples through her.

"Xytel?!" Karal takes her rough palm and squeezes. Xytel weakly squeezes back.

Fento mimics the action on her other side. "We are here, Xytel." He speaks the Sinna phrase for friend.

Moments pass. Spasms course through her, less violent now. Weakly, she points to the tree.

"Do you want us to take you there?"

A faint hum.

"Come on, Karal." Together, they drag her body just beneath the tree.

Xytel's breath deepens when they stop. Her eyes open to slits, then close. Before she slips under, she shakes her head back and forth.

The tree envelops them in the shadow of its heavy branches and sprawling limbs. The bark smells of mold. Yellow-green growths climb up the trunk, sickish and swollen. Fleshy. Shriveled seed pods bump against each other whenever a gentle breeze blows, sounding like hanging rattles. Thunder rumbles again, closer.

"What do we do, Fento?" Karal's voice barely carries.

"I don't know. We can't leave from here. This place is forcing us to stay." He looks up at the tangle of wood above. "We should prepare to camp for the night. I can only hope Xytel recovers with rest, and we can run away in the morning. Otherwise, we'll have to drag her out and risk killing her."

Thunder rolls overhead, drawing closer as a light drizzle begins to fall. Fento and Karal huddle together. When lightning flashes, they clasp hand in paw while Xytel starts mumbling incoherent words. Fento leans down, trying to make them out.

"Can you hear anything?" Karal watches lightning inch closer.

He listens, then shakes his head. "I can't make it out. It doesn't sound like her usual little noises. This is 'orum' over and over again."

A sudden clap of thunder pulls him back to Karal's side. Lightning dances in the skies with steady regularity. Thunder rattles the seedpods above in a haunting melody. They say little to each other as the storm threatens. Rain drips in tiny droplets around them. The tree shelters them from the worst of it.

Daylight fades beneath the dark canopy.

Xytel suddenly sits up.

Lightning illuminates her profile. Fento and Karal crawl to her.

"Xytel, are you—" Karal stops. An overhead sizzle of lightning reveals Xytel's eyes are shut. She repeats the phrase Fento mentioned, louder now.

"orum—orum—orum—"

"I don't think she's awa—"

Xytel's hand shoots out and wraps around Karal's neck and squeezes. Choking, Karal struggles while Fento grasps at Xytel's fingers. Karal strikes at the rigid arm.

The chant never changes from Xytel's mouth: "orum—orum—orum—"

Fento pries two fingers loose, giving Karal enough room to wrench free. She collapses to the ground, coughing and gasping.

"Are you okay?" He rushes to her side, helping her sit.

She coughs until she can speak. "Yes." Another cough. "I think she's dreaming. I don't know what she's doing." Karal watches as Xytel begins crawling toward the base of the tree.

The chorus from Xytel speeds up, louder now.

"orum—orum—orum—orum—orum—jah."

Fento's eyes go wide. He looks from Xytel to the tree and again.

"Karal, we need to stop her!"

He runs to Xytel and grabs an arm. His strength is like a feather against her bulk. She barely slows. Karal joins him, wrapping around the same arm. "I don't understand, Fento! Why are we doing this?!"

"Listen!" He grunts, pulling back.

"orum—orum—orum—jah—orum jah orum."

"No!" Karal digs her heels in. The effort nearly halts Xytel's progress, but her legs keep crawling. Her free arm extends toward the tree, fingers coming within inches of the swollen sacs on the trunk.

"orumjah orumjah orumjah orumjah."

The cadence slows as the words combine.

Fento pulls back, claws failing to find purchase. Karal yanks opposite the tree.

Sizzle-Crack!

A nearby strike surprises her. Her grip loosens.

Xytel surges. Her fingers brush the swollen sacs.

Pop. Pop. BOOM!

Tumors detonate around the tree in rapid succession—the sacs burst like overripe bladders, spraying thick clouds of dark spores. The seedpods rattle overhead as the massive trunk shudders. Wave after wave of spores billow out, coating everything in black dust.

All three cough violently, struggling to breathe as they crawl away from the trunk, spewing dark fluid from their mouths. Xytel's eyes jolt open, freed from whatever had possessed her. Choking up a dark mixture of blood and snot, she tries to speak. "Ba—baaa—baadd— tre—treeeeee."

Fento and Karal tip over, their faces covered in dark residue. They fall onto their sides in a pile, unconscious.

Xytel lurches forward, crawling toward her friends, eyelids drooping. Within inches of reaching them, she collapses.

As consciousness fades, she exhales one final word:

"—Sorumjah."

FRAGILITY

Fento wakes with a start. Pain courses through his body in waves. His left arm hangs limp, broken—several bruises throb. Darkness surrounds him, and the air is thick with decay. Lying on dank earth, he raises himself and crawls forward, reaching a wall of dirt and rock. Round stones mix with jagged ones. Following the wall along its length, he finds no end. The room feels circular. Gradually, he stands, reaching as high as he can.

There is no ceiling.

It dawns on him that he is in a pit and has been here before. This is beneath the Central Gardens.

His breath quickens. He sinks back to the ground. Touching his face, he feels wetness and tastes blood on his fingers. Several cuts are at different stages of healing. He can't recall how he ended up this way.

Forcing his eyes closed, images flash in his mind. A girl and a Sinna. They were...heading somewhere, but the destination is murky.

Agony bites with any movement. Instead of lying down in misery, he leans back against the wall until he finds a comfortable curve. He crosses his legs, drops his arms, and stills. He tries to clear his mind of all the harsh sensations. With focus, he alters the cadence of his breathing, forcing his heart to slow. The aches recede enough to grant him a respite. He burrows deeper into the meditative calm that overtakes him. Everything dulls as his connection to his physical self dims. The heaviness of the moment lifts. Awareness is temporarily suspended.

He is weightless, ethereal, adrift, edging on sleep.

Thwack!

An unexpected kick to his side jolts him back. Pain erupts from his ribs. From above, a blinding light shimmers, bathing him in a pearlescent glow. As his eyes adjust, he sees her—a nightmare in white. His Klenzeer.

She speaks in a low, harsh voice. "Beast, how low you have fallen. You were always my favorite little pet. You made me do this to you. You earned every ache that you feel. Your weakness shows that YOU ARE NOT WORTHY OF ME!" Her yell echoes throughout the pit. She kicks him again.

He stifles his moans. "I am sorry, my dearest love. I failed you. Fen are not brave. I am unworthy of your strength, divine one." He slithers on his side and bends uncomfortably to kiss her pristine boots.

"*Cur*, don't touch me. I have ascended, my pet. I am now in the best class. I am an Alpha. I am A13 now. She smiles. "I forgive you, though. You are weak, but I will make you stronger. You will ascend with me. Your god is merciful."

His head thrums with searing pain. This moment feels like a memory, yet—

"Beast, pick yourself up and follow me. We have much to do. You will be cleaned and prepared to follow me in my ascension. You will use your keen senses to help me become the greatest Alpha." A13 lifts an ebony staff and bangs it on the ground. The earth shakes as the chamber walls drop. Fento feels the platform rise toward the overhead light.

The pair ascends together.

When they reach the top, attendants of the Klenzeer take him away. They are among the few remaining first version Ones—the original progenitors. Most died out or were preserved for study, but the Ones here are old and twisted into bent shapes, kept alive by machines pressed to their backs. Tumors cover their bodies. They move with the grace of broken toys. Yet they are gentle with him. Broken and battered, they know his importance to A13. They have witnessed many of his beatings and healed him, time and time again.

They bathe and groom him, cleaning and combing his fur. His wounds are treated with a salve known for its accelerated healing. A device is affixed to his broken arm that repairs fractures in days, not weeks. He is returned to his mistress's side in hours, healed, yet hollow.

A13 walks the hallowed halls of the Central Garden in a robe of purest white. She is tall—over six feet—lean and strong. Her neck is long and graceful. Dark hair with faint, pale streaks of gray is pulled tight into a bun. Her stride is confident and elegant.

Fento scurries behind her, as is expected of him. Unfailingly obedient, he takes notes on everything she says. There are no limits to what he will do to serve her, under the threat of punishment.

When they arrive at the living quarters, they walk into her new apartment. Everything is bright white—the rugs, the walls, the furniture, even the books. Anything that isn't wood is made of silver or glows like gold. A13 touches every surface, asserting ownership over it all. She caresses every curve and checks for dust. She finds none. She cackles.

Her yellow eyes fall on Fento. A smile from her dark, thick lips reveals dull, yellowed teeth. Lines furrow her brow as she focuses on him. "Come lie next to me, pet. I wish to stroke your tail, my handsome little boy." She drapes herself on the bed, reveling in its luxury.

Fento gulps as he approaches, wearing the smile he has been trained to wear. It must never falter, lest she beat him. "I am here for you, my love." He deepens his voice, as she prefers.

A13 takes her long, thin hands and strokes the lily-white fur of his tail. He tenses, not looking back, unless commanded. Each caress of her dark hands intensifies the ache in his head. Rings of obsidian and pearl flash in his periphery.

"I have missed you, my little beast. How I wondered *when* I'd see you alive again." Her smile is brutish, her tone dulcet. "I did not intend to be so thorough in my last thrashing of you, but *you* upset me." Her voice lowers. "You embarrassed me on my special day."

Fur is ripped from Fento's tail. He winces with each tug but maintains his affectionate speech. "It was my fault. I was weak and soft-skinned. I was afraid. I could not hope to win." He holds back his reaction as she pulls. "I am sorry, my love."

She grunts and drags him closer by his tail, her tone shrill against his ear. "I will not *have* you disappoint me again, beast."

He swallows as a lump grows in his throat. A13's acrid breath is like acid. "I will do what I must to make you happy."

She stands up and paces her chamber, speaking more to herself than to him. "Now that I *found* my place as an Alpha, I must keep *it* at all costs."

Fento's ears droop. "I will do anything to elevate you higher."

"*You* will help me find the anomalous," she hisses.

Fento stiffens at the word. His hands reach for his throbbing head. A low groan escapes him, followed by an impossible, "No."

"What did you say?" A13's face becomes stony.

He collapses to the ground, teeth gritted. He grunts, "No."

Her face contorts. She kicks him in the ribs and bellows, "You *must* find the anomalous!" She reels back and unleashes again, striking his chest with the tip of her boot. He spits blood, pale fur stained red. "Do not *press* me. You will find the anomalous for me, BEAST!"

Another kick elicits a groan from his bloody lips. He struggles to breathe, but he forces out, "No."

"YOU WILL FIND *THE* ANOMALOUS!" Her tone burns into him as she winds up and drives her boot toward his head.

A13 kicks. Fento yowls and resists until he has no strength left. Every inch aches. Tears obscure his vision. His will shatters, and he whimpers a weak, "Yes."

A13's tone softens as she lowers herself to his ear. Right before he passes out, she whispers, "You would swallow a *button* if I told you to. Never disobey me. That's my good little *cur*."

Her laughter is all he hears as everything fades to black.

KARAL'S EYES drift open in bed. Grunting, he places his palms on the sides of his forehead. A pulsating headache syncs with the rhythm of her heart. He knows the familiar sting of a hangover. From under the covers, she paws for the water pitcher on the bedside table and feels it slide off with a resounding crash.

Feng!

The Cycle ended last night, and he—she—the memory escapes. How did they make it home, much less take their boots off or slip into bed? Who helped them?

She groans, wavering between getting up and staying in bed, but Clara is coming today. She can't see him like this. She whines as she gets out of bed, blinded by the bright room. He shuffles to the window and feels a ceramic shard embed into his foot. She yelps and curses for failing to remember the shattered pitcher.

He hobbles to the window and closes the shade just enough to provide relief. With some effort, she pulls out the shard and staunches the blood. It didn't penetrate too deeply, but it's painful. When he looks up at his home, he deflates.

What a mess.

She tries to remember anything about the night before, but nothing comes to mind. Just as he's about to give up, images of a pale male and a Sinna startle him. It's a brief flash, but the familiarity disrupts her concentration, making her headache pound harder.

Yubu! It's the first thought that makes sense so far. He needs it to focus. She loosely laces her boots, grabs a bucket, and heads for the outside door. Bracing him—herself for the sunlight, they open it.

Something's off.

The sun is dull, and the world is drenched in shadow. He carries the bucket to the well and fills it, distracted. The water she pulls has a rank smell.

When he turns around, she gasps.

A tree towers over the center of Gallow. Its height and width swallow the sun. Several branches weave in and out like dark webs. They limp back inside, unease trailing them through the door.

Setting the kettle to boil, he sits down and tries to remember anything from the previous night. Cradling her face, she rubs it roughly.

Think, Karal, think.

The haunting image of a man in darkness flashes before him, making him jump. When she looks around, the nervousness won't fade.

The boiling water pulls him back. He brews some yubu and gulps it too fast, burning her throat. The headache doesn't ease. He makes a disappointing breakfast, hoping to combat the pain, but can't stomach more than a few bites.

She tidies her home and prepares for work while her food digests. At this point, his misery is almost crippling. When she glances toward the window, she feels flustered. The sun is shining again. No tree. He looks out to confirm. Rubbing their eyes doesn't restore it to their vision.

Last time I drink, I swear.

A vow broken countless times. A nagging feeling of déjà vu gnaws at them.

She realizes she has just enough time to clean up before Clara arrives. Filling his basin with water, he splashes their face. When he looks in the mirror, he pauses.

That's odd.

His hair is already short. It hasn't grown. Even the sides are short, and they grow quickest. Only short stubble shows.

The Cycle ended last night. It should be longer.

Perplexity grows. Nothing else needs attention except wiping away some dark dirt around his nose and mouth.

When he looks away from his reflection, he notices nothing

unusual. An empty space lies adjacent to her bed, though she could swear something used to be there. His headache threatens to overwhelm them as they step back—a disjointed feeling tugs at them.

Something is wrong.

Each percussive throb brings stars to their vision.

He lurches toward the shop, pausing at the doorway to say— nothing.

Is there something to say?

She can feel a wave of nausea rising as a migraine threatens. The door into the smithy sticks, and they smack into the rough wood, blinding pain rising to an incapacitating level. He pushes, but the door doesn't budge. Curses flow as they struggle. Veins throb. The worn wood shakes, threatening to burst off the hinges, but they falter. It's too much. Hope fades to a glimmer. Strength ebbs. He slides down to his knees, too weak to cross.

I'm the blacksmith of Gallow.

Just as he gives up, the door swings open and she stumbles across the threshold.

She stands, breathing it in.

Everything suddenly aligns.

The confusion, the headache, the memories, they all recede. She is exactly where she's supposed to be.

Every tool, every piece of ore, and the warm flame of the forge calm her and melt away the headache. Nothing is as pleasurable as being in this room. A fulfilling smile spreads across her lips.

A knock on the outside door startles her. "Come in," she yells, expecting Clara.

The door opens on creaky hinges, and a figure blocks the light. Stooping low to enter, the Klenzeer steps across the threshold, bathed in shadow. Her face shifts from fear to anger. Memories of Ives and Lindor dying at his hands flood her. Screaming obscenities, she snatches two solid hammers from her workbench and charges, swinging with unchecked ferocity.

He deflects the blows with his rod, metal clanging and reverberating. He shoves, swings, sends one hammer flying from her hand, then kicks out, staggering her backward.

She issues a guttural roar and charges again, flailing the hammer, but he counters each time. The ringing of metal on metal vibrates through her hand. Each defended hit shakes her to her core.

Never leaving the shadows, he strikes her nose with the staff held horizontally, followed by a swift swing that thuds into her side. A retaliatory hammer swing almost breaks through, but he trips her and she hits the floor.

He springs on her, exiting the darkness, pinning her beneath his weight, driving the rod against her throat.

The Klenzeer's face is—is her dad's.

He mocks her, face inches from her own. "Weak girl. You never stood a chance. If I'd only had a son."

Screaming, she writhes under his weight. He counters every attempt to move, leaving her feeling powerless.

He laughs. "You anomalous are weak!" His eyes light with a subtle, red glow.

The lack of oxygen brings stars to her vision. She opens her mouth, struggling to speak.

She manages two words before she passes out.

"—kill you—"

Everything fades to black.

XYTEL'S EYES slowly blink open. The taste of mold and ichor hangs in the air. Vile. She raises to a sitting position with slow, careful movements. Above, the towering branches of the haunting tree spread out in vast tangles. The seedpods rattle.

Dark patterns of shadow shroud her as the moon breaks free from the cloud cover overhead. She scans her surroundings, hoping to spot Fento or Karal, but neither is in her line of sight. As she prepares to rise, she wipes her face and feels dried streaks. She tastes it—blood. With care, she takes a moment to clean it off.

Feeling whole again, she stands. Her tongue drifts out, tasting the air. There is no trace of Fento or Karal. The taste of rot is overwhelming. She walks around the base of the tree, searching, but finds no sign of her friends.

When she completes the revolution, she exhales. Dread builds as she gazes at the surrounding terrain. The charred grass around the base of the tree looks like midnight in the dim light, but then she yelps. A red door sits in the middle of it all, framed in gold, glowing like a beacon in the pale moonlight. She walks toward it.

"Where are you going, Sinna?" A deep, disembodied voice echoes through her.

She stops, refusing to turn around. This voice. This presence. One and the same. It had controlled her. Made her do things against her will. "I am leaving this dream," she says, anger sharp in her voice.

"How perceptive. You are intelligent for a Sinna." A humph of satisfaction. "There is nowhere to go. I am Ra, Ra is me. You cannot escape."

"Xytel. My name is Xytel. I am not yours. I will find a place far from you."

"Oh, a Sinna with a spoken name. How novel. Will you breed with Ones next? Once a Sinna, always a Sinna." The Sorumjah's tone darkens. "Thank you for your assistance, Xytel the Sinna."

"I would not help you!"

A pause. "Do you believe your senses to be incorruptible, Sinna? Your journey, to me, pure luck?"

She hesitates, shaken.

"It took considerable resources to bring you all to me. Manipulating weather. Causing avalanches. Flooding the river." A harsh, grating inhale. "I wondered how to steer you to me from the mountains, but a Sinna's senses are easy to sway. All it required was manipulation of the air—a subtle change in taste. It was simple to guide you here."

"Wha—what? Why?" Her voice trembles.

A long silence.

"A purpose. A very special purpose."

It laughs mockingly.

Furious, she gathers her courage and turns to face the tree. She flinches.

Midway up the trunk, a decrepit face lined deep with ridges of bark stares back. Glowing, red orbs protrude beneath a heavy brow. Two vacant holes serve as nostrils. Most alarming is the wide mouth, dripping a thick, oozing, dark fluid. It grins at her. Sharp wooden teeth jut out at odd angles, black with rot.

Her stomach drops.

"Are you afraid, Xytel? Where is your bravado now?!"

She firms her stance, tightening her body and narrowing her gaze. "I am not scared now."

"Will you stand up to me? There is a Klenzeer who will find you interesting to play with."

"My friends and I will fight. You will not find us." Her tone rises defiantly.

"Your friends are subdued, and soon you will join them. I have—"

"We will fight!" Her knuckles crack. "I will fight!"

"SILENCE!"

A resounding vibration knocks her down.

"Enough of this prattling. Accept your role. A Klenzeer will come to collect you, and you will be processed. I await you at the Gardens."

The ground vibrates as the earth loosens around thick, serpentine roots that begin to animate. Xytel springs up, moving quickly to avoid their grasp. She dodges left, then right, as heavy roots burst from the ground. Her fists push against the earth as she dashes. She reaches the edge of the charred grass, but falls as loose soil gives way beneath her. She is just inches from the door when an errant root coils around her ankle and drags her back, her hands clawing at the burnt grass for any hold.

"You will not escape, Sinna!" The Sorumjah howls as she's dragged toward the base.

She seizes a stiff embedded root, abruptly stopping her momentum.

The Sorumjah scowls. The root sprouts a serrated edge, spikes piercing her flesh and drawing blood—but she doesn't let go. She screams as her body is pulled in two directions. The root around her ankle tightens. A second cinches around her waist. The serrated root snaps at its base, launching her toward the tree as more roots bind her torso and one wrings her neck. Her arms and legs go limp as she is lifted to within feet of that heinous face.

"You will die, Sinna, as will your friends." The grin widens, oozing black fluid. The root around her neck tightens, cutting off her air. She spasms, flailing, fighting the steel grip.

Remembering the jagged root in her hand, she swings with everything she has. The ridges slice through the coil at her neck. She catches a breath and swings again, cutting through the roots ensnaring her torso and ankle. She drops several feet to the ground, rolling, tendrils snatching at her as she scrambles away.

The Sorumjah laughs.

"HE IS COMING, SINNA! HE WILL FIND YOU!"

She spins and rolls through outstretched shoots, wielding the jagged root like a sword, cutting through with impunity. The uneven ground trips her as she crawls toward the doorway. A thick root seizes her ankle—she twists and swings down with a fierce grunt, cleaving through. Her hand finds the handle. The door swings open.

A reflection of her world lies before her.

Fento and Karal lie on the ground, unmoving.

She surges forward as a root snatches at her weapon. She releases it and bounds through. The door slams shut behind her.

The Sorumjah's laugh echoes in her ears.

SCATTER

Xytel wakes with a start and sits up. She looks toward the horizon. The sun rises above the plain. She scans for Fento and Karal and finds them unmoving on the ground, their chests rising and falling in a slow rhythm. Dark stains mark their faces.

She closes her eyes and extends the tip of her tongue. All of her missing sensations rush back, and the taste of the world feels normal again, but doubt rises. The Sorumjah's words surface. The manipulation of the air. The tastes. She looks behind her. An ordinary tree with damp bark. Nothing like the spectacle of the previous day. No trace of it lingers in the air.

The plateau they sit on is covered with grass and bushes for several hundred feet. Only this ordinary tree grows from it. There is no ring of burnt grass.

She stands and wobbles forward. The world spins, forcing her to her knees. She closes her eyes. An echo surface in her mind: *He will come to collect you—*"

She crawls to Karal and shakes her. "Karal, you must wake. He is coming." She does the same to Fento. "Wake up, Fento. The Klenzeer. He is coming to collect us."

Both fail to stir.

"Wake up! Karal! Fento! You must wake."

Neither moves.

She stands but collapses to her hands and knees. Dark fluid spills from her mouth as she expels the black spores from her lungs.

Turning to Karal, she wipes her friend's face, removing residue from her nostrils and mouth. Then, she opens her mouth and takes care to remove what substance she can reach, repeating softly, "Karal, wake up."

Desperate, she opens Karal's mouth wider and sticks a finger down her throat.

Karal gags, and she starts coughing up streams of dark mucus, eyes opening as she chokes out the fluid.

Xytel watches. Tears stream down Karal's cheeks as she breathes fresh gulps of air. When the coughing finally slows, she falls to her side. Xytel crawls to her, stroking her head. "I am sorry. You would not wake. The darkness kept you asleep."

Karal speaks in a low, dry rasp. "Water, I need water."

Xytel crawls to a canteen and shakes it, hearing the water slosh within. When she hands it over, Karal manages one word between thirsty gulps: "Tree."

"It is gone. All tastes are gone. I don't understand." She stiffens. "Klenzeer is coming. We must run."

Karal's eyes widen. She gets up and falls. Xytel points to Fento, and they both crawl to him. She rubs his face with rough hands and repeats the same steps as with Karal. In minutes, Fento is hacking the dark residue onto the grass, eyes streaming as he crawls on shaky arms. When he manages a clear breath, he gasps, "Where is the tree?"

"We do not know. When I woke, it was gone. You were both sleeping. I could not wake you."

Fento falls backward, breath shallow. "How did you wake up? This could be a dream."

"I escaped my dream. There was a door. The tree tried to kill me."

"We should talk about our dr—"

"No!" Xytel interrupts.

They both turn to her as she rises. "Klenzeer is coming. Sorumjah said so. It tried to stop me. It said many things."

The color drains from Fento's face. He tries to stand but keeps failing. Xytel lifts him, carrying him in her arms, while Karal finds her footing. She straps on the backpack and nods. Xytel tastes the air once more, praying the results are authentic. Turning several times, she finds a hint of the Ormanti.

They leave the plateau.

MORNING FLASHES by as they journey east. Their pace is slow, with few words exchanged. The mild descent shows no traces of the environment from the day before. No tall or twisted trees. No paths to follow. No unnatural spectacles. Subtle dry grasses mask their passing as the land flattens. Midway through the morning, Fento gathers enough strength to walk on his own.

When they find a fruit-bearing bush, they devour all they can stomach. Many hours have elapsed since they last ate. After several handfuls, Fento sits on the ground, spitting out remnants of the dark spores.

"What did you see, Xytel? I didn't see the tree." He shivers, looking away. "The memories were jumbled. I could see that something was wrong, but my head—"

"It hurt, didn't it?" Karal speaks up. "Like a headache that kept getting worse."

Fento nods. "Yes. I knew something was wrong, but couldn't pinpoint it."

Karal growls to herself. "My dad was in my dream, but he was also the Klenzeer. I was so hell-bent on my revenge that I didn't realize who he was. Even in my dream, I was overpowered." She looks away.

Spitting, Fento asks, "And you, Xytel? Did you see a Klenzeer? I saw my old Klenzeer. She—she felt so real." He draws his knees up, whiskers twitching as he stares at the ground. "But this memory never happened."

Xytel nods, tasting his terror. She rests a hand on his back. "I only saw the tree. It said many terrible things, and—" She stands, walking a short distance away. Tears fall, which she swats away angrily. "It is my fault. We were guided to tree by me."

"What? I don't understand Xytel. You didn't—" Karal starts, but Xytel interrupts.

"No! The tree said it made the storm. Made the flood and rocks fall. Made the trees. And—and—it made the tastes." Another tear leaks out. Her shaky hand wipes it away.

Fento opens his mouth to speak, but finds no words. Karal stares at Xytel.

"The worst is Klenzeer is coming." Xytel continues, voice shaking. "He is coming to us. We must go and lose him in town. He must not find us."

"Oh, Xytel." Karal pulls her into a hug. Xytel's shoulders shake.

Fento's voice reaches them, somber. "We have all been used, but we can't let it beat us. We have each other."

Xytel breaks the embrace and wipes her eyes. She inhales and releases a series of sounds mixed between breaths. "I am ready."

"Me too. Let's get to Ormant."

Fento nods. Xytel guides them to a mature forest lined with wild bushes. Natural-looking trees shelter them from the sun, shedding any unease from the day before.

When they finally reach the river, they are ready to collapse. The journey from the plateau, while not taxing, drained them of any remaining vitality. They gather edible roots and herbs they have on hand and place them in a pot to boil. Starting a fire is the hardest thing any of them has done all day. They slump to the ground around it—Karal against a tree, Fento on his side in the dirt, Xytel standing, looking around.

"Xytel, you need to rest, too." Karal's eyes are heavy.

Xytel straightens. "Sinna are strong, and I must protect my friends. Sleep. I will watch for danger."

With little stamina left to argue, both Karal and Fento fall asleep almost instantly.

It is early evening when Xytel rouses Karal. Waning light illuminates the Sinna's sturdy silhouette. Karal blinks away the grogginess, preparing to yawn, but Xytel clamps a large hand over Karal's mouth, placing a finger before her own mouth for silence.

Karal nods and crawls to Fento. He almost springs up from being touched, but Xytel's hand presses against his chest. He breathes rapidly, shocked into consciousness. Several seconds pass before he recognizes what's happening, and his breath slows.

In the dim light, they sip the broth. The Ormanti flows by, still swollen from the recent rains. Zizzers and nighttime scurriers blend into the background. Stars twinkle through gaps in the trees. An occasional night flutter swoops overhead, obscuring the stars in its path.

"Will we be safe tonight?" Karal whispers.

"I truly hope so." Fento's voice is low, full of caution.

Xytel shifts closer. "I will stay up and—"

"Stop it, Xytel." Karal's words carry gentle reproach. "You owe us nothing but your friendship. That tree was sent to find us. Ever since we lost the Klenzeer, it has likely been searching for us, and it found us somehow. We had forgotten about it when we found you. Fento and I got careless. We were excited about meeting you, and then the idea of the Village blinded us."

Xytel sighs, releasing a low breath. She opens her mouth, but only air escapes. She tries again and whispers, "It brought us to it for a purpose."

"What do you mean? What purpose?" Fento asks.

Xytel shrugs. "It did not say. It said it was a very special purpose."

"That doesn't make any sense!" Karal's voice comes out louder than expected.

"Shhh!" Fento's brows rise. She shrinks back. "We escaped, and it's all that matters."

A night flutter swoops low. Noiseless. It snatches a bug out of the air, flapping away.

Karal clears her throat. "Something doesn't sit right." Fento and Xytel turn to her. She licks her lips. "It had us. We were unconscious. Yet somehow, we escaped."

Fento hums. Xytel blinks, thinking.

"Isn't it strange that Fento and my dream were specific to our past, and both had Klenzeer in them. Xytel did not. It was different. Direct." She sighs. "Something about that nags me."

"Xytel, you have faced two Klenzeer, have you not?" Fento asks.

She nods. "One took me to the Gardens. Another killed my father."

"See?" Karal's voice rises. "Why not assault her with one? Why speak to her? Why give her a way out?"

Fento's ears flatten. "She might be the only one among us not afraid of Klenzeer."

Karal nods but shrugs, unsatisfied. She yawns quietly. Further yawns follow from her friends. Night presses, and they fall fast asleep.

WHEN KARAL AWAKENS, dew blankets the ground. Xytel sleeps beside her, snoring, mouth wide open. The world feels chill and damp. She glances at Fento, who is curled up in a ball.

She walks to the Ormanti. Clear, cold waters rush south. She washes her face and rinses her mouth. The temperature shocks her awake, clearing the fog from her mind. She turns to leave but notices a piece of floating wood. It's charred and dark. Several pieces follow, all resembling the first. Pieces of metal—bolts and fasteners—are embedded in some of the wood.

"Fento, get up. There's a problem." She startles him awake. "Come to the water!"

He scurries to the water's edge and studies the current while Xytel joins moments later. Pieces of wood, some darkened, float downstream. Upstream, more are coming. Fento jumps up a nearby tree and climbs effortlessly towards the top.

He scrambles down hastily, out of breath. Karal and Xytel wait for him.

"There are traces of smoke. It's not a forest this time. I think bridges are being destroyed. We need to hurry north."

CHOICES

Fento leads them north, following the river. He scouts ahead, with Xytel behind him and Karal at the rear. They creep forward at a snail's pace, anxious and alert. As they approach a sharp bend, he asks them to wait by a tree while he climbs. Disappearing into the canopy, he strides from tree to tree like a ghost. When he spots what he's looking for, his ears droop.

When he returns, Karal lets out a held breath. "What did you see?"

He guides them around the bend with careful steps. The collapsed skeleton of a bridge comes into view.

"What is this?" Xytel strokes the blackened wood on their side of the river. "It is cold."

Fento folds his arms across his chest, ears drooping further. "There are three bridges into Ormant. One was this old footbridge. It is the one furthest south. It was decrepit but would likely have held us. The next bridge is the main one, called the Junction. It is large and sturdy—the largest of the three. The last is furthest north. It's another footbridge, but stouter than this one. I can't say for sure, but the floating remains may be from one of those bridges. There may just be one left."

"I don't understand," Karal stammers. "What happened to this bridge? Why was it burnt down?"

"It may have burned previously." Fento swallows, eyes drifting to the wreckage. "Or very recently."

"But why would anyone—" Karal starts, but Xytel cuts in.

"We are meant to be here. They know where we run to. To Ormant." Her voice hardens. "This is a trap."

Fento's face falls. His tail sags. "You were right, Karal. Something was wrong." He tenses. "They guided us here." He turns to Xytel. "Told you what you needed to hear so we would rush to Ormant and make it easier to hunt us."

"Is this the special purpose?" Karal's words come out hollow.

Silence falls. Fento stares at the rushing waters. Karal bores holes in the ground with her eyes. Xytel shakes.

"Stupid Sinna! Friends in trouble. My fault. My fault." She hits the sides of her head.

Karal grabs her wrist. "Xytel, please stop! Please! Look at me." Xytel's dark eyes find hers. "They reasoned out where we were headed. Guided us." She winces. "Whatever the case may be. They forced us here." She looks away. "Now, we need to figure out how to fight them."

"You can't be serious!" Fento's hackles go up. "There is no fight, Karal! His rod burnt down half a forest."

She looks at him, gritting her teeth as a tear streaks down her freckled cheek. "You said it yourself when we first met—he won't ever stop hunting me." She pauses. "You said you should have let me drown!" Another tear races to her lips. "What's the point of running? He's never going to stop chasing me, Fento!"

She breaks down.

He moves to comfort her, but she pulls away. "No!" Between sobs, she manages, "I don't want to run anymore. Whatever fate is before me, I'm ready to face it." She sniffles and wipes away tears.

Fento backs away. "What about you, Xytel? Are you determined to fight, too?"

Xytel looks from one to the other in silence. When she turns to

Karal, Karal averts her gaze. Turning to Fento, she reaches out and pats his head. "You are a good friend, Fento, but you are afraid. I am not."

Karal turns and hugs her.

Fento's shoulders sag.

When Karal breaks the embrace and turns back, Fento is gone.

Sprinting through the woods, Fento has no idea where he's going. He can't be captured. He won't go back. Never again. Nothing in the world would ever bring him back to his Klenzeer. Tears blur his vision. Sobs choke his breath. He pushes away thoughts of Karal and Xytel. The guilt is overwhelming.

He missteps and trips down an embankment, tumbling in a chaotic flurry of limbs. A thick tree at the bottom welcomes him as he hits his head with a resounding thud. He struggles to stand. The world dims. Trees, ground, and sky swirl before his eyes, before he drops back to the earth, breath coming in labored gasps as his eyes shut.

Minutes pass before his eyelids rise. Flutter songs reach his ears. He stares up at an awkward angle at the boughs of a large tree. A pulse of pain reaches him when he moves. A bump on his forehead stings to the touch.

He lets out a shallow breath.

"What are you doing, Fento?" The words sound foreign, his voice low, though he knows he uttered them.

"You cannot abandon them. You need them."

He blinks back tears.

Words spill out.

"Tree, fire, bridge, Klenzeer."

His breath quickens.

"You are supposed to be here."

He knows he's right. The fear is overwhelming anyway.

He weeps, full-bodied.

Seconds pass before he reacts, standing shakily. Wiping his tears, he gazes at a path away from the Ormanti, aching to run—then turns back.

The sun sits high in the sky, shifting toward early afternoon.

He swallows, then turns to the nearest tree, climbing to the top, claws digging deep for purchase. When he finds his bearings, he descends with resolute determination.

Gritting his teeth, he heads toward the Junction.

SEVERAL HOURS HAVE PASSED, and it's dark when Fento finds Karal. She's digging a hole with the flat edge of a rock. He makes a sound, causing her to jump up with her hammer in hand. They regard each other in a silent standoff. Her face reveals little. When she turns back to her digging, Fento's chest tightens.

A fire blazes in the center of a campsite. Several patches of loose dirt surround a figure meant to represent Karal sleeping by the fire, dressed in her old, stained tunic.

He approaches, avoiding freshly dug dirt traps, but Karal keeps digging. When she speaks, her words cut. "Your backpack is hanging from that tree behind us. Everything is in there. We haven't touched it."

"Karal." His tone is soft.

"What?" She continues digging.

He looks down. "I didn't mean to—"

"Run away?" She shouts it.

"Yes," he whimpers.

She stops digging and rises to her full height, eyes narrowing. "Friends don't treat each other this way."

"I—"

"You can run away, Fento! I understand what you're running from. But you don't leave without saying goodbye." Tears fall from the corner of her eyes. "You don't do that to people you care about." Her mouth quivers, but she stiffens. "I've lost too many friends this Cycle, and I never had a chance to say goodbye to them." She rubs her eyes with rough, dirty hands. "You somehow hurt the worst." She drops her gaze to the ground.

"Karal, I'm sorry." He tries to hug her, but she raises her hand.

"Just grab your things and go. Xytel and I—"

"Karal, the Klenzeer is not alone." Desperation edges into Fento's words. "He has a Kaitan with him."

Karal glares. "How do you know this? What's a Kaitan?"

Fento stiffens and looks to the ground. "After I ran away, I had a change of heart. I went to the Junction using the trees and any stealth I could manage. I hoped I wasn't too late. When I got closer, I spotted his Sinna hiding in the brush. The Klenzeer was on the bridge, inspecting wagons and their contents. Below him, in the water, tethered to the bridge, was a Kaitan. It's like a wagger crossed with a long-snouted, scaly thing. They're used for tracking.

"I watched for several hours waiting for you both, but you never showed up. No others joined the Klenzeer in that span. Toward the end of the day, I saw him take a torn leather apron out of a sack. The Kaitan inhaled the scent and tore it to shreds." He swallows. "He will be hunting you, Karal. Three very deadly opponents will be coming this way. You have to run." His voice cracks. "Please."

Karal turns around and picks up her rock. She doesn't look at him when she speaks. "Thank you for the information, Fento. It was brave of you to go there." She lowers herself and resumes digging.

He runs around to face her, dropping to the ground. "He isn't going to capture you. He's going to kill you."

Karal looks up from her work. "I'm not leaving, Fento. I'm done running. He can come and get me." She sighs. "You should go before he finds you, too."

"I'm not leaving."

Karal stops digging. "You don't want to die, Fento. You shouldn't—"

"And neither do you," he interrupts. "That is why I am here. To help in any way I can to keep you both alive."

Her shoulders fall. "Why now, Fento? I gave up on you when you left. It hurt, but I understand your fear. Now you come back here, and you're ready to die? Don't lie to yourself. There—"

He talks over her. "I have lived in fear my entire life, Karal. Only once did I fight back, and I was abandoned by my family. That left a scar." He clenches his fists. "I can't abandon you as they did me. I won't repeat that same mistake." He stands up. "I choose to die with my family."

Karal rises, brushing the dirt from her hands, facing him with tired eyes. Fento returns the gaze with a hopeful smile. A minute passes before she returns it. He relaxes and smiles wider.

Then she punches him.

He drops, unprepared for the swing. His cheek swells, a throbbing ache spreading as he looks up. She offers her hand. "Welcome back."

He accepts the gesture, and she pulls him up. Rubbing his jaw, he says, "I deserved that."

"Be thankful I held back for my friend." She pauses. "Now, find a shovel and start digging. We need to prep."

Fento grins despite the ache. "Where is Xytel? She could help us dig faster."

Karal laughs. "If you haven't noticed her, she's doing her job well."

She looks away, and Fento follows her gaze. His eyes go wide.

"Oh my."

JUNCTION

Mist floats above the ground when the Kaitan breaks the surface of the Ormanti. Twilight casts the forest in blues and grays. The Kaitan's spiked tail swishes in the water with excitement. It exits the riverbank on silent feet into the waiting mist.

Nothing stirs.

Ahead, on the ground, bundled blankets lie beside a dead fire, the warmth of the coals long faded to ash. The silent predator slinks forward. Water streams from its fur. Noiselessly, it stalks toward the blankets, its gait unhurried. One webbed foot moves, followed by another at stop-motion speed. It long-snouted mouth opens, revealing rows of thick, sharp teeth. Saliva drips from the roof of its mouth. Inch by inch, it approaches: twenty feet, fifteen, ten.

It stops, muscles flexing in tense anticipation. Its chest expands rapidly. It sniffs. The vertical slits of its eyes flare.

Lightning-quick, it leaps, spiky legs and clawed feet angling downward, mouth open wide as it drops onto the blanket, snapping and ripping. Clothes tear in two as it rolls the blanket and bites down. Its mouth pierces flesh and bone. Blood whips from the carnage. A large, dead hopper—a crafty decoy—lies lodged in its jaw.

CRACK!

A branch shakes as if released. The Kaitan looks upward, too late. Xytel plummets, needle-like leg extended. The piercing tip drives through both skull and brain. The impact flattens the head to a mash. Her other leg pierces the torso. The Kaitan splatters into blood and fur. Xytel's momentum drives her a foot into the ground, leaving a crater.

Karal whoops from several branches above, covered in mud, leaves, and sap. Fento watches from an adjoining tree, smiling widely, similarly camouflaged. They clamber down to assist Xytel. The Kaitan's carcass is a pile of pulverized meat, the ground soaked dark beneath it. Karal offers Xytel her hand while Fento grabs the other. Together, they help pull Xytel free.

She walks a few feet, then staggers. A fine crack runs along her leg in the dim light.

"Xytel, your leg! Are you okay?" Karal runs to her. Fento pulls out his bag from behind a bush and looks for a rope to wrap around the appendage and create a splint.

"I do not eat ironweed. Bones are weak. I will heal. Sinna do not jump, but we fall. We are tough." Xytel walks with a limp.

Fento searches for a branch sized to her height for a crutch. As he walks past the carnage, a red flash catches his eye. Under the flattened wreck of the Kaitan lies a black collar, with a pinprick of light blinking at regular intervals. He recognizes it instantly.

"We have to go! This collar was around the Kaitan's neck." He holds it up, then throws it into the river. "I wore something similar in my first few Cycles as a pet. It works as a tracker. The Klenzeer might be following the Kaitan. He may be hurrying here now."

He gathers their remaining supplies and stuffs them in the bag. He and Karal each take an arm and help Xytel move. Her limp isn't severe, but it slows them down. They head west, away from the Ormanti, putting distance between themselves and their camp.

Karal whispers as they hobble away. "Xytel, I can't believe the impact you made. The earth shook. Your plan was amazing!" She smiles from ear to ear. "Where do we go from here?"

Fento answers. "We need to separate him and his Sinna. If we can—"

Xytel moves quickly, suddenly alert, shoving Fento.

A shadow darts from their right. A thin point narrowly misses Fento's head as he drops to the ground, the point burying itself deep in a nearby tree. The Klenzeer's Sinna turns and lunges at Karal. She dodges left. Xytel rolls beneath his reach and rises on shaky legs.

The Sinna dislodges his spike and moves toward Xytel. A tracker blinks red at his wrist. He clamps both palms over her face and drives her head back, aiming to crush her windpipe—then a hammer whips around and smashes him in the eye. He releases her. Xytel stumbles back from her injured leg. The Sinna's eye swells and weeps blood but stays open.

Karal stands ten feet away, hammer in hand.

The Sinna backs up and charges. His bulk covers the distance in an instant. He slams his shoulder into Karal's chest as her swing skips off his skin. A pop sounds. She flies back and hits the ground hard, breath knocked out, chest burning, head ringing. He backs up and comes again, aiming to finish it. Xytel tackles him at the last second.

They grapple—closed fists, locked holds, broken free. Trees shudder as they crash against them. Bushes snap as their bodies roll through, entangled. Dust and debris billow around them. Fingers jab at eyes, clutch jaws. A clean punch from Xytel flattens his nose as she tries for his uninjured eye. He bucks hard when her hands close around his throat, thrashing until he throws her clear.

Karal rises to help but clutches her ribs, breathing in ragged bursts. Fento rushes to steady her, and she clings to him as blows thunder between the two Sinna.

Fento watches helplessly, avoiding getting mixed in the melee, one hand rummaging through the pack for anything useful.

Xytel readies herself for another clash, pounding her chest, flexing her shoulders.

They square off again, both rising, fists up, several feet apart. Xytel drops her fists to the ground and extends her legs behind her. The opposing Sinna mirrors the stance. They roar at each other, circling, then charging.

Xytel goes high. The male goes low—directly at her injured leg.

Whack!

The fissure widens to a crack, nearly shattering. She falls, clutching the wound. The Sinna looms over her, spike raised at her chest.

Fento launches from behind, driving his claw into the Sinna's remaining good eye and grinding. As the Sinna screams, Fento loops rope around its open mouth and pulls hard, riding the back of its head. The Sinna wails and thrashes, trying to reach him. It bites down on the rope, but it holds with tensile strength. Teetering blindly, it bucks and nearly pitches Fento free, but he adjusts, pulling harder. The rope bites the corners of the Sinna's mouth.

The Sinna crashes into a stout tree, rebounding. Leaves rain down from the impact, yet Fento hangs on, feet buried in the Sinna's shoulder blades.

The thrashing slows. Its arms drop. It sways.

Then it falls forward, landing on its face. It fails to move again. Shallow breath. Nothing else.

Fento lets go and drops off, panting. He looks up at Xytel's pained face. She reaches for him, but he holds back his hands. "Please don't touch them. I have a paralytic oil on my fingers. If this comes in contact with your saliva or an open wound, it will do something similar to you. I don't know how long it will last." He rinses his hands with water, discards the rope, then rubs them with dirt.

Karal hobbles toward Xytel and eases her into a seated position. The cracked bone bleeds steadily. Xytel gurgles in pain. Fento speaks quickly, "Karal, go to my pack! I have navid leaves we can spread on her wound. It will numb her senses, but it will also take away the pain."

"No!" Xytel gulps air between words. "Only one is left. If we fight, we win. If he is tracking us to our camp, the bridge is open. We go!" A pained groan follows.

"You are severely injured. He has the advantage. If we try to attack him, we'll lose." Karal struggles to get the words out between her own shallow breaths.

Fento adds, "But if we give him time, he will get reinforcements."

"We must go, Karal." Xytel's voice is labored.

Karal growls in frustration but reluctantly agrees. She tears a strip from her shirt and ties it around Xytel's leg. Xytel yowls but endures. They get her off the ground with effort.

"What do we do with him?" Fento points to the paralyzed Sinna. Drool leaks from his slack mouth. "We can't leave him. He's a threat. He almost killed us."

"I cannot injure him more. It hurts my heart to fight Sinna. He is not my enemy." Xytel looks away.

Karal's hammer hangs heavy in her hand, pulling her sideways with each breath. "He was there when Ives died. I owe him this much."

Fento and Xytel walk away. The sounds that follow are excruciating. Xytel closes her eyes and lets the tears come.

Karal returns to them, bloody and hollow-faced. Together, they limp to the Junction, without looking back.

It is late morning when the bridge comes into view. The journey through the woods has been somber. The cloth around Xytel's wound drips steadily. She makes no sound, though the effort shows on her face. Fento slows to a crawl and hides among the bushes just south of the bridge.

The main entryway to Ormant, the largest town this far south, lies devoid of people. An occasional bushtail hops branch to branch. The Ormanti rushes swollen below.

"What do we do? This has to be a trap." Karal lies on her belly, watching the road.

Xytel leans against a tree, breath shallow, staring at the bridge.

"I'll climb and try to get a different view." Fento scrambles up and works his way toward the crossing, hopping from branch to branch.

Where the forest ends, he stops. Menacing clouds drift overhead, sunlight fading in steps. Shadows pool near the bridge. Everything remains still. The bridge is abandoned.

"He is here," Xytel speaks between pained breaths.

A lone figure appears on the road. Clad in all black, the Klenzeer makes his appearance, striding with confidence.

Fento yells, "Run!"

Karal springs from her spot and grabs Xytel. They hobble toward the bridge. The Klenzeer doesn't react. Fento scans the opposite end of the bridge for an ambush, but nothing moves. He signals his friends forward, eyes wide with fear.

They join hands. The Klenzeer stops.

"Beeeeasst!" The voice cuts across the distance. Fento twitches but holds his ground, turning to face the tall figure in black.

"You travel with ill company, beast! I thought I recognized you near Paldor. The Sorumjah confirmed it when it spotted you with this girl and a Sinna. Of all the people in Ra, I never expected to hear of you again. A13 will be thrilled. It is time to come home."

"I am never going back!" The hairs on the back of his neck stand on end. He takes his friends' hands and walks backward onto the bridge. He feels Karal's hand squeeze his as their feet touch wood.

"And you!" The Klenzeer points at Karal. "You murdered my prize. That Sinna took ages to train." He walks to within paces of the bridge and stops.

Xytel spits. "You use us. Sinna are not like him. You make monsters. You are truga!"

The Klenzeer laughs. "You are a surprise. A Sinna with intelligence and cunning. I will enjoy dissecting you."

They walk backward across the bridge, halfway over, when the Klenzeer yells, "STOP!" He drives his staff into the ground. The orb glows green. A boom erupts from the far end of the bridge as wood explodes. Splinters fly like shrapnel all around them, and a wall of black flames flares up, cutting off their route.

"Who do you think you are dealing with? I am a Klenzeer. You still live because I will it, not because you have beaten me." He lowers into a fighting posture.

Xytel charges, grunting through the pain. The Klenzeer smiles. "Now!"

From beneath the water, a second Kaitan erupts and launches itself, latching onto her left hand. Its momentum drives her into the railing as it bears down on her arm. Her tough skin holds against tearing flesh, but the rows of sharp teeth do damage.

Karal runs to help. The Klenzeer rushes the bridge simultaneously, swinging his staff at her head—she ducks back, barely. He adjusts. She brings down the hammer. Metal rings out. They lock together, each pushing for leverage. He smiles. "How weak you are, blacksmith. Perhaps if you were born male, you might stand a chance."

Fento backs toward the burning end of the bridge, fumbling through the pack in search of the two dull blades inside.

The Klenzeer forces Karal back, kicks out, and trips her. She hits the wood, landing solidly, nearly losing her grip on the hammer. He drops onto her, pinning her beneath his staff, pressing his weight down. The pain in her ribs intensifies.

"You will watch your friends die, and then—"

Fento lands on his back after bouncing off the railing. He stabs his blades—five, six, seven times. The Klenzeer releases a hand, seizes him by the scruff, and hurls him toward the fire. The knives stay buried. Fento lands just short of the flames and rolls clear before his fur can catch.

The bridge groans. Fire spreads to the deck and piers.

Karal pulls her arm free and swings. The hammer finds his temple with a dull thwap. He drops with a bloody gash and rolls away.

Xytel struggles with the Kaitan—it gnaws and tears at her arm, exposing bone, blood pooling as the flames smolder closer. She pulls her arm in, tries to grip the beast with her jaw, but its dense fur prevents purchase. She slams its head into the railing. Again. Again. Its grip loosens, yelping, body twisting to escape. She balls flesh and fur under an iron grip and keeps driving, pummeling relentlessly. *Thwack. Thwack.* It stops moving. Dead. She collapses onto the planks.

The Klenzeer turns at the sound. He snarls, stands, unsheathes the knife, and drops the staff. He sways once, then shakes it off. His eyes find Karal, struggling with smoke and her ribs. Fento intercepts with an agile leap, claws out, but the Klenzeer swings wide, blade slashing, and sends him spinning. A snap sounds on impact.

Fento hits the wood on his injured arm, and a deep, gushing wound bleeds out. He stands anyway, his arm hanging wrong.

Karal rises. Her face is sooty and set, flames reflected in her eyes. Heat pushes toward the bridge's midpoint. The Klenzeer drives at her, knife swinging—across, then down. She dodges both slices within a hair's breadth. On the third swing, he angles high, lurching forward. The Katian's corpse strikes his back. He staggers, losing a step. Karal drives the hammerhead up in an uppercut that catches his neck and chin with enough force to lift his feet from the wood. Before he lands, she brings it down on his face, pouring every ounce of hatred into the shot. His nose and jaw collapse. He crashes onto the bridge and stops moving.

She drops, coughing. The Klenzeer is still.

Xytel drags herself to Karal, leaving a red trail. Fento joins them, one shoulder slumped wrong. Black flames rise around them.

Karal reaches for Xytel, but Xytel stops her with a raised hand. "You have to go." Her voice is low, almost scratchy. Tears wet her face.

"We can't leave you." Karal's mouth trembles. "I won't." She takes Xytel's bloody hand.

Xytel shakes her head. She turns to Fento. "Care for her."

A black dagger punches through Xytel's chest.

A weak breath leaves her, wet with blood. The Klenzeer sits up behind her—face collapsed, eyes burning.

Fento grabs Karal and pulls her back toward the bridge's edge. Flames close in. The Klenzeer crawls towards them, then falls onto his face. Xytel's large hand closes around his ankle.

He kicks. The grip tightens. Xytel gurgles, blood in her throat, streaming from her mouth. The bridge groans and buckles. Karal kicks the flaming railing, and it collapses away. She turns and pulls Fento tight against her chest.

"No! The pack! I need the pack!" Fento grabs for it desperately, squirming out of her grasp.

"Why?"

The bridge tilts.

Fento returns, desperation in his eyes, clutching the pack desperately. The Klenzeer reaches toward them, his face a ruin of flesh and broken teeth. Xytel turns her head.

She nods.

Karal holds her gaze for as long as she can. Then the flames pull her back.

She jumps, taking Fento with her.

The cold water shocks through her. Hard strokes bring her to the surface. She drags Fento onto her chest and swims for shore with one arm, breath shallow, vision sparking at the edges, fighting the current until her hand touches land. She pulls them up. Fento rolls onto the ground and expels water.

They turn and face the burning remains of the Junction Bridge. Neither speaks. Karal shakes as adrenaline drains and grief rushes in. She feels Fento's paw find hers. She takes it.

Tears cut through the soot on her face.

They stare at the burning husk until the skeleton falters and the Ormanti swallows it. Scarred wood falls in heavy piles. Fento speaks low, voice rough. He says, "Cheen cheen yaun," and pounds his chest twice, then lets out a low yowl.

Karal does the same. Her face is still. She watches until the last of the bridge goes under.

Nothing bubbles up.

PART II

SNARES

PORTENT

Thunk, thunk, thunk.

Two daggers pierce the eye sockets, the third pierces the mouth.

Thunk.

A fourth finds the heart.

A13 moves with predatory grace—another blade whipping from her hand stabs a wrist. Mid-somersault, she buries a strike into the opposite joint. Landing in a roll, she unleashes a volley—two piercing critical thigh arteries, the last impaling the groin. Sweat beads on her dark skin as two more blades pierce each ankle. The next severs an artery in the neck.

The thirteenth remains sheathed. Her trump card—never used for training.

Stuffing pools onto the ground, the dummy emptying to a husk. A13's breathing remains controlled, heart rate already dropping. She approaches the target, scrutinizing each black dagger with practiced efficiency. Six inches long and dense, forged from a durable obsidian metal that rarely dulls—they reflect no light. She inspects the edges for flaws.

There is no room for mistakes in the field.

Overhead, the lights shift to red, pulsing three times before returning to white. The pattern repeats twice more. "I wonder who died this time?" She sniggers, striding out of the training room.

She dons her uniform while walking toward the Council of Wisdom, which sits at the pinnacle of the Central Gardens. Brilliantly white, her attire clings like a second skin to her athletic body, layered with a snug jacket whose gold buttons shimmer. Her boots echo through the pyramid-style building as she ascends the two hundred steps from bottom to top, barely elevating her breath. Stepping into the circular chamber with its central dais, she finds eleven council members already gathered in matching pristine uniforms.

Atop the dais sits a gnarled tree, its black bark twisted into the shape of a body writhing in agony. Two arms sprout three-quarters up the trunk, spreading like many-limbed snakes. Leafless branches pulse with black fluid while tendrils crack the marble beneath, rooting deep into the dais. Above the arms, a head protrudes from the trunk—bald, shaped like a One, perched on an imperceptible neck. A wide mouth full of sharp teeth grins at the assembled Alphas. Its twig-like nose juts out between round, beady eyes that glow red. The bark's striations form smile lines across its expressive brow. Standing two and a half feet tall atop the three-foot dais, it sways and creaks with each movement.

When it speaks, its voice rings shrill and tinny.

> *Oh my heavens, it would appear,*
> *We have lost a Klenzeer.*
> *On a mission, was he trying to procure,*
> *A male or female, I am unsure.*

It laughs as the dais turns, the tree ogling each Alpha in turn.

A3 steps forward. "Where did they meet their end? How do you know this?"

The tree fixes its gaze on the speaker.

> *Sent him I did to find his lost prize.*

I guessed it turned into his sorry demise.

The tree spins and shimmies.

> *A One he sought near the town of Ormant*
> *Found it, he did, though now he might not want.*
> *Gone two weeks he has been from here,*
> *His Sinna found dead, somewhere near.*
> *Two Kaitans were found, killed as well,*
> *A costly mistake this Klenzeer that fell.*

Its expression darkens. The Alphas shift and whisper. A Klenzeer, a Sinna, and two Kaitans—formidable alone, but their combined downfall is alarming. None address the tree.

A13 speaks. "I knew this missing Klenzeer. He was competent, and his Sinna formidable. What killed them?"

The Sorumjah turns to face her and lowers its voice.

> *A hammer blow felled his beast,*
> *A smith, likely the one who made it cease.*
> *A rare Sinna was there, intelligent and bold,*
> *Unknown its future or if it now grows cold.*
> *Lastly, there was a beast familiar to you,*
> *Useless to all, but now with purpose anew.*

"Who was I familiar with?!" A13's eyes narrow. "I'll find them and stick them full of knives."

The Sorumjah squeals, shaking its branches.

> *No harm is needed at this moment,*
> *Unless this figure starts to foment.*
> *An observance will be made of this death,*
> *A future endeavor we study with bated breath.*

The Alphas mutter. A7 steps forward. "Will we not pursue this murderer? A formidable Klenzeer has gone missing. We must investigate."

Silence fills the chamber. The Sorumjah rotates on the dais, mouth curling.

> *Are you afraid or vengeful, I wonder?*
> *How many more will be sent in to blunder?*
> *No body was found, and no evidence as of yet.*
> *Only a burnt bridge and no other threats.*
> *Useless a search for a trail gone cold,*
> *This death is meaningless; this news is old.*
> *Go now and ponder the life you have left,*
> *Bolder become Ones; bolder you must get.*

The tree falls silent, eyes fading to black. An uproar erupts. A13 stands apart, watching them bicker.

Abruptly, she speaks above the chatter. "This is a warning!"

A hush falls.

"The tree tells us we're failing to enforce the Laws with sufficient authority. If Ones are growing bolder, they don't fear us enough." Her voice grows colder. "Whoever this smith is, he considers us vulnerable. Pray he doesn't inform the masses and embolden them. Pray they don't fight back."

"What do we do?" A7's voice rasps.

"We incentivize those ranked below us to spread fear, threats, and violence. They must enforce their will on the populace. Bend them into submission. Fear begets obedience. Never rest on your laurels— dissent always exists. We must quell it quickly."

She glares at her fellows, then turns and leaves.

∽

Tap, tap, tap.

Her boots announce her descent. Any Klenzeer within earshot

alters course, knowing her penchant for unpredictable violence. Her frown deepens as she reaches the fourth level of the Central Gardens.

In her apartment, she retrieves parchment and a writing utensil and works through the Sorumjah's words and her memories of the deceased Klenzeer.

C111317 — capable Klenzeer, sent by Sorumjah to retrieve a One, body missing

Sinna — strong, controlled by Klenzeer, killed by the Smith? Accident? Luck? Was this smith the prize? Who helped him?

Kaitans — two dead, unknown causes

Location — Ormant, burnt bridge

Second Sinna — status unknown, intelligent, how did it get this way?

Lastly, there was a beast familiar to you.

She circles the last line, working through it aloud. "Who is this? Why are they familiar to me?" She recalls the next statement. *Useless to all, but now with purpose anew.* "What manner of beast is this?"

Below, she writes the Sorumjah's final words to her.

A future endeavor we study with bated breath.

Her brow furrows. "The goddamn tree is toying with us, keeping secrets." Her hands clench, knuckles cracking as she balls up the parchment. "If the Overseers didn't need it, I'd watch it burn."

She returns to her practice. Whatever the Sorumjah is plotting, she will be ready. Licking her lips, she savors the opportunity to strike flesh. A flick of her wrist sends a dagger into her palm.

She is an Alpha. Obstacles in her path only face death.

The first blade flies true.

SOLEMNITY

Fento's blunt throwing knife sails through the air, spinning end over end in a lazy arc.

Clink.

It strikes the metallic target and tumbles harmlessly to the ground. A clatter rings out as it joins several similarly pitted and rusted blades—dull edges catch the waning sunlight.

Another knife flies, then another, and another.

Dusk settles over the training ground.

Fento's scarred, calloused paw gathers the collection, and he returns to his starting position. One elongated paw skirts the edge of a slashed line in the dirt, while the other rests a foot and a half behind. He closes his eyes. The shrill voice of his Klenzeer rises in memory. "*Focus. Know the target. Feel the target. See the target. Imagine yourself in a life-and-death situation. Now throw!*"

Another knife darts through the cool air. Another clink. Another failed kill.

The knives come in quick succession. The target vibrates with each impact, yet they continue to fall like broken toys. Anger builds as failure consumes him.

"Xytel," he whispers.

A surge of rage directs itself toward the painted target.

THUNK!

The blade embeds deep into the metallic surface. A wisp of a smile registers as he channels his anger. Another embeds, then another. Five, six, seven—all striking in a tight pattern. Still, he knows this isn't enough. Hitting the target means nothing.

He must obliterate it.

"*Kill it. Never let it get back up.*" A13's words echo.

He approaches the target and retrieves all the knives. The fifty-pace walk back has worn the ground smooth from countless repetitions.

Fento stands, eyes hardening with fresh determination. Every strike must be lethal. The knife launches once more, spinning end over end through the gathering darkness.

Thunk!

Night descends, and the practice continues.

SENTENCE

Karal blinks open her eyes, weariness settling into her bones. Her arms ache, shoulders complaining from endless hours at the forge. Next to her, Fento snores softly. His familiar presence comforts her yet confirms that this torture has become her life.

She stretches, but the aches linger, dulling to mild annoyances. Rising, she surveys the smithy that has become her prison. Dirty wooden walls trap her in a rectangular box, maybe twenty by thirty feet. Small and cramped, it's hardly an architectural masterpiece. Pieces of wood are nailed over holes caused by rot. Two small windows, streaked with dirt and impossible to open, frame the sole door.

Karal sighs. Moving to the wash basin, she pumps her foot on a pedal, forcing fresh water to flow into it. The indoor plumbing remains the smithy's lone redeeming feature. The ice-cold water on her face offers brief revitalization. She'd make yubu, but Fento would complain about the floating bits in his favorite drink. His always turns out perfect anyway.

She yawns as she passes a table filled with freshly made wares. Cambra cleats, a metal box, and a bridle sit among dozens of other items, awaiting delivery. To her left, dozens of parchment orders hang from twine—an exhaustive list compiled by Fento that grows each day as he secures work throughout Ormant as a Runner. His knack for undercutting the local Guilds brings in work.

Too much work.

Reading each order, she recalls the joy of making wares for Gallow. Here in Ormant, they feel overwhelming. She threatens to tear apart the least desirable parchment: new shackles for the Posts in the town center.

She pounds her fist on a table, sending items to rattle.

"Good morning to you, too." Fento smacks his lips, roused by the sudden noise.

"Sorry."

He gets up, stretching. Pops and clicks mark his movements until he shakes them off. His tail swings as he walks to the basin. "Were you admiring your hard work or lamenting having to do more?"

"The latter," Karal grumbles as she organizes the twine pieces in her preferred work order.

Fento watches her. "I did warn you that you'd smith again someday." He offers a wry smile.

"You didn't mention I'd only get ten percent of the profit and no enjoyment from it."

"We had no choice, Karal. We were bloody, broken, and watched Xytel die at the Junction. We were desperate." His voice cracks. "No one was going to offer aid, except..."

"Beo." She barks the name. "I know. No need to remind me." She examines her swollen hands, flexing them into fists despite the minor cuts and bruises—proof she needs to work more carefully, less frantically. "Sorry, I'm in a mood today."

Fento approaches, gazing into her hazel eyes. They shimmer green in the dim light. He slides his scarred paws into her worn, calloused hands. "We'll find a way out of this mess." The warmth in his tone breaks Karal's malaise. She offers a faint grin.

"Now, how about some yubu to keep us going?"

~

THE MORNING PROCEEDS as it has for the past two Cycles. Karal works relentlessly, forging items from the parchment list, while Fento delivers finished pieces and procures more business.

As he's leaving, Fento asks, "Do you need more ore? I can put in an order, or is there enough for a couple of days?"

Karal waves him off. "All set!" She focuses on a tricky metal fold.

He turns toward the door, loaded with deliveries. The morning sun almost blinds him as he opens it—the dreary hole they inhabit lets in scant light to appreciate the day.

The shop sits south of Ormant's center, near the bend where the road turns southwest. Heading north, Fento waves at a pair of friendly carpenters he knows. Homes and businesses are packed along the main road, with lines of barracks and shops competing for access. Numerous laborers, tradesmen, and residents move between shops or head toward their workplaces.

Traveling north, he reaches the town center. Called the square despite its circular shape, its center features a large, flashy three-tiered fountain topped with a Fantil aiming a bow and arrow to the sky. Surrounding it, several taverns, the town brothel, a lone theater, and the mayor's opulent home gaze into Ormant's heart.

Arriving at the mayor's residence, Fento gazes up at the four-story monstrosity of brick and finely crafted wood. He knocks three times.

A tall man with a long, thin face and notable overbite invites him in. "Hello, Rondu. How's your day?"

The name 'Fento' ceased to exist the day he arrived at Ormant.

"Good day, Gregan. The sun's out, and business keeps me dry and fed. No complaints." He admires the lavish interior as Gregan retrieves the owed credits. "You're my first stop of many. Here's Nanda's kettle." He hands over the heavy, newly repaired kettle and bows gracefully.

Continuing north with his load lighter, he makes three stops before passing larger residences and small specialty shops. He knocks on a stained yellow door and is greeted by a sturdy man who invites him inside. The interior heat is oppressive as a craftsman blows glass into a round, bowl-shaped form. Rondu retrieves the forged shears used for cutting glass and waits while another craftsman tests their quality.

A large mirror with a cracked top lies on its side near the doorway. Rondu gazes into it while waiting, examining the black and brown dye splotches that obscure his usually white fur. These stains cover his arms, legs, tail, and face. His once-albino body will remain stained as part of his new identity.

As long as there's a risk of an investigation into the dead Klenzeer at the bottom of the Ormanti River, he and Karal will always face danger.

A firm hand on his shoulder startles him. A sturdy man politely thanks him for the shears and offers a generous tip. Rondu shakes his hand and heads toward his final stop at the distant farms on the town's northern edge.

After delivering some cleats, he turns toward the road and looks north. Ormant's edges fade into wetlands connected by spidering streams. A narrow dirt road extends into the distance, winding over gentle, grassy hills before disappearing from view.

Seconds pass in perfect silence as gentle breezes sway the grasses east to west. Rondu speaks reverentially. "We'll make it out of here, Karal. We'll find a way."

He turns back toward town, feeling refreshed.

It's nearly noon when Rondu returns to the shop, carrying several parchments and receipts from his morning sales. He's careful not to startle Karal as she perforates a metallic strainer with a delicate touch, boring fine holes. Once she steps back to admire her work, he clears his throat.

A smile springs to her face. "When did you get back?"

"Maybe about five minutes ago. I didn't want to disturb your work —it looked delicate."

"Nah, I'm just a perfectionist. Doesn't need to be that precise. I like making it look even. It'll distribute water better that way."

"Your dad would be proud."

She rolls her eyes and turns away, hiding her smile. When she looks back, her eyebrows rise. "Can we spar? Please?! It's been days, and I need a break."

Rondu rolls his eyes. "You and your sparring. Is that all the fun you want these days? Normal people gamble or watch plays, but all you want is sparring." He looks toward Karal, who smiles with child-like anticipation. "Fine, but just a few minutes. I'm behind on deliveries."

Karal hops with excitement, removing her heavy apron and gloves. She grabs the cross-peen hammer with its repaired handle—carried from Paldor. Assuming the fighter's stance Rondu taught her, she taunts him. "Don't think I haven't noticed what you've been doing at dusk behind the shop."

He shrugs. "That's nothing. Just throwing some dull blades around."

"No way, mister. You're practicing. And you're damn good at it, too. I watched you last time."

Rondu sighs. "Fine, I'm getting rid of the rust. My Klenzeer was very stern and taught me well."

"She must have taught you loads of fighting techniques. And you never used them?"

He quiets, his gaze dropping to the ground. "I was the practice dummy she released her anger on. I learned to defend myself to avoid further injuries and became adept at fighting and countering her. And because I discarded it all when I left the Gardens, Xytel died."

Quiet settles between them as they share the memory of that day. It feels like a lifetime since that moment, but sorrow still burns inside them. When he lifts his piercing blue eyes, they harden.

"I won't let another friend die like that. Prepare yourself, Karal. Here I come."

DESPERATION

"Parry, parry, thrust. Good. Now swing—not so wide, it leaves you open for counters." Rondu breathes heavily, sweat beading on his forehead as they practice moving forward and backward in a line. "Don't just focus on offense. Defense keeps you alive." He blocks a swing with his stick and taps her wrist. "You have one weapon hand, and I just disarmed you."

She surprises him by dropping the hammer, rolling to the right, and grabbing it with her left hand. "I have more than one hand, teacher."

His eyebrows raise. "He made you forge with your left as well?"

She swings with precision, knocking his stick away. "Dad was pragmatic." She lowers her voice to a husky tone, mimicking her father. "If you lost your right arm, what would you do with your left? Why, keep forging, of course."

Rondu delights in this and switches to his left hand. "Your dad and my Klenzeer were equally demanding. No wonder we get along so well."

Their sparring continues for several minutes, Rondu snapping instructions as their pace picks up. "Not so low. You can't recover quickly enough to counter. You have to—"

The door bursts open. Backlit by sunlight stands Robichard Dillard, the shop's owner. His eyes are wide, mouth open enough to invite bugs. He staggers through the doorway, reeking of alcohol. Bloodshot eyes blink rapidly in the dim interior. He wipes dirty gray hair from his face, glancing around. "How do—do you forge so damn much?" A long burp escapes from his wide mouth, obscured by a mangy gray and white beard.

Karal lowers her hammer. "By not drinking all day and working hard. If I owned this shop, I'd—" Rondu's calming hand on her back steadies her. She swallows the rest.

"What was that, Toby?" Dillard mutters mockingly. "Owner of which shop? I'm the owner, and you listen to me."

The stupid adopted name rankles her. Karal ceased to exist when they entered Ormant—they use their real names sparingly now. She crosses her arms, counting backward from twenty.

Dillard walks along the tables, unaware of Toby's death stare. When he reaches the strainer, he admires the craftsmanship. "You don't have to make the holes so perfect. It's just a strainer."

Rondu steps in front of Toby, shaking his head, whispering, "He's just goading you."

Toby turns away, cursing under her breath. She rakes her hands through the stubble on her head, pulling on the short black mohawk she wears as part of her disguise.

Dillard continues critiquing. "This cleat is too heavy. That axe is too long. That box could use more sanding."

"Enough, Dillard." Rondu's voice silences the old man. The commanding tone causes Dillard to flinch.

"Fine. Fine." His dirty, thick hands rub against the warm anvil. He avoids Rondu's gaze. "So what were you two doing with the hammer and stick?"

"None of your damn—" Toby begins, but Rondu cuts in. "We were practicing self-defense. You never know who might try to rob you at night."

"Thieves? In Ormant? You'd have to be—"

"Better safe than sorry." Rondu's tone brooks no argument.

Dillard coughs for several moments while Toby and Rondu glare. His heavy frame shakes with each dry hack. "Good work, you two. Keep the profits coming."

He turns and stumbles through the main door, still coughing, shutting it with a rough pull. Toby hurls her cross-peen hammer across the shop. It strikes the door with a resounding thud, embedding itself in the wood.

Dillard's muffled scream can be heard, accompanied by quick footsteps fading away.

"THAT TRUGA!" Toby seethes. "If I hear one more criticism about my work—" She kicks the table repeatedly, growling with each impact.

Rondu sighs, walking to remove the hammer. He admires the hole, rubbing the wood around the wound. "Maybe we should lock the door next time we spar."

"Yeah—" Toby curses under her breath. She adjusts the wooden binder under her shirt. She refuses to repeat what happened in Gallow—only Rondu knows her secret now. She puts on the heavy leather apron, ready to go back to work. Staring at the anvil, she lets out a weak snivel. A single tear rolls down her soot-stained cheek, which she furiously wipes away.

"It's not fair."

"I know, but this is what we agreed on for Beo's discretion. He gets fifty percent of the profit, Dillard gets forty, and we get ten. He has our signatures and blood-soaked thumbprints on a contract. I can't see us getting out from under it."

"Then we should run!" Toby's anger boils over. "We owe three thousand credits each to Beo—six thousand total. And that selfish piker still takes half our daily profits on top of it. How is that fair? How do we survive? We work day and night for a pittance and still have to pay down our debt. We'll be trapped here for endless Cycles. We'll never reach the Village of—"

Rondu rushes to her, gritting his teeth. "Keep your voice down!

Don't speak that name aloud. I've warned you before—towns have ears." His breathing quickens. "I can be paranoid about certain things, but that's one I'll always insist on. Please, Karal." He uses her real name sparingly.

She raises her hands, signaling peace. "I'm sorry. It's always on my mind. So is Xytel." She pulls on her gloves, preparing to return to the forge again. "More than anything in this world, I'd love to live as myself, in a place that won't judge me for being a woman in a role only men are allowed."

DUSK ARRIVES WITH FEW INTERRUPTIONS. Rondu enters and leaves the shop multiple times throughout the day. Toby works tirelessly at the forge. It takes his shouting to break her concentration.

"Come on. Let's go to the yard." His smile softens the exhaustion on her face. "You'll enjoy this."

He guides her behind the shop, where a long, narrow alley stretches about seventy feet. Rusty heaps of scrap and abandoned projects clutter the space, surrounded by tall weeds and scattered trash. At the end of the row, Rondu has set up a sturdy wooden barrel with a painted target.

"What's that bizarre thing for? Showing off tonight?"

He shakes his head. "No, it's for you." He grins. "I saw how you threw your hammer at Dillard. That's a tough skill to master, but you pulled it off. I thought you might appreciate some practice."

She examines the target, then looks back at Rondu. Her eyes sparkle. "For me to practice? Really?" Her face lights up for the first time in weeks.

Toby walks to the barrel and examines the target, muttering to herself about ways to reinforce it. Rondu taps her shoulder. "Are you going to study it all night, or throw something at it?"

It takes her three tries to get the aim right. She aims too low or too high at the start. On the third try, she hits the lower edge of the barrel, causing it to tumble. She claps. "This deserves a drink!"

MINUTES LATER, they head to their favorite spot, the Tipsy Tavern. Facing the town square, it's one of three local taverns surrounding Ormant's circular center. Inside, familiar tradesmen greet them with jokes and complaints about difficult customers. The crowd swells with patrons. A fiddler leads a chorus of songs, while quiet conversations fill the darkest corners. Dillard sleeps in one corner, drool pooling around his face, with a half-drunk mug of ale keeping him company.

Toby and Rondu find a quiet corner where they eat and sip tall tankards of ale. Their favorite server, Sela, chatters about town gossip while not hiding her cleavage or her interest in Toby. When she walks away, her hips sway seductively.

Rondu leans close. "If you and Sela want some time alone, just let me know." He winks.

Toby kicks him under the table, causing a wince and a faint "ouch."

As the night goes on, they sing raunchy songs inspired by the fiddler and enjoy several ales and visits from friends. The evening is filled with merriment until partway through, Toby quiets. Sipping her beer, watching the drunken tradesmen's antics, her smile fades.

"Are you okay?" Rondu asks.

She shrugs. "Just tired, I guess."

Rondu nods toward the door. Offering a hand, he stumbles as he rises. "Oh my," he exclaims, not having been this drunk in quite some time. Toby catches him and offers an arm. They wave goodbye and meander back to the shop. Rondu leans most of his weight on Toby, babbling incoherently about receipts and grabbing more work from the mayor's residence along the way.

When they finally reach the shop, they wash up and get ready for bed. Rondu sobers slightly, remarking about the night. "What was the sad face for earlier? You were having a good time, and then you weren't." His eyes are half-closed, yet his ears are alert.

"Don't worry about it. Something I have to work through." Toby deflects. She lies on their shared bed of hay, staring into the darkness.

Rondu stifles a yawn and burps at top volume while approaching. "Nuh-uh. You don't slip past my instincts that easily." He drops onto the hay. "What's going on? We're friends, right? It's Sela, isn't it?" A wan smile crosses his lips.

Toby flicks his ear, then stares into the darkened shop. She fights the urge to speak before giving in. "I just hate being this—this person. I hate being Toby. I'm imaginary. No one sees me. No one sees who I really am."

"I see you," Rondu says, his paws moving to hold her hands. His ears droop with shared sadness. "I see how wonderful you are, no matter what you wear or what name you use."

"I know. You're the one person who keeps me going. You're my only friend, but I'm tired of hiding myself from everyone else. I've done it most of my life." She hesitates as an idea forms. "Can we—can we?"

"What?" Apprehension rises.

"Can we talk to Beo tomorrow? Maybe you can talk him down, or we can renegotiate?"

Rondu groans, rubbing his face. "Karal, I don't think—"

"Please! Maybe he appreciates our hard work and would be willing to give us a discount. You can do all the talking," She pleads with her eyes. "I need to see an end! I don't know how much longer I can take this."

"If we run, they have the authority to send a Klenzeer after us. We might not be so lucky next time."

"All the more reason to talk to Beo. If we at least try, it might give us a goal or direction. Anything. I just need hope." She lets out a shaky breath.

"Ugh—stupid ale. I can't believe I'm agreeing to this." He shakes his head. "Fine. But I do all the talking. Okay?"

"Yes!" She hugs him, giving him a quick kiss on the cheek. She pats the hay beside her, inviting him to lie down.

He sighs, regretting his decision, but smiles when her warmth reaches him. Together, they welcome sleep as another day in Ormant fades into darkness.

Ormant

BEO

Morning dawns quietly in the shop. Toby rises early and tries making yubu, pouring hot water through filtered leaves. She fumbles with the amount and misses most of the filter. The result is a robust flavor that leans toward overpowering, with floating bits added for texture. The scent awakens Rondu as he recovers from a night of excess.

"Morning, partner," Toby calls from across the shop, reading the day's parchment orders.

Rondu's rough "hmm" is his sole reply. He rises gingerly, stretching with his hands pressed against his temples.

"There's yubu if you need something to wake you up." She points to a metallic jug near the forge. Vapor drifts from the top.

"I'm getting there." He yawns, shuffling through the shop while rubbing his face. When he reaches the jug, he takes a gentle whiff and cringes. With trepidation, he pours himself a cup, using a filter to catch the floating bits of shriveled leaves. The first sip rudely awakens him. He follows with a rough "thanks" and takes a second involuntary sip.

A warm smile greets him as Toby plants herself before him, hands on her hips, expectant.

"Yes?" Rondu asks.

Her eyebrows arch. "When are we going to see Beo?"

Rondu squirms as memories of their last conversation flood back. Toby pipes up. "I won't say a word to him."

He lets out a long exhale and gives a stern look. "He's a predator, Karal. He senses weakness. Day after day, he exploits people when they are at their lowest. That's why he always wins. If you say anything, do it with confidence. Got it?"

She nods.

"We'll go after lunchtime. Hopefully, a full belly will help him start talking and make him more open to renegotiation."

Toby nods again and skips to the anvil, donning her gear. Rondu watches her, shaking his head. He collects the morning deliveries and starts his day.

THE BUILDING Beo uses as an office is plain. It's a one-story square with windows centered on each wall; its exterior is faded and dull from weathering. The small windows let in light but are high enough for privacy. The pitched roof and stone fireplace show the marks of age. Surrounding buildings look similar in size and style. In this sea of unremarkable structures, the sign outside reading "Beo Luca, Broker" solely sets it apart.

As Toby and Rondu enter, a small foyer leads to another door into the main office. Rondu exhales, taps lightly, and waits.

"Come in."

Inside, Beo Luca sits at a worn wooden desk that wobbles as he writes in a ledger with a pen dipped into an inkwell next to his hand. Several older ledgers sit in the corner of the desk, their pages yellowed. He lifts a finger on his free hand, pausing his visitors as he finishes an entry.

Two uncomfortable wooden chairs jut out at odd angles—the room's only other furniture. No wall hangings or rugs decorate the space. The fireplace is worn and dirty, in need of cleaning or repair.

Beo puts his pen down and lifts his face. A warm, disarming smile spreads across his handsome features. "Toby, Rondu! My favorite blacksmiths. How lovely to see you both. Please, sit."

He stands to his full six-foot height and clasps his meaty hands around theirs. A tight black long-sleeve shirt stretches across his torso, revealing his musculature. He sits only after they are seated.

"What can I do for you both today?" He glances at the window. "I've been focused on balancing books all day. What time is it?"

"A little past the usual lunch hour," Rondu replies. "I apologize if we're interrupting your work."

"Not at all." Beo swipes a hand, dismissing the comment while flicking long auburn hair over a shoulder. "I always make time for my clients, especially profitable ones." He smiles, showing pearly white teeth with two canines that look larger than the rest.

Rondu swallows. "Well, Beo, Toby, and I were curious about our balance and wanted to check in."

Beo grins. "I like clients who stay on top of their debts and balances. It gives them goals to aim for each Cycle. With the current Cycle ending soon, it makes sense. Forty-two days come and go so quickly. Isn't that right, Toby?"

Toby nods, her expression neutral.

"Let's see. I don't have receipts from today as Chavin hasn't checked in yet, so I only have balances through yesterday," He leafs through the ledger, stroking his goatee. Several pages flip before he finds their account. 'Toby & Rondu' marks the top of the page. Neat cursive entries line up in columns showing quantity, customer, charged rates, and percentages per party. An entry for fifty credits reflects twenty-five under 'Beo,' twenty for 'Dillard,' and five divided between 'Toby & Rondu.' Rolling entries display a balance after each line.

Beo looks up. "After yesterday, you each have a balance of Two Thousand Eight Hundred Sixty-Two credits. Impressive after roughly two Cycles' worth of work. Bravo, Toby. At this rate, you're sure to reach your goals. What should you set for the next Cycle? I keep hearing compliments from customers. I might have new clients who would benefit from your work. Wouldn't it be lovely if you could make a new kettle for my neighbor? He drones on about his leaky one. Oh, and there's a—"

"Ahem," Rondu interrupts. Beo trails off.

"I get carried away sometimes. You know me, always thinking about ways to help people." He winks at Toby.

Rondu sits upright, his ears matching his posture. "Beo, we appreciate the opportunity you've given us to work in Ormant and benefit from Dillard's forge. We hope the profits we've made for you are helpful. It should come as no surprise that the labor required comes at a cost to our health and well-being."

Beo shifts. Charm still accents his voice. "Go on."

"It would benefit both of us if we could reduce our balance burden by some amount. Maybe a bonus for our efforts and Toby's continued quality work."

Beo leans back, fingers interlocked, evaluating them. He turns to Toby. "What do you think? You've been pretty quiet. Don't you have a say in this?"

Rondu attempts to speak, but Beo cuts him off. "Go on, Toby. I'd like to hear from you as well."

Toby looks to Rondu for guidance, but he stays focused on Beo. She turns back and stammers, "Well, it's hard working day and night at the forge. It's taxing on the body and mind. We get limited breaks for food and drink."

Beo's face softens with sympathy. "That's a shame, Toby. I didn't realize it was so burdensome. Perhaps if you worked fewer hours, it would be more rewarding. Less time at the forge."

"But we would make less money," her voice rises. "It would take too long."

"Too long for what?" Beo asks, studying her. Concern flickers across his expression. "To pay your debt? So what—it'll just be there, but pay it no mind. Your health and well-being are what matter most. Make enough to get by. That's all you need to worry about."

"No," Toby spits, her face turning angry. "I can't keep living under your thumb forever."

"Under my thumb?" Beo winces, hurt by her words. "Have I exerted pressure on you? Hounded you daily for profits?"

"No, but—" She looks to Rondu.

Rondu tries to interrupt, but Beo speaks over him. "Not now, Rondu. We're getting to the heart of this matter for Toby, are we not?" His eyebrows knit, eyes narrowing. "Please continue, Toby. Help me understand where my thumb is pressuring you."

Toby's breath quickens, her face flickers between anger and confusion. She shifts her gaze between Rondu and Beo. "I can't do this forever. I don't want to die slaving away at Dillard's forge. I hate this—"

"Arrangement?" Beo's word silences her. She folds her arms, looks away, but nods.

Rondu slumps in his chair.

Several seconds of silence pass before Beo stands and closes his ledger. His dark eyes lock onto his clients. Rondu meets his gaze, but Toby looks away. Beo steps from behind the desk and walks to a window. He adjusts his wrinkled black pants, pulling them tighter against his slim hips. He elevates his voice as he starts pacing around his office. "So my clients, who showed up bloody and wounded from an altercation at a now-defunct bridge, think their arrangement is unfair?" He pauses. No response. "And now they want a boon to ease their pain? Am I hearing it right, Rondu?"

"Yes."

"Did you both agree to the contract terms, which I'll gladly retrieve if you need a visual reminder of your commitments?"

A curt "Yes, Beo" comes from Rondu.

"If I recall, your contract states that in exchange for services provided, you will work at Dillard's Blacksmith Shop for a profit of no more than ten percent per sale, and you will owe a debt of three thousand credits each to Beo Luca." Beo's voice remains steady as he continues his promenade.

"Yes," Rondu whispers.

"Now, Toby, please relate what services were provided."

"You provided us employment to repay the debt, a place to sleep, and your continued silence."

"Thank you, Toby. Very enlightening. However, if I were to add details, it would be to justify my continued silence about whatever mess you two caused while fleeing the Junction bridge, which experienced a catastrophic fire that day. When Chavin found you both, he dragged you here—bloodied, injured, and in shock."

Rondu begins to reply, "And we are thankful—"

"You should be grateful. I risked my neck taking in two arsonists. There was a Klenzeer in the area the day before, and I could have easily reported you, but I showed mercy. Instead, I found medical care and managed to get you employment, despite your strange behaviors."

"Strange behavior?" Toby asks.

"Of course! You refused medical care for your ribs and wouldn't undress out of bloody clothes in front of people." Turning to Rondu, he states, "And you barely winced when your arm was stitched and set. I would have thought you both intoxicated if not for Rondu's calm that day."

Beo finishes his reprimand at his desk and leans in, lowering his voice. "Now, if you truly want a discount on your balances, I'll listen to your account of what happened at the bridge. There might be useful gossip in your story that could benefit me."

Neither responds. The silence feels tragic.

"Very well then, I believe our conversation is at an end, don't you?" Beo returns to the gracious host he was at the start of the meeting.

Toby gets ready to leave, feeling crushed, but Rondu remains seated. Beo tilts his head. "Yes, Rondu?"

Rondu clears his throat. He stares icily into Beo's dark eyes. "Beo, while we appreciate all the kindness you've shown us, you should reconsider the limits of your clients. Though we seem mild-mannered and simple, I would argue that we hide our true potential." He stands with his hands on the desk, his gaze steady. "Toby and I have faced many challenges to reach Ormant. Many would shake you to your knees, but we remain firm in our pursuits. When we set a goal, we accomplish it regardless of the Laws. If there's a time when you need a task that skirts the Laws, we are willing to do whatever is necessary to help you achieve your goal." An unsettling smile spreads across his face.

Beo remains motionless, then looks away, replying quickly. "I appreciate your statement and will consider you both should the need arise. Thank you for your visit. I need to return to my ledger entries." He stands to offer his hand, but Rondu, followed closely by Toby, leaves without a farewell.

THAT NIGHT, Beo is restless. Something about Rondu's statement unsettled him. In the morning, he calls in a client while pacing.

Zebu, a local caster contractually indebted to Beo, listens intently. "Go to the old Junction bridge, not the new one upstream. I want you to dredge it with your hooks. Dive down if you need to. Find any evidence of what might have burned the bridge down and bring it here. Understood?"

Zebu nods and leaves.

SEVERAL DAYS PASS AS Beo wears down a square track inside his office. The weather becomes damp and gloomy, worsening his impatience. When Zebu finally returns, he looks as pale as a ghost and reeks of ale. His hand shakes, and he avoids meeting Beo's eyes.

"What is it, man? What did you find?"

It takes four shots of liquor before Zebu calms enough to speak.

His voice drops to a nervous drawl approaching a whisper. "Mr. Beo, I did the task yesterday evening. I tried casting from the river's edge, but I kept hooking something heavy I couldn't move. The river was swollen, so it was hard to tell what it was." He gulps, begging for more spirits. After another swallow and several minutes, he continues. "I tied a rope to myself and the other end to a tree upstream, then swam out. When I got midstream, I dove down. It was cloudy from the rushing water, but I managed to trace my casting line to where my bramble was stuck. I pulled with all my might, dislodging something heavy. When I pulled the rope to get back to shore, whatever I was holding snapped off, and the rest of the weight fell back to the bottom."

Beo grips the edge of his desk. "What did you find, Zebu?"

Zebu pulls a package out from behind him and places it flat on the desk. Beo looks at it, unsure what to do next.

"We're square, Mr. Beo. I want nothing more to do with this. I ain't told nobody nothing about it." Zebu backs toward the door, nods, and leaves in a hurry.

Beo looks from the door to the mysterious package, tension building. He finds the opening and upends it, spilling the contents out. The arm bones that clatter onto his desk don't unsettle him—he's seen death before, but shock registers when he sees metal fused with them.

What makes him yelp, however, is the cloth melted onto the bone.

The unmistakable black and gold fabric of a Klenzeer's uniform clings to the blackened remains.

RECON

"His name is Rondu. I don't care where he goes. Follow him for a week. He is not who he seems," Beo barks at Lievus. "Write down who he speaks to and where he goes. He's the smith's runner, so he'll be all over Ormant."

In his office sits a short, thin man. Burn scars blemish the left side of his face. Shifty eyes flick around Beo's desk. He adjusts in the uncomfortable wooden chair. "Why him?"

Beo grimaces. "Because I'm paying you to. Stop asking questions."

"Fine," Lievus frowns. "Where does he live and work? Give me a physical description. Also, who does he work with? They might know something."

"He works at Old Dillard's smithy. I rent him a room at the red barracks near the square, room thirty-two. He's a Fen who is mostly white, with gray and black splotches on different parts of his body. I think he dyes his fur. He works with Toby, a strong boy with a black mohawk. I doubt he'd betray him—they seem like good friends. He's not a concern. Focus on Rondu."

"A Fen?" Lievus responds questioningly. "Aren't they kind of skittish and work for 'them'?"

Beo narrows his eyes and lowers his voice to a whisper. "That's what I'm trying to determine."

Lievus's eyes widen. "This will cost extra. There's a greater risk."

Beo dismisses Lievus with a nod and a wave, grumbling from behind his desk. Lievus smiles as he leaves the office. The coin for this kind of work is profitable when he squeezes at the right moment. The noontime sun forces him to squint. He pulls the tattered gray hood of his cloak—an effective way to hide his face. Remaining anonymous with such visible scars makes his line of work challenging.

Lievus, however, is skilled at staying covert.

HIS FIRST DESTINATION is the barracks. The red ones near the town center cover a large area and house over a hundred residents. It's easy enough to slip in unnoticed amid the busy activity. Several males walk in and out on the first floor as he makes his way through. The second floor is reserved for females, so he avoids the stairs. He passes by the door marked thirty-two, knocks once, then continues to the end of the row. No one answers. He reverses direction and knocks twice. No activity. He knocks three times, staying put this time, his ear pressed against the door.

With an abundance of discretion, he unlocks the door with a pricey master key he obtained several months earlier. When money runs low, he's willing to do a little theft to get by.

He sneaks inside and finds nothing. A single unmade bed sits in a corner, sheets neatly folded on top. Next to it, the bedside table is empty. No personal belongings hang in the closet. The sink looks dusty and unused. Even the floor is spotless.

Lievus shakes his head. "Maybe he stays with someone he knows, or is this a cover?" He vacates the room, checking for witnesses as he opens the door a crack. When he leaves, he locks the door, disappearing without a trace.

His next stop is the taverns in the square. They offer the best snippets of information for the cheapest price. He stops at the Charltan, then the Oak, but no one seems to have heard of the mysterious Fen. When he enters the Tipsy, he greets the bartender warmly. "Ho, Tomas, what's new?"

"Lievus, you sly one, where have you been hiding?" Tomas, a stout man shaped like a barrel, greets him with a cheery smile. "I have some info for you for the right credits."

"I knew I saved my credits for a reason." Lievus palms some currency and exchanges it with a handshake.

Tomas lowers his bald head to Lievus's ear. "I heard Arten has been dealing ore on the side. Rumor has it he might have found a new vein and is skirting the guilds." He winks.

Lievus rubs his hands. "That's juicy news. Thank you, friend."

"So, what trouble are you bringing my way?" Tomas asks.

Lievus looks around, but the Tipsy is pretty empty at this hour. The lunchtime crowd has cleared out, and a few day drinkers remain. He clears his throat. "Some Fen has Beo spooked. Goes by the name of Rondu."

Tomas pulls back, eyebrows raised. "Rondu? I know him. He and Toby come in here from time to time. They're pretty innocent if you ask me. That Toby has Sela all twisted up." He yells across the bar. "Hey Sela, how's your flame doing these days?"

Sela flips him a rude gesture as she approaches, causing Lievus to chuckle. She snaps, "Toby is mine. You can't have him, Lievus," then smiles, blowing a kiss as she walks away.

"She always picks the pretty ones, that girl."

Lievus mocks, "Then I have no shot," causing Tomas to laugh.

They exchange barbs for a few minutes. As Lievus prepares to leave, Tomas suggests, "Why don't you talk to Dillard? Sure, he's a drunk, but he swings by his shop now and then. He might have seen something."

With a nod and a slap of the bar, Lievus gets up and walks toward Dillard on his way out. He kicks the stool Dillard is sitting on while his head hangs over the bar, asleep with drool on his face. "Wake up, old man," he yells in his ear.

Dillard's head shoots up, dazed, tipping backward if not for Lievus's steady hand. "What? What do you want? Beo paid my debts. I don't owe nobody." A stream of curses escapes him.

"Hah! I've always wondered how you got an apprentice so quickly. No wonder you never do any smithing anymore. Toby running the show?" Lievus mocks the old man mercilessly. He lowers his voice. "Never mind that. Tell me about the runner, Rondu. What do you know about him?"

Dillard squints and sneers. "That Toby stole my shop. Rearranged everything and ruined my business. Truga threw a hammer at me." Spittle flies with each word.

"Oh, please, you waste. I'm sure they run rings around you. If you had enough wits about you, you wouldn't have accumulated all that debt. Useless truga." Lievus shoves him forward, walking away, angry at having his time wasted.

Dillard yells out, just out of earshot, "Stay away from that Fen. He's not what he seems." Curses and grumbles keep dropping from his mouth as Lievus waves him off.

OUTSIDE IN THE SUNSHINE, Lievus squints and pulls up his hood. He checks several usual places for more information. The brothel is a dead end because Toby is unusually chaste. The gambling hall has no record of either of them. The distillery also comes up empty. Even the theater shows no signs of them. Frustrated, he kicks a rock aimlessly as he moves through the growing crowds. Dinnertime is slowly approaching, and he has no leads.

As he walks along the main road, who should he notice but a Fen walking north toward the supply house. "Of course." He mutters. "They need to resupply with ore at some point."

He waits outside in the shadows while Rondu places an order. When the Fen leaves ten minutes later, instead of following him, Lievus enters the supply house and browses until the store empties. He approaches the counter, where a younger clerk sits looking bored to tears. Lievus slides some credits forward. "What can you tell me about the Fen that just walked out?"

The young man raises his eyebrows, then looks down at Lievus's hand and nods. Lievus adds another ten credits.

With a scratchy voice, the clerk says, "He comes in once a week, buying ore. Doesn't say much and then leaves. Friendly enough fella, mentions the weather now and then."

Lievus lowers his voice. "Does he meet up with anybody? Friendly with the staff? Stay longer than necessary?"

The clerk shakes his head and resumes his watch, leaning back away from the counter. Lievus curses himself for having spent so much on worthless information and heads to the Tipsy for dinner.

Inside the tavern, it's loud and hard to hear anything over all the conversations and the fiddler starting his show. Tomas makes eye contact and tilts his head to his left. Lievus turns casually and spots his target in a dark corner. Rondu is there with someone he assumes is Toby. He can see why Sela is drawn to Toby—he's handsome in a soft way. Toby and Rondu laugh as they exchange comments, unaware of Lievus's watchful gaze.

Lievus secures a stool at the bar with a good vantage point. He orders a plate of food and eats leisurely, nursing a large tankard. Skilled at reading lips, he lifts his eyes from his plate every few bites to analyze their conversation. They mostly talk about work—the most monotonous kind of conversation. When Sela arrives with fresh drinks, Lievus watches her flirt mercilessly with Toby, who appears shy and lacks confidence.

The rest of the night continues with chatter, even as the fiddler strums. Lievus yawns, growing tired from the day's work. He becomes overconfident, watching his quarry with less finesse. He raises his eyes and catches the Fen looking in his direction. When they make eye contact, Lievus looks away as if caught. He glances again a minute later, but the Fen keeps staring.

Feeling self-conscious, Lievus looks away and waits five minutes, maybe longer, watching the fiddler gyrate on stage, singing a familiar ditty. When he takes a furtive glance back toward Toby and Rondu, Rondu is gone.

From over Lievus's right shoulder, a light male voice orders a drink, "I'll take some wine, please. I want to change it up tonight." Lievus turns slightly and spots a paw in his periphery. Sharp black nails tap to the beat of the music. Lievus stiffens.

Rondu lingers for a few seconds, then sneezes, blowing his nose on a handkerchief. Lievus continues to watch the stage. He feels a light touch on his back and snatches a look behind him, catching the rear of a Fen walking away, his tail swinging lazily.

Lievus grimaces and promptly leaves the tavern. *Tomorrow*, he promises himself. He'll follow Rondu around then.

THE NEXT DAY, Lievus rises with the sun to position himself near the blacksmith shop, hiding in an alleyway several buildings away. Tucked within the shadows, he remains unseen in his gray cloak. He keeps the hood up to conceal his face and wears gloves to hide his skin.

An hour after dawn, the smithy door opens. Rondu leaves with a generous load of packages, weighing him down. He bounces on his feet as he heads north toward the square. Lievus follows, moving from shadow to shadow, blending in with the townsfolk. He pauses each time Rondu enters a home or shop, recording the residence and how long he stays inside. Each visit lasts a handful of minutes, and Rondu always exits with a cheerful smile and a kindly farewell.

The pattern repeats throughout the day. Occasionally, Rondu sneezes, blowing his snout on a cream-colored handkerchief. Twice, he gets turned around and has to backtrack, asking for directions.

When evening comes, Lievus is spent. He has chased Rondu up and down Ormant's main street, covering several miles. He reaches the Tipsy early and finds a table in a quiet corner. As Sela arrives with a tray of food and a tankard, he offers her credits in exchange for any information she can gather from Toby and Rondu over the next few days. She winks and slips the credits into a pocket near her bosom.

Later in the night, Rondu arrives with Toby in tow. Toby appears tired. Unlike the previous night, they station themselves in a bright, wide-open area near the stage, away from Sela's usual section. The vantage point makes it difficult for Lievus to observe them or read their lips. They lean in frequently, talking into each other's ears, annoying Lievus for having his surveillance thwarted so easily. Grumbling, he leaves the tavern earlier than expected, avoiding his quarry and slinking out through the shadows.

ON THE THIRD DAY, rain comes. Thankfully light, it forces Lievus to wear his darker, stained leather cloak. Like clockwork, Rondu starts his rounds of deliveries early, but instead of walking, he runs to avoid getting wet, causing Lievus to chase after him.

Puddles form on the road as rain persists, wetting Lievus' trousers and adding to his misery. This time, Rondu stays inside the buildings he visits for longer periods, leaving Lievus to wait impatiently in the shadows. Rondu sneezes, but less often than the day before. The familiar cream-colored handkerchief appears again.

The day ends similarly to the previous one, though the rains end before evening. Lievus ends his watch early to eat at the Tipsy. He positions himself towards the middle of the bar, giving him good vantage points to either side of the tavern.

Tomas greets him with a smile, speaking in a low, casual voice. "Ho, Lievus, how's your assignment going? Find anything juicy?"

Lievus grumbles. "Long days with little to show for it. The Fen is ordinary. Maybe a bit cautious, but nothing special. I don't get Beo's concern."

Tomas shrugs. "Maybe Beo's losing his mind or makes too much money. He's likely paranoid, and Rondu set him off somehow." He walks away, greeting patrons and serving ales. When he returns, he leans in and whispers, "If you get tired of this chasing, I have an acquaintance who's reliable and gets answers in mysterious ways. He's pricey, but effective."

"No, Tomas, I'm not desperate yet. If I become so, I'll let you know. For now, I'll keep chasing this Fen."

Tomas suddenly looks up. "Three nights in a row, masters Toby and Rondu—our ale must be exceptional."

Toby's voice rings out in a cheerful tenor. "We're taking some extra breaks this week. It's been tough working at the forge. Plus, the Cycle's end is coming up. Gotta eat a little extra."

Rondu speaks next, his voice upbeat. "I've been doing lots of running today. I might need a double plate!"

This time, they settle at a table almost directly behind Lievus. He grounds his teeth, annoyed that he lacks a good vantage point from behind. If he were to turn around, he'd be staring right at them. He wolfs down his meal and moves to stand near the stage, periodically glancing in Rondu's direction. When the crowd surges, the drunken chaos blocks his view.

Frustrated, Lievus leaves the tavern, but instead of going home, he heads toward the smithy. With Toby and Rondu at the Tipsy, he'll have plenty of time to search. As he approaches the door, a distinct scent stops him—wood stain. Before he lost his parents to the fire, they would send him to the lumber yard to pick up stains for their business. He recalls carrying them with a steady hand to avoid spilling the foul substance.

The aroma is most potent at the door. He slides a sliver of his finger down it and notices it's coated in the substance. He nearly screams, wanting to pick the lock, but unable to risk upsetting the drying pattern. He tests the windows, but they're hard to move, let alone see through.

At a loss, he turns to leave and startles at the familiar shape of a Fen, and likely Toby, walking down the main road. He hides as they enter the smithy and end their night. He listens from his vantage point but struggles to hear their muffled voices through the wooden walls.

He heads home, another day lost.

❧

THE NEXT MORNING, he wakes feeling tired and groggy. The days have been long, and the assignment more frustrating by the day. Heavy rain pours down. Thunder rumbles overhead. He mumbles to himself and looks for his leather cloak—but it's missing. He is positive he was wearing it the night before, but now it has vanished.

When he goes to retrieve his lighter cloak, he finds an unexpected piece of parchment on it. He looks around, worried and fearful of having slept through a burglary. He runs to the loose floorboard under his bed. Digging his hand into the crevice, he retrieves an empty sack.

His credits are missing—all of them.

He tears open the parchment. A sole word is scrawled in neat script: *Beo*.

He puts on his cloak and rushes to Beo's office. He enters the foyer and notices his leather cloak hanging from a rack, soaking wet. He can hear Beo talking to someone inside. Just as he's about to knock, the office door swings open, and Rondu steps out.

Lievus steps back several feet. Rondu greets him all smiles. "Good morning. Or at least morning. It would be better if it were drier."

Unsure how to reply, Lievus stammers, "Yes. It's wet."

Rondu sneezes violently and paws at his person for a handkerchief. He looks up at Lievus. "Would you happen to have a handkerchief?"

Lievus reaches into his cloak pocket and pulls out a cream-colored one, unfamiliar to him.

"Thank you," Rondu replies, blowing fiercely and returning the cloth.

Lievus watches Rondu slip on the heavy leather cloak and lift the hood. Rondu sniffs and turns to Lievus. "Have we met? You smell familiar." His piercing blue eyes trap Lievus's gaze, probing him. An eerie, menacing smile spreads across Rondu's lips, revealing jagged teeth.

The expression disappears instantly. "Maybe it's my cold. My mistake," and then he turns and walks away.

Heart pounding, fear firmly rooted, Lievus enters Beo's office, pale as a ghost.

Beo rushes to Lievus, checking the foyer for signs of Rondu. "What are you doing here? Rondu was just here."

Lievus strolls to a chair and slumps down, his hands trembling. "What was he doing here?"

"Lievus, are you okay?"

"What was he doing here?!" Lievus snaps.

Disarmed, Beo sits on the corner of the desk, arms crossed over his chest. "He and Toby have been hoarding credits and just deposited a fair amount. Why?"

Lievus's body shakes with rage, his eyes narrow. "Was it one hundred thirty-two credits?"

Beo's eyebrows arch with surprise. "Why yes, how did you know?"

Lievus screams.

CYCLE 240

"Are you out of your damn mind?!" Toby shouts, her face upset, even as a grin inches across her lips.

Rondu folds his arms across his chest. "I was merely testing the waters. If this person were relaying information to a Klenzeer, he wouldn't have gone to Beo's so quickly or reacted like he did. He was working for him."

Toby shudders, leaning close. "What does that mean for us?"

"I don't know." Rondu sighs, his voice turning dour. "He either knows something about us or is investigating because he's suspicious. Either way, we should be careful around him."

"Well, I don't need more attention from my least favorite person." Toby washes her hands. "Let's avoid him for a while."

Rondu nods, sighing as he hangs up the wet leather cloak.

Unexpectedly, Toby walks over and hugs him. She whispers in his ear, "You are something else, you know that?" She releases the embrace and steps back, studying her companion. "You've changed, Fento. And I'm thankful to have you in my life."

An embarrassed look crosses his face. He walks away, hiding a smile, as he gathers several packages and arranges them for delivery.

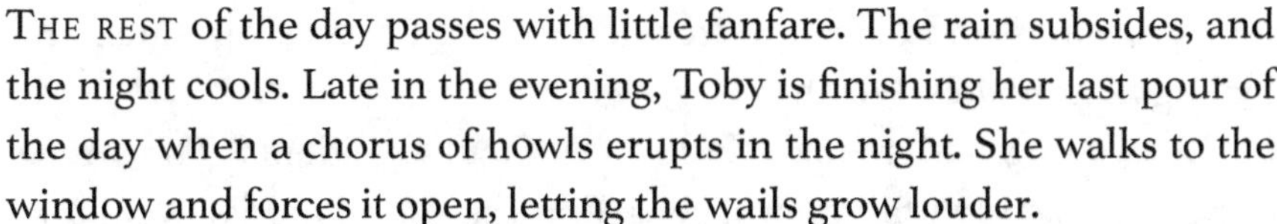

THE REST of the day passes with little fanfare. The rain subsides, and the night cools. Late in the evening, Toby is finishing her last pour of the day when a chorus of howls erupts in the night. She walks to the window and forces it open, letting the wails grow louder.

"Gods, I love that sound." Cool air washes over her.

"They're kind of annoying if you ask me," Rondu responds from a far table.

She sticks out her tongue. "How can you tell a slopeback's howl from a Loper's? You said Lopers are like slopebacks, but bigger, and the unusual mating transformation."

"Yes, they're similar, but not quite. Lopers have a sharper howl and a longer wail. Slopebacks have shorter intervals and sound more like growls. For Lopers, it's usually a mating call—they get lustful at Cycle's end. Slopebacks just enjoy howling at the moon."

Rondu joins her, sniffing the air. "I can't believe another Cycle's end is upon us. Are you prepared? Scissors ready? Fresh clothes?"

"Yes, I'm ready. I've been doing this long enough." She whines over his mothering. She looks contemplative as she listens. "It's unnatural. The Cycle's end, I mean. It feels like something the Overseers would create."

"Hmm, I never thought of it that way." Rondu tilts his head. "I guess it is odd. I'm so used to it that I haven't given it much thought. We all suffer through it equally. Most people live through it. Some die. We all move on somehow."

Silence fills the room as they listen. The howls gradually fade, and the moon rises high, nearly full.

The next day, the current Cycle ends.

THERE'S a flurry of activity in the morning. Almost everyone is out and about, buying food to cook or eating prepared meals. The infirm and elderly get extra attention, while children are force-fed heaping spoonfuls of sugary treats.

Toby and Rondu join the frenzied feasting, eating too much and feeling their bellies stretch.

By evening, satiety takes hold of Ormant's residents. The streets grow quiet as nightfall approaches, and the sounds of its occupants disappear.

Ormant turns into a ghost town.

Toby and Rondu lie on their backs on the shop floor. The forge sits silent and cold. A lone candle burns low.

"If I don't survive the Cycle, I'd want you to burn my body in the forge and spread my ashes in Gallow so I can live in my home again properly." Toby smirks as she relays her final wishes.

Rondu looks at her aghast. "You must be mad if you think I'm going to cut you up just to burn you to ashes. That sounds too messy. Yuck!" He rolls his eyes. "I'll just light this old shop on fire and collect the ashes afterward. Much cleaner that way." He chuckles.

Toby flicks his ear in reprimand.

"As for me," Rondu begins, his face growing serious, "just leave me and go find the Village."

"Fento, no—" she begins, but he interrupts. "Karal, you deserve happiness and freedom. There's no sense in suffering here alone. Go north and find it, wherever it may be." He touches her face softly with a paw, sliding it down her cheek.

As if on cue, a low chime echoes in the air, vibrating through everything. Their minds waver as if attuned to the sound. They don't yawn, but their eyes shut, and they drift into a deep sleep.

IN THE SKY, the moon's pale yellow glow darkens to deep red, casting a crimson veil over the land. The island of Ra is bathed in the chilling light.

A sudden, suffocating pressure fills the air, squeezing every surface. Ripe fruit begins dripping sweet nectar. Sap oozes from open pores on trees. Toby and Rondu expel the air from their lungs. The moon compresses, squashed by an unseen force. Red, viscous fluid oozes from its craters, covering its surface in roiling waves like an ocean.

The pressure increases, almost tearing the world apart.

Just when everything feels fit to shatter, a haunting whistle pierces the night, and the tension eases with a sharp crack.

Lungs fill with air, breathing life back into creatures everywhere. The moon rebounds violently, decompressing like a coiled spring. The rapid expansion blasts the fluid away from its surface, expelling sheets of liquid across the island like a heavy red rain. The deluge lasts seconds, not minutes, with the remnants dripping from surfaces in steady drops.

The fluid moves lightning quick, sentient, seeking living organisms. It infiltrates them through their orifices.

It invades the host, multiplying like a virus, triggering physical changes—the affected body ages.

Cells divide at an accelerated rate. Hair and nails grow out. Children grow taller and mature, and adults age. Females experience a menstrual cycle in seconds if their bodies are mature enough. For the elderly and infirm, they decline rapidly as their bodies break down at a blistering rate. All these changes are exhaustive, leading to death in some.

As the effects complete in each organism, the remaining viable fluid departs the body, seeking a new host.

Vast amounts of heat are released in the form of sweat as the body consumes calories to produce these changes. The aging is equivalent to three months of elapsed physical time. Almost no one escapes the effect programmed by the Overseers. Those who don't prepare consume themselves—their bodies cannibalizing their own reserves to achieve the accelerated aging. Pregnant women and infants are unaffected. The fluid's detection is guided by specific instructions after countless Cycles of experimentation.

The process takes minutes in each body. Toby's hair lengthens while her nails grow out, cracking from the speed. She goes through a full menstrual cycle—blood absorbed by strategically placed cloth. Rondu's fur grows out and sheds, restoring his bright white hair. His claws grow long and sharp, though thin near the tips.

By the time every organism in Ra has been affected, several hours have passed.

An eerie silence falls over the land as bodies recover from the exhausting process. Its task completed, the fluid slows to a stop, color drained from deep red to dull pink.

A loud crash, like a cymbal, echoes in the sky. Silent minutes pass as the moon shifts from deep red to an electric green, its light growing warm and gentle. Pooled on the ground, the fluid drifts to the shimmering rays, attracted to the light. It reaches a boiling point on contact with the rays, aerosolizing in seconds. Vapor floats through the skies across Ra, forming a faded pink cloud that drifts toward the moon.

Mechanical suction draws in the cloud from within its craters as the moon reabsorbs the spent liquid.

A final sound—a sharp electronic ping—rings out.

The moon fades to pale yellow, returning to its original state, ending the current Cycle.

In every village, town, or city across Ra, glowing golden doorways of light rise from the ground. Measuring eight feet wide and ten feet high, as thin as slivers of wood, these rectangular structures radiate with a sinister brilliance.

From them emerge the Overseers.

Like floating wraiths, they hover inches above the ground. Ranging from seven to nine feet tall and three to four feet wide, they arrive by the dozens within each community. In their long, bony, gloved hands, they carry instruments that send beams of light along their paths, analyzing the population size, overall health, and genetic composition. They wear long, flowing robes made from a sparkling material that twinkles with their movement. No feet touch the ground as they float, taking readings and collecting data. Their heads are topped with large spherical helmets that reflect light. The crystal is smoky in color, with dense fog floating within, revealing little. Around their necks, rectangular boxes sift air, producing quiet electronic whizzes and crackles with each inhale and exhale.

They operate with practiced efficiency in swarms spread throughout Ra. Their observations are limited but sufficient for their needs. When satisfied, they return through the doorways, vanishing into the Beyond. The lights fade from the portals, dissipating to nothing.

In forty-two days, they will return to examine the evolution of their thralls.

IN ORMANT, an unusual sound echoes through the deserted streets.

Footsteps.

A figure, cloaked in black from head to toe, walks freely, unaffected by the Cycle's end. They march through the square, relaxed, carrying a lantern, accustomed to their lone immunity.

They walk straight to Dillard's smithy without deviating from their path.

Rusty hinges creak as the door opens. In walks the stranger, uninvited and stealthy. On the ground, Toby and Rondu sleep soundly, twitching from their dream state.

The figure approaches them, observing the changes in their bodies. Rondu is bright white, his fur grown out, the dyed patches faded. The claws on his paws are long and cracked near the tips.

Toby sleeps peacefully, her hair longer on the sides, brown with black curls from her faded mohawk. Some strands, dyed black, drape her face. Her face is ashy with soot, and she smells strongly of sweat. The mysterious figure inhales Toby's scent and winces. They step back and notice something unusual. Near Toby's groin, blood stains the fabric. Her khaki pants are dirty, yet a few red blotches seep through.

Their eyes flit between Toby's pants and face, highlighted lightly with hair. They lower themselves again, hand floating an inch above

Toby's loose shirt, wavering. When they press a finger on her chest, they feel the binder.

Satisfied with their assessment, they stand back.

Pressed for time, they search the smithy. When they find a pack shoved in a corner, they rifle through it, removing the contents. Several camping items are wedged inside, along with casting gear and various dried roots and ointments. Near the bottom, they discover a black bundle. When they unfold it, the familiar cloth of a Klenzeer's uniform, Rondu's size, is revealed. They stumble backward, hands shaking, nearly knocking over several staged delivery items.

Two last items remain in the bag. One is a small, misshapen brass orb with an indentation that would fit a finger perfectly. The other is a curious wooden box made of ornate wood.

Pressed for time, the figure stuffs the pack's contents back inside and rises. On their way out, they pause, listening to Rondu's voice babbling in his sleep. They stand still, attentive.

Rondu's voice slows, then stops. His head tilts toward the mysterious figure. Eyes closed, no expression on his face, he growls:

"DO NOT RETURN!"

Horrified, the figure backs into the door, exits hastily, and runs.

Rondu's head returns to its original position, expressionless. He continues babbling and falls deeper into sleep.

DAMNED

As morning dawns in Ra, the spell of sleep lifts from its inhabitants. The survivors of the Cycle wake to a new day. Many are mourned who couldn't survive the ordeal—a common experience accepted by all.

Toby and Rondu tidy up as usual, though reapplying their disguises adds an extra step to the routine. Soon, Toby restarts the forge and returns to her usual tasks, reading parchments and deciding the proper order of things. Rondu leaves with several packages, planning to deliver them before noon.

It is midday when he returns, panting. "Karal, Karal!" He jumps in her peripheral vision to get her attention while she focuses on hammering a piece of metal.

"What?" She stops mid-swing. "What are you all riled up about?"

"Dillard's dead," He drops his voice. "He died from the Cycle. He drank himself into a stupor and didn't prepare. They found him dried like a husk."

Toby almost smiles, then thinks better of it. She looks around. "What does that mean for us? Who owns the shop?"

Rondu's face falls. "Beo owns it now. He keeps ninety percent of our profits. Chavin told me this morning when I was dropping off receipts."

Toby throws her gloves across the room. "That truga?! He could do anything. He owns us more than he ever has. Dillard was an annoying pain, but he still wanted the shop."

Just then, a knock sounds on the door. "Come in," Toby shouts.

As if on cue, Beo Luca walks in.

"Good day, both of you." His voice is somber. He wears finer clothes than usual—a gray top hat with a black band, long soft gray pants, and a white shirt snug against his torso. He removes black gloves as he enters, dragging his feet.

"I regret to inform you that proprietor Dillard has passed with the Cycle. He was part-owner of this fine establishment. His gambling debt was settled with my fifty percent ownership, and his remaining share transferred to me upon his death."

Toby and Rondu watch him without expression.

Beo strolls the shop, touching tables and wares. He clears his throat. "I regret to inform you that I will be retiring the shop and establishing a new, more profitable business on these grounds."

"What?!" Toby is on her feet. She's on the cusp of throttling Beo, but Rondu holds her back.

Beo glances at the exit, but continues. "Patches and glue hold this shop together. There's no value in maintaining a business likely to collapse at any moment. Dillard didn't invest in his operation."

"And how is that our fault?!" Toby yells. "I put my heart and soul into making you and that worthless old man money, and now you're going to dump us on the street? What about the money we owe?"

Beo swallows. "You will still owe the money, but will have to manage a different trade to obtain it as a laborer or otherwise."

She punches a wall and knocks over a table. "How is this fair?! You get everything you want, and we get nothing but debt! We hardly receive any profit already. What is life as a laborer going to lead to?"

Beo opens his mouth. Rondu speaks first. "It's time to leave, Beo." His voice brooks no argument, icy blue eyes piercing the dim lighting.

Beo recoils. He put on his hat and offers a quiet farewell. The door shuts. The shop falls silent.

TOBY CURLS into herself near the warm embers of the forge, watching the hypnotic dance of flames. The dark orange glow flickers across her soot-streaked face.

"There was a time when living outside of Gallow seemed like a great adventure. I dreamed of it when I was younger. Told my dad I would have incredible stories to tell him." She releases a long, sorrowful exhale. "Now, older and wiser, I wish it were still just a dream."

She looks back at Rondu. A tear rolls down her cheek, splashing onto the dirt floor. "When do we get to win, Fento? Why are we always on the losing side of things?"

He sits beside her, resting his head on her sturdy shoulder. His sigh matches hers in length and sorrow. "I wish I knew, Karal. Every time we win, we somehow lose more."

They stare at the dwindling flames. Rondu wipes away her tears as they fall. "I wouldn't want to ruin your disguise," he teases, offering a weak grin.

Toby's mouth twitches after a few seconds. A faint smirk appears. "You should have let me punch him."

Rondu chuckles. "I almost did."

"I'd feel better if he had a gap in his teeth. His smug face irritates me."

Rondu raises his eyebrows. "Did you notice his personality changed?"

Toby shakes her head.

"When you threatened him, I saw him break character. He was afraid of you—deathly afraid." Rondu huffs. "I think the real Beo is a scared man. He puts on a brave face, but when I've confronted him, he shatters quickly."

Toby snickers. tilting her head to study Rondu. "Maybe I'm used to you or know you too well, but you aren't threatening." She rubs his ears and smiles.

Rondu clenches his teeth and shoots her his harshest glare. She laughs and tackles him, tickling him in every spot she knows he's most sensitive. They wrestle until she finds a vulnerability.

"I surrender! Please!" Rondu shrieks as she attacks his armpits.

She takes a deep breath and stands, offering her hand. "The shop is closed. I refuse to give Beo any more money today. I'll donate my efforts to the Tipsy Tavern."

He takes her hand and stands next to her, nodding. They put their arms over each other's shoulders and head out the main door, work forgotten, the forge left to die down.

THE TAVERN IS QUIET, even for noon. Tomas greets them, surprised to see them so early. Sela lights up as the pair sits at their usual corner table. Toby is unusually chatty as drinks are served. She eats a light lunch and drinks several more tankards than she should.

She sings naughty songs and drags several drunk patrons into the chorus. Rondu joins a few of the ditties, keeping watch as he holds back from drinking himself.

When Toby dances with Sela, Rondu almost interrupts, but Tomas teases him about letting the lovebirds dance for a while.

They twirl around the empty tavern in an uneven dance, keeping a foot apart, Sela doing most of the navigating.

"You are so handsome, Toby. I like your soft face. Stubble makes me itch." Sela talks with a lisp that Toby enjoys.

"And you are so pretty, Sela." Toby slurs. Sela keeps her upright.

Sela grins across at Tomas, giddy. She asks Toby to flex, impressing Sela with her strength.

Rondu watches their dance grow less casual by the second.

Sela moves closer and lowers her head to Toby's chest. She looks up in surprise.

Rondu is there in an instant. "I'm sorry, Sela. It's getting late. We have orders to fill, and I need to sober this boy up, or we'll be working all night." He smiles as he steers Toby away.

Sela drifts back to the bar, disappointed, as Tomas watches her with a wide grin. "How was your dream boy?"

Sela snorts. "Stinky. And wearing armor or something."

"What do you mean?"

She watches the pair disappear through the door. "He was wearing something hard on his chest. I couldn't lie my head and feel his pecs." She sighs and returns to her duties.

Tomas watches them go, curious.

RONDU GUIDES a drunk Toby out into the early afternoon sun. They both squint as they move through the crowd. A large assembly has gathered near the Posts.

Weekly, several individuals are disciplined for violations of the Law—mostly whippings and other corporal punishment. Toby and Rondu always avoid the display. Memories of Gallow still haunt Toby. But today, she drunkenly drifts toward it, drawn by the size and rowdiness of the crowd.

The masses hurl curses and rotten fruit at a figure that Toby can't see through the press of bodies. The frenzy grows until they all suddenly go silent and part swiftly. Toby turns to see what they're staring at when she spots the unmistakable figure of a Klenzeer approaching.

She tumbles backward into Rondu. "They're coming for us," she mumbles.

He catches her and holds her steady, his own face still. He whispers, "The Klenzeer isn't here for us. Look at the Posts."

Toby turns. The figure comes into view, and her mouth drops.

"That is a Twun," Rondu says quietly.

Hanging from the Posts is a wretched figure. His face is divided— half resembling a Loper, half a One, split by a muddled line where both halves meet. The Loper side carries an orange eye, fur, and a scarred snout. The other side is a boy of fourteen or fifteen—brown eye, bushy eyebrow, scars, no nose, only a breathing hole. Loper ears top both sides of his head; the One side also has a malformed One ear. His mouth is tipped with fangs and a partially formed muzzle. Excess skin is pulled tight on the One side—a fuzzy chin sports both stubble, skin, and fur in spots.

His body tells a different story. A strong, broad chest glistens with sweat. Veins cross tightly formed abdominals. Fur mixes with flesh across his stomach, puckered with old scars. Broad shoulders support scattered fur down his arms and back. His hands end in long fingers tipped with black claws. He wears torn, stained pants cut at the knee. His legs are shaped like a slopeback's—the knee at the front of the hind leg, a sharp hock joint angling back where the ankle would be, ending in large pawed feet with long black nails. A prominent skeletal tail, partially furred, extends behind him.

The Twun growls as the Klenzeer approaches. She grips a broad, square-headed hammer on a long metal shaft, tipped with a dull black pike.

When she turns, Toby snarls.

The square falls utterly silent.

The Klenzeer surveys the mass, frowning, eyes cold. She spits on the ground. "What you see here violates the Law of Purity. One of your own mated with a Loper, producing this beast. Look upon it and understand why your benevolent Overseers created this Law. This monster is an aberration. He shames us with his deformity. He is a stain upon us all."

The hush holds. Then the Twun speaks—and the crowd flinches.

"Is it a crime to live? I had no choice in my birth. I had no choice in my parentage. My sin was to be born undecided in my nature. What punishment should I face for—"

The Klenzeer swings the flat head of her hammer into his chest. The air leaves him.

He takes a deep breath and presses on. "What punishment is birth if you cannot control it? Don't I deserve—"

Another blow. "SILENCE! You have no power or rights here!

Blame your parents for coupling where it is not allowed. What I do is merciful. You will be taken to the Central Gardens, where you will be disposed of. You are here as an example to this community, to help them understand what evil befouls Ra when Laws are not obeyed."

The Twun lifts his head. "Don't I deserve to be judged by those who look upon me in disgust and pity? Don't I—"

The hammer strikes his face. The crack echoes through the square. His head lolls. He goes limp.

Toby looks away. Rondu does not.

The Klenzeer raises her hammer in triumph. The crowd stirs to a cheer. She flexes, her tight black uniform hugging every muscle.

Toby and Rondu leave hurriedly. At the edge of the square, Toby turns and curses at the crowd with a hand gesture. Rondu lowers her hand, eyes wide.

"How can they do that to a person? It's not right. He's a living, breathing person,"

"This is not the place to debate the Laws. We have no control over this."

She stops. "Feng to the Laws. They are built to oppress us, not guide us."

"Karal." His voice is low and careful. "We have to be careful to stay safe. Ormant, Gallow—they're all like this. They're taught to hate things that counter expectation."

Rondu leads them home.

From a recessed alley, a cloaked figure steps out and watches them go.

INVITATION

When Toby and Rondu arrive at the shop, Toby is sobering—she lost most of her lunch somewhere on the walk home and now lies on the floor groaning, the world spinning.

"What did I do to myself?"

Rondu sits beside her and strokes her short mohawk, rubbing her head with his claws.

"That feels nice." She breathes softly between moans. "What is a Twun?"

Rondu sighs. "It's complicated." He looks around the quiet shop, darker with the forge extinguished, then back at her waiting face. "Twuns are born like this, or so I'm led to believe. I've only ever seen one other. My Klenzeer told me that Lopers and Ones are tied together. They're intimately related branches from the same family tree. If they mate, it's like mating with a close sibling. Mutations happen. It doesn't make sense to me—neither species looks anything alike.

"Generations of each have been born over many Cycles, but the results are always the same. Their bodies are volatile when pairing. That sad creature on the Posts is the result of an unfortunate union."

Toby looks incredulous. "And somehow it's justified to kill him? As easy as that?" She shakes her head. "He's the example to parade in front of all these gullible people, so they can keep living in fear."

Rondu nods.

"I can't believe—" She winces, head throbbing. "Can you get me some water or maybe something to eat?"

Rondu bounces up and scans for his pack. "I have something better than that." He finds it and rummages through it, head popping up between searches. "Have you been going through this? Everything's out of place."

Toby shakes her head, remaining quiet.

"Found it!" He sets a pot to boil on the flat top of the forge. Even cooler than usual, it still resonates with impressive heat. When the water bubbles, he pours it into a large mug with several pieces of brown root floating in the liquid. "Ovega tea will fix you right up."

Toby thanks him and drinks.

A peaceful silence settles between them. After a few minutes, her face eases, and she lets out a grateful moan—then a rapid, pounding fist slams on the smithy door. She groans. "We're closed!"

More knocking, a bang, and a young voice. "Dillard?!"

Toby hauls herself to the door and opens it, nearly fainting from the sunlight. A boy around ten or eleven rushes in.

"Where's old Dillard? I need him!"

"He's dead. The Cycle took him."

The boy runs in circles, talking to himself. "What will I do? She'll kill me. I can't come back empty-handed."

Toby catches him by the hand and kneels to his level. "What do you need and who needs it?"

"More shackles! We have to restrain the beast with more shackles! The scary woman demands it!"

Toby's jaw tightens. "I can get you more shackles if you'll shut up."

The boy quiets from the reprimand, staring at the ground.

She releases his hand and crosses to an old wooden box, sifting through Dillard's junk. She pulls out two shackles and holds them up.

The boy's face splits into a wide smile. He reaches for them, but Toby lifts them high out of his reach and looks down at him. "That woman in black is afraid of your beast. She's nothing but a bully. You should learn to stand up to bullies."

The boy blanches. "That beast would eat me if he had the chance. He's got those big claws and that horrid face. I'll stand behind the lady in black. She's less scary."

Toby drops the shackles. "Get lost."

The boy rushes out, slamming the door behind him. Toby winces, palms her face, and ambles towards the straw bed. She swallows the rest of the tea. "You're in charge. I'm going to sleep this thing off."

Rondu shakes his head, smiling at the absurdity of the scene. He grabs a broom and starts sweeping.

~

IT IS late afternoon when a solitary knock sounds from the door, sounding more like an accidental tap. Rondu pauses what he's doing, scans for feet below the threshold, then moves to the door. He takes a deep sniff and detects nothing. He opens the door to no one.

He's scratching his head when he notices a note tacked to the hole Toby made with her hammer.

He steps outside and looks up and down the road. People pass him by without noticing, going about their routines. He removes the note and reads it, stopping halfway through. He looks up and examines his surroundings with greater scrutiny, inhaling the nearby scents. Nothing familiar. He shuts the door with a solid pull.

He's rereading the note for a third time when Toby yawns from across the shop. She stretches, rubs her face, and eventually stands.

"Whatcha got there?" She yawns again, trying to shake off the last traces of sleep.

He passes the note without a word. Toby reads it aloud.

"North Road past the square. White, two-story house on the west side of the road. Orange door. Look for the 'X' mark on

*the lower left of the door. Knock three times, wait a moment,
then knock a fourth time. Tonight for dinner."*

"Who left this? When did you get it?"

"I have no clue who left it or how long it's been on our door. I thought I heard a knock a few minutes ago, but no one was there."

"What should we do with it?"

Rondu hesitates. "I don't know."

"Well, should we go? Do you think it'll be safe? I'll admit, I'm curious." Toby flips the note over and finds no clues.

Rondu rereads it. "If we go, we go armed and ready to fight. I can't imagine this came from that Klenzeer. She seems like the loud, action-oriented type. This is someone more cautious."

Toby nods and takes a sip of water. A small smile. "Sparring practice to prepare?"

Rondu grins. They should prepare for anything.

As the sky darkens and stars fade in, Toby and Rondu leave the shop. Toby carries her hammer. Rondu palms short, sharp knives in his pockets.

When they near the square, a small crowd still throws rotten food and harsh words at the Twun. The Klenzeer is nowhere to be seen. They rush past without looking.

Heading north, they scan the area for a two-story house on the west side. In the dark, white homes are hard to distinguish from light gray ones. As the houses become more spread out, they find their destination tucked between two others.

Rondu points to the X on the lower left of a door, sketched in charcoal.

They walk past the house, watching for anything off.

"Well, what do you think? It doesn't seem like an ambush," Toby whispers.

Rondu nods. "I guess we should try it."

Toby moves to the side of the doorway out of sight, raising her hammer. Rondu palms his knives in his pockets. He swallows and nods at her.

Three knocks. A pause. A fourth.

His hackles rise at the sound of approaching footsteps. He drops into a defensive stance.

The door swings inward.

Surprise flashes across Rondu's face.

UNUSUAL ENCOUNTERS

Standing at the doorway is Beo Luca.

Rondu darts his eyes around and sniffs, but only notices the smell of food cooking and sees nothing unusual. His tension eases.

"Did Toby not come?" Beo looks past the threshold.

She steps out from the side, hammer in hand, face filled with confusion. "Did you write the note?"

Beo nods. "Come inside, hurry. I have nosy neighbors."

Inside, the home is lavish and tastefully decorated. Beo walks ahead and signals them to follow. Their mouths fall open. The home has an unexpected decadence, reminiscent of an art gallery. Beautiful paintings decorate most walls, several displaying landscapes from various regions of Ra. A few portraits hang in gold leaf frames. One notable portrait of Beo standing beside a wrinkled old woman hangs above a fireplace. Sculptures of slopebacks and forest animals sit on pedestals and tables throughout. The couches and chairs in the sitting area look new and unused. Several rooms branch off from the central foyer, each decorated with a unique theme. The kitchen is large and well-used, shelves filled with ingredients and cookware. Stew bubbles over a fire, its aroma immediately sharpening their hunger. Wine bottles of various vintages sit in a polished wooden rack.

Toby glares at Beo while he samples the stew. When he turns, he stops at her expression. "Would you like some wine?"

She shakes her head. "Why are we here?"

Beo fumbles. "Not up here. Somewhere more private. Follow me."

He grabs the pot and leads them down a set of stairs to a basement. Broken furniture and old crates crowd the corners. In the middle, a table is set with cloth, plates, and utensils. Two candelabras drip wax from long, thin silver candles. A mix of fruits and cheeses already sits on plates alongside mugs of water.

"I'll grab some wine." Beo heads upstairs, Rondu following close behind.

When they return, Beo carries four bottles. Rondu carries one and sips from a glass, nodding at Toby. "It's a good vintage."

Once settled, Toby's patience runs out, "Why are we here, Beo?"

"After dinner, I promise." He offers a wary smile.

Her anger eases after a full meal. The stew is tasty and thoroughly enjoyed. She even sips wine, mostly because everyone else is.

She and Rondu stare as their host looks around nervously. He rises unsteadily, wine glass in hand, and drains it. "I know you both have secrets." He points to Toby. "I know you are female." He points to Rondu. "And you were a Klenzeer or wore their cloth somehow."

Both chairs tumble as they stand, weapons drawn, eyes sharp.

"Are you turning us over to that Klenzeer?" Toby shouts.

Rondu's hackles rise, eyes narrowed.

Beo drops to his knees, trembling. "No—no. I wanted to clear the air. I'm sorry. I've never done this before." He swallows. "I'm a—I'm a —Twun."

"What?! No, you aren't!" Toby shouts.

Beo nods.

"Prove it!" Rondu growls.

As slowly as possible, Beo raises his hands and moves his hair away from his ears. Behind them are a second set of clipped ears sewn into his flesh. He lowers his hands to his mouth and removes false teeth. Only two large canines remain, jutting out like fangs. He drags a fingernail against another, revealing black beneath.

Toby and Rondu stare.

"Well, that changes things." Toby rights her chair, sits, drains her glass, and pours another.

Rondu stands with his arms at his sides, working through it. "This is the real you, isn't it?"

Beo nods. "I have to be somebody different to survive. My mother, bless her heart, was tough and got me through many hardships. This is just one of the things she made me become to keep surviving."

"How long have you been in Ormant?"

"Fifty or more Cycles. It's hard to remember."

Rondu tilts his head. "You don't look that old."

A tepid smile. "I don't sleep during the Cycle's end. I'm unaffected by it."

Rondu sits down. "How is that possible? Everything sleeps."

"Not me," Beo grimaces. "Not since my age of reckoning."

"What is the age of reckoning?"

Beo pours himself more wine nearly to the brim. His face goes melancholic. "It is the age when a boy changes to a Twun."

"So you didn't start off as a Twun?" Toby asks.

"No." He pauses, eyes drifting to the floor. "For a Twun, it happens at puberty. When your hormones are ready to mature a boy into a man, the blood of a Twun becomes reactive to the aging at a Cycle's end. It's a violent change that wakes you with intense pain in the middle of it all. The body gets confused about whether you are a One or a Loper. It feels like your body is actively splitting while you're awake; parts of you change, others don't. Since that moment, I haven't experienced another unnatural aging. I am immune to it."

Rondu leans in. "So you've watched Cycles end? You know what occurs during them?"

Beo stands and paces. "It's an incredible process, unlike anything you've ever seen. The moon turns red. Sounds fill the air. Streams of blood-red liquid approach everything and cause you to age. I watched it happen many times to my mother before she passed. The liquid ignores me like I don't exist." His voice drops. "And the Over-seers come."

Toby and Rondu go still. Neither moves for an extended moment. Then Toby leans forward, hands on the table. "What do they look like?"

As Beo begins to speak, Rondu loses focus. His eyes glaze. The room fades to black. His own voice echoes back to him from some-where far away—*rain, chains, choking, howling, woods, rain, chains, choking, howling*—repeating endlessly. Then another voice joins, bass and unfamiliar. *Fento, you will live to the end. You must. You must.* It rises to a scream. *YOU MUST!*

A shudder runs through him. He snaps back. Beo is talking, but the words have slipped past. When Beo stops, he looks at Rondu. "Are you alright?"

Rondu nods. Toby watches him. He mouths, *don't worry*, and she turns back to Beo.

"How do you know about us?" Rondu asks, steadying himself.

Beo looks down. "I was afraid of you two. Something about our meeting a while back left me feeling ill." He takes a long sip of wine. "I had the bridge investigated, and traces of a dead Klenzeer were found." He raises his hands when he sees their faces change. "Don't worry, I've told no one. Only one other knows, and he's not aware of you two."

He drains more wine and continues.

"When the Overseers float about at Cycles' end, I pretend to sleep. It's the only way to avoid them. I almost got caught once. After they leave, there's a quiet period. I went to your shop and looked around." He describes the blood on Toby's pants and the Klenzeer uniform, then falls silent, his eyes settling on Rondu.

"What?" Rondu asks.

"You spoke in your sleep."

"I did? Maybe I was dreaming? What did I say?" Rondu tilts his head, confused.

"You turned your head to me, eyes closed, and said, 'DO NOT RETURN'." Beo's face tightens. It frightened me to the bone."

Toby and Rondu exchange glances. Rondu stays quiet, shaking his head slowly.

Beo continues when no response follows.

"I'd had enough by then, so I decided to sell the shop. It was impulsive. I'm sorry." He looks away.

"Then why are we here?" Toby asks.

A wry smile. "It's because of you, Toby."

She points to herself. "Me?"

"It was quite by accident, really. I heard about the Twun in the square and decided to see him from the shadows—out of curiosity. He was much more disfigured than I became, and I felt sorry for him the moment I saw him." Beo's voice softens. "That's when I heard you both arguing near the edge of the crowd. You railed against his treatment. It filled me with such joy." He smiles. "I had to meet you. The real you."

Toby returns the smile, but Rondu's brow draws in.

"What's the matter? Toby asks.

Rondu leans forward, arms crossed. "What do you want from us, Beo? Your timing is suspicious. You could have waited days or weeks to talk to us. Why tonight?"

Beo stares at the floor. His breath holds. Several seconds pass.

"Spit it out," Rondu snaps.

A long exhale. Beo eyes lift slowly. "I want to contract both of you to help me free the Twun."

DECISIONS

"**A**re you out of your damn mind?!" Rondu doesn't rein in his anger. "It would be madness to try and free that Twun with a Klenzeer so close."

Beo begins pacing. "I understand this request is risky but—"

"No, not risky—it's suicidal!"

Toby watches him pace. "Beo, how are we going to free the Twun? He's chained to the Posts day and night. There's no way we'd get access to him."

"I have a plan that might work. There are risks for all of us, but I'm set on trying it if it will free my brother."

Rondu raises his voice. "Your brother? You hardly know who he is! What if he's deranged? You know nothing of his background or upbringing. For all we know, he could be as evil and dangerous as the Klenzeer proclaims."

"Beo, this is unreasonable." Toby stands, rubbing her temples. "There's nothing in the world that would make us want to do this. We got lucky at the bridge."

Beo stops pacing. His voice goes steady. "The shop. I would give it to you."

Toby and Rondu look up.

Beo's confidence builds as he speaks. "You both came into my office expressing how you would do anything to get out from under my thumb. Well, this is it." He looks up, voice dropping. "I'm alone in Ormant. My mother was my only friend, and she passed long ago. There's no one here who is closer to me than an acquaintance. I shared my secret with you to build trust. I have no one else I can share this plan with without someone summoning the Klenzeer. I'm asking—no, begging you to help, because I have no one else to ask. I am in agony watching someone else who resembles me in spirit suffer in front of the masses. My heart breaks for him. And if I could do one thing in my miserable life that's positive, it would be to free him."

Thunder booms overhead. Beo sinks into his chair. He pours more wine. "I'm a charlatan, Toby. Rondu reads me well. I'm weak and fearful, but I'm not cold."

Rondu sips his wine, watching Beo. "What is your plan?"

Hope flashes across Beo's face. "I've been told that the Twun will be moved in two days, so our options are limited. I planned to invite the Klenzeer to speak with the Town Council away from the Posts. She seems excitable. We would drink and eat with her there, distract her, while you both release the Twun and help him escape."

He reaches beneath his collar and unties a necklace. From it hangs a single canine tooth, old and chipped. "To the north of here, there's a pack of Lopers with whom I was raised. The chief, Amarack, was like a father to me. His son, Jowao, was like a brother. If you bring this Twun to them, they will adopt him into the pack, I'm certain of it." He holds the tooth out. Yellowed with age, it dangles like a medallion. "This will announce your friendship to the pack. Tell them, brother Jarden sent you."

Toby and Rondu watch it uncertainly.

"There's so much risk, Beo." Toby rubs her temples. "Any one of us could slip up."

"Or the Twun could be a deranged lunatic." Rondu's voice is flat.

Silence. Rain falls overhead. Beo sinks deeper into his chair.

"I don't know if we can do it, Beo." Toby's voice is quiet. "You're dangling something valuable, but the risk doesn't balance the reward."

Beo hands ball into fists. He shakes his head. "I'm sorry to hear this. It's hard to hear. Thank you for listening to me. I'm honorable—I won't sell the shop, but the contract remains."

Toby clenches, about to protest, but Rondu's hand and gentle shake of his head stop her. They thank Beo and climb the stairs from the basement.

Outside, the rain falls in sheets. They dash home, dodging swelling puddles. As they cross the square, Rondu slows to a stop.

The Twun lies on the wet ground, arms shackled above him, rain bouncing off his flesh. Even in the faint glow of the posted lanterns, the bruising from the Klenzeer's hammer is visible. His face is swollen, and the mark of the chest strike is clear.

He looks up at them. His face is steady. He sniffs the air and studies Toby head to toe, tilting his head. When he turns to Rondu, his expression shifts. His eyes narrow. A low growl escapes him. Rondu holds the glare, eyes steady.

As Rondu walks away, Toby follows and whispers, "What was that?"

"We were taking a measure of each other."

"And?"

"We have much to talk about."

KNOCK, KNOCK

Morning dawns dark gray. A heavy hand thuds against the shop door. "Where are you, smith?" The Klenzeer's bass voice carries through the planks.

She stands outside in her black uniform, broad as a tunku and just as impatient. Townsfolk give her a wide berth. She scratches her head, turns, and mutters as she walks away. "I will seek you again, Toby and Rondu. I'll have to thank Tomas for the tip. Suspicious individuals should always be followed up on."

Her hammer swings at her side as her scarred, sturdy body lopes down the main thoroughfare. Rain begins to sprinkle. She pays it no attention. She is impervious—she is a Klenzeer.

⌒

THE CHARCOAL X has faded in the rain. Rondu knocks on Beo's door, three knocks, then a fourth seconds later. The rain falls in sheets, soaking them both.

"Maybe he's not home?" Toby pulls her hood up.

Rondu grins. "He's home. His kind don't wake this early. He's likely hungover." He crouches before the lock and picks it while Toby shields him from prying eyes.

They step in and relock the door. "Go make us some yubu," Rondu says. "Beo will need a stiff drink this morning." He winks and heads upstairs.

Beo's snores echo from the end of a hall. Rondu follows the sound into a luxurious bedroom with a bed larger than any he's ever seen. Vibrant oil paintings and sturdy wooden furniture opulently decorate the space. Even the soft, white rug looks pristine. The luxury is obnoxious.

A wild smile forms on Rondu's face. He jumps onto the bed and draws his knife.

Beo wakes in a panic. "Mercy! What are you doing here? Are you robbing me?"

Rondu lowers the blade to Beo's throat. Cold steel against flesh. A high-pitched gasp escapes. Clattering sounds rise from the kitchen below.

Rondu asks, his voice coarse, "How do you take your yubu?"

Beo's face flickers between terror and confusion. "Sugar—sugar with some nectar."

Rondu removes the knife as he winks. He leans out the door and calls down the order, then exits the bedroom, leaving Beo staring at the ceiling.

A loud, exasperated sigh echoes.

Beo enters the kitchen to find a disaster. A towering pile of burnt toast sits on a plate. Greasy, charred jambo rests in a bowl. Runny eggs spill onto his once spotless table. He takes a sip of the offered yubu and nearly spits it out.

Toby speaks with a mouthful of toast, black crumbs spreading across the table. "We talked about it last night. We're in. But your plan needs to be foolproof. We need to review every detail. This has to be perfect."

Rondu's voice is friendly but grave. "We're walking a fine line, Beo. If there are any doubts, we will pull out."

Beo looks at them both, burnt toast in hand. They are vastly different in personality, in style, in everything. But the confidence behind their grave faces is satisfying.

He grins and explains the details.

THE RAIN CONTINUES, alternating between heavy and light. Near noon, Beo stands before an ornate wooden door, in a soaked black leather cloak. He knocks and waits.

A stiff man with a pronounced overbite bows slightly. "Good morning, Master Beo. If you're looking for the Master, he's upstairs."

"Thank you, Gregan. It's pitiful outside."

Gregan leads him to the second floor, where a short, portly man wobbles forward with an outstretched hand. Bald on top with dark hair on the sides, he has warm, youthful eyes. He grins with too many teeth. "Beo, how wonderful to see you again. How is business? Have any new gossip I might be able to use?"

"Raveno, it is a delight to see you, my friend." Beo extends his arms for a hug, and they embrace. He whispers, "Nothing concrete to offer, though news of a new vein of ore is circulating."

Raveno settles into his throne-like chair behind a gleaming reddish desk, while Beo takes the simpler seat across. "And what do I owe the pleasure of your company? I heard it might rain all day. How disappointing."

"It gives us more time to count our coffers." Beo smiles.

A light chuckle. "You're witty, Beo. I appreciate you. What can I do for you?"

Beo's expression darkens as he leans in. "I've been receiving complaints. My clients are worried about that beast in the square. They're threatening to pull out if this becomes a regular occurrence."

Raveno rolls his eyes. "Oh, Beo. That beast. It's all I hear about. Everyone's upset and worried it will break free. I tried to convince the Klenzeer to take it away, but she insists on keeping it here for a few more days. She says it's educational." He throws his hands up. "Bah! It's disgusting and a threat."

"Is there something you can tell her to discourage her from bringing more?"

"I wish it were that simple. She's a Klenzeer. They're beyond reason." Raveno huffs.

They fall into silence. Beo's face brightens, then falls.

"Have you got something?"

"I don't know, it's tricky." Beo waffles.

"I'll take anything at this point. I'm desperate."

Beo lets the idea form slowly. "Perhaps we can convince the Klenzeer that the best lessons require no examples. Maybe we can invite her to speak on the evils we should avoid so she can feel confident that Ormant has learned from her example and needs no refresher."

Raveno tilts his head, his eyes narrowing. "How so? She's a Klenzeer."

"She seems like a person who exists for praise. I've flattered plenty in my lifetime. She just needs convincing. We can honor her and let her educate us. I'm sure she's a normal person at heart."

"She's a lunatic!" Raveno moans. "I've offered her my assistant, but she constantly requests my presence. Even the slightest bend of the Law, and she's raging through the town. Townsfolk are terrified of her. The Council is up in arms, demanding I do something."

"Then we must meet with her! Show her that we'll listen to her and become stricter in Ormant. Bring in the constables and the Council. We can persuade her that we're ready to meet her standards. That way, she leaves satisfied that she doesn't need to bring more examples to town."

Raveno goes quiet. The frustration drains from his face, replaced by something that looks almost like excitement. "That might work." He sits up. "That's genius!"

EVENING APPROACHES. Puddles line the main road. Toby and Rondu walk south from the shop at a hurried pace. When they reach a stout wooden door, Toby raps with her fist.

Impatient, she's about to knock again when it swings open.

A tall, elderly man with a stern face looks out. "Yeah, what do you want?"

Rondu presents a note kept dry under his cloak. The man snatches it and reads it by the light of his home. When he returns to the door, something eases in him. He points to each of them individually. "Friends of Beo or caught in a favor owed to him?"

Both answer, "Favor."

The man laughs, sarcasm woven through it. "Which one of you is Toby?"

She nods.

"You're Rondu, then?" He arches an eyebrow at the other.

Rondu returns a smile.

He shakes their hands. "The name's Noly. Like you, I owe Beo for some trouble he got my son out of." A regretful shake of his head. "As I read it, you're both heading north to visit Toby's family. Rondu, you're the navigator, but Toby's in charge?"

"Yessir," Toby answers.

"And you two need my Buttercup and a wagon to haul some furniture out of Beo's to burn on the way up north?"

Toby nods. "You read it right, Noly."

Noly looks out at the heavy rain. "Hell of a storm to burn stuff in."

Rondu chuckles. "We'll figure it out."

"That Beo." Noly shakes his head. "Such a truga."

LATER THAT EVENING, back at the shop, Toby and Rondu prep for their operation. Buttercup hisses outside, rain pelting her scaly hide. Steady pings emit from the tin roof, a rhythm that should be soothing but amplifies the tension growing in Toby's chest. In an hour, the Klenzeer will be at the meeting hall.

"Tonight," she says. "We're actually going to do this tonight."

Rondu nods, his blue eyes catching what little light filters through the grimy windows.

She flexes her swollen hands, feeling the ache in her knuckles. Two Cycles of servitude. Two Cycles of being owned by Beo, working herself to exhaustion for scraps. Two Cycles since they watched Xytel fall at the bridge.

"Do you think she'd approve?" The question escapes before she can stop it.

Rondu's tail stills. "Xytel?" He's quiet for a long moment. "I think she'd tell us we are doing the right thing, even for a stranger."

"And then?"

A small smile touches his muzzle. "And then she'd insist on coming to help."

Toby blinks away the burn behind her eyes. She's cried enough. This task requires clear eyes and steady hands.

"We could still decide not to do this," Rondu says. "There's a lot of risk."

"I'm not quitting. It's the right thing to do. We can't let them win."

"Xytel would be proud of you."

"We'll succeed. Fulfill our pact with her."

"The Village of Any." Rondu's voice is quiet.

He reaches across the darkness and finds her hand. His paw is warm despite the chill. "Tonight changes everything. If we free this Twun—if we actually do this—we'll earn our own freedom. No one will own us."

"We'll be free to go north." Toby squeezes his paw.

The rain intensifies. Somewhere in Ormant, the Klenzeer prepares for her meeting, confident in her power. On the Posts, the Twun lies miserable, chained and wet. At the meeting hall, Beo drains a glass of wine as the seats begin to fill.

Toby closes her eyes and thinks of Xytel—of her strength, her loyalty, her sacrifice. *We won't waste it.*

"We should go," Rondu says softly. "The meeting starts soon."

"I know." She doesn't move yet. "Just one more moment."

They hold hands in the darkness, letting the weight of what they're about to do settle over them. This isn't like fleeing the Klenzeer at the bridge. This is choosing to walk into danger. This is choosing to act instead of react.

"For Xytel," Rondu whispers.

"For us," Toby adds.

They rise together, check their tools one last time—the hammer, the knives, the wagon waiting outside—and step out into the storm.

ACCORDING TO PLAN

Seated at the bar at the back of the spacious meeting hall, Beo settles into a high-backed chair. The wine in his trembling hand leaves red streaks down the glass. He downs it in one gulp.

Thunder rumbles overhead. The rain pings in a steady percussive beat. His heart hammers in time with it.

The window near the bar shows nothing but darkness and rain. His own pale reflection stares back.

What is happening out there?

Sudden applause jolts him from his watch.

The doors to the hall open wide. The Klenzeer enters, black-and-gold uniform immaculate, stretched tight against her sturdy frame. Her tight braid of dark hair is brushed out, softening her appearance, but authority emanates from her like heat from a forge.

She nods and waves politely, her smile uneasy.

Beo takes his cue and rushes to her, wine glass extended for a toast. She stares at the offered goblet. Her mouth twitches—something threatening flashes across her face. Then it's gone, replaced by a smug grin. She drains the glass in one pull.

Cheers erupt. More drinks appear. By the time the Klenzeer settles at the lectern, she's downed four glasses with a fifth in hand.

Raveno waddles to the front, keeping his distance. Sweat glistens on his forehead. "I would like to welcome everybody to a special meeting of the Council. We have an esteemed guest tonight. Representing our benevolent Overseers, please welcome their Klenzeer."

The throng of two hundred stands and claps. The Klenzeer bows, a flushed grin on her face.

From the front row, the town council applauds lightly. Constables sit directly behind, their rougher appearance a stark contrast to the affluent council. Behind them, guilds and trade union reps form a wide barrier, while exuberant citizens stand in the back, eager to curry favor.

Beo watches the masses from the back. All inside. All distracted. All away from the Posts.

Raveno drones through town business. Minutes crawl by. When he finally yields the floor, tepid applause trails his departure. He squats next to Beo, reaching for a bottle, whispering, "I hope you're right about meeting with the Klenzeer, Beo. My reputation is on the line."

Raveno's pour is heavy-handed.

At the lectern, the Klenzeer straightens, growing taller, puffing her chest. She looks at her notes, then the audience, clenches her jaw, and clears her throat.

"Ormant, as a town, is failing to meet the standards of excellence expected from it."

Eyes blink. Faces fall. A loud cough. Silence. She swallows a large sip of wine and speeds up.

"However, I feel that there's great growth potential here." Engagement returns. "I've analyzed the town during my inspections and offer the following suggestions. The benefits of extended hours for the lowest class and the requirement for farmers to work daily are essential. Tilling and plowing fields should be a priority, not—not—"

She trails off. Her expression goes slack.

Her mouth moves. Words spill out, barely audible. "A large old farmhouse. Tunkas and woolies graze in the meadow. Grandma is speaking to me about the harvest."

A rough shake of her head, followed by a clearing of her throat. The moment evaporates like mist in the sun.

Members of the audience glance at each other, murmuring. Beo's attention pulls from the window.

She presses on. "The assignment of jobs for laborers should be enforced first by age, followed by gender. The strongest persons—should—be—"

Again, she stops. Her eyes find the ceiling. Words slip out, growing louder.

"A Klenzeer is here? Why is he here, Momma? Momma?" She shudders. "Don't touch me! Where are you taking me?! Help me Momma—"

Blinking rapidly, she resumes where she trailed off, unaware of the break. "—first in line to receive credits. We should encourage hard work and reward credits, followed by the first choice of partnering for those of breeding age."

Beo stands, slowly. His eyes dart to the window. Nothing.

"Beo." Raveno's voice is tight. "What is wrong with her?"

A loud gulp. "The wine," Beo mumbles.

The audience speaks in low tones. The Klenzeer continues unaffected.

"Additionally, we should enforce the privilege of—"

She gasps as if the air has been drained from the room.

Her mouth vibrates. Fear floods her face. Her eyes go dead.

"Why am I strapped down?!" Her pitch climbs toward a shriek. "Who are you?! What—what is that machine?!"

Tremors overtake her hand. Wine spills. Notes scatter to the floor.

"What are you going to do with tha—"

She howls.

Tears stream down her face.

"IT'S BURNING ME! MY FLESH IS BURNING!"

Her whole body convulses.

"STOP! IT HURTS SO MUCH! DON'T! PLEASE! NO MORE!"

Chairs scrape. People back away. Every face turns to Raveno.

He is as white as a sheet. "Beo, what do we do?"

Beo's glass drops, shattering in a spray of crystal. His breath quickens. He forces himself forward, one foot in front of the other, floorboards creaking with each step. His heart pounds in his ears like a fierce drum. Audience members watch slack-jawed as he plods to the front of the grand hall down the main aisle.

He stops before the lectern.

The Klenzeer rocks back and forth, reciting the Laws in perfect order, eyes vacant. Each swing grows more violent.

Tremors run through Beo's hand as he moves toward her—voice shaking. Sweat pours down his temples.

"My—my—my Klenzeer, are you okay? Do—do you need help?"

He waves his hands before her face. Nothing.

Closer—his hand inches toward her shoulder.

His eyes dart from her face to his hand and back.

One foot away.

Six inches.

Three.

He swallows loudly.

One.

His fingertip grazes the deep black threads.

CRUNCH!

The wineglass in her hand explodes.

She moves like lightning, grabbing Beo's wrist, twisting, then forcing him to the ground.

"DON'T TOUCH ME!"

The yell echoes in the silent hall.

Staring down at him, she hesitates. Her mind realigns with her surroundings, eyes rising to look at the assembly. She releases his wrist. Blood drips from glass shards embedded in her palm.

A stern warning surfaces from her training. "Do not consume their poisons." She says it to herself, quietly.

She licks her lips, tasting the remnants of wine, then clears her throat. "I need water. The alcohol has upset my speech. We will recommence in ten minutes. Until then, stay quiet and still!"

Her footsteps echo as she leaves.

A forced calm descends. Council members sit with their hands folded.

Beo returns to his perch, flexing his wrist, wincing. He quietly requests a new glass of wine, drains it, then begs for another. Raveno slides close, "This talk might get us killed. We need to salvage this."

Beo nods.

WHEN THE KLENZEER RETURNS, her braid is tight, her face stone. Whatever broke in her has been sealed away. She stomps to the lectern, frowning at the audience.

She dissects every Law. Catalogues every failure. Her voice cuts like a blade.

Beo stops hearing her words, listening instead for sounds outside —shouts, alarms, anything.

Distant thunder. Heavy rain. Nothing else.

His eyes dart to the window. Blackness stares back.

His grip tightens on the wineglass until his knuckles go white.

When the Klenzeer finishes her speech, a chill spreads.

Beo stands clapping exuberantly. The only one.

The audience stares. No one joins him. Chairs scrape.

Raveno walks grimly to the front. A short bow to the Klenzeer is all he musters before turning to the solemn crowd. He clears his throat. "Thank you for attending. It's been a historic opportunity for us."

Silence.

Beo winces, watching audience members standing. *I have to do something. They need more time.*

Raveno continues. "Thank you, my Klenzeer, for sharing your assessment of our town and the many improvements needed to enhance its standing in your eyes. We'll reconvene at a later time and discuss the hundreds of alterations you suggested to improve our situation." He swallows.

Just as Raveno prepares to leave, Beo rushes to the front. He stands before the audience, smiling cheerfully.

"Grand Klenzeer!" his voice cracks slightly. "Your criticism is invaluable. But—" He smiles wider. "—perhaps you could share what we're doing right? As the largest town in the south, surely there's something worth recognizing?"

The Klenzeer appraises him, then turns to the audience. Her mouth twitches.

"I suppose you deserve some praise. There are things you're doing well. Don't flatter yourselves. The list isn't nearly as exhaustive as you might hope, but Ormant surprised me in some areas."

Beo bows and returns to the bar, exasperated, wrist throbbing. He switches hands to pour another glass.

The Klenzeer speaks again with authority but softer accusations. Faces light up. Council members engage, asking about quotas. Even the constables lean forward. The discussion breathes.

Beo exhales. Minutes tick by.

Raveno slides close. "You're getting better at this by the minute. If I weren't Mayor, the Council would elect you instead."

Beo forces a laugh.

"I was about to fake a fatal illness and be carried away," Raveno smirks.

"Still might," Beo takes another drink. His hand shakes.

He looks toward the window one last time

Darkness stares back.

He's done all he could.

Whether it was enough—he'll know soon enough.

ABSOLUTION

Leather reins bite into Toby's hands. Her breath remains steady despite the shivering. Cold rain pelts relentlessly like an avalanche of tiny rocks. The rusted axles of the wagon grind with each rotation. Loose wooden boards shake with the constant friction of wheels on rutted dirt.

Beside her, Rondu is silent. His watchful eyes stare into the darkness.

"You ready?"

A subtle nod. Nothing else.

The few pedestrians they pass ignore them, too busy fleeing the rain. Toby guides Buttercup around large puddles hiding deep furrows in the road. The cambra clops easily enough in the dim light, her scales deflecting the deluge. Two lanterns tied to the wagon's side provide thin light. The streets themselves are dark—most lamps waterlogged or extinguished.

Toby and Rondu huddle together for warmth, cloaks hiding their faces. They are shadows drifting in the night.

When Ormant's heart comes to view, the square is quiet. Too quiet. Too empty.

Toby guides Buttercup around the fountain, scanning doorways and windows. The brothel is dark. Most surrounding buildings too. The Oak appears to be the only open tavern. At the edge of the square, almost out of sight, the meeting hall glows.

Inside sit Beo and over two hundred townsfolk.

Inside is the Klenzeer.

"Now or never." Rondu's voice sounds unsteady.

Toby stops the wagon diagonally across from the Posts. Thunder rumbles overhead. Her pulse hammers.

The square is empty. No constables. No pedestrians. Just rain and darkness and the Twun watching them from the Posts.

Rondu hands her the key Beo secured for the manacles. His hand is steady. Hers isn't.

"Ready?" he whispers.

She's not. She nods anyway.

Toby's footsteps are agonizingly slow.

The central fountain spills beyond its boundaries, forming a small lake around it. She avoids it, her rhythm steady.

A sharp whistle cuts through the rain.

Her heart stops.

Rondu's signal. Someone's coming.

She drops into a crouch behind the fountain. Water soaks through her cloak. Footsteps. Voices. A high-pitched laugh.

A couple stumbles past, drunk and giggling, heading north. They don't look back.

Toby waits. Counts to ten. Twenty.

The square empties again. She rises and continues.

Ten feet from the posts, her nerves tighten. Her boots feel heavy. One foot in front of the other.

The Twun appears larger than life. Razor-sharp claws. Coiled muscles. He watches her with his uneven face. Faint bruises from the day before are still visible on his body.

They stare at each other in the rain.

"We've come to rescue you."

"Then why are you afraid of me, rescuer?" His tone is brusque, neutral.

Thunder rumbles.

"I'm not afraid of you." Her voice cracks. "I'm afraid for you." She wipes rain from her face. "The last time I was this close to the Posts, I was chained to them—like you. I was stripped of my clothes, my dignity, and my identity. They changed who I am. Forever."

The Twun tilts his head and surprises her with a smile. Heart-breaking and pained. "They may break my body, but never my will." His gaze drifts away from her. "Get behind me quickly. We have company."

Two patrons stagger out of the Oak, intoxicated and boastful. They approach the Twun, who goes still. One squints past the Twun. *Does he see her?* His companion distracts him.

"Okay, Jonah, I—I—bet I can get within five feet." Eli stumbles over both words and feet.

"Don't do it, Eli. That thing will bite you, and you'll start turning into one of them." Jonah's words are less sloppy. He spits water from his thick mustache.

"Nah, I can—I can do this. You watch. He's asleep or dead." He hiccups. "Not sure."

Jonah steps back. "Be careful, little brother."

Eli approaches in short, sober steps. Nine feet. Eight. Seven. He takes a bold step forward, turning to his brother, boastful—when the Twun growls and lunges, snapping inches from Eli's fingers. The chains hold firm.

Jonah yelps, yanking Eli back, feeling him frantically for wounds. Eli joins in, counting his fingers.

"Come closer, and I'll show you how strong a Twun's jaws are." The words drip with sarcasm. A devilish grin. The Twun rattles his chains.

Eli and Jonah scramble away on hands and knees, leaving a muddy trail. Toby covers her mouth, holding back her laugh. The Twun grins over his shoulder. "They will never break my will."

She pulls the key and unlocks a manacle. The Twun lets out a full-bodied sigh of relief, shaking his arm vigorously, wincing as pins and needles force a growl from his lips. She opens the other arm, and he nearly collapses.

"Thank you, rescuer." Genuine gratitude softens his face.

She moves to the ankles and finds one shackle stuck. "Feng. Stay here."

The Twun chuckles. "I have no plans to leave my legs behind."

At the wagon, Rondu touches her arm. "Are you okay? Is he hurt? Can we free him?"

"He's fine. He's not broken. At least not yet. One of the ankles won't open. We need to start sawing." She digs through the cart for their tools.

"This is taking too long. I'll come with you. We have to be quick about this." Rondu gathers everything and carries them across the gap.

The Twun growls as he approaches. "I do not trust you, Fen. Your kind has blood on their hands."

"And you'll have blood all over ours if you don't shut up and work with us," Toby barks back. "He's my best friend, and any grudge you hold against Fen don't matter here. We can leave you behind if you can't handle him."

The Twun grumbles and looks away.

They saw the chains. The blade bites into metal with a grinding shriek. Toby looks up.

The square stays empty. She saws faster.

"Why are you cutting the chains? Only one is stuck."

Rondu responds quickly. "We risk many lives freeing you. They cannot know that a key sets you free. We'll cut partway through a link, but you need to do the rest. You're strong, and we'll help you pull."

"Clever, Fen. We are to fake my escape. I would expect such trickery from you."

Rondu grunts and keeps sawing. About a third of the way through a leg chain, the Twun tells them to step back. He wraps his arms around one of the posts and pulls. Muscles strain. Metal digs into the ankle, blood running dark.

"Stop!" Toby hisses. "You're hurting yourself—"

He ignores her. Face contorted. Pulling harder.

Deep-seated growls escape as the strain vibrates the chain.

Ping.

The link snaps. He collapses, breathing heavily.

The square stays empty.

After a moment, he pushes himself up. "Time is wasting, rescuers. Three more to go."

THREE CHAINS BREAK with increasing difficulty before exhaustion overtakes the Twun. Toby and Rondu add their strength for the last until the entire chain assembly rips from the post.

The chain whips free and slams into the lantern.

Clang!

Glass explodes. The flame dies.

Darkness swallows them whole.

Toby's breath catches. "Rondu?"

"Here." His paw finds her hand. "We need to move. Now."

They half-carry, half-drag the Twun to the wagon. He's heavier than he looks. The remaining chain clinks with every step. At the wagon, he tries to climb in—his legs give. Rondu catches him, grunting. Together, they heave him into the bed. He lands hard, groaning. The wagon shudders. Buttercup hisses.

"Sorry," Toby whispers.

The Twun doesn't answer. He's already snoring.

Rondu studies the unconscious body. Bones protrude from an emaciated frame. "He looks starved. The constables were too scared to get close enough to feed him." He looks up at Toby. "And look at his state." A strong scent of feces and urine emanates from him. "They weren't even kind enough to give him a means to relieve himself."

"I can't believe they were going to kill him." She unwraps a dark tarp and covers him, tucking in the corners. "This is the right thing to do, Fento. Let's hurry."

They climb onto the wagon, hands shaking. Adrenaline fading. Cold seeping in. Toby clicks at Buttercup. The cambra moves forward, slow and steady.

Every window feels like it's watching them.

Toby exhales. "I can't believe we still have furniture to move."

Rondu glances back at the tarp-covered shape. "That's the least of our worries." He pulls back his hood, ears erect, and extends his palms face up. A grin slowly forms. "At least the rain is stopping."

Toby clicks Buttercup into a faster walk.

Ahead, the road disappears into darkness.

EXPECTATION

"We did it, Beo!" Raveno claps his back.

Raucous applause showers the Klenzeer as she bows slightly. Members of the Council stand and nod. Droves of attendees approach, but her solemn expression keeps them at bay.

Tomas is among the remaining community members. He smiles and waves. The Klenzeer addresses him directly. "I will follow up with those two individuals in the morning. They were unavailable earlier."

Beo watches from his spot, eyes split between the window and the Klenzeer. Any moment, someone might be shoving through the door with news from the Posts.

Just a little longer.

The crowd disperses. Raveno approaches the Klenzeer as she walks by the bar, keeping a respectful distance. "I'm thankful for your speech this evening. It was well received, and the Council will soon meet to discuss implementing your proposed changes. I'm eager to see the changes in the Town. Your presence has been very enlightening." He bows deeply and then excuses himself.

Beo looks anxiously at the main door, then back to the Klenzeer, with a charming smile. "I just wanted to thank you again for sharing your valuable knowledge this evening. It's wonderful to hear from someone who has met with our benevolent Overseers."

She nods curtly and steps toward the doorway.

He steps into her path. "My Klenzeer—please, a moment. There's something you should know." His hands shake. He clasps them behind his back. "Something I couldn't say in front of everyone."

"Listen—" she begins.

"Beo," he responds quickly. "My name is Beo Luca, my esteemed Klenzeer."

"Listen, Beo Luca. I appreciate your words, but the hour is late."

His face goes pale. "Oh, please, forgive me for being forward. I didn't mean to overstep. I just have insight to share, but wasn't sure if the public forum was the right place." He lowers his voice. "I might have noticed something in town."

She pauses. An eyebrow rises. "Go on."

Beo surveys the hall. "I'm not certain, but I suspect there may be a Twun living in this town."

She goes very still. "Continue."

"During my walks, I've noticed a suspicious-looking fellow from the farms. I see him every few days at the market." He shifts on his feet. "He's strong, like the Twun in the square, though he looks like us. He's quite hairy on his arms and legs." He looks about, then leans in. "Once, I thought I saw sharp ears beneath the bushy hair on his head. It might have been my imagination, but it stayed with me all this time. With you here, I thought I'd report it."

The Klenzeer pulls out parchment. "Describe him. Everything."

Beo's mind races. He describes the most obnoxious farmer he knows—the one who shortchanged him last season. Bushy hair. Crooked nose. Scar on the left cheek. He adds detail after detail, stretching it out, giving her enough to occupy the entire morning.

All the while, his eyes dart to the windows. The square is still dark. Still quiet.

The Klenzeer finishes writing. "Good work, citizen. I'll investigate at first light." She tucks the parchment away and strides toward the door.

Beo watches her go. The moment she's out of sight, his legs give. He sinks down into a chair, hands shaking.

THE KLENZEER WALKS toward her lodgings, mind full of promising leads. The farmer. The blacksmiths. Ormant may quickly help her ascend through the ranks. She'll find them at first light.

She passes the square, then stops. Something's wrong. The Posts are dark. Both lanterns are out. That's not protocol. There should be light on the prisoner at all times.

Her pace quickens.

NO!

Running now.

IT CAN'T BE!

In the pale light, she sees it. The chains hang empty. Broken links are scattered on the ground. He's gone.

For a moment, she can't breathe. Can't think. Then rage floods in, hot and overwhelming.

She roars.

The sound tears from her throat, primal and furious, echoing off every building in the square. Windows light up. Doors crack open.

She storms Raveno's house, fist pounding like a battering ram. Gregan opens the door with bleary eyes that nearly leave his head. He rushes to Raveno, practically dragging him from bed.

"The Twun has escaped! There's danger in Ormant!"

Raveno snaps out of his stupor. He's moving before the implications register. "I'll get the Constables." He runs down the street in mismatched clothes.

The Klenzeer returns to the square, voice going hoarse, "The Twun has escaped! Do not exit your homes! He's dangerous!"

Constables arrive, lanterns swinging. Breaths heightened.

The Klenzeer focuses on the ground, seeking clues. She yells. "Examine the Posts. Now!"

They circle nervously. The ground is littered with broken chains, links snapped clean.

"He must have pulled them apart," one mutters. "How strong is he?"

"Search the area," she growls. "Some of you get to the bridge and the river to eliminate escape. Question pedestrians and the homes around the square. Check for tracks, blood, anything."

They split and spread out.

Rain puddles cover the square. Tracks are nonexistent. He could be anywhere. Miles away. Hidden. Starving. Slow, with chains still attached. Desperate.

The Klenzeer stares at the road north. Her room is north—her hammer, her gear.

She can still catch him.

She turns and runs, jaw set.

The hunt starts now.

JUSTICE

"Gods, why is this furniture so heavy?!" Toby's hands still shake as she hauls a drawer from Beo's basement.

"Louder," Rondu hisses. "The neighbors need to hear us."

"Stinking Beo!" She forces the complaint to carry.

Behind them in the wagon, under the tarp, the Twun sleeps on.

"I wish we had a third person!" Toby drops the drawer near the wagon with a crash.

A window lights up across the road. Good. Witnesses.

"I can't believe Beo is making us get rid of his junk." Rondu struggles with a large crate.

As they remove the furniture piece by piece, they carefully stack most of it around the Twun or lean lighter items against him. Despite the noise and constant movement, he continues to snore, undisturbed.

Minutes later, the task is done. Windows in the surrounding homes are lit. Nosy neighbors watch the proceedings, strengthening their alibi.

Toby smiles as they head north. Wagon wheels churn into the wet ground, now heavier. Buttercup whines but pulls.

As the northern farms come into view, the waning moon emerges from behind broken clouds and lights the way. Rondu relights an extinguished lantern. Their path forward is fully lit.

Toby claps and hops in her seat. "I can't believe it! I think we've done it."

Rondu grins. "You were amazing! I'm so proud of you."

"Oh, stop it. I didn't do anything."

"You were fearless. Our passenger could have been a psychotic killer. You confronted him without flinching."

She shrugs. "You could have done it."

Rondu shakes his head. "That boy would have torn me limb from limb just for being there. You made the right call."

She leans in, lowering her voice. "Why is he so angry at Fens?"

Rondu shrugs. "He's got some issues to work out while he's living with his new pack."

The farms come and go in silence. A wave of joy washes over Toby as Ormant's border slips from sight.

She hugs Rondu, kissing his head. "We're free, Fento! Free to make money. Free to get packed. Free to find the Villa—"

A shout cuts through the night.

Toby's heart stops.

In the distance, a figure sprints toward them under pale moonlight. Long pole. Lantern swinging wildly.

Rondu's voice drops to almost nothing. "No, no, no—"

Her black-and-gold uniform is unmistakable.

The Klenzeer.

Toby's hands freeze on the reins. Behind them, the Twun shifts under the tarp.

The Klenzeer's voice carries across the field, breathless: "Be careful! The Twun has escaped!" Deep inhales follow. "Have you seen any signs? Where are you headed?"

"That terrible beast has escaped?" Toby looks to Rondu, then back at the Klenzeer, feigning fear. "Oh no!"

"Where are you headed? What are you doing here so late at

night?" Her hammer rests on the ground. She leans on it as she recovers.

"I have some days off and am heading to visit family. We borrowed this wagon from Beo to get there faster. It got late. Work was busy. He made us promise to burn some old furniture in exchange." She points to the awkward pile in the back. "What should we do?"

"Friends of Beo, you say? He's a good man. Trustworthy." She scans the expansive landscape. Nothing stirs. A few streams bubble, swollen from the rains. "I can't imagine the Twun would bother you. You could probably outrun him with a cambra and wagon."

Her posture relaxes. She glances back at Ormant. "You may go. Be careful. Avoid the beast if you see it. It's fierce and deadly."

Rondu mutters, "Thank you. We'll stick to the road."

The Klenzeer lifts her lantern for a better look and studies Rondu. "Are you a Fen?"

He leans forward from behind Toby. Lantern light catches his ears and his features.

An uncomfortable silence passes between heartbeats.

The Klenzeer shifts, eyes narrowing slightly. "What are your names?"

"Rondu. And this is Master Toby."

Her head tilts. Doubt flickers. "Are you smiths?" She steps back, tightening her grip on her hammer, lifting it to her shoulder.

"Yes. We closed up shop for a few days for the trip. Rondu is my navigator. I'm not good in the dark."

A contemplative hum.

Below the line of sight, Toby's right hand drops to the hammer at her waist. Rondu palms his two knives.

"Do you have need of a smith?"

The Klenzeer ignores the question. Her eyes move to the back of the wagon. "You were going to burn this furniture tonight?"

The question hangs.

Toby's grip tightens. "Or tomorrow if it's too wet. As long as we get rid of it is all Beo wanted."

The Klenzeer walks slowly to the rear of the wagon, hands tracing the edge. Toby and Rondu turn at an awkward angle to watch. "Why not leave in the morning?"

"I wanted to be sure to spend as much time as I could with my family. I haven't seen my brother in ages."

The moon emerges fully from the clouds, casting pale light. Toby's face is stone. Rondu's head catches a faint glow. The Klenzeer's face stays in shadow, though a frown is clearly visible.

Her hand reaches for the tarp.

One finger hooks the corner.

Slowly, she pulls.

Her eyes stay locked on Toby and Rondu—watching for tells, for guilt, for fear.

She lowers herself inches without breaking eye contact. Then darts her eyes beneath the tarp.

An orange eye blazes back.

The Twun explodes from the wagon.

Furniture flies as if detonated. Crates shattering. The tarp whips free.

The Klenzeer stumbles back, fumbling with her hammer—
Too slow.

A chain wraps her throat. Once. Twice. The Twun yanks her off her feet like she weighs nothing.

Her hammer thuds to the ground. Both hands claw at the chain. Her mouth opens. No sound comes.

Toby and Rondu sit frozen.

Muscles flexed like steel cables, the Twun vibrates. The Klenzeer punches behind her. She sputters, chokes, fights for air.

"She's dying!" Toby snaps out of her shock. "You have to stop!"

The Klenzeer's struggles weaken. Her punches become taps.

Her arms slow. Reaching. Failing.

A weak sound escapes. A plea.

Then nothing.

Her face is black in the moonlight. Eyes bulging. Mouth open.

The Twun pulls tighter.

Crack.

The sound is small. Quiet. Like a stick snapping.

Neither Toby nor Rondu breathes.

The Twun holds her a moment longer. Then he drops her.

She hits the edge of the wagon and tumbles to the ground, landing in a heap, twisted wrong.

Utterly still.

The Twun faces the moon and howls. Raw and mournful—torn from somewhere deep. A chorus of slopebacks answers from the north. Another pack joins from the east. The cries build and gradually fade into silence.

His face is brutal in the moonlight.

He looks down at the body and speaks to the dead woman.

"So you shall ascend."

He faces Toby and Rondu, his expression menacing.

Rondu's voice is hollow. "What have you done?"

The End Of Ra - Book One - ANoMALoUS

ABOUT THE AUTHOR

William Beltre is a first-generation Dominican-American and the son of immigrants. Growing up in a household without the traditional academic roadmap, he initially viewed reading as a chore-until the day he discovered Tolkien. That encounter sparked a lifelong fascination with the transformative power of storytelling.

While studying Computer Animation at UMass Amherst, a Comparative Literature course titled "Brave New World" introduced him to the visionary works of Orwell, Stephenson, Atwood, and Butler. This exposure to iconic speculative fiction didn't just expand his library; it blew his world open, fueling an insatiable appetite for narratives that challenge the status quo.

What began as a hobby, trading late-night "doom-scrolling" for creative output, has evolved into a vital passion. For William, writing has become as necessary as breathing-a way to kindle for others the same spark that redefined his own life years ago.

Above all, William considers his family his greatest success. This journey is shared with his wife, Jo, and their children, Marley and

Javi, who reflect the blended values he holds dear. He lives in New Hampshire with his family and a chaotic menagerie of two dogs, three cats, and one remarkably misbehaving bunny.

Visit the world of Ra at endofra.com